Kate
HEWITT
Highly Unsuitable

RISING STARS
COLLECTION

July 2015

August 2015

September 2015

October 2015

Kate Hewitt discovered her first Mills & Boon® romance on a trip to England when she was thirteen and she's continued to read them ever since. She wrote her first short story at the age of five, simply because her older brother had written one and she thought she could do it too. That story was one sentence long—fortunately they've become a bit more detailed as she's grown older. She has written plays, short stories and magazine serials for many years, but writing romance remains her first love. Besides writing, she enjoys reading, travelling and learning to knit.

After marrying the man of her dreams—her older brother's childhood friend—she lived in England for six years, and now resides in Connecticut with her husband, her three young children and the possibility of one day getting a dog.

Kate loves to hear from readers—you can contact her through her website: www.katehewitt.com.

Published in Great Britain 2015
by Mills & Boon, an imprint of Harlequin (UK) Limited,
Eton House, 18-24 Paradise Road, Richmond, Surrey, TW9 1SR

HIGHLY UNSUITABLE © 2015 Harlequin Books S.A.

Mr and Mischief © 2011 Kate Hewitt
The Darkest of Secrets © 2012 Kate Hewitt
The Undoing of de Luca © 2010 Kate Hewitt

ISBN: 978-0-263-91570-9

024-1015

Harlequin (UK) Limited's policy is to use papers that are natural, renewable and recyclable products and made from wood grown in sustainable forests. The logging and manufacturing processes conform to the legal environmental regulations of the country of origin.

Printed and bound in Spain
by CPI, Barcelona

Mr and Mischief

KATE HEWITT

CHAPTER ONE

'IT LOOKS like I missed the party.'

Emily Wood turned from her rather dour perusal of the leaving-party detritus, surprised that anyone was left. Stephanie had gone an hour ago, full of high spirits and plans for her wedding in a month's time, and the rest of the employees had trickled away afterwards, leaving nothing but a few tables of crumb-scattered plates and glasses of now-flat champagne in the office's party room.

'Jason!' The name burst from her lips as she stared in surprise at the man lounging against the doorway. 'You're back!'

'My plane landed an hour ago,' Jason replied, glancing ruefully around at the mess. 'I thought I might make the end of the party, but obviously I was mistaken.'

'Just in time for the clean-up,' Emily replied lightly. She crossed the room and, standing on her tiptoes, reached up to kiss his cheek. 'How lovely to see you.' His skin was warm and she inhaled the citrusy tang of his aftershave; the scent was more pungent than one she would have associated with stoic, straight-as-an-arrow Jason, the boy who had kept her out of trouble, the man who had left Highfield for a high-profile career in civil engineering. He was her boss and oldest family friend, although whether he was *her* friend was another matter altogether. Looking at his rather cool expression now, Emily remembered how Jason always seemed to disapprove of her just a bit.

She stepped back with a brisk smile. Jason hadn't moved, but Emily was gratified to see the tiniest quirk of his mouth. Amazing, but it almost looked like a smile. 'I didn't know you were due back in London.' As founder and CEO of Kingsley Engineering, Jason travelled for most of the year. Emily couldn't even remember the last time she'd seen him beyond a flash of sober suit in the hallway, or amidst the chaos of a family gathering back in Surrey. He'd certainly never sought her out like this.

Although, she acknowledged as she began to gather up the icing-smeared plates, he wasn't really seeking her out. He'd just missed the party.

'I thought it was about time I came home,' Jason said. He glanced around at the empty tables. 'It looks like it was a successful party. But then, of course, I wouldn't expect anything less.'

Successful, Emily thought, rather than *fun*. So typical of Jason. She arched her eyebrows. 'Oh, and why is that?'

'You're quite the busy little socialite, Em.'

Emily bristled, because the words did not sound complimentary coming out of Jason's mouth. Just because she enjoyed a party hardly made her some kind of scatty socialite. And the childhood nickname surprised her, even though it shouldn't. Jason had been the only one to call her that. Little Em, he'd tease, yanking her plaits and giving her a smile that wasn't quite condescending. More just…knowing. Yet he could hardly say he knew her now; despite working for his company, with his intense travel schedule she'd barely seen him in the five years she'd been at KE. And she couldn't remember the last time he'd called her Em.

'I wasn't aware you kept tabs on my social activities,' she said, only half-joking.

'I'm honour bound to, considering our history. And, in any

case, you've made the social pages enough it would be hard not to notice.'

Emily gave him a playful smile. 'And you read the social pages?'

'I eagerly await them every morning.'

Emily burst out laughing, for the thought of Jason poring over photos of ageing debutantes and profligate playboys was utterly ludicrous, though she'd hardly expect him to joke about it—or joke about anything, really. More than once she'd wondered if he'd had his sense of humour surgically removed.

'Actually,' he continued, his tone serious and even severe once more, 'my PA scans them for me. I need to know what my employees are up to.'

Ah, there he was. The real Jason, the Jason she knew and remembered, always ready to deliver a scolding or shoot her one of those stern looks. Emily gave him a sunny smile. 'Well, as you can see, this was quite the wild party. Cake and streamers, and I believe someone *might* have brought out the karaoke machine. Scandalous.'

'Don't forget the champagne.'

Emily reached for several empty plastic flutes. 'How did you guess?'

'Actually, I provided it.'

'You did?' She couldn't keep the surprise from her voice, and Jason's mouth quirked again in a small smile. He propped one shoulder against the doorway.

'Really, Emily, I'm not quite that stern a taskmaster. And I did actually try to make it to this party. Stephanie has been with the company for over five years.'

'Ah, so that's the reason. You probably give out some kind of honorary plaque.'

'You only get one of those for ten years' service,' Jason told her, and Emily's mouth dropped open. He had to be kidding—then she saw a telltale glint in his eyes and realised he was. Two jokes in one day. What had happened to him in Africa?

Surprised and a little discomfited by their banter, Emily paused in her clearing up to look at him properly; he wore a suit—of course—of expensive grey silk, a muted navy tie knotted at his throat. His hair, chocolate brown, the same colour as his eyes, was cut short. He looked crisp and clean and neat, remote and untouchable with that small, rather superior smile Emily had never completely liked but accepted as part of who Jason was, the exalted older brother-in-law, separated from her by twelve years, distant and just a little disapproving.

He'd never taken part in their silly childhood games. She, her sister Isobel, and Jason's younger brother Jack had always got into the most amazing scrapes, and Jason had been the one to bail them out and lecture them afterwards. She'd accepted and resented it at turns, yet never questioned his innate authority. It was too much a part of him, and the relationship he'd had with them all. Yet it had been months since she'd seen him, years since they'd really talked.

Five years ago, when she'd arrived in London looking for a job, he'd directed her to Stephanie, then Head of Human Resources, and then barely seen her settle in as a secretary before he'd been off again, directing a building project in Asia. The times he'd seen her since then had been at the office, where he kept a cool, professional distance, or back in Surrey at various family gatherings, where he was no more than what he'd always been—Jason, as good as an older brother, bossy and perhaps a little bit boring but still…Jason. An essential part of the landscape of her life, steady and staid and *there*.

'So are you back for long this time?' she asked, turning back to the table of paper plates.

'A few months I hope. I have some business locally to take care of.' He spoke casually enough, yet Emily sensed an undercurrent of intensity that sparked her curiosity, and she glanced back at him. Jason's impassive face gave nothing away.

'Local business?' she repeated as she dumped another load of paper plates into the bin. 'I didn't know KE had a local project going on.' As a civil engineer, Jason's speciality was water management in Third World countries. It was a rather impressive line Emily trotted out when conducting interviews, although she'd yet to really understand just what it entailed. He'd never done a local project before, as far as she knew.

'It's not to do with the company,' Jason replied, his voice mild.

'Personal business?' she asked. 'You mean family?' She thought of Jason's taciturn father, his tearaway brother, now married to her own sister. Was someone in trouble or ill? Her brow furrowed, and Jason's mouth quirked once more in that knowing little smile as he shook his head.

'You're full of questions, aren't you? No, as a matter of fact, it's nothing to do with family. But *personal*.' He stressed it lightly yet pointedly, making her feel a bit like the bratty little girl she'd undoubtedly been to his very cool teenager. Or twenty-something. He'd always been a little god-like in his maturity and sophistication. When she'd been getting braces, he'd already started his own company and made his first million.

'Sorry. I'll stop.' She smiled just as teasingly back, determined to keep it light and breezy, although now her curiosity was well and truly whetted. What kind of personal business could Jason Kingsley have? There had always been a fair amount of office speculation about the boss's personal life, for while he was in London he always had a different woman on his arm at various social functions, usually someone glamorous and shallow, and in Emily's opinion totally unsuitable for Jason. Yet she'd never seen him with a serious girlfriend and, despite the office's occasional forays into speculation about that aspect of their employer, Emily hadn't given too much thought to Jason's personal life. Of course, she'd hardly seen him at all. And although their families were intertwined through the marriage of her older sister to Jason's younger brother, he hardly ever went back to Highfield, the village in Surrey where they'd both grown up. And he'd already said it wasn't family-related, so what was it?

After another few seconds of silent speculation, Emily shrugged it aside. Clearly Jason's personal business had nothing to do with her. It was probably something incredibly boring, like taking care of an old debt or an ingrown toenail. She thought of Jason sitting on a doctor's examining table, and a sudden, bizarre image of him in nothing more than one of those awful little paper robes flashed across her brain. The mental picture was both ridiculous and yet strangely enthralling, for her overactive imagination seemed to have a rather good idea of what Jason's bare chest would look like.

An unexpected bubble of laughter erupted from her and she clapped her hand over her mouth. Jason glanced at her, shaking his head. 'You've always been able to see the lighter side of life, haven't you?' he said dryly, and she dropped her hand from her mouth to dazzle him with her brightest smile.

'It's a great talent of mine, although it takes some work in certain company.' His eyes narrowed and her smile widened. She knew Jason disapproved of her breezy attitude. She still remembered how sceptical he had looked when she'd come to London and asked him for a job. In retrospect, she *had* been a bit scatty, blithely assuming that Jason would have something for her to do, and pay her for it as well, but still it had been all too clear just how much Jason had doubted her capabilities.

You're here to work, Emily, not for a lark...

Well, she hoped she'd proved herself in that area at least over the last five years. She was poised to become the youngest Head of Human Resources the company had ever had—admittedly there had only been two before her—and Jason himself had suggested her promotion, according to Stephanie.

Despite that, as she looked back at him watching her with that knowing little smile, his eyes crinkled at the corners and she couldn't help but still feel like the silly young girl she'd once been. And, despite the promotion, he apparently still thought she was.

'So Stephanie is to be married in a month,' Jason mused. 'This Timothy fellow—he's all right?'

'He's lovely,' Emily said firmly. 'I had a hand in getting them together, actually.'

Jason arched an eyebrow, coolly sceptical as always. 'Really?'

'Yes, really,' she replied, slightly nettled. 'Tim is a friend of a friend of Isobel's, and she told me that Annie told her—'

'This is sounding far too complicated.'

'For you, perhaps,' Emily shot back. 'I found it quite simple. So Annie said—

'Give me the condensed version,' Jason cut her off, and Emily rolled her eyes.

'Oh, very well. I invited them both out to a party—'

'Now that part I have no trouble following.'

'Actually, it was a charity fund-raiser,' Emily informed him. 'For terminally ill children. In any case, they met there and—'

'And it was love at first sight, was it?' he filled in mockingly, and Emily pursed her lips.

'No, of course not. But they never would have even met if I hadn't arranged it, and in point of fact Tim was a bit shy after his wife died, and Steph has an absolute horror of blind dates, so—'

'It took a bit of handholding?'

'Or helping them to hold each other's hands. You can't make someone love you, of course—'

'I should think not.'

Emily glanced at him curiously, for there was a sudden, darker note to Jason's tone she didn't expect or understand. She shrugged it aside. 'In any case, they're getting married in a month, so it all worked out nicely.'

'Very nicely indeed.' Jason had closed the space between them so she inhaled the citrusy whiff of his aftershave once more, felt the sudden heat of his body, and a strange new awareness prickled along her bare arms and up her spine. He really was awfully close.

'You have icing in your hair,' he said, and reached out to brush a sticky strand away from her cheek. His fingers were cool, the touch as light as a whisper, yet Emily stiffened in surprise anyway. She was conscious of how dishevelled she must look, with her hair falling down and a coffee stain on her skirt. Definitely not at her best.

She laughed lightly and pushed the unruly tendrils behind her ears. 'Yes, I'm rather a mess, aren't I? I just need to finish this clearing up.'

'You could leave it for the cleaning lady.'

'Alice? She's taken the day off.'

'You know her name?'

'I am about to become the Head of HR,' Emily reminded him. 'Her mother's ill and she's gone to Manchester for the weekend to see her settled in a care home. It was a terrible wrench for her to make the decision, of course, but I think it will work out—'

'I'm sure,' Jason murmured, effectively cutting her off yet again, and Emily gave him a knowing look.

'So sorry to bother you with details, but I thought you kept tabs on your employees' lives? Or just the ones who make the social pages?'

'I'm more concerned about how a social scandal reflects on Kingsley Engineering,' Jason replied, 'rather than the hows or whys of a cleaning lady taking the day off for her elderly mum.' He gestured for her to keep speaking. 'But do go on.

It's fascinating how you take such an interest in other people's lives.'

Emily felt herself flush. Was that a criticism? And while she'd been high-spirited on occasion, she'd never involved herself in an actual scandal. Although she supposed high-spirited and scandal were synonymous in Jason's view. 'I suppose,' she told him rather pointedly, 'it's what makes me good at HR.'

'Absolutely, among other things.' He smiled, a proper one, not just a little quirk of his lips, revealing a dimple in one cheek. She'd forgotten about that dimple, forgotten when Jason smiled properly his eyes turned the colour of honey. They were normally brown, just as his hair was brown. Brown and boring. Except when he smiled. Abruptly, Emily turned back to the table. She could tell Jason was watching her, felt his assessing gaze sweep over her. Strange, how you could *feel* someone watching you.

'Are you planning Stephanie's wedding, as well?' he asked now. 'Some big fancy do?'

Emily turned around, brushing another unruly strand of hair from her eyes. 'The wedding? Heavens, no. That's far above my capabilities. And she's having it back home where she grew up.'

'But you'll be there, won't you? Maid of honour, I suppose?'

'As a matter of fact, yes.'

Jason's smile deepened, and so did his dimple. Something flashed in his eyes, something dark and unsettling. 'And you'll dance, won't you? At the wedding?' His voice had dipped to a husky murmur, a tone Emily didn't think she'd ever heard him use before, a tone that brushed across her senses with a shiver. She frowned, then froze as she realised just what Jason was alluding to with that little murmured remark.... Jack and Isobel's wedding, when they'd danced, and she had been seventeen years old and very, very silly. In the seven years since that episode had occurred, Jason had never mentioned it. Neither had she. She'd assumed he'd forgotten it—just as she had. Almost…until now. Now it was suddenly taking up far too much space in her brain.

'Of course,' she said after a moment, her voice light. She decided to ignore any implication he might have been making. They hardly needed to talk about that unfortunate episode now. 'I love to dance.' She glanced at him again and, despite her now almost twenty-five years, she felt every inch the gauche girl she'd been at that wedding. She'd made *such* a fool of herself, but at least she could laugh about it now. She *would* laugh about it.

'I know,' Jason said, his voice still no more than a murmur. 'I remember how we danced.' The corner of his mouth quirked up again, only for a second, as his gaze held hers. His eyes really were the most amazing colour…like whisky, or chocolate, but with golden glints.… 'Don't you?' he pressed, a lilt of challenge in his voice.

So he was going to mention it—and make her mention it, as well. From that knowing glint in his eyes, he intended to tease her about it, although why he'd waited seven years to do so, Emily had no idea. She smiled wryly, determined to ride it out. 'Ah, yes. How could I forget?' Jason didn't say anything, and Emily shook her head, rolling her eyes as if it was no more than an amusing little anecdote. It *was* a silly enough episode, seven years in the past, and surely it had no power to embarrass her now, even if she'd been mortified at the time.

It was just, Emily told herself, that they'd never talked about it, not when he'd hired her, not when he'd kissed her cheek at their niece's baptism, nor when he'd sat at the far end of the table at Christmas dinner. On all of those occasions he'd remained rather remote, and only now was Emily realising how glad she'd been to retain that little distance. Yet here he was now, standing so close, bringing up all these memories, and behaving in a very un-Jasonlike way. It unnerved her.

She let out a light little laugh and gave him a self-mocking smile. 'I made quite an idiot of myself over you.'

Jason arched an eyebrow. 'Is that how you remember it?'

Of course he wouldn't make it easy for her. He never did. Not when she was six, not when she was seventeen, and not even now she was almost twenty-five. She should be used to his lightly mocking smiles, the eloquent arch of a single eyebrow, but somehow with the distance in their professional relationship she'd forgotten. She'd forgotten how much he could affect her.

'You don't remember?' she asked, pretending to shudder. 'That's a relief, I suppose.'

Jason didn't speak for a moment, and Emily busied herself with organising the dirty cutlery into a tidy pile. 'I remember,' he finally said, quietly, without any humour at all, and she felt a strange, icy thrill all the way down her spine.

And suddenly, without either of them saying anything more, Emily felt as if that memory was right there with them, living and breathing and taking all the air. She certainly remembered it, could feel even now how young and happy she'd been—and so very silly.

Jason had asked her to dance, the obvious and polite thing to do since he was the brother of the groom and she the sister of the bride. He'd been a worldly twenty-nine to her naive seventeen years, and she'd been breathless and giddy from three glasses of champagne when he'd taken her in his arms and led her in a gentle and unthreatening waltz. It had been a dance of duty, and Emily had known it for what it was—she hadn't even *wanted* to dance with boring Jason Kingsley in the first place. All he'd ever really done was tease her or scold her.

Yet somehow, when he'd taken her in his arms, keeping her a safe six inches from his body, she'd felt something else. Something new and tingly and really quite nice, in a disquieting sort of way. She'd been an innocent at seventeen, and had never felt that sweet rush before. And so, despite Jason's serious expression and boring waltz, she'd tipped her head up and smiled at him with as much flirtatious charm as she thought she might ever possess and said, 'You're quite handsome, you know.'

Jason had looked down at her, his face so aggravatingly solemn. His expression hadn't changed one bit. 'Thank you.'

Somehow Emily didn't think that was what he was supposed to have said. She wasn't sure of the script, yet she knew she didn't like these lines. And yet he *had* been handsome, with his dark hair and eyes, the white of his smile and the strength of his arms as he held her that proper distance away from his body. She could still feel the heat and strength of him and, fuelled by the champagne fizzing through her veins, Emily had added, 'Perhaps you'd like to kiss me.' She'd tilted her pretty little chin up further, and had even had the audacious stupidity to pucker her lips and wait. She'd let her eyelids flutter closed, so suddenly desperate to have him kiss her. It would have been her first kiss, and at that moment she'd wanted it so very much. She'd wanted Jason, which was ridiculous because she'd never once thought of Jason that way—never even considered such a possibility—until he'd asked her to dance.

The moment had gone on too long, several seconds that had made agonising awareness, as well as a punishing sobriety, steal over Emily. She'd opened her eyes and seen Jason gazing down at her in what was almost a glare. His eyes had narrowed, his mouth had tightened, and he hadn't looked friendly—or boring—at all. All of her flirtatiousness had drained out of her, leaving her as flat and stale as the dregs of her own champagne. She'd almost felt afraid.

Then his expression had changed, the glare wiped clean away, and he'd smiled faintly and said, 'I would, rather. But I won't.' And with that, before the dance had ended or even really started, he'd set her gently and firmly from him and walked off the dance floor.

Emily had stood there for several seconds, unmoving and incredulous. The public humiliation of being left on the dance floor was bad enough, but far worse was the private humiliation of being so summarily rejected by Jason Kingsley. She'd been quite sure, at that moment, that he really wouldn't want to kiss her. And because she'd been seventeen, tipsy, and it would have been her first kiss, she hadn't been able to lift her chin and throw her shoulders back and saunter off the dance floor like she'd meant to. Instead she'd stumbled across the parquet, dissolving into drunken tears before she'd even left the ballroom.

Definitely an idiot.

She turned to smile brightly at him now, forcing the memory—and its accompanying mortification—back to the far recesses of her brain. 'Well, I shan't ask you to dance again, I promise you,' she assured him. 'Never fear.'

A smile flickered across Jason's face like a wave of water. His gaze rested on her thoughtfully, as if he were taking her measure. 'But, Em, I was counting on you to ask me to dance.'

Slightly thrown, Emily laughed and replied, 'Well then, I certainly won't ask you to kiss me.'

'Then I shall be especially disappointed,' Jason returned, his voice soft, and Emily felt shock slice through her, rendering her quite speechless, until she realised that of course Jason was just teasing her, the same as always. Except he'd never teased her quite like that before.

Jason watched as shock widened Emily's jade-green eyes, her tongue darting out to moisten her lower lip. He felt a sudden jolt of desire at the sight of that innocent little action, and it both surprised and annoyed him. He had no business feeling that way about Emily…again.

He hadn't even meant to seek her out tonight. He had only a few months to be in London, and spending time with Emily Wood was low down on his list of priorities. In fact, *not* spending time with her was a priority. He had other more suitable women to pursue. Women who were sensible, level-headed and businesslike, perfect for his purpose. Emily, with her cat's eyes and teasing smile and endless legs, was definitely not any of those things. Even more importantly, she was off-limits. She'd been off-limits seven years ago, and she was still off-limits now—for more reasons than he cared to name or number.

'How does it feel to be the Head of Human Resources?' he asked, determined to move the conversation back to business. 'Youngest in the post.'

'Strange,' Emily admitted. 'I hope I'm up to the task.'

'I'm sure you will be.' He'd watched her grow into her position in HR from afar, and he'd been both surprised and encouraged by the way she'd taken to the role. Her promotion had been a smart business move, even though some—including Emily herself—might think it hinted at nepotism. Jason never let feelings get in the way of business. Or of anything.

'As for your first duty,' he told her, 'there's a woman I'd like you to interview on Monday, for a receptionist position.'

Emily glanced at him rather sharply. 'Oh?' she asked, her tone a bit diffident.

'Helen Smith. She's just come to London and could use a bit of help.'

'A friend of yours?' Emily asked, her voice sharpening just a little, and Jason suppressed a smile. Sometimes Emily was so easy to read. Could she actually be jealous? Did she still harbour a bit of the adolescent affection she'd shown him seven years ago?

The possibility was intriguing...and dangerous.

He still remembered the moment she'd tilted her pretty face up to his and said, *'Perhaps you'd like to kiss me.'*

And he *had* wanted to, more than he'd been willing to admit, even to himself.

That sudden, fierce jolt of lust had nearly knocked Jason to his knees. She'd been seventeen, practically a child, completely innocent and utterly naive. The strength of his own response had shocked and shamed him; he'd left the wedding immediately afterwards, near trembling with the aftershocks of surprising and suppressed desire, determined to put Emily completely from his mind.

And he'd accomplished just that, almost forgetting her completely, until three years later when she'd traipsed merrily to London without a plan—or a job—and he'd reluctantly offered her an entry level post.

He remembered how she'd sprawled in the chair across from his desk, her honey-blonde hair tumbling over her shoulders, her green cat's eyes alight with mischief. She'd worn an indecently short miniskirt and a top in a vivid green that matched her eyes; he suspected she considered such an outfit business attire. He couldn't keep his eyes off her long tanned legs, or the way one foot swung back and forth, a spiked heel dangling from her scarlet-polished toe.

Jason had stood behind his desk, his hands shoved in his pockets, doing his best to appear stern and disapproving. She'd been only twenty at the time and had looked artless and beautiful and so very young. And while he'd managed to forget how Emily had affected him three years ago, it had come back to him then with an overwhelming rush of memory and feeling.

'You can have me do anything,' she'd told him. 'I'm not fussed.' He'd stood there, looking grim, trying not to let it show on his face just what he could imagine having her do. It had been three years since they'd danced at the wedding, three years when he'd barely seen or thought of her at all, and yet he'd still felt that fierce dart of lust. When she'd leaned forward her hair had swung around her face and he'd smelled the scent of her shampoo. Strawberry.

She'd looked up at him from underneath her lashes, her eyes dancing with amusement. 'Honestly, Jason, you look positively dire! I'm not that bad, I assure you.'

From somewhere he'd summoned a smile. 'And whatever I have you do—I assume you want payment for it?'

She'd looked momentarily thrown, her expression unguarded and vulnerable, and with a stab of self-loathing he'd realised again just how young and inexperienced—in every way—she was. Then she'd laughed, a rich, throaty gurgle that had made Jason shove his hands even deeper into his pockets, a scowl marking his face. Emily had the laugh of an experienced woman, a sexy, sultry laugh, and it *did* things to him. When had she started laughing like that? When had she started to really grow up?

'Well, yes, that was the idea,' she said, smiling with that artless honesty that exasperated and endeared her to him at the same time.

And so he'd given her the post, as she'd undoubtedly known he would, and then he'd kept his distance. He'd had no intention of involving himself with an innocent like Emily, especially considering how their families were related. And he'd succeeded...until now. Now, when he'd seen her in the party room, wearing a candy-pink business suit that was so short it nearly showed her bottom when she bent to pick up a bit of rubbish from the floor. He'd stared at her, noticing the long, tanned length of her legs, the way that ridiculously short skirt moulded over her curves.

He should have walked away before she'd seen him. God knew he'd done it before. Yet something had compelled him to come into the room, and he'd spoken. Stayed. Seeing Emily after so long had been like finally finding a drink in the desert. Her warmth and humour had reached out to him, enveloped him and made him want more. And so he'd remained, joked and flirted, and then most damaging and dangerous of all, he'd mentioned that almost-kiss they'd shared seven years ago. Jason could not fathom why he'd done that, when he'd been perfectly happy never to think about it again, much less talk about it.

And surely Emily felt the same way…unless she did still have some vestige of that schoolgirl crush? The thought should alarm him, but it accomplished something else entirely. He wanted to watch her eyes darken to moss and see her tongue swipe at that lush mouth once more.

Annoyance prickled through him yet again. He needed to get a grip. This was Emily. *Emily.* Inappropriate, unsuitable and off-limits. Full stop.

'Helen Smith,' Emily repeated, and Jason could tell she'd recovered her equanimity. 'I'll keep an eye out for her CV—'

'My PA emailed it to you this afternoon.'

'I see.' She gave him a quick, curious glance from under her lashes and then turned away. 'I'll make a note of it.'

'Good.' He was determined to keep the rest of their conversation purely professional, even as his gaze rested on the falling-down chignon of her glorious golden hair, one curling tendril resting on the curve of her breast. Determinedly, Jason yanked his gaze away, his mouth settling into a grim line, yet something still compelled him to add, 'I've never met her, actually. She's a friend of a friend, and I'd like to help her out. She should be suitable for an entry level position.' Why on earth was he explaining himself? There was absolutely no need.

'Fine,' Emily said briskly. 'I'll do what I can.'

'Good.' Jason matched her brisk tone and then gave one more glance around the cleaned-up room. He still had several phone calls and emails to answer, as well as a charity fund-raiser to attend. All part of the personal business Emily was so curious about…and which he had no intention of telling her.

She would, he thought with a grim twist of his mouth, find out soon enough.

Jason was looking grim again, which was a good thing, Emily decided. For a few moments there he'd seemed like someone else entirely, and the thought unsettled her. Her reaction had unsettled her even more, because when Jason had dropped his voice to that husky murmur and actually said he'd be *disappointed*…

Quickly, Emily pulled that train of thought to a screeching halt. Not something she needed to think about. At all. She glanced around the empty room with satisfaction, making sure her gaze was averted from Jason, and then went to turn off the lights.

She hadn't realised how dark it had become, twilight stealing softly over the city, so that the room was pitched into sudden darkness when she flicked the switch.

'Oops…' She laughed a little as she stood there in the dark, conscious how a lack of light made things seem almost…intimate. She could hear the gentle sound of Jason's breathing, and when she groped for the switch again she came into contact with Jason's chest instead, a hard wall of muscle that tensed against the flat of her palm. She hadn't realised he'd come so close. She jerked her hand away as a matter of instinct, even though the feel of that hard wall of muscle seemed to have imprinted itself on her palm. The last thing she wanted was Jason to think she was throwing herself at him…again.

'Sorry,' she muttered, yet she still didn't move. Her brain and body both seemed to have frozen, so she'd become incapable of either thought or action. Her hand tingled. 'I…I just need to find the light.…' she finally managed, stammering slightly. *Why* did Jason always reduce her to the gauchest kind of girl?

'It's here.' Jason reached past her and flicked on the switch. Emily took a hasty step back as the room was cast into unrelieved fluorescent light.

She felt a blush heat her cheeks, which made no sense because surely there was nothing to be embarrassed about. Yet she felt, strangely, as she had seven years ago, when she'd offered herself to him so innocently, only to be rejected.

And Jason was glaring at her again, just as he had then. Really, he looked quite cross. Emily felt a flicker of annoyance and the emotion relieved her. At least it was familiar. She took another step back. 'Thanks,' she said briskly, tucking her hair behind her ears. 'I suppose I'll see you around, if you're staying in London for a bit.'

'Most certainly.' Jason's face was expressionless yet his gaze was steady on hers, steady and unsettling. He really didn't know her any more, she reminded herself. She was completely different and far more experienced now than she'd been at seventeen. A bit more experienced, anyway. And hopefully a little less scatty.

'I'm sure you have things to do,' she said in that same brisk, brittle voice. 'And I must get home. Goodnight, Jason.' And without looking back, she hurried down the hall to the safety of her office, strangely and annoyingly disconcerted, almost as much as the seventeen-year-old who'd run from the ballroom in tears.

CHAPTER TWO

EMILY gazed at the woman seated across from her desk, noticed how her fingers nervously pleated the rather wrinkled fabric of her cheap black skirt, a cautious smile brightening her lovely features. Helen Smith was a beautiful young woman, a few years younger than Emily, with a cloud of dark hair like a soft halo around her pale face.

'So.' Emily smiled encouragingly as she scanned Helen's scanty CV. 'You worked as a waitress up in Liverpool...'

'And I temped for a while in an office,' Helen offered helpfully. Her voice was soft and lilting. 'I answered the telephones. Mr Kingsley thought I might do the same here. He said one of your receptionists was on maternity leave.'

Emily wondered—not for the first time—just what Jason's relationship to the lovely Helen Smith could possibly be. Did she have anything to do with this mysterious personal business? 'Yes, Sally just had a baby boy.' Emily returned the CV to her desk; there really wasn't much to see there. 'So Mr Kinglsey is right,' she said with a smile. 'We have an opening.'

'He's a nice man,' Helen whispered, looking down at her lap. Her hair fell forward, obscuring her face, and Emily wondered if she'd ever seemed this young and...clueless. Probably. She felt a stab of sympathy for Helen Smith even as she glanced at her bitten, ragged nails and worn jumper. She could certainly use a manicure and a makeover.

Could it actually be possible that Jason was interested in Helen? She *was* beautiful, despite the nails and clothes, although Jason's dates had always been socialites or starlets. Still, he'd never taken them seriously. Maybe a woman like Helen Smith, lovely and fragile, would capture his heart. Why on earth did she care anyway? Annoyed, Emily turned back to Helen's scanty CV. 'He's a very nice employer,' she said firmly, and Helen nodded shyly.

'It was good of him to listen to Richard about me.'

Emily raised her eyebrows, curiosity sharpening inside her. 'Richard?'

Helen blushed, which made her look lovelier, her cheeks as pink as roses, her complexion like a china doll's. Emily had never doubted her own basic attractiveness, yet right now she was conscious of her rather round-cheeked, healthful appeal, a bit different from Helen's fragile loveliness. 'My...well, he's just my friend, I suppose. We grew up together, back in Liverpool, and...' Helen's blush deepened and she pulled the sleeves of her worn jumper down over her hands, just as Emily remembered doing as an angst-ridden teen. 'Well, I'm older now,' Helen continued hesitantly, 'and Richard thought if I moved to London, and we spent a bit more time together...' She trailed off, nibbling her lip. 'Richard said that perhaps—in time—we might make a go of it,' she finished almost apologetically.

'He said that?' Emily asked before she could stop herself. It sounded most unromantic.

Helen stared at her with wide grey eyes that reflected every emotion, including now a woeful uncertainty. 'Yes...you know, to see if we're a good fit.'

Like a pair of shoes. Emily suppressed a shudder. She could not imagine anything less appealing. Still, she was hardly one to judge. The two relationships she'd entered into in a spirit of cautious optimism had been, if not disasters, then surely disappointments. She most certainly wasn't looking for a third. Still, if you were going to have a relationship, surely you wanted something a bit more than what this Richard was offering.

'Sounds very sensible,' she said. Too sensible. Where was the romance? The *love*? There was nothing sensible about either, as far as she was concerned, although she had no first-hand experience. She'd never been in love, not even close, and she doubted it would ever happen. True love matches—like her own mother and father's—were rare, which was why Emily had been happy to help Steph and Tim along. She'd just about given up finding it for herself. 'Does Richard work for Kingsley Engineering?' she asked, mentally going through the several hundred employees Jason had on his payroll. There were several Richards.

'Yes, he's worked on a project with Mr Kingsley in Africa,' Helen answered. 'He just got back.'

Emily nodded, for now she knew just who Helen's Richard was. Richard Marsden, one of a handful of Jason's protégés, a solid-looking engineer with an earnest expression, a nervous tic and absolutely no sense of humour. Of course he would suggest such a thing. She could just see him sitting Helen down on his sofa and outlining his five-year plan for their relationship, with accompanying PowerPoint presentation. It all sounded rather dreadful. 'Well,' she said diplomatically, 'it will certainly be nice for you to be able to spend some time with him.'

'Yes…' Helen sounded hesitant and, although Emily didn't blame her, she decided they'd had enough personal conversation. Part of her success in Human Resources was to know both when to employ and to curb the personal aspect of her position. 'Well, since Mr Kingsley can vouch for you, I'm certainly willing to hire you. We'll just fill out some forms and then I'll show you around the reception area.'

Helen beamed. 'Thank you, Miss Wood.'

'Please, call me Emily. We're all friendly here.'

Emily watched as Helen bent her dark head to fill out the forms, a sudden, gentle sort of protectiveness stealing over her. The girl really did seem terribly innocent. She would certainly need someone to look out for her, show her the ropes. And, more importantly, a bit of fun. Clearly Richard wasn't going to do it.

'Come on, then,' she said when Helen had finished the forms. 'We can grab a coffee before I show you 'round. You can meet a few people.' A few people other than Richard Marsden, she added silently.

The rest of her first day as Head of Human Resources passed uneventfully enough, with no more than the usual common complaints and banal paperwork to round out the hire of Helen that morning. She was surprised to find it already past five o'clock and most of her department gone when she finally finished her last email and pressed send.

'A successful first day, it seems.'

Emily looked up to see Jason standing in her doorway, and she wondered how she could have missed his approach. Her heart certainly gave a sudden, surprising lurch now.

'Jason, you startled me.' She smiled up at him, noticing the deeper grooves from his mouth to nose, the faint fanning of wrinkles at the corners of his eyes. The African sun had aged him a bit, but it was not unattractive. Jason could certainly carry off a rather dignified look. And he was quite a bit older…he was nearing forty. Time to think of marrying, perhaps. The thought was unsettling, only because she could not imagine Jason with a wife. He would probably pick someone to suit him just like Richard was with Helen. She could just see him compiling some sort of list. *Must be handy with an iron, a golf club and a gardening spade….*

'Yes, it was successful,' she said, stressing the word lightly. 'No less than you'd expect, of course.'

'Of course.' He strolled into her office. He wore, as usual, a dark suit with a crisp shirt and blue silk tie, a woollen trench coat over one arm. He looked utterly put together and as always a little remote, and yet he seemed somehow different too. Or perhaps she was the one who was different, for she couldn't quite keep her gaze from roving over him as that citrusy scent of his aftershave assaulted her senses.

She rose from her desk, glad she'd chosen a cherry-red power suit with a fitted jacket and miniskirt for her first day as Head. Admittedly, her skirt was a *bit* on the short side, and she saw Jason's gaze flick to her bare legs before his mouth tightened into a faint but familiar line of disapproval.

Feeling a little impish, Emily held one foot out for him to examine. 'Oh, do you like my shoes?' she asked, widening her eyes innocently. Today she'd worn a pair of matching red stilettos with diamanté straps. She wasn't generally that into shoes, but these had been hard to resist. And they matched her suit perfectly.

Jason stared at her stretched-out leg, looking decidedly unimpressed. 'Very pretty,' he said after a moment. 'Although not necessarily work attire.'

'Well,' Emily told him, unable to resist the opportunity to bait him just a bit more, 'I had to liven up this suit somehow.'

For a split second Jason looked positively thunderous, and Emily wondered if he was actually angry. Then he glanced at her, smiling, his eyes lightening to the honey colour she'd seen last night, and he said, 'Trust me, Emily, your clothes do not need livening up. Now, how about a bite to eat and you can tell me all about your first day?'

Emily blinked in shock. She had been half-expecting Jason to check up on her since it was the first day of her new position, but this? 'Dinner?' she repeated rather stupidly, and Jason's smile widened.

'That is the idea. Usually, around six o'clock, people like to eat and drink. Sustenance, you know, as well as a social habit.'

Emily's mouth twitched in a smile. She'd forgotten about Jason's dry sense of humour. And, despite her surprise at the invitation, she realised she'd like to have dinner with him. She was curious about how he'd changed, and even what this personal business was. And there was something about Jason—something oddly different—that she wanted to understand. Or at least explore. 'Actually, I'm famished,' she told him as she reached for her coat. 'I skipped lunch. So yes, you can treat me to dinner.'

Jason watched as Emily slid a form-fitting trench coat over her already clinging suit. It didn't even cover her legs. For a coat, it was remarkably revealing. He felt himself frown, already regretting his impulse invitation. He hadn't even meant to come down to Emily's office; he had plans that evening, and he'd meant to walk straight outside to his car. Yet somehow he'd taken this little detour, and once he'd seen Emily hold out one perfectly shaped golden leg, her eyes sparkling with laughter, his resolve had crumbled to dust.

He'd kept away from her for seven years; she was nearly twenty-five now. She was experienced, if the social pages were anything to go by, and surely a single evening—a little bit of light flirting—wouldn't harm anyone. It was just, Jason told himself, an itch he needed to scratch. It wouldn't go anywhere. It couldn't. He wouldn't even kiss her.

Yet already he was reaching for his BlackBerry, and he quickly sent a rather terse text to cancel the rest of his plans for the evening. He clicked the button on his keys to unlock the car, and Emily started in surprise.

'You own a Porsche?' she said, clearly surprised.

Jason opened her door, breathing in the strawberry scent of her hair and something else, something warm and feminine that had lust jolting through him yet again. *Just dinner.* 'It appears that I do,' he said, and she rolled her eyes as she slid into the sumptuous leather interior.

'Quite a nice ride. It's not what I'd expect at all.'

'Oh?' Jason slid into the driver's seat. 'I didn't know you had expectations about my mode of transport.'

'Yes, but that's it exactly, isn't it?' Emily said with a laugh. She shook her hair back over her shoulders in a golden waterfall. 'Your "mode of transport". I'd expect something basic and, well, boring for you, just a car to get you from point A to point B. Of course,' she teased, 'the colour is a bit dull. Navy-blue doesn't do it for me, I'm afraid.'

Jason stared at her for a second, utterly nonplussed by her rather brutal assessment of him. *Boring?* And he'd been thinking she still had a little crush on him. Well, that was him sorted. 'Boring,' he repeated musingly as he started the car. 'And dull. I wonder if I should be offended.'

'You can hardly be offended by that, Jason!'

Now he really *was* offended. Most women didn't think he was boring at all. Most women were eager to spend an evening with him. Yet here Emily sat sprawled in the seat across from him, her skirt riding up on her slim thighs, looking at him as if he were her doddering old uncle whom she had to humour.

Yet she hadn't looked at him like that last night. He still remembered the brief, enticing touch of her hand on his chest. She'd been startled by the electric current that had suddenly snapped between them; he knew she'd felt it. He certainly had. Now he slid her a sideways glance as he revved the engine, causing Emily to laugh a little as she instinctively grabbed the door handle. 'Can't I?' he murmured.

'Well, honestly,' she said once he'd pulled out of the office's underground car park and begun to drive down Euston Road at quite a sedate speed. 'You've always been—'

'Boring?' He heard the slight edge to his voice and strove to temper it. This was not how he'd pictured this evening starting.

'Well, not boring precisely,' Emily allowed. 'But… predictable. Cautious. Steady.' Jason kept his face expressionless although he felt his brows start to draw together in an instinctive glower. She was actually *patronising* him. 'You never took part in the games and scrapes we got into—'

'By "we" I assume you mean you, Isobel and Jack,' Jason returned dryly. At Emily's nod, he continued, 'You might do well to remember, Em, that you're twelve years younger than I am. While you were getting into these so-called scrapes, I was in university.' His hands tightened on the wheel as the difference in their ages struck its necessary blow. Emily might be twenty-five, but she was still young. And in many ways, naive. Innocent, if not utterly, not to mention scatty, silly and far too frivolous. She was entirely wrong for him. Wrong for what he wanted.

Wrong for a wife.

'Well, of course I know that,' she said. 'But, even so…you've always been a bit *disapproving*, Jason. Even of Jack—'

'You didn't have to live with him,' Jason returned, keeping his voice mild. Of course everyone loved Jack. Jack was *fun*, except when it was Jason fetching him from boarding school after he'd been expelled, or from a party where he'd passed out. Fortunately, Jack had settled down since he'd been married, but Jason still remembered his younger brother's turbulent teen years. He'd helped him out because their father never would, and Jack had no memories of their mother. He had precious few himself…and the ones he did, he'd sometimes rather forget.

'Still,' Emily persisted in that same teasing tone, 'I remember the lectures you gave me. When I picked a few flowers from your garden, you positively *glowered*. You terrified me—'

'By a few flowers you mean all the daffodils.' They had been his mother's favourite, and he'd been furious with her for beheading them all, as he remembered.

'Was it all of them?' Her eyebrows arched in surprise. 'Oh, dear. I was a bit of a brat, wasn't I?'

'I didn't want to be the one to say it,' Jason murmured, and was rewarded with a gurgle of throaty laughter that made him feel as if he'd just stuck his finger in an electric socket. His whole body felt wired, alive and pulsating with pure lust. This evening really had been a mistake. He was playing with fire, and while he could handle a few burns, Emily surely couldn't. That was why he'd always stayed away, and why he should keep at it. Right now he could have been sitting down to dinner with Patience Felton-Smythe, a boring woman with a horsey face who liked to garden and knit and was on the board of three charities. In short, the kind of woman he intended to marry.

Emily gazed out of the window at the blur of traffic, the streets of London slick with rain. Although it was only the beginning of November, the Christmas lights had already been strung along Regent Street and their lights were streakily reflected on the pavement below.

'Where are we going?' she asked as Jason turned onto Brook Street.

'Claridge's,' he said and Emily let out a little laugh.

'I should have known. Somewhere upscale and respectable and just a little bit stodgy.'

'Like me?' Jason filled in as they pulled up to the landmark hotel.

Emily smiled sweetly. She *had* offended Jason with her offhand remark. 'You said it, not me.'

'You didn't need to. But, in any case, Claridge's has had a bit of a remake over the years. You might find it's the same with me.' He tossed the keys to the valet and came around to help Emily out of the car, his hand strong and firm as he guided her from the low-slung Porsche—not easy to manage in her stiletto heels and short skirt—and continued to hold her hand as he led her into the restaurant. Emily didn't protest, although she surely should have. There was something comforting and really rather nice about the way his fingers threaded through hers, his grip sure and strong.

It reminded her of when she'd been younger, and no matter what she'd done or where she'd gone, she'd trusted implicitly that Jason would be there to save her. Scold her too, undoubtedly, but she'd always known with him she was safe.

Yet as Jason glanced back at her, his eyes glinting, turning them the colour of dark honey, she had to acknowledge that something about holding Jason's hand didn't feel like when she was younger at all. In fact it felt quite different—different enough for a strange new uneasiness to ripple through her, and she smiled and slipped her hand from his as the maître d' led them to a secluded table in a corner of the iconic restaurant.

'So what's the occasion, exactly?' Emily asked as she opened the menu and began to peruse its offerings.

'Occasion?'

'I can't think the last time you took me out to dinner, if ever.'

Jason's lips twitched. 'There's a first time for everything.'

'I suppose, but…' Emily paused, cocking her head as she gazed at Jason; his hair was a little damp and rumpled from the rain and he had an endearingly studious expression on his face as he perused the wine list. She could see the faint shadow of stubble on his jaw, and it made him look surprisingly attractive. Sexy, even, which was ridiculous because she'd never thought of Jason that way—

Except for that once, and that was *not* going to be repeated.

'Are you checking up on me?' she asked, and Jason glanced up from the wine list.

'Checking up on you? You sound like you have a guilty conscience, Em. Too many parties?'

'No, it's just…' She paused, uncertain how to articulate how odd it was to be here with Jason, almost as if they were on a date. Which was ridiculous, because she knew Jason didn't think of her that way—hadn't he proved it on the dance floor seven years ago? Emily was quite sure nothing had changed there.

Except *she* had changed, of course. She'd grown up and moved long past that silly moment of infatuation with staid, stuffy Jason. And while she was perfectly happy to have dinner with an old family friend, she wasn't sure she wanted some kind of lecture. Had her father asked Jason to keep an eye on her, now he was back in London for a fair bit? It was quite possible.

'Just no lectures,' she said, wagging a finger at him, and Jason shook his head.

'I think you're a little too old for lectures, Em. Unless you misbehave, of course.' There was something almost wicked about Jason's smile, his eyes glinting in the candlelit dimness of the room, and Emily felt her stomach dip again. He turned back to the menu and she decided she must have imagined that suggestive undercurrent, that little glimpse of wickedness. There was nothing wicked about Jason Kingsley at all. He was the most law-abiding citizen she had ever known.

'I promise not to,' she replied, tossing her hair, and Jason beckoned the waiter over to the table to take their orders.

Emily ordered and then glanced around the room as Jason ordered for himself, a low murmur she didn't really hear. Most of the diners were businessmen making deals, or well-heeled pensioners. This place really was a little stodgy.

'The chicken? Adventurous, Em,' Jason said, slanting her an amused look as the waiter left.

Emily gave him her own flippant look right back. She'd

been a notoriously picky eater as a child, as Jason undoubtedly remembered. 'The braised calf livers aren't to my taste.'

'Still picky?'

'Discriminating is the word I'd use. And not as much as you might remember, Jason. I have changed, you know.'

'I don't doubt it.' He paused, his long, supple fingers toying with the stem of his water glass. 'I suppose,' he said musingly, 'there's quite a bit I don't know about you now. I've been gone, most of the time at least, for so long.'

'But now you're back to stay?'

He shrugged. 'For as long as needed.'

Emily nodded in understanding. 'On this personal business of yours?'

A frown creased his brow before his expression cleared and he flashed her a quick, knowing smile. 'Yes.'

She couldn't help but laugh; he wouldn't give anything away. He never did, but then she'd never thought Jason had any secrets before. Or at least secrets worth knowing. 'You're a man of mystery now, aren't you?'

'Rather than boring?' Jason filled in, one eyebrow arched.

'I think I hurt your feelings when I said that.'

'Only a little bit. As retribution, I told the waiter to bring you the calf livers rather than the chicken.'

Her eyes widened as she realised she actually hadn't heard what he'd ordered. 'You did not!'

'No, I didn't. But you believed me, didn't you?' His faint smile, for a second, formed into a fully fledged grin, and the effect of that smile had Emily unsettled yet again. She'd forgotten how white Jason's teeth were, how the dimple in his cheek deepened.… He really was a handsome man, which was, of course, what had compelled her to flirt with him seven years ago. She would not make the same mistake again.

'Only because you've always told me the truth, no matter how ungracious it is.'

He cocked his head, his gaze sweeping over her in considering assessment. 'Would you rather I lied?'

Emily thought of times Jason had told her the unvarnished truth when no one else would: when she was fourteen, she'd had a terrible spot on the tip of her nose. She'd been horribly embarrassed, and in a moment of desperation she'd asked Jason if he'd noticed it.

Straight-faced, he'd said, *Em, how could I not? But I still like you, spots and all.*

And when she'd been fifteen and missing her mother, who'd died when she was only three, she'd asked him if one ever stopped missing one's mum. She'd never met his mother; she'd died when he was eight years old.

No, he said, *you never stop. But it does get easier. Sometimes.*

His words had comforted her because she'd known them for truth rather than mere sentiment.

'No,' she said now, with her own surprised honesty, 'I wouldn't rather you lied. I suppose you need someone in your life who will tell you the truth.'

'I'll always do that.' His gaze lingered on her for a moment longer than she expected, so a sudden warmth spread through her limbs, a new unsettling awareness that she could hardly credit. This was *Jason*. She felt a rush of relief when the sommelier came with the wine and Emily watched as Jason, with that same easy assurance, swilled it in his glass before taking a sip and then nodding his approval. When the man had left, he raised his glass, the deep ruby-red of the wine catching the candlelight, in a toast.

'To old friends and new beginnings,' he said, his gaze still lingering, Emily raised her own glass, as well.

'Hear, hear.'

'So,' Jason said once they had each taken a sip of wine, 'how is Helen getting on?'

'Ah, I knew there was an ulterior motive to this dinner.'

'Not at all,' Jason replied blandly. 'But, since you interviewed her this morning, I thought I might as well ask.'

'Well, I hired her as you asked me to. I think she'll do well enough. She hardly has the experience, though.'

'I didn't expect her to.'

Emily raised her eyebrows. 'A charity case?'

'Just a kindness,' Jason replied mildly.

Emily reached for her wine again, suppressing a sharp stab—of something. Whatever uncomfortable emotion was assailing her was not one she wanted to name. 'She's quite beautiful, you know.'

'Actually, I don't. As you might recall, I told you yesterday that I'd never met her.'

'Ah, yes.' Emily pursed her lips. 'I do recall now. You wanted to hire her as a favour to Richard Marsden.'

Jason cocked his head. 'I don't think I mentioned him by name, but yes.'

'Because,' Emily continued wryly, but with a little bite to her words, 'Helen and Richard are going to make a *go* of it.'

Jason paused, his wine glass halfway to his lips. 'You sound as if you don't approve.'

'Who am I to approve or disapprove?' Emily replied, her eyebrows arching innocently.

'It sounds eminently sensible to me,' Jason said with a brisk reasonableness Emily didn't like.

'Oh, yes, very sensible,' she agreed. 'Hardly romantic, though.'

'Romantic?' Jason frowned. 'Is it meant to be romantic?'

He sounded so nonplussed that Emily almost wanted to laugh, yet something in her—some deep, hidden well of emotion—kept her from amusement. Instead, she almost felt hurt, which made no sense at all and so she pushed the thought away. 'Well, in general, Jason,' she said, as if explaining basic arithmetic to a slightly backward child, 'the kind of relationship Helen was talking about with Richard is meant to be romantic rather than *sensible*. You're hardly choosing a…a pair of shoes when it comes to a girlfriend or even a wife—'

'I'm a great believer in sensible shoes.'

Emily narrowed her eyes, unable to tell whether Jason was joking or not. She had a feeling he wasn't. 'A girl likes to be swept a little bit off her feet, you know.'

'It sounds dangerous,' Jason replied, straight-faced. 'If you're swept off your feet, you could lose your balance. You might even fall.'

'Exactly,' Emily replied. 'You might fall in love, which is the whole point, isn't it? Rather than making a go of it.'

He eyed her thoughtfully. 'You seem to have taken exception to that expression.'

'I have,' Emily agreed with a bit more passion than she would have preferred to show. The glass of wine must be going to her head; she'd had hardly anything to eat since breakfast. 'I'd much rather stay single my whole life than be with someone who asks me to make a *go* of it,' she finished, her voice still sounding a little too loud.

'Duly noted. And are you planning to stay single, then?'

'As a matter of fact, yes,' she said, glad to see surprise flash across his features. 'I've no reason to get married.'

'No reason?'

'I'm not lonely or unhappy or dying to have children,' Emily replied with a shrug and a bit more conviction than she actually felt. She didn't want to admit to Jason that she had no reason to get married because she hadn't met anyone worth marrying. Worth taking that risk for. 'I'm not going to wait around for Prince Charming to come and rescue me,' she declared, her tone starting to sound strident. Jason raised his eyebrows, a small smile playing about his mouth, clearly amused. 'I want to have fun.'

'Now that I can believe.'

She made a face at him. 'What's wrong with that? There's plenty of time to settle down.'

'For you, perhaps.'

'Oh, yes, I forget how old you are. One foot in the grave already.' She smiled at him, determined to stay light and teasing although for some reason she was feeling less and less so. 'In any case,' she said dismissively, 'I have friends, a job I love, a niece and nephew to cuddle and a man who adores me.'

Jason stilled. 'A man who adores you?' he queried in a tone of polite interest.

Emily couldn't help but laugh at Jason's suspicious look. He looked as though he thought she had some sort of toyboy on retainer. 'My father, of course.' She eyed him mischievously. 'Did you think I was talking about someone else?'

'I wondered,' he admitted blandly. 'But since you've been wittering on about your determination to stay single, I had to assume we were not talking about a romantic interest.'

'I wasn't wittering,' Emily said with some affront, and Jason raised his eyebrows.

'I apologise. You were waxing poetically.'

She made a face. 'That sounds worse.' To her surprise, she found she was enjoying this little repartee. She leaned forward, a sudden, sharp curiosity making her ask, 'And what about you, Jason? Any plans to be swept off your feet?'

His mouth quirked upwards, revealing that dimple. 'I thought I was meant to do the sweeping.'

Emily laughed ruefully in acknowledgement. 'It sounds as if we're talking about cleaning a house. Do you intend to marry? Fall in love?' She'd spoken lightly, yet the question suddenly felt invasive, intimate, and she half-regretted asking it even though she wanted to know the answer. Badly.

Jason rotated his wine glass between his strong brown fingers; the simple action was strangely mesmerising. 'One does not necessarily require the other,' he finally said, and Emily felt a bizarre flicker of disappointment.

'And which would you prefer?' she asked, keeping her tone light and teasing. 'Love without marriage, or marriage without love?'

Jason took a sip of wine, his eyes meeting hers over the rim of the glass, his gaze now flat and forbidding. 'Love, in my opinion, is overrated.'

'A rather cynical point of view,' Emily returned after a moment. She felt that flicker of disappointment again, and suppressed it. What did it matter what Jason thought of either love or marriage? 'What made you decide that?'

He lifted one shoulder in a shrug. 'Experience, I suppose. Anyone can say they love someone. It's just a bunch of words you can choose to believe or not. They don't make much difference, in the end.' He lapsed into a sudden silence, frowning, as if his own words had triggered an unpleasant thought—or memory. Then his expression cleared, as if by force of will, and he glanced up at her, smiling. 'Much better, in my opinion, to marry and, yes, even make a go of it than witter on about love—or wax poetically, as the case may be.' His eyes glinted with knowing humour, and Emily conceded the point with a little laugh although she wondered just what experience had made Jason so cynical…and what had made him frown quite like that.

'Be that as it may,' she said, 'a little poetry surely can't go amiss.'

'Yet you've written off both marriage and love, it would seem?'

Written off seemed a bit strong, but Emily didn't intend to debate the point. As far as Jason was concerned, written off would do very well indeed. 'I told you, I'm happy as I am.'

'Happy to have fun.'

'Yes.' She stared at him defiantly. He made fun sound like a naughty word. She knew he thought she was a bit scatty, perhaps even a little wild, and she took a perverse pleasure in confirming his opinion. Even if she still felt that bizarre flicker of hurt.

'Yet you seem to be interested in finding love and marriage for others,' Jason noted dryly. 'Stephanie and Tim being a case in point.'

'Just because I don't want it for me doesn't mean it isn't right for other people,' Emily replied breezily. 'I'm a great believer in love. Just not for myself. Not now, anyway.' She took a sip of wine, averting her eyes. She wasn't quite telling Jason the truth, but she had no intention of admitting that she wasn't looking for love because she didn't want to be disappointed when it proved impossible to find, or didn't live up to her expectations. She'd witnessed a love match first-hand—or almost. Even though her mother had died before she had any real memories of her, Emily had heard plenty of stories about Elizabeth Wood; she knew from her father—and his grief—that they had loved each other deeply and forever.

That kind of love didn't come to everyone. She was afraid it would never come to her. And it was much easier to convince herself—and Jason—that she'd never wanted it in the first place. 'In any case,' she continued in an effort to steer the conversation away from such personal matters, 'we were talking about Richard and Helen. And I think it's safe to say that I know a bit more about these things than you do.'

'These things?'

'What women want when it comes to romance. Love, even. I may not be looking for it myself, but that doesn't mean I don't know what most women want.' She'd had enough late-night sessions with friends over a bottle of wine or even just the idle chatter by the coffee machine at work to be quite the expert.

'Is that right?' He sounded amused, which annoyed her. She did, in fact, know what she was talking about, much more than Jason ever would. She could just imagine Jason sitting some poor woman down and asking her to make a go of it just like Richard Marsden had. Knowing Jason, he wouldn't ask; he'd insist. He'd probably propose marriage with a drawn-up business contract in his breast pocket. The thought sent an unreasonable flame of indignation burning through her.

'Yes, I do,' she told him firmly. 'Women want a man who will romance them, Jason. Woo them with flowers and compliments and thoughtfulness and…and lots of other things,' she finished a bit lamely. The wine was really going to her head; her brain felt rather fuzzy. 'And what they *don't* want is to have someone sit them down and tell them they *might* be suitable, but first they need a trial period.'

'I doubt Marsden said it like that.'

'Close enough. The meaning was clear.'

Jason cocked his head. 'And you don't think Helen Smith could tell Marsden just where to put it if she didn't like his idea?'

Emily let out a reluctant laugh. 'Perhaps—if she had more backbone. She's young and impressionable. In any case, another man will surely come and sweep her off her feet while Richard is deciding whether they can make a go of it or not. She's very beautiful.'

'So you've told me.' His mouth curved upwards once more. 'But if you ask me, which I am quite aware you are not, Richard's suggestion is very sensible. And, in the long run, far more romantic than a bunch of plastic-wrapped bouquets and meaningless compliments. I think he could be just the thing for her.'

'You make it sound as if Helen has a head cold and Richard is a couple of paracetamol,' Emily protested, her mind spinning in indignation over Jason's dismissal of everything she'd just said. Plastic-wrapped bouquets and meaningless compliments! God help the poor woman he decided to approach with his own sensible plan. 'That's not what a woman wants out of love or marriage, Jason.'

Jason leaned forward, his eyes alight. They really turned the most amazing colour sometimes, Emily thought a bit dazedly. Almost amber. She swallowed, aware that she probably shouldn't have had a second glass of wine. And where was their food?

'But you said you weren't interested in love or marriage,' he reminded her softly.

Emily swallowed again. Her throat felt very dry. How had this conversation become so personal and…and *intimate*? 'I told you, I'm happy as I am.'

'With no intention of ever falling in love?'

With no intention of telling Jason any more about her own love life, or lack thereof, Emily amended silently. 'Perhaps love *is* overrated,' she said, throwing his own words back at him. 'I've had two relationships and although I didn't love either of the men involved, they were still definite disappointments. I'm not interested in searching for something that might never actually happen or even exist.' Or being hurt when it couldn't be found or didn't work out. She thought of her father's two decades of mourning. No, love wasn't overrated. But the aftermath might be underestimated.

Jason sat back, seemingly satisfied. 'Wise words. I quite agree.'

'So no love or marriage for you?' Emily said, meaning to tease, yet the question came out a little too serious.

'I didn't say that,' Jason said, and his dark gaze settled on Emily with a frown. 'I'll have to marry some time. I need an heir for Weldon, after all.'

Now *that* sounded positively medieval. She could see Jason arranging some awful marriage with a sour-faced socialite just because she was of good breeding stock. She shuddered. 'How practical of you,' she told him. 'I hope I'm not on your list of candidates.'

Jason's expression darkened, his brows snapping together

rather ferociously. 'Never fear, Em. You most certainly are not in the running.'

Well, he didn't have to sound *quite* so certain, Emily thought, feeling rather miffed by his hasty assurance. Of course they'd make a terrible couple—they were far too different—but did he really have to look as if the thought of marrying her was utterly repellent?

'Well, that's a relief, then,' she said lightly. 'So what kind of woman are you looking for?'

'Someone who shares my view on love and marriage.'

'Someone sensible, then.'

'Exactly.'

Emily made a face. It all sounded really rather horrible. 'Not one of the starlets or models you've usually had on your arm?' she said, trying to tease even though she still felt a bit miffed, and perhaps even hurt.

Jason frowned. 'Those were just dates,' he said. 'Not wife material.'

Emily shuddered theatrically. He sounded as if he were talking about a lump of clay, moulded to the shape he preferred. 'Well, good luck with that,' she said, her voice sharpening despite her intention to still sound so insouciant.

Jason inclined his head in acknowledgement. 'Thank you.'

Emily smiled back, but inside she found she really didn't like thinking about Jason and his sensible bride-to-be—whoever she was—at all.

CHAPTER THREE

THE rest of the meal passed pleasantly, and Emily was relieved to have the conversation move on to more innocuous matters. The chicken, although unadventurous, was delicious, and Emily found she enjoyed chatting with Jason about things as seemingly insignificant as the weather or the latest film. She'd forgotten what a dry sense of humour he had, so sometimes it took her a few seconds even to realise he was joking.

'Will you miss travelling?' she asked as the waiter cleared their plates. 'Since you're planning to be in London for a time.'

'I'll have other things to occupy me,' Jason replied easily.

Emily pursed her lips. 'This personal business.'

'You're quite curious about that.'

'Only because I can't imagine what it is. You've always been such an open book, Jason. No secrets. No surprises.'

Jason drummed his fingers on the table. He had rather nice fingers, Emily thought distractedly. Long and tapered. She'd been noticing them all evening. 'Boring again.'

'I really did insult you with that!' She laughed as Jason pulled a face.

'I never realised you thought me so stodgy,' he replied as he poured her another glass of wine.

'I shouldn't drink that,' she protested. 'I'm already feeling a bit tipsy.' Tipsy enough to have admitted it, as well.

Jason's lips curved in a knowing smile. 'And I recall that you say some quite interesting things when you've had a glass or two too many.'

Emily felt herself flush, for she knew just what Jason was referring to. *You're quite handsome, you know. Perhaps you'd like to kiss me.* Yet again he'd referenced that evening, that single dance when, buoyed by champagne and her own youthful naivety, she'd offered herself to him. Why did he keep mentioning it? Did he think it some great joke?

'Don't,' she said, trying to still sound light and teasing, and yet not quite pulling it off. She found she couldn't pretend it was all a joke, as she had the other day. Somehow, in the quiet candlelight, with Jason holding her gaze over the table, she couldn't summon that light, airy insouciance that she always covered herself with, almost like armour. 'I'm a bit sensitive about that,' she managed lightly and Jason sat back, his expression turning speculative.

'Why?'

Emily choked back a startled laugh. 'Because you humiliated me, that's why!'

Jason stared at her, his expression so utterly nonplussed that once again Emily was torn between laughter and a strange sense of hurt. 'I humiliated you?' he repeated, his tone quietly incredulous. 'Sorry, Em, but I don't quite see how that happened.'

She shook her head, refusing to discuss it. They'd gone over it once already, and it really was time to relegate that episode to the dim and dusty past. 'Never mind. It hardly matters, Jason. It was seven years ago. I was practically a child.'

'I know,' he said, so softly Emily almost didn't hear him. 'I was quite aware of that at the time.'

Discomfited again, Emily said, 'In any case, we were talking about Helen and Richard.'

'Is there more to say on that subject?'

'You might not think so, but as someone newly arrived to London, Helen surely would like to experience all it has to offer and meet a few—'

'Oh, no, you don't, Emily.' Jason put his glass down and looked at her with a certain knowing sharpness that Emily didn't really like, but at least she recognised it. This was how Jason had always looked at her, how he *was*, and it almost relieved her to have him treating her the same as he always did. Then she could treat him as she always did, and she'd stop feeling so unsettled, so…restless. 'You aren't planning to organise Helen, are you?'

'Organise?' Emily repeated, widening her eyes.

'Yes, just as you did with Stephanie. She might have been your work superior and several years older than you, but you had her well in hand within months.'

Emily stared at him in surprise and with a little bit of affront. He made her sound like a bossy know-it-all when she was just *outgoing*. Unlike some people. 'How would you know?' she demanded. 'If I remember correctly, you'd swanned off to Asia at the time.'

'Swanned off?' Jason repeated in wry disbelief. 'I don't think working twelve hours a day on a flood retention basin in Burma involved any swanning.'

'How would you know what I was up to?'

Jason shrugged, his face impassive. 'I have my sources. I know you organised her on a round of dinner parties and drinks outings, and Tim wasn't your first attempt at a blind date—'

Emily's mouth dropped open most inelegantly. 'You've been *spying* on me—'

'Keeping tabs,' Jason cut across her. 'I hired you when you came to London, and of course I had a vested interest in making sure you were keeping safe. Especially considering your father, Isobel and Jack would all have my head if anything happened to you.'

'Nothing did,' Emily said a bit sulkily. She didn't like the thought of Jason knowing what she was up to. Here she'd been thinking to show him how sophisticated and poised she'd become in the last few years, only to discover he'd been keeping an eye on her all along, as if she were some recalcitrant child.

'In any case,' Jason continued, 'my point is that while I'm perfectly happy for you to welcome Helen into the company and even show her around a bit, I draw the line at having her *meet* people or, God help us, involving yourself in any more matchmaking.'

'So you do admit I had something to do with Steph and Tim!' Emily said in triumph, and Jason reached for his wine.

'Undoubtedly, but I'd like you to leave Helen and Richard alone so they *can* make a go of it, if they so choose.'

Emily sighed, rolling her eyes for dramatic effect. 'Very well. It is quite clear to me that you do not have a romantic bone in your body.'

'On the contrary,' Jason replied equably, 'I think it shows a remarkable sensitivity on my part, that I concern myself with them at all.' He smiled blandly. 'You, however, need not concern yourself.'

'As Head of Human Resources, it's my responsibility to make sure Helen settles in—'

'I'm sure Richard has that well in hand.'

'Ha!' Emily shook her head. 'He probably thinks inviting Helen over for some television and takeaway is enough.'

Jason narrowed his eyes. 'You really do have something against him, don't you?'

'No—' Emily protested, but Jason cut across her.

'Or is it just more amusing—and easier—to involve yourself in other people's lives rather than consider your own?'

Emily blinked; the banter had suddenly turned a bit too personal. His accusation hurt. 'Are you saying I'm a busybody?'

'I'm giving it to you straight,' Jason corrected, a small smile barely softening his words. 'Don't meddle.' He signalled for the waiter. 'And now I think I should take you home.'

Emily was irritatingly aware that Jason had just ended their conversation whether she had something more to say or not. So typical of him, and even though she'd fully intended to show him just how sophisticated and poised she'd become, she still felt like a scolded child in his presence, complete with braces and plaits. She rose from the table as gracefully as she could, well aware that although she wasn't drunk, she was definitely operating with a little buzz.

'Thank you for dinner.'

'The pleasure was all mine.' Jason's lips twitched as he gazed at her; Emily knew she probably looked a little sulky. 'Literally,' he added.

She felt compelled to say, 'I don't meddle.'

'And I'm not boring,' Jason whispered, his breath fanning her ear, his hand on the small of her back as he guided her from the restaurant. 'It seems we have to get to know each other all over again, Em.'

Before Emily could think of a reply, or even untangle just what Jason might have meant, the valet was fetching his Porsche and she was sliding into the leather interior, her head resting against the seat as the world spun dizzily around her. Definitely too much wine.

'Poor, Em,' Jason murmured as he pulled away from the kerb. 'Did you have anything to eat today?'

'A few crackers at lunch,' Emily said with a sigh. 'I'm a notorious lightweight, but even this is a bit much for me.' She felt her stomach lurch and grimaced.

'I hope,' Jason said, 'you're not going to be sick all over my car.'

Emily tried to laugh, although the idea was alarmingly possible. 'If I am,' she said, 'it's because the chicken was off, not because I drank too much.'

Jason laughed softly. 'Perhaps you should have tried the calf livers.' He reached over and laid a cool hand on her forehead, his fingers massaging her temples with deft lightness. She inhaled the citrusy tang of his aftershave, felt the graze of his thumb on her cheekbone. The touch managed to both soothe and stimulate her, which made her body feel even more confused. Jason had never touched her like this before; he'd never really touched her at all. 'Maybe you should close your eyes,' he suggested.

Emily obeyed, her head resting against the seat as she took a few deep breaths and her stomach finally settled itself. Jason left his hand on her forehead, the pressure cool and comforting. Emily had the bizarre desire to put her hand over his own, to keep his palm there, pressed against her. 'Sorry,' she said after a moment, and then added, compelled to honesty, 'And here I wanted to show you how sophisticated I am.'

'Sophisticated?' Belatedly, Emily realised she probably shouldn't have said that. 'Sophistication is overrated, Em.'

'Like love?' The words slipped out of their own accord. She felt as much as heard Jason's hesitation.

'Yes,' he finally said, removing his hand, and she opened her eyes. Jason had stopped the car, and she saw they were in front of her building. The car suddenly seemed very small and dark and quiet, the only sound their breathing.

Emily curled her fingers around the door handle. 'Well, goodnight, then,' she said, her voice a whisper in the dark, and Jason reached for his own door.

'I'll see you home.'

Emily fumbled in her bag for her keys, conscious of Jason next to her, looming like a dark shadow. She lived in a block of mansion flats, with separate keys for the front door as well as the door to her own flat. Now, in her befuddlement, she shoved the wrong key into the door, jamming it uselessly.

'Here, let me,' Jason said, and his fingers wrapped around hers as he took the key from her and replaced it with the other, then turned the lock easily and opened the door.

The elegant little foyer was lit only by a small table lamp and in the shadowy light Emily could see Jason's expression, his gaze solemn and yet somehow intent in a way that unnerved her. This whole evening had unnerved her because even though Jason had, for the most part, acted exactly as she expected him to, authoritative and a little annoying and yet still affectionately, impossibly Jason, he'd been different too. The whole evening had been different and, at this moment, with Jason still gazing at her in that intent, *intense* way, Emily could not articulate even to herself why. She couldn't think at all.

'You don't have to come upstairs,' she said, and then blushed at what sounded like some kind of ridiculous innuendo. 'I'm fine—'

'I'll leave you to it, then,' Jason said and, after a second's pause where they simply stared at each other, he lifted his hand, his fingers suspended in air, a whisper away from her face. Emily held her breath, unsure of what he intended or why she felt a strange swooping sensation in her stomach, as if she'd missed a step, or the floor had fallen away completely. Then Jason let his fingers brush her cheek, no more than a whisper of a touch, his fingertips barely trailing her jaw as a smile softened his features. Yet before Emily could even process it or the feel of his fingers on her skin, his expression hardened once more, his brows snapping together as he dropped his hand. 'Goodnight, Em,' he said, and then he was gone.

Emily sagged against the stairs, her mind spinning more than ever before, and this time it had nothing to do with the wine.

* * *

Jason slid back into his Porsche, cursing himself for almost kissing her. Or maybe for not kissing her. His body and mind were clearly at war, both seething with unfulfilled desire. This evening had been incredibly enjoyable, and therefore a big mistake. Why was he wasting his time with Emily? It so clearly couldn't go anywhere. He wouldn't let it.

And yet still here he was, wanting to be with her because it was so intensely pleasurable to listen to her banter, to hear her throaty laugh, to watch the lamplight pick out the golden glints in her hair. He'd felt vibrantly and vividly alive in her presence, and when she drew close to him he couldn't keep himself from touching her. Her skin had felt like warm silk.

This time Jason cursed aloud. This was *Emily*. Emily Wood, his nearest neighbour, his sister-in-law, the girl whose plaits he'd tugged and tears he'd wiped. She was a woman now, yes, but she was also scatty and silly and a little bit wild, and a completely inappropriate choice for a wife. As for anything else…that was, if not unimaginable, then impossible.

He could not have a cheap affair or easy fling with Emily Wood. He thought of all the reasons why being with her was a bad, bad idea: their families were related; she was young, more naive than she'd like him to believe; and most importantly, most disastrously, she had ideas about love. Romance. She might not be looking for love or marriage now, but *convenient* and *sensible* were clearly not in her vocabulary. He'd seen the stars in her eyes.

Just as he'd seen the stars in his mother's eyes wink slowly out. He'd lived with the resulting darkness, and it made him all the more determined to find the kind of wife his father should have had, the kind of wife he needed: convenient, sensible, practical. No romance. No love. No Emily.

Yet still the thought of her slid into his mind with a slyly seductive whisper and he found he could picture having an affair with Emily Wood all too easily. He could quite vividly imagine the silken slide of her lips against his, the heavy weight of her hair under his hand. And more…much more than that. Her body fitted close to his, her legs entwined with his…

Jason called a halt to that line of thinking, pleasurable as it was. No matter what her age now, Emily was still off-limits. He'd told her the truth when he'd said she was not on his list of candidates for a wife. He'd returned to London on *very* personal business, and that was the matter of finding someone to marry. He was thirty-seven years old and his father's health had begun to fail. He needed an heir. Emily might think that was awful and archaic, but Jason preferred to see it as practical.

Practical and without the kind of emotional expectations that had made his own mother miserable, and his father a widower. Love wasn't just overrated, it was inadvisable. Fraught with disappointment and danger, which was why Jason chose to avoid it altogether…as would his wife. No meaningless words, useless gestures, nameless disappointments. Just mutual respect and affection, the most solid basis for a lasting union.

What was not practical was envisioning Emily Wood in that role. Scatty, silly, teasing and tempting Emily Wood. Spoiled darling of the social pages, not to mention her father. Looking for love, even if she didn't realise it. Hell, she was arranging it for other people.

She was not remotely suitable to be his convenient, carefully chosen wife.

And she thought he was boring.

He laughed aloud, the sound rueful, as he acknowledged just how much Emily's careless remark had annoyed him. He really had thought she was still a little besotted with him, and the fact that she wasn't made him realise the extent of his own foolish arrogance. Although she hadn't thought he was boring when he'd touched her. He'd heard that slight indrawn breath, felt the crackle between them. Emily had definitely not been bored then.

And he'd barely been able to keep himself from cupping her face and drawing those lush lips towards his for the kiss he'd long denied himself.

And would continue denying himself, even if he longed to prove to Emily just how *exciting* he could be. He was in the business of finding a wife, not a lover. And despite the lust that still fired his body, he knew Emily could never be either.

CHAPTER FOUR

EMILY woke up with a vicious headache, which did not endear her to anyone, including Jason. She still had a vague sense of unease from their dinner last night, although she could not articulate why. It had been kind of Jason to take her out and, since she could be a bit more rational about things in the cold light of morning, she was honest enough to acknowledge that it was perfectly right and fair for Jason to be checking up on her. She'd expected it, years ago, and had been surprised and even a little hurt when he'd left so abruptly after he'd hired her. So why should it bother her now?

That part of their conversation, Emily acknowledged, didn't bother her. No, it was the other, hidden part, the way his eyes had glinted so knowingly and his mouth had quirked up at the corners and he'd murmured in that low hum of a voice that made her feel as if she wasn't with Jason at all, at least not the Jason she knew and depended on and sometimes—often—was irritated with, the Jason who teased and scolded and kept her in line. She was with a different Jason, someone she wondered whether she knew at all.

It was most unsettling.

Emily pushed *that* Jason out of her mind as she hurried to dress for work. Her headache had made her slow and after popping a few paracetamol she quickly dressed, grabbed her bag and hurried out of her flat.

She was looking forward to seeing Helen again, who was reporting to HR to start her first day at nine o'clock sharp. Helen was already waiting when Emily arrived, wincing slightly at the bright office light, at five minutes after nine.

'Sorry…a bit of a slow morning.'

'Oh, it's all right,' Helen said quickly. 'It's just so good to be here.' She smiled, a faint blush tinging her cheeks. 'I am a bit nervous, though,' she admitted.

'I'm sure you'll be fine,' Emily assured her as she put her things away and reached for Helen's paperwork. 'Come on then, let's get you sorted.'

Fifteen minutes later, Helen was seated comfortably at the front reception area, with Jane, the other, more senior receptionist, showing her how to work the bank of blinking telephones. There had been a push a few years ago to move to a more modern automated system of taking calls, but Jason had refused, and Emily could guess why. Two receptionists would be out of jobs. Besides, she supposed he was a bit old-fashioned that way, and the personal touch of a real human voice on the other end of the line was always appreciated. It was one of the many things that made Kingsley Engineering head and shoulders above other engineering firms, and Jason Kingsley a wealthy man.

Now Emily watched as Helen's eyes rounded at the seemingly complicated system of buttons and switches, her expression glazing over as Jane explained how to hold a call while answering another one, and then reeled off a list of employees who never liked to take calls, and other ones who preferred to be interrupted.

'Goodness,' Helen murmured. She'd been writing down what Jane was saying, but had abandoned the effort mid-list and simply stared around her in what looked to Emily like growing dismay. It reminded Emily of how she'd felt—and probably looked—when she'd started in HR, with Steph explaining a filing system that had been alarming in its complexity.

'Don't worry,' she told Helen, squeezing her shoulder. 'You'll get the hang of it in no time. I know it seems overwhelming at first, but it just takes a few calls before it's easy peasy.'

'Easy peasy,' Helen repeated, as if reassuring herself.

'I'll be back in a few hours to check on you,' Emily promised. 'And take you out to lunch.' She wasn't going to make the mistake of skipping lunch again, she thought, even as she acknowledged that Jason wasn't likely to ask her to dinner two nights in a row.

She hadn't seen him this morning, which was hardly surprising, yet she still felt a tense expectation prickling between her shoulder blades as she took Helen down to reception. It wasn't until she saw Jason come through the front doors of the building that the tension eased and her shoulders relaxed, making Emily realise just what had been causing it in the first place.

'Ah, you must be Helen,' he said, smiling easily as he held a hand out to shake, and Helen's blush deepened so she looked truly lovely, all cream and roses.

'It's so nice to meet you, Mr Kingsley.'

'The pleasure is all mine,' Jason assured her, and his voice had that low, steady thrum that reminded Emily of how he'd been with her last night, how it had made her feel, and she stepped forward, smiling brightly.

'I've just been showing Helen the ropes. But I'm sure she'll be running rings around Jane within hours!' Emily smiled conspiratorially at Jane to let her know this wouldn't *quite* be the case, and Jason turned from Helen to Emily, his gaze resting on her with that quiet sense of assurance that still, after all these years, had the power to unnerve her.

'I'm sure she will, if you have anything to do with it,' he said, and Emily wondered if she was the only one who heard the faintest thread of mocking laughter in his voice. He turned back to Helen, smiling again as he wished her well, and then went to head towards his executive office. After saying her own goodbyes to both receptionists, Emily fell into step with Jason, matching his long stride, and he slid her a sideways glance. 'You seem to be taking quite an interest in Miss Smith.'

'I take an interest in all the people I hire,' Emily replied briskly. 'It's my job.'

'Of course,' Jason agreed. 'And an admirable dedication to your job is the only reason, I suppose?'

He was laughing at her, she knew, but somehow she didn't really mind. She'd reached the door of her office, and she turned to face him, surprised and a bit breathless by how close he stood to her. She could smell the citrusy scent of his aftershave again, and underlying it was a fainter, muskier scent that she knew had to be just *Jason* and the thought made her stomach flip over in a way she was starting to get used to, it had been happening so often in the few days since Jason had returned. Despite its now familiarity, it still felt strange, unnerving, because this was Jason and save the thirty humiliating seconds when she'd asked him to kiss her, she'd never reacted this way to him before. She could only imagine how horrified he would be if he knew. 'Of course,' she said innocently. 'What else would it be?'

'As long as you aren't planning to meddle,' he said. Although he kept his tone light, Emily heard the warning in his words.

'Meddle or matchmake?'

'They're one and the same.'

'Only in your opinion.' She placed a hand on his chest, her palm flattening against the crisp fabric of his shirt, her fingers instinctively seeking the heat of him underneath the cloth. She felt his heart thudding steadily under her palm. She'd meant it to be a light, even impersonal touch, no more than a playful poke in the sternum, yet as if driven by a deeper, baser need, she found it couldn't be that; her hand acted of its own accord, fingers stretching, seeking, while every thought flew from her head.

'You don't need to worry about Helen—or me,' she finally said, fishing for the words that seemed to have pooled deep in her consciousness. She looked up to meet his gaze, saw the gold flecks in his eyes. They weren't brown at all. They weren't boring either. She swallowed. 'You don't need to keep an eye on me, Jason. I'm all grown up now.'

'As I'm coming to realise,' Jason said, his voice so low Emily felt it vibrate through her. His chest tensed under her hand. They remained silent, unmoving, and Emily felt as if everything had slowed down, distilled into this one moment, which was crazy because it wasn't a moment at all. They were just talking. And she was touching his chest.

'Well.' She cleared her throat and somehow managed to remove her hand from his chest; it flopped to her side like a dead thing, useless, awkward, and she suddenly didn't know what to do with it. She was acting ridiculously, Emily thought. Almost as bad as when she'd asked him—

Her mind skittered away from that memory. *Seven years ago.* Old hat, ancient history. Yet it felt close now—far too close—so even now she was half-inclined to tilt her head up and— 'I should get to work,' she said, a little too loudly, and she made her mouth curve into something close to a smile as she turned from him and opened her office door.

Jason watched her go, not moving. It wasn't until she was at her desk that Emily heard him walk down the hall, his steps quick and assured as always, as if he hadn't a care in the world.

She collapsed into her chair. What was *wrong* with her? Why was she acting so strangely around Jason—Jason, who had always been so predictable, so safe, so *ordinary*?

Even as she asked herself the question, Emily knew the

answer. She was acting so oddly around Jason—feeling so odd—because no matter how she tried to convince herself otherwise, some vestige of girlish longing from that dance long ago remained inside of her, needing only to see Jason properly again to unfurl and blossom once more.

Some part of her still wanted Jason. Wanted him to kiss her, even. Wanted him the way a woman wanted a man, if only to prove to the girl she'd once been that she was desirable. Desired…by Jason.

Which was ridiculous, because the last person she should be thinking of that way was Jason Kingsley. He'd surely be appalled if he knew the nature of her thoughts. *She* was appalled, because of all people to be even the littlest bit attracted to—well, Jason Kingsley was low down on her list. Sometimes she wondered if he even liked her all, beyond the most basic affection. He'd certainly always been quick to point out her faults. And as for his faults…well, boring was the least of them. Stodgy and stern and *horribly* practical…

She had no business feeling oddly about him at all. So she wouldn't. It was, Emily decided, a simple matter of mind over body. Whatever latent, leftover feeling she might have secretly nurtured for Jason would be stamped out by self-control right now.

She had more important things to do, better things to think about—

'Emily?'

Emily jerked her head up from where she'd been blindly gazing at a mindless doodle on a spare bit of stationery. It looked suspiciously like a J. She crossed it out viciously and then smiled at the woman who stood in her doorway, her skirt six inches shorter than Emily's, her nails curved talons, ruthlessly manicured. Gillian Bateson, the Head of Public Relations.

'Gillian, hello. Good to see you. Can I help with something?'

'I don't suppose Stephanie told you about the charity fund-raiser?' Gillian said in that rather lofty tone that Emily had never liked.

'I'm afraid not,' she replied equably enough. She knew the basics: every year Jason hosted an exclusive fund-raiser for a water-based charity, usually in one of London's best hotels. It was an intimate, expensive event that Gillian organised, apparently with help from HR.

'It's a very big do,' Gillian said, seating herself down across from Emily. 'Last year we raised three million pounds for wells in the Sudan.'

'That must have made for a lot of wells,' Emily said politely. She just managed to keep the mischief from her voice. Gillian had always been rather full of her own importance.

'It's a *very* important event,' Gillian confirmed, rolling her eyes dramatically. 'Of course, I'm in charge of it since it's essentially PR, but Stephanie always wanted to know what was going on—I suppose I'll have to fill you in, as well?' She made it sound as if that would be a terribly tiresome thing to do, and Emily smiled in understanding.

'If you'd be so kind, Gillian.' She had to remind herself that Gillian had been divorced three times and had lost custody of her only daughter. All the nail varnish and hairspray surely hid a deep heartache. Or so she tried to believe.

'Well…' Yet another eye roll. If she kept at it, Emily thought wryly, she'd have her eyes permanently aimed at the back of her head. 'We're raising money for a desalination plant in Namibia. The fund-raiser is meant to have a black and white theme, and since Jason's flat is decorated in black and white we're going to have it there—'

'The fund-raiser is at Jason's flat?' Emily could not keep the surprise from her voice as she digested this information, unsure how she felt about it. Or Gillian calling him by his first name in that intimate way.

Gillian arched her ruthlessly plucked eyebrows, a smug

smile curving that over-lipsticked mouth. 'You *have* been there?'

Actually, she hadn't. And no doubt Gillian knew it. She'd been there, obviously. Emily did not want to ask herself why. She smiled, shaking her head regretfully. 'No, I'm afraid I haven't had the honour, but I'm sure it's stunning. And Mr Kingsley is certainly generous to lend the use of his flat for the fund-raiser.'

'Yes, he is, isn't he?' Gillian swung one foot, her spiked heel dangling. 'I don't know why he hasn't married,' she mused.

'I'm sure he hasn't found someone sensible enough for him,' Emily said, her voice sharpening for the first time, and Gillian gave her a knowing glance.

'You think he needs someone sensible? He's hardly gone for the sensible types before.'

Emily shifted in her seat, uncomfortable with the nature of the conversation, or the sharp stab of something that felt almost like jealousy at the thought of Jason *going* for anyone.

Still, Emily was forced to acknowledge that Gillian was right. Jason had never taken out sensible types, but then he'd never been seen with the same woman twice. All they'd been were dates, just as he'd said. Arm candy. So just what kind of woman would he want to be the mother of his all-important heir? What woman would fall in line with his no-love qualification? Plenty of women, Emily supposed, including sweetly biddable Helen Smith or worldly Gillian Bateson.

And why, oh, why, was she thinking like this?

'In any case,' Gillian said with another cat-like smile, 'I'm sure he's getting ready to settle down. He's quite a catch.'

'I suppose.' What awful expressions, Emily thought. A catch, like you had to run after somebody and wrestle them to the ground before convincing him to marry you. And settling down was even worse. It sounded so...disappointing. She could just imagine what kind of woman Jason would choose:

someone coolly composed and perhaps just a little bit horsey; someone who would arrange flowers and place settings with contemptuous ease and give him an heir and a spare right off the bat. She'd have no sense of humour at all. A woman like that would be perfect for Jason. She would be so very sensible and stodgy, just as he was.

Except he hadn't seemed so stodgy last night.

'Well, that's probably all you need to know,' Gillian said, unfolding herself from the chair. 'The head of every department gets an invite, but that's all.' So that was why she'd never been to one of Jason's fund-raisers before, Emily thought a bit sourly. Gillian strode towards the door. 'I'll take care of all the arrangements. You can just show up.' Emily had a feeling Gillian was keeping her out of the loop on purpose, especially since the fund-raiser would be at Jason's flat. No doubt Gillian had her eye on him as husband number four.

And that unpleasant feeling still spiking through her was *not* jealousy. Emily gave Gillian her sunniest smile. 'Thank you so much, Gillian, that's lovely.' She breathed a sigh of relief when Gillian finally stalked out of the room, leaving behind a waft of cloying perfume.

Emily let out a tiny sigh. Why was she irritated by Jason's offer to host the party? Or was it simply the possessive way Gillian had talked about Jason—as well as the thought of him finding a wife?

None of it had anything to do with her, and it shouldn't affect her mood at all. It wouldn't, because she wouldn't let it. Determinedly, Emily turned back to her desk and she spent the rest of the morning taking telephone calls and sending emails, purposefully busy, before she headed down to the reception area to meet Helen for lunch as promised.

'How are things going?' she asked cheerfully as she approached the circular marble desk that was the focal point of the building's lobby. Jane was busy on a call, but Helen sat there looking pale and a bit woebegone. 'Got the hang of it?' Emily asked, smiling, and Helen darted an anxious look at Jane.

'I disconnected three calls,' she confessed in a whisper. 'And I got the lists wrong—'

'The lists?'

'The ones about who likes their calls and who doesn't,' Helen explained. She sounded frantic. 'I mixed it all up, and gave the calls to people who don't want them and not to those who do—'

'Oh, well, no one was too bothered, were they?' Emily said, quick to reassure Helen. 'I told you, we're quite a friendly bunch here.'

'Mr Hatley came down right to the desk,' Helen said in a low voice. 'Shouted at me that he didn't want the bloody calls.' She blinked up at Emily, who felt her heart give a little twist at Helen's obvious misery.

'I should have warned you about John,' she said. 'He's an old bear, but his bark is much worse than his bite. Or growl, I suppose. Come on.' She reached for Helen's coat, which hung on a nearby hook, and handed it to her. 'There's a pasta place around the corner that does a wonderful lasagne. Let's forget our troubles for a bit.'

Helen rose gratefully from her seat and Emily waved to Jane, who gave her a rather despairing shake of her head and a pointed look at Helen before Emily sailed through the building's front doors. It appeared it was going to take more than a morning for Helen to figure out the phones, but she'd get there in the end. Emily would make sure of it.

In any case, everything looked better from a cosy table in a restaurant, as they tucked into huge bowls of pasta and crusty garlic bread.

'How are you finding London?' Emily asked as she twirled some linguine around her fork. 'Is Richard showing you around a bit?'

'A bit,' Helen allowed. She sounded cautious, perhaps even unhappy. Emily could hardly pretend to be surprised.

'He's busy, I suppose?' she said in sympathy; she could just imagine Richard getting on with his flood retention basins and hydraulic mechanisms and who knew what else, leaving Helen quite on her own.

'I didn't realise he worked quite as much as he did,' Helen admitted. 'And I don't understand a word of it—'

'Neither do I,' Emily confessed cheerfully. 'And I've worked here for five years.' She was interested in people, not mathematical formulas or desalination plants, for that matter. 'Surely he's been around sometimes, though?' she asked, and Helen gave a little shrug.

'Occasionally,' she said softly. She hesitated, then confessed in an anxious rush, 'I suppose it's bound to be different than you think, isn't it? We've been friends for so long, you know, and of course things will be bumpy at first—'

Bumpy? Emily felt a swell of self-righteous indignation. Surely Helen deserved a bit better than *bumpy*, a little more than sitting at home waiting for Richard to ring. 'Tell you what,' she said suddenly, an idea lighting her mind and firing her heart, 'I've an invitation to a party tonight—it's a launch for a new clothing designer, I think.' Actually, she wasn't sure what it was for; she received dozens of invitations every week, so that Emily mixed them up in her mind. Yet any of them would be a good opportunity to dance and laugh, and that was just what Helen needed. 'Why don't you come with me?'

Helen's face slackened in shock. 'Me? You want to go with *me*?'

Richard had already done a number on her, Emily thought sourly. 'Of course. It'll be fun.'

'I don't have proper clothes—'

'You can borrow something of mine.' Emily eyed Helen assessingly, acknowledging that she was probably a size or two

smaller than Emily was. Well, she had a few things she didn't
fit into any more, alas. And the idea of a makeover energised
her. 'We'll have a real girly evening getting all done up,' she
said, 'and then have a night on the town! Richard won't know
what's happened to you.'

Slowly, shyly, Helen brightened. 'That does sound lovely,'
she began, 'but—'

'No buts. It will be fun.' And successful, as Jason liked to
say. Quickly, she pushed him out of her mind. He didn't need
to know about this.

By eight o'clock that night Emily was shepherding Helen
into the foyer of one of London's grandest hotels. Helen was
looking around in awe, clearly overwhelmed by the sheer
luxury of the venue, with its glittering chandeliers and marble
floor, the ballroom bustling with a thousand guests, all of
them well-connected and wealthy.

Helen had transformed into a swan quite wonderfully,
Emily thought in satisfaction. The black cocktail dress was
unfortunately two years out of date as it was one of the only
things of hers that had fitted Helen, but its lines were simple
and classic and made the most of the younger woman's slight
frame. Emily had piled her luxuriant dark hair on top of
her head, and emphasised Helen's huge grey eyes with dark
shadow and eyeliner. And she'd given her a manicure. She
looked gorgeous.

Buoyed by her own efforts, Emily worked her way through
the crowd, plucking two flutes of champagne from a circulating tray as she introduced Helen to the numerous acquaintances she'd cultivated over the years. No matter that Helen
mumbled her greetings as she ducked her head; she'd get the
hang of it soon, and she was pretty enough that it hardly mattered what she said.

'How have I missed you two gorgeous ladies?' A smooth
voice interrupted Emily's latest introduction and she turned
to see Philip Ellsworth standing just a little too close, his

gaze taking in Helen even as he smiled at Emily. Philip was charming, wealthy and definitely had an eye for the ladies. Emily watched Helen blush under Philip's appreciative stare. Well, her confidence could use a little bolstering.

'*So* charmed to meet you,' Philip said after Emily had made the necessary introductions. 'I can't believe I haven't come across you before. I'm sure I would have remembered.'

'Helen is new to London,' Emily interjected. Philip was still gazing at Helen with obvious admiration, and it compelled her to say, 'The music is just starting up. Philip, I'm sure Helen would love to dance.' All right, it was a little obvious, but he clearly enjoyed her company, and why shouldn't Helen have a dance? 'You do like to dance, don't you, Helen?'

'Yes,' Helen admitted in a shy whisper.

'In that case, I'll have to oblige,' Philip said with a charming and very white smile. He must use artificial whitener, Emily thought with a tiny flicker of distaste. Yet there could be no denying he was incredibly handsome and suave. And just the thing to cheer Helen up a bit. 'I'm always at Emily's command,' he added, throwing Emily a sleek and even sly look. She firmly ignored it.

'Go on, then,' she said, and watched in satisfaction as Philip led Helen to the dance floor with obvious expertise. And Helen wasn't too bad a dancer herself. Who knew what could happen there, Emily mused. Philip was in his thirties. Perhaps he was looking to marry, as well. Settle down. She smiled wryly at her own choice of words. No doubt Jason would accuse her of matchmaking again, but she could hardly be blamed if Helen and Philip made a go of it—

Emily laughed aloud. Those unfortunate phrases really had got stuck in her head. Her gaze returned to Philip and Helen. He was holding her quite close, and she was looking up at him with a rather dazed smile. Emily could not suppress the sharp stab of triumph at seeing Helen out and enjoying herself, flourishing under the approval and attraction of a handsome man. Take that, Richard Marsden.

She lifted her champagne flute, only to pause with it halfway to her lips as her body tensed of its own accord, a shiver of awareness rippling over her. She felt as if she were being watched, and before her brain had processed this her body already knew.

Her gaze swivelled to the entrance of the ballroom and she felt as if an electric current had just pinned her in place. Jason Kingsley stood there, and he was looking right at her.

CHAPTER FIVE

EMILY took a hasty sip of her champagne, then promptly choked, causing an ageing socialite to give her a frosty frown. Such behaviour was hardly decorous.

Emily smiled weakly and watched as Jason made his way towards her, threading through the well-heeled crowd with an arrogant assurance, seemingly indifferent to the people mingling around him. He was a head taller than most of them, and they looked no more than a swarm of insects buzzing about him, an annoyance he dealt with easily as he made his way towards her. Emily swallowed, her chest still burning from when she'd choked. Jason didn't look angry precisely, but he didn't look happy either. Nervously, her gaze flicked to Helen and Philip, now swaying to the music. She had a feeling he wouldn't be happy about that.

Jason surveyed Emily and tried not to scowl. She wore a tiny slip of a silver spangled dress that glittered like water on the scales of a fish, her hair falling down her back in golden waves. She looked, he thought, like an X-rated mermaid.

'What a surprise to see you here,' she said, tilting her head and giving him a flirty smile, her cat's eyes slanted at the corners, alight with mischief.

Jason held on to his temper, but just. He'd arrived a few minutes ago with Margaret Denton, a girl he'd gone to Cambridge with and who was now a solicitor, very elegant, understated and perfect wife material. And then he'd seen Emily...and Helen. He'd watched as Emily pushed Helen towards Philip Ellsworth, who was the biggest waste of space Jason had ever encountered and was steadily partying his way through his daddy's trust fund. Jason's annoyance had increased as Philip took Helen to the dance floor and Emily practically preened with satisfaction. She was matchmaking. Again. And this time she—or at least Helen—was quite out of her element. He'd left Margaret with a cluster of mutual acquaintances and headed towards Emily, drawn to her with a force he could neither stem nor stop.

He smiled at her now, coolly. 'I do attend social events, Emily,' he said, keeping his voice mild, 'although perhaps not as many as you do.' He nodded towards Helen and Ellsworth. 'Now I *am* surprised to see her here.'

'I invited her,' Emily informed him with a hint of defiance beneath her blithe tone. 'I thought she could use a night out—'

'Don't you think this might be a bit much?' Jason surveyed the crowd with a jaundiced eye. Most of the guests were shallow, petty, vain and insipid. And they'd devour Helen Smith in one bite.

'It's just a good time,' Emily said with a defensive shrug. 'And it's better than Helen waiting for Richard Marsden to ring.'

'You've really got it in for him, haven't you?' Jason said. He took a flute of champagne from a tray and downed half of it in one sip. He'd never seen a dress quite as revealing as Emily's. Her legs looked endless, ending in silver skyscraper heels. She'd painted her toenails silver to match. He yanked his gaze upwards, but there was no hope to be found there. Admittedly, the dress wasn't particularly low cut, but the silver material moulded itself to Emily's breasts, outlining every luscious curve. He settled his scowl on Emily's face, for he was indeed scowling now. She seemed to have that effect on him.

'I don't have it in for anyone,' Emily told him, sounding defensive. 'But I don't see any harm in inviting Helen out—'

'And are you going to pretend you didn't just push her towards Ellsworth?'

Emily flushed, and Jason couldn't help but notice how the heightened colour brightened her eyes. Her chest heaved, drawing his attention downwards again. His scowl deepened. 'All I did was ask him to dance with her—'

'Usually, it's the man who does the asking.'

'This is the twenty-first century, in case that had escaped your notice—'

'You're matchmaking again, Emily,' Jason cut her off softly. 'And this time I'd really rather you wouldn't.'

'Why? You're matchmaking as much as I am, clearing the way so she can be with someone like Richard.'

Jason stilled, every muscle tensed. He didn't like her scoffing tone. Or her implication. 'Someone like Richard?' he repeated, his voice lowering dangerously. He *felt* dangerous.

'Yes,' Emily replied with some heat, 'someone earnest and dull who can't be bothered to romance the woman he allegedly loves—'

'You've witnessed this? Talked to Richard, perhaps?'

Emily's flush deepened. 'It's fairly obvious from talking to Helen,' she finally said. She bit her lip, taking its fullness between her teeth, and Jason's fingers clenched around his flute of champagne.

'What does it matter to you?' he demanded roughly. 'I didn't think you were a great believer in love anyway.'

'I do believe in love!' Emily returned with sudden force. Her voice rose and Jason wished he had thought to have this conversation somewhere more private. She was making a scene. 'I believe in it very much,' she continued, her voice thankfully a notch lower. 'Just because I haven't found it for myself—'

'But you're looking after all?' Jason enquired. Why was he asking? Why did he *care?*

Emily looked troubled, and trapped. She lifted one shoulder in a shrug, and the skinny strap of her dress fell down her arm. Her dress had just become a bit more revealing. 'I'm happy as I am,' she said firmly, 'and I don't have anything against Richard Marsden.'

Jason's mouth curved in a cool smile. 'No, indeed, you just find him—let me think—*boring*. Predictable. Cautious.'

Emily stiffened in surprise, her eyes widening. 'This isn't about you, Jason.'

No, it wasn't, Jason thought savagely. Yet it *felt* like it was about him, and her rather dire assessment of him that still, stupidly, stung. Deliberately, he reached out and slid the strap back up to her shoulder, his fingers sliding along her skin. Emily jerked in response, and he saw desire flare in her eyes. A feeling of triumph raced through him, headier than champagne, followed by another flash of lust. He smiled. 'No, of course not,' he murmured. 'It's not about you or me at all.' His hand lingered on her shoulder, his thumb tracing the arc of her collarbone. Emily had frozen, staring at him in dazed shock, and Jason knew he should remove his hand. He was doing it again. Playing with fire. Yet he just couldn't seem to stop.

Emily felt as if her mind and body had both frozen, so shocked by the way Jason was touching her. Although that wasn't quite true; all he'd done was fix her dress strap. No, she was shocked by her own response, the desire coursing through her in a molten flood she had neither expected nor experienced before. And she couldn't move—or think—or even breathe. The crowds shifted and swirled around them, and she felt as if she and Jason were pinned in place. His thumb stroked her collarbone again, his eyes hard and blazing on hers.

Somehow, slowly, as if she were in quicksand, Emily moved. She took a shaky step backwards, shaking her head with more force than intended or necessary, her champagne sloshing and her hair flying. 'This argument is pointless,' she said. 'Helen is a grown woman and she can do as she likes. And so can Richard—and Philip—and you.' Jason had dropped his hand and was simply staring at her. Too disconcerted to say anything more, Emily gave him one last pointed look and pivoted on her heel, intent on finding the only safety on offer: the Ladies.

Yet just as she'd entered the empty, quiet corridor that led to the loos, Jason was there, his long strides overtaking Emily's, so he cut her off from her escape and with the simple turn of his body left her trapped against a wall.

'Jason—'

His body was close enough that she could feel the heat of him, sense his strength. 'You're absolutely right, Emily, Helen can do as she likes. And so can Ellsworth. And Richard. And me.' She looked up at him, his face alarmingly close to hers. His hair was rumpled and colour slashed his cheekbones. Emily was conscious of his nearness, the very scent of him, the way his chest rose and fell under the crisp whiteness of his shirt. Her mind spun with the sensory overload, blanking as she stared up at him, felt the heat of his body like a pulse against her own.

He braced his hands against the wall on either side of her head so that she was effectively imprisoned, although standing between the strength of his arms did not feel like being trapped. Instead, as her heart started to pound and her cheeks flushed, Emily felt a glorious sense of anticipation that rose up inside her like a bubble, so she felt almost as if she could float right off the ground, anchored only by the heavy thud of her heart. Jason's gaze remained on her, his eyes the colour of dark honey, and Emily could not look away. From somewhere she found words.

'Well, of course, Jason, they can all do as they like.' She looked up at him, felt her lips part in what surely was expectation. *Invitation*. Her voice lowered to a breathless, husky murmur. 'And just what is it you'd like to do?'

'This.'

As he lowered his head to hers, Emily could hardly believe this was happening. He was going to kiss her. Alarmingly. Amazingly. At last.

And then he *was* kissing her, his lips cool and firm on hers, one hand coming to curve possessively about her waist, his fingers splaying along her hip. With his other hand he touched her cheek, cradling her face in a gesture that was as intimate as the kiss itself and infinitely more tender.

Emily remained frozen under that gentle touch of his lips, too shocked to respond, at least at first. Then her body began to become aware of just how wonderful it felt to be kissed by Jason, every nerve and sinew suddenly, gloriously alive, overwhelmed by a tidal wave of sensation. As Jason gently explored the contours of her lips, his mouth so firm and persuasive on hers, her body clamoured for more and then took control despite the sputtering protests her mind still insisted on making.

This is Jason—Jason! He can't be kissing me. He can't want to kiss me...

Her body was defiant; Emily found she was taking hold of Jason's shoulders, almost as if she meant to push him away, except of course she didn't. Instead, her hands slid from his shoulders to his head, her fingers threading through the crisp softness of his hair as her mouth opened under his like a flower in the sun and the gentle touch of his tongue to hers sent her body spinning into a deeper whirlpool of sudden, intense feeling.

Yet Jason did not deepen the kiss further and, even as she

pressed closer, her hips bumping his, she became aware of his restraint. He did not pull her closer; he did not move at all and as her brain came up to speed with her body, Emily realised this kiss was not a kiss of passion, but one of proof. Jason was proving something to her; he was telling her something with this kiss, and Emily wasn't sure it was anything she wanted to hear.

Yet before she could pull away in appalled indignation, which was what she intended, Jason broke the kiss and stepped away with his own cool little smile. Emily stared at him, her chest heaving, her lips tingling.

'What was that for?' she demanded in a raw voice.

He looked nonplussed for a tiny beat before his lips curved wider in a satisfied smile. 'Does there need to be a purpose?'

Emily had no answer, because now that her body had stopped its restless clamour—although it still *ached*—her mind had taken over, spinning out incoherent protests, impossible ideas.

'Very well,' Jason said coolly, his voice edged with impatience. 'Then this. Now you know I'm not boring… and neither is Richard Marsden.'

'And a kiss is meant to convince me of that?' Emily scoffed, which would have been a lot more believable if her voice hadn't wobbled.

'Considering how much you enjoyed it,' Jason replied, his gaze sweeping over her flushed face and heaving chest with knowing assessment, 'yes.'

'I didn't—' Emily protested uselessly, for it was surely a lie and Jason was already walking away from her.

Jason stalked away from Emily, furious with himself for losing his self-control. For kissing her. And yet his body wanted—demanded—more, and he was both aggravated and amazed by how that one simple kiss had affected him so much. Affected her as well, to both his satisfaction and shame.

'Jason, where *have* you been?' Eyebrows arched, too elegant to look annoyed, Margaret Denton glided up to him, one thin hand on his arm, her nails biting into his flesh. The smile she gave him was both imperious and reproving, and annoyed him all the more. She smiled as if she were his mother, as if she already owned him.

And this was a woman he was considering for his *wife*?

Not any more.

Carefully, Jason detached his arm from Margaret's biting grasp. 'I'm sorry, Margaret, I had business to attend to.' She pursed her lips, unimpressed, and Jason's gaze settled on the woman across the ballroom who stood alone, watching the crowds with a lonely longing. 'Excuse me,' he told Margaret and, without looking back, he headed across the ballroom.

'Mr Kingsley!' Helen Smith looked at him in both surprise and more than a little relief. How long had she been standing alone? Jason wondered. How long had it taken Ellsworth to ditch her?

'Good evening, Helen. I hope you're having a good time?'

'Oh…yes.' She smiled, but he saw the uncertainty in her eyes. This kind of crowd was far from her own experience, and standing alone like a wallflower had to be a miserable introduction to it.

'I wonder if you could do me a favour,' Jason said, and Helen nodded, her eyes wide.

'Of…of course—'

'Emily wasn't feeling all that well, and I believe she's gone to the Ladies. Would you mind checking on her?' He glanced at his watch as if he cared what time it was. 'I'm afraid I have to run.'

'Of course, Mr Kingsley—'

Smiling his thanks, Jason turned to leave the ballroom behind. He'd done enough damage for one night.

* * *

Emily stood in the elegantly upholstered ladies' room, gazing at her shocked reflection in the gilt mirror. Her face was flushed, her lips reddened, her hair a tousled mess. She looked as if that one kiss—just one kiss!—had utterly affected her, changed her, and in some ways it had.

Jason Kingsley had kissed her. Why? What had he been hoping to accomplish? He'd certainly never expressed any interest in kissing her before—and after he'd kissed her he'd stepped away so easily, giving her such a cool little smile.

Emily felt her stomach lurch in panicked protest. He wasn't interested in kissing her at all. He hadn't been affected like she was, even now, her face flushed and her mind spinning in dazed, dizzying circles.

The door to the ladies' room opened and Helen slipped in, frowning in hesitant concern. 'Emily—are you all right?'

Emily pushed her hair behind her ears and lifted her chin. 'Of course. Why shouldn't I be?'

'It's just that Mr Kingsley said you were in the Ladies and I ought to check on you—'

'Jason worries too much,' Emily said with a laugh that sounded just a bit brittle. It both stung and soothed her that Jason had thought it necessary to send someone to check on her. It was considerate—and annoying. He'd probably been trying to detach Helen from Philip, and this was simply an excuse. 'Honestly, I'm fine. The noise is giving me a bit of a headache, that's all.' She ran some water over her wrists and then quite deliberately took her lipstick from her handbag and reapplied it, her gaze fixed firmly on her own reflection. Her blush had faded, she saw, and her lips did not look so swollen. Slipping the lipstick back into her bag, she turned to Helen. 'There. Shall we go back out?' Helen nodded and Emily smiled, her equanimity almost restored as she led the way back to the ballroom. 'Philip Ellsworth is very nice, isn't he?' she said, and from the corner of her eye she saw Helen blush and felt another little stab of satisfaction.

Take that, Jason Kingsley, she thought and, smiling, reached for another glass of champagne. She glanced around the ballroom, instinctively seeking out that tall, purposeful figure but she could tell from the emptiness she felt inside that Jason had already gone.

Emily kept her thoughts from Jason—and that kiss—for the rest of the evening. She was on full form, sparkling and chatting and posing for photographs until well after midnight, when common sense finally told her she—as well as Helen— had to return to work tomorrow, so they might as well call it a night.

Yet, alone in her flat, the rooms all dark around her, she found the memory of Jason's kiss came rushing back to her, overwhelming her senses and making her ache deep inside in a way she didn't like but recognised as the onslaught of unfulfilled desire.

Why had Jason kissed her? Why had it stirred up this longing and need inside of her, when surely it couldn't be sated? *She* couldn't. Not by Jason, for that kiss—that little kiss—had been nothing more than a proof, a punishment for pushing Helen and Philip together.

The more Emily considered it, the more she felt, like a leaden lump in the pit of her stomach, that she was right. Jason had not kissed her out of desire or attraction or anything like that. He'd kissed her to prove something to her, simply because he could. The thought sent a blush firing Emily's body and scorching her face, even in the empty darkness of her own flat. She was reminded, painfully, of Jason's rejection on the dance floor seven years ago. She'd so desperately wanted to prove to him—and herself—how beyond that moment she was, how grown-up and sophisticated and worldly she'd become, but she'd done the opposite. Now, with the aftermath of that kiss sending a riot of ricocheting emotions through her, Emily realised she wasn't sophisticated at all... at least not when it came to Jason. With Jason she would forever be an adoring, annoying little girl, and she'd never felt so more than now.

Jason stared at the social pages of the newspaper that his PA had laid out with other relevant articles. Tumbled, golden curls, a tiny silver scrap of a dress. Three separate photographs, each one more damning than the last. He scanned the captions: *Emily Wood dazzles the fund-raising scene in an exclusively designed dress... Emily Wood and unidentified guest toast their evening... Emily Wood and Philip Ellsworth dance together at last night's charity gala.*

With a grimace of disgust, Jason pushed the pages away. He didn't need to see any more photographs. He'd already been convinced that as charming as Emily was, as desirable as he knew her to be, she could also be silly, scatty and most unsuitable. He had no business expressing any interest in her at all. No business kissing her.

She was not wife material. Not even close.

So why couldn't he get her out of his mind? Why couldn't he forget that kiss?

Why did he want more?

He'd returned to London for the express purpose of finding a wife. With his father's health failing, it had become all the more urgent. He had no time to waste with Emily Wood, and yet he was honest enough to realise he had trouble resisting her. His self-control had deserted him, his willpower at an all-time low. How he'd managed to keep his distance from Emily for seven years he had no idea, since he certainly couldn't seem to manage it any longer.

With another grimace Jason pressed the intercom for his PA. 'Book my ticket for Nairobi, Eloise,' he said. 'I'm going back to Africa after all.'

By the next morning, Emily had pushed the kiss and all its accompanying realisations completely out of her mind. Almost.

He still lingered on the fringes of her consciousness like a mist, and she found herself gazing blankly at her computer while her hand went inadvertently to touch her lips, remembering the touch of his mouth against hers, how firmly his lips had moved over hers, that thrilling touch of his tongue and the very taste of him—

Stop. She had to stop. Yet, despite her determination not to, she spent the entire morning in a state of high tension, waiting to see Jason, preparing herself for the pointed barbs he would no doubt direct her way. Yet he did not stop by her office and despite her half-dozen forays to the lobby—to check on Helen, of course—she did not see him enter the building. At lunch his PA informed her that Jason was out of the office for a few days, preparing for another trip to Africa.

'I thought he was back for a while,' Emily said, hating that she actually sounded disappointed. 'A few months, at least.'

The PA, Eloise, shrugged. 'An emergency came up.'

Emily stopped by Helen's desk on the way back upstairs. 'Richard's going off to Africa again?' she said, and Helen nodded, her expression downcast.

'Yes, it's very important, he said. Just a week, though, this time.'

'Well, that's good, then,' Emily said after a moment. 'Did you have fun last night?'

'Yes—' Helen smiled rather shyly, and Emily smiled back in encouragement, sensing the younger woman wanted to say something more. 'Philip is very nice,' she finally admitted in a whisper, and Emily felt a thrill of triumph—as well as trepidation. Suddenly she was glad Jason wasn't in the office today.

'He is,' she said after a second's pause. 'Perhaps you'll see him again.'

'Do you think?' Helen's face lit up even as she chewed her lip nervously. Emily felt another flicker of trepidation. Philip really was charming, she told herself. Yes, he moved in a fast crowd, but he was always unfailingly polite—if a little smooth—and she'd never heard anything *that* bad about him. Helen, with her sweetness and innocence, could be perfect for him. Surely there was nothing wrong with enabling them to spend a little time together.

With another smile directed at Helen, she headed back up to her office. Work took up too much of her time to think about Jason, or anyone else for that matter. When the phone rang at the end of the day, she was surprised to hear Philip's plummy tone.

'Philip! You've never rung me at work before.'

'There's a first time for everything.'

Emily leaned back in her chair, anticipation racing through her. Philip had never rung her before at all, and there could only be one reason—one person—why he would do so now. 'So what's the occasion?' she asked.

'No occasion. I have spare theatre tickets and, after seeing you and your lovely companion last night, I thought you might want to go with me.'

'The theatre? I'm sure that would be lovely.' Of course he didn't know Helen well enough to ask her alone, Emily thought, her excitement mounting. She was the perfect cover. He really was interested in Helen. After making arrangements with Philip, she disconnected the call and hurried downstairs to tell Helen the news.

Several hours later they were having drinks in the theatre bar, waiting for the curtain. Philip was charming as always, and had even kissed Helen's cheek when he'd seen her. Emily stepped away so she was on the other side of the little table, and Philip and Helen sat next to each other on tall stools. Philip, Emily decided firmly, would be just the right man for Helen. He'd wine her and dine her and sweep her off her feet, just as she deserved. And Emily could show Jason how wrong he was. Now *that* thought was immensely satisfying. All it would take was a little nudge in the right direction…

For a moment Emily felt a ripple of concern for the hapless and absent Richard. She really didn't have anything against him, did she? No, of course not. If Richard wanted to be with Helen, he could certainly make a bit more effort. Perhaps Philip's attention towards Helen would motivate him. Or… She glanced at the pair across from her; Philip was tucking a tendril of hair behind Helen's ear while she ducked her head and blushed. Or Philip and Helen could fall in love and live happily ever after, the way it was supposed to happen. The way her parents had, until her mother had died.

The way she wanted for herself, even if she'd told Jason otherwise. Even if she was afraid that she'd never find that kind of man, that kind of love.

The bell rang, and Emily stood up from the table. The show was about to begin.

Emily's mood remained buoyant throughout the evening and all the way home. Philip had suggested they all share a cab, but Emily had insisted she could walk and left the two of them speeding away in the darkness. She imagined telling Jason the news that Philip and Helen were together, even engaged. She pictured the huge wedding, hundreds of guests. Perhaps she'd even be bridesmaid. She'd wear something understated, and look modest and quietly proud—

Chuckling softly at her own flight of fancy, Emily let herself into her flat. Her mobile phone buzzed with a message and Emily flipped it open as she shed her coat and kicked off her heels. There were two messages which she'd missed while at the theatre: one from her sister, asking her if she was coming to Surrey for Christmas, and then another from Stephanie, reminding her of the rehearsal dinner for her wedding in two weeks' time. Emily could hardly believe the wedding was so soon. She wondered if Jason would be attending, and then quickly banished that thought. It hardly mattered anyway.

Emily was dying to know how the evening turned out for Philip and Helen, and she finally got the low-down when she stopped by reception on the way to lunch the next day. Helen was getting ready to leave for an afternoon appointment at the dentist's and they walked out together into the brisk November afternoon.

'So…' was all Emily needed to say for Helen to launch into a hesitant yet happy description of Philip and all his charms.

'He's so gorgeous, isn't he?' Helen said with a sigh. 'And he says the funniest things…and he looks at me as if he likes me…' She paused, nibbling her lip, her lashes sweeping downward for a moment before she looked up anxiously at Emily. 'He looks at me and I go all tingly. I feel so *alive*. Have you ever felt like that?'

'Alive?' Emily repeated dryly. 'Yes, I think so.'

'I meant—'

'I know,' Emily said quickly, suppressing a pang of remorse at her rather facetious reply. 'And to tell you the truth, Helen, I've never felt like that with a man.' She thought briefly of Jason's kiss, and hurriedly suppressed the memory. Her two dismal attempts at a relationship hardly counted either. No, love looked set to pass her by, and that was fine. Hearing about it from Helen was good enough. Almost, anyway. She smiled down at her. 'So what you've got must be special.'

'Do you think so?' Helen asked. 'Do you think he likes me?'

Emily thought of the way Philip had sat next to Helen, had brushed her hair away from her face, had slid next to her in the cab, their thighs touching. 'I'm sure of it,' she said.

'Richard will be so disappointed,' Helen said quietly. 'We were meant to use this time to get to know one another—to see if we suit—'

'And obviously you don't,' Emily replied briskly. 'If he'd

wanted to be with you so much, he should have asked you out. Sent you flowers—'

'He did give me a house plant,' Helen said quickly, and Emily only just kept herself from rolling her eyes.

'How very nice of him,' she said. 'Still, it's not your fault if you don't…suit. And since Philip is here and Richard isn't…'

'He leaves for Africa tomorrow,' Helen said in a low voice. 'I should tell him, I know, but…' She nibbled her lip again and Emily smiled kindly.

'But?'

'We've been friends for so long,' Helen said. She sounded miserable. 'And Richard really is a nice man—'

'Of course he is. But you don't date—or marry—someone just because he's nice. I think you need a bit more than that, Helen. You deserve it.'

'Do I?'

'Yes,' she told her firmly, 'you do.' Every woman did. Helen was just one of the lucky ones who might actually get it.

Helen nodded, accepting, and Emily waved her off to her dentist's appointment, expansively offering to let her take the rest of the afternoon off. 'I know what that novocaine can do to you. You'd be lisping into the phone!'

'I should be back by four,' Helen said. 'I don't want to leave Jane in the lurch. And actually I kind of enjoy the work now.' Smiling with a new self-confidence, Helen headed down the street. Emily watched her, feeling proud of Helen and all she'd accomplished, and yet…she could not keep a strange, empty feeling from rattling around inside her. She felt a little forlorn, a little lonely, as she headed up to her office. She knew she should be happy for Helen, and she was, of course she was. Yet as she sank into her chair she also realised she felt a bit adrift herself. She had since Jason had kissed her and scattered all her certainties. *I'm happy as I am.*

Was she? Was she really?

Staring blankly at her computer screen, Emily wasn't sure she was any more. The thought was frightening. Depressing too. Because if she wasn't happy, what on earth could she do about it?

Forcing the question—and its impossible answer—aside, she kept her head down and focused on work until a hesitant knock on her door at half past three. She looked up and stared straight at Richard Marsden.

'Hello,' he began, awkward and uncertain, and Emily simply stared, shock rendering her temporarily speechless. A creeping sense of discomfort immediately followed, for while she'd been telling Helen it was perfectly fine to forget Richard just hours ago, she hadn't had to deal with the man face to face.

Now he stood here in an ill-fitting suit, round-shouldered and a little dull, yet, Emily acknowledged fairly, with a rather nice smile.

'Sorry to bother you, but I'm looking for Helen Smith. Jane down at reception said you might know where she is.'

'She's at the dentist's,' Emily said, her voice faintly cool despite her intention to sound both friendly and professional.

'Oh.' Richard's face fell, the corners of his mouth turning down almost comically. 'I was hoping to catch her before I leave for Africa. I'd stop by her flat but my flight leaves at eight—' He paused hopefully and Emily did not attempt to fill the silence. 'Do you know if she'll be back today?'

Emily hesitated. Clearly Helen had not told Jane that she intended to return by four. Of course, Helen's appointment could run long—dentist appointments often did—and there was no saying for certain that she would be back in the office today. There was no saying for certain at all.

Emily looked at Richard Marsden's slightly droopy eyes, his kind smile, and then quite suddenly pictured Jason saying coolly, *You most certainly are not in the running.* She remembered how easily he'd walked away from that kiss, and how shattered she'd felt in its aftermath.

Her own mouth hardened and she heard herself saying, 'I'm afraid I don't know, Richard. She told me she planned to take the entire afternoon off.'

Richard nodded slowly in acceptance, clearly defeated before he'd even begun. Emily felt a flicker of regret but also a stab of self-righteous scorn. If Richard wasn't going to try harder than *that*—

'Well, if you see her, will you tell her I stopped by? And that…that I'm thinking of her?'

Emily knew she would have no difficulty in delivering Richard's paltry message. 'Of course I will.'

'Thank you,' he said, and Emily, her throat suddenly tight, just nodded.

As he rounded the corner, she managed to call out, 'Have a safe trip, Richard.'

Then, as he finally disappeared down the hallway, she let out a long, slow breath she hadn't realised she'd been holding.

It didn't matter, she told herself. Helen would have said something to Richard anyway. She was planning on it— mostly. And, in any case, Richard was only going to be gone for a week or so…although, Emily thought, by the time he returned Philip and Helen could very well be an established couple. Philip was, among other things, a fast worker.

She turned back to her computer screen and the email she'd been in the middle of composing, but the words danced before her eyes. All she could really see was Richard's defeated look, his disappointed smile, and she wondered if for once she'd interfered just a little too much.

CHAPTER SIX

EMILY pulled at the tight satin bodice of her bridesmaid's dress and grimaced in the mirror. The hot pink colour made her look like a piece of bubblegum, and the skirt belled out around her knees so she was halfway to wearing a tutu. Stephanie, however, had been enamoured with what she thought was a fairy tale dress, and insisted Emily looked gorgeous in it. Emily silently disagreed with Stephanie's assessment, but offered no resistance. This was Stephanie's day, not hers.

The wedding was to be a small, intimate affair, the ceremony taking place in the church of the Hampshire village where Stephanie had grown up, and the reception a dinner at a local hotel afterwards. Emily had arrived last night just in time to make the rehearsal, and then fallen into bed, exhausted and a bit overwhelmed by the general pandemonium and near hysteria an imminent wedding caused. Seating plans. Bouquets. A last minute alteration to Stephanie's dress. Emily's head swam.

Since last night she'd only seen Stephanie and Tim and their families and attendants, and she hadn't had time to ask Stephanie if Jason would be coming to the wedding.

No, that wasn't really true, Emily acknowledged to herself as she fixed her hair into what she hoped was a neat chignon. She'd had plenty of time to talk to Stephanie over the last two weeks. She hadn't *wanted* to ask about Jason because she didn't even want to think about him, or that kiss, and she certainly wasn't going to give her friend any reason to think there was something between her and Jason. Because there wasn't. How could there be? The thought was beyond ludicrous.

All they'd shared was a single kiss—a kiss that had been part punishment and part proof, as Jason had said himself. As if that kiss proved anything about Richard Marsden. Or even Jason. All right, it proved Jason was a decent kisser, but that was hardly relevant to anything. Or anyone. Certainly not to her.

And yet Emily could not quite forget the feel of Jason's lips on hers, how they'd been both hard and soft, warm and cool, and even more aggravatingly—and alarmingly—how she'd responded to that kiss, as if he'd lit a candle inside of her. Not just a candle, but a roaring fire. And it still hadn't gone out.

A knock sounded at the door of the spare bedroom in Stephanie's parents' house, where Emily had been getting ready.

'The car's here,' Joanne, Stephanie's mother, called. 'Are you all set, dear?'

'Yes…just about.' With a last rather despairing look at her tutu-like dress, Emily turned towards the door.

The ceremony was beautiful, just as Emily had known it would be. The church sanctuary was bedecked with ivy and white roses, and a hushed silence prevailed as Tim and Stephanie exchanged their vows, their voices ringing with heartfelt sincerity and love.

This was why people got married, Emily thought with an unfamiliar wrenching inside. She'd consider it herself if she ever met a man who would look at her the way Tim looked at Stephanie. Not with disapproval, or amusement, or—

She was thinking about Jason. Again. Emily forced the thoughts away and let her gaze wander around the church. There were a handful of people from work but, other than that, few she recognised. Then she heard a quiet creak as someone opened the door to the church and slipped into the last pew.

It took Emily a stunned second to process who it was.

Jason.

His gaze locked on hers and held it, refusing to look away, his eyes calm yet his jaw tense. He looked…*determined* was the only word for it, as if he had a goal in mind and he fully intended to achieve it. Perhaps that was the way he looked at a flooded river, or a swamped stream, or—

But, no. He was looking at her, and Emily could not look away. She couldn't move. It was as if Jason's gaze was actually trapping her, and her hands clenched around her posy of rosebuds, the dress cutting into her ribcage, her gaze locked on Jason's. Her gaze, of its own accord, moved to his mouth, took in those firm, sculpted lips. How had she never before noticed what amazing lips he had? They'd been on hers. Hard on hers.

One kiss. Just one kiss, and yet she couldn't forget it. She had a feeling she never would. She swallowed, her throat suddenly unbearably dry. Jason still gazed at her, steady, unyielding.

'And by the power invested in me, I now pronounce you man and wife.'

Finally, Emily possessed the ability to tear her gaze from Jason's and she clapped along with everyone else as Tim, beaming, took his wife in his arms. She watched as he kissed her, a kiss filled with passion and love and happiness. That kiss was a declaration, a celebration, a shout of joy to the world.

Jason hadn't kissed her like that. No one had.

Swallowing again, Emily glanced back at Jason. He was chatting with the person in front of him, oblivious to her now. Emily wondered if she'd actually imagined the intensity of the moment before; surely Jason hadn't been looking at her quite like that.

Like what? her mind mocked, for she didn't even know.

Stephanie and Tim had broken their kiss and were now beaming at everyone around them. Emily felt another wrench of what could only be envy. She'd meant what she'd said to Jason; she was happy, and she certainly didn't need anything. The search for the kind of love Stephanie and Tim shared was exhausting and uncertain, and she had no desire to embark on it only to end up frustrated and alone. Better to be happy and alone, surely.

Yet that didn't keep her from wanting for a moment—just a moment—what Stephanie and Tim had. She wanted it desperately. She longed for someone to look at her the way Tim had looked at Stephanie, with love, his face softened with adoration. She wanted to be desired, treasured, adored. Wined and dined and romanced. Swept off her feet.

It wasn't going to happen.

Determinedly, she shrugged the feeling aside. Surely it was no more than even the most hardened heart would feel at a wedding as lovely as this one. It would pass.

Smiling at her radiant friend, Emily followed them down the aisle. She made sure to keep her face averted as she passed the last pew.

Of course she couldn't avoid Jason for ever. She tried to, and managed it through drinks and dinner. Her duty as bridesmaid kept her close to Stephanie's side, straightening her veil, fetching her a glass of water, smiling until her cheeks ached for the requisite round of photographs.

Yet when the dancing started and Stephanie and Tim took the floor, Jason headed directly to her and she realised she'd been waiting—and even expecting—him to. Emily's heart started a heavy thud of anticipation as she watched him stride across the ballroom, as purposeful and self-assured as always. His hair and eyes both glinted near-gold in the dim lighting and she could see the ripple of muscles under his immaculate suit, the easy shrug of his shoulders as he walked.

She wondered what he was going to say to her, if he would mention the kiss. Should she act unconcerned, indifferent, as if she'd already dismissed it as the nothing encounter it surely was—for him, at least? Yet that would be an act, and he would surely know it. He'd probably tease her about it, but at least then they would be on familiar footing.

Her palms grew slippery as she clutched her flute of champagne. She wished she'd reapplied her lipstick. She also wished she wasn't wearing a poufy, too-tight bridesmaid dress in shocking pink satin.

'Care to dance?'

The words shocked her, brought her back to the last wedding she'd attended with Jason, when he'd asked the same question and held his hand out in just the same way...and she'd been wearing pink satin then too. Some things never changed.

'Fine,' she said, realising that sounded a bit ungracious.

Jason, however, just smiled, although Emily saw his eyes didn't respond. They still held that same hard determination, and Emily wondered at its source.

She placed her hand in his, let his fingers enfold hers as he led her onto the small parquet dance floor. His other hand rested on her waist, warm and large, his fingers splaying across her hip.

The band was playing a low, lazy tune, something you only needed to sway to. Emily kept her gaze focused in the region of Jason's chin as they moved to the music. They were closer than six inches apart this time, and this was no boring waltz. She could feel the heat from his body, inhaled the tang of his aftershave. He was a good dancer, she realised with some surprise; he swayed well, his movements languorous, even sexy, his sure hands guiding her to his own lazy rhythm.

Emily could not look him in the face. She felt agonisingly aware of him, and also of the memory of dancing with him seven years ago. She'd been so affected and overwhelmed by him then. Clearly nothing had changed.

Jason touched her chin with his finger. 'Can't you look at me?'

Reluctantly, Emily forced her gaze upwards. 'Of course.' Yet when she took in the blaze of his eyes, the wry twisting of his lips, she wished she hadn't risen to his challenge. She couldn't look at him. She couldn't tell what he felt. Or if he was thinking about their kiss the way she was…with every nerve and muscle of her body.

Involuntarily she'd stiffened, the memories and uncertainties causing her to stop their slow dance, and Jason gently nudged her hip with his hand, forcing her to move again. Sway. Her hip came into gentle contact with his and she felt a lightning shaft of awareness. Bone against bone. She angled her body away from his, which was difficult considering how close he was holding her.

'Are you acting so skittish because I kissed you?' he asked in that practical, matter-of-fact way that was so essentially Jason, and at this moment Emily did not know how to respond. All her witty retorts seemed to have evaporated. Banter was beyond her.

'Ah, yes, that kiss,' she finally said, her tone sounding cringingly false and even hearty. 'How could I forget?'

'It would be a poor reflection on me if you had forgotten,' Jason observed.

She risked a glance upwards; he was gazing at her with a steady, intense assessment that was more unnerving than any glower or scowl. He looked like he was trying to understand her, and surely she didn't want *that*. 'You mean on your kissing abilities?' she queried flippantly. Or at least as flippantly as she could.

'Quite. However,' Jason continued, pulling her closer again so their hips gently collided once more, sending a shaft of agonising awareness low through her pelvis, 'I know you didn't forget, and I'm in no doubt of my own abilities.'

Emily let out a little huffy laugh. 'That's a bit arrogant.'

'Is it?' Jason touched her chin with his thumb, angling her face upwards. His mouth was a whisper away from hers. 'You wanted me to kiss you seven years ago, Em. Things haven't changed that much, have they?'

'Actually, they have,' Emily retorted, her words sharpening. She did not want to be reminded of that night, not when Jason's kiss—and her own humiliating response—was so fresh and raw in her mind. Her heart. Things *had* changed; she was different. 'In any case, Jason, if you meant that kiss as some kind of proof, I'm sorry to say it failed.'

'Proof?' Jason repeated. He sounded genuinely puzzled. 'Proof of what?'

'That Richard's not boring,' Emily said impatiently. He'd told her so himself, so why was he looking at her as if she had just said something utterly nonsensical? 'You said,' she reminded him. 'Remember?'

In one quick yet fluid motion, Jason guided her off the dance floor. Emily could barely keep up with him, tripping in her heels, his hand now encircling her wrist, as he led her from the crowded ballroom to a small secluded lounge off the lobby of the hotel. The sudden silence unnerved her, left her defenceless. All she could hear was the ragged tear of her own breathing, and all the words that hadn't yet been said.

Jason stared at her for a long moment, spots of colour high on his cheekbones although his eyes were assessing and cool. 'What?' Emily demanded. 'You told me yourself, Jason.'

'I know I did,' he said, his voice as calm and measured as always despite the colour still flaring in his face, 'but only because you needed a reason.' A faint smile flickered over his features. 'As far as responses to a kiss go, "What was that for?" is fairly insulting.'

'But logical,' Emily returned. 'Why else would you kiss me, Jason?'

Jason's eyebrows rose. 'Why *else*?'

'You never wanted to before.'

He kept staring at her, his brow furrowed now as if he were figuring out a complicated maths problem...or her. Emily crossed her arms over her chest, the pink satin stretching alarmingly across her breasts. She was really beginning to regret this dress.

'Is this about the time we danced at Isobel and Jack's wedding? All those years ago? How I supposedly humiliated you?'

He sounded so disbelieving that Emily knew he didn't know. Hadn't seen how she'd bolted from the dance floor in tears. Although it amazed her that he hadn't noticed; she'd felt so obvious and exposed. 'It was a long time ago, I know,' she said stiffly. 'And of course it hardly matters now—'

'Of course it does matter,' Jason cut across her, 'since we're having this conversation.'

'I just felt very rejected,' Emily said, her words stilted and stiff, each one drawn from her with the utmost reluctance. She had wanted to banish this memory, had convinced herself she had. Yet seeing Jason again—having him mention it after so many years of silence—brought it all rushing back, made her realise afresh how painful that little episode had been. She couldn't laugh about it now; maybe she never had been able to.

And now she felt as if she were giving Jason more ammunition to tease her, or at least give her one of those coolly mocking looks. She waited for one eyebrow to arch as he gave her some dry rejoinder. *If you're going to offer yourself on a plate, Em...*

Instead, he said something else entirely. 'Emily, I told you then how I wanted to kiss you.'

She stared at him, shocked, totally unprepared for this admission. 'No, you didn't—'

'Yes, I did,' Jason replied, his words sharp, as if he were angry about the truth of it. As if he hadn't wanted to want to kiss her. Perhaps he hadn't. 'In fact, I remember exactly what I said. You asked if I'd like to kiss you, and I told you I would, *rather*.'

'But I won't,' Emily finished woodenly.

Jason stared at her for another endless moment before the corner of his mouth quirked upwards. 'And clearly you only paid attention to the second clause of that sentence.'

'And clearly you aced grammar,' Emily threw back at him. She didn't want to talk about this any more; she didn't want to remember. 'Look, it really doesn't matter. It was seven years ago.' She let out a long breath that shuddered only slightly. 'It was just a moment. A silly moment.' Why had she ever asked him to kiss her? And why hadn't she been able to forget when he finally had?

'It wasn't,' Jason said quietly, 'a silly moment for me.'

Emily froze. Forgot to breathe. She could not make sense of his words; they fell into the taut stillness between them and lay there, demanding she do something with them. *Ask*. 'What are you talking about?' she finally whispered.

'I wanted to kiss you, Emily,' Jason said. His voice was quiet and yet so very matter-of-fact. 'I wanted to kiss you very badly, but I didn't because you were seventeen years old and I doubted you'd ever been kissed before.'

Colour washed her cheekbones. 'I hadn't,' she admitted, her voice still no more than a thread of sound.

'I was twenty-nine. Older than you are now. And the realisation that I could want to kiss you, want *you* so much terrified and shamed me. You were too young.'

Emily stared at him as she tested the truth of his words. She remembered how he'd glared at her; he'd looked so angry. 'But you…you pushed me away like you couldn't stand the thought of me—or kissing me!' she finally burst out, amazed that it could hurt even now. For years she'd convinced herself that silly little moment between them had been nothing more than that. Silly. Little. Yet now she knew she couldn't pretend, not when Jason was being so honest. That silly little moment hadn't been silly—or little—at all. Not for her, and perhaps not even for Jason.

'I pushed you away,' Jason said, his patience clearly starting to fray, 'because I didn't want to humiliate myself—or you! There couldn't be anything between us then, not when you were no more than a teenager.'

Then. He made it sound as if it might be different now. As if something—what?—could happen between them now. The thought was so overwhelming, so alarming and exciting and yet somehow preposterous, that Emily could think of nothing to say. She didn't even know how she felt, how to untangle this confusing rush of emotions—shock, fear, anxiety, excitement, hope—that raced dizzily through her and left her robbed of speech or even breath, so she could only stare at him, helpless, hopeful, waiting.

Jason watched several different emotions chase themselves across Emily's features. He'd shocked her, he knew. He'd been honest—more honest than he'd intended—and now she didn't know what to say. Think. Feel.

And neither did he. His mind and body had been in a ferment for too long. He couldn't keep himself from Emily, despite every intention to do just that. Time and time again he'd sought her out, been drawn to her in a way he could not resist. The realisation was aggravating. Humbling too. He'd always prided himself on his sense of self-control, his iron resolve—both had crumbled to nothing when he'd finally given into desire and kissed Emily, felt her sweet, yielding response, her lips parting under his, her body curving against him. He wanted Emily. He'd gone to Africa to escape her, escape the attraction he'd felt, and instead he'd endured days of remembering just how she'd felt and tasted, nights where he'd relived that one kiss in his mind. And imagined a few other things besides.

Even work hadn't been enough of a distraction, and after a week of it he'd realised what he wanted. What he needed.

To get Emily out of his system. And the only way to do that, to move forward, was to have her. In his arms, in his bed.

Why not?

She'd told him she wasn't interested in love. Not for herself at any rate. She wanted to have fun. She'd had several relationships already and was wise to the ways of the world. So why shouldn't they indulge in what would be a very basic and pleasurable affair? She wasn't seventeen any more. She wasn't innocent any more.

He'd been afraid of hurting her back then, of course he had. But Emily had already shown him how unimpressed she was with him already—she thought he was *boring*, out of bed at least; Jason saw the positive side of that assessment now. It meant she wasn't in love with him. She didn't want to marry him.

But she wanted him. He knew that. And as long as he didn't hurt or disappoint her—which he wouldn't, since her heart wasn't involved—why shouldn't they enjoy themselves? It had suddenly seemed wonderfully simple. And easy.

Although from the way Emily was looking at him now, with so much dazed uncertainty, Jason knew it didn't seem so simple to her. She hadn't believed he desired her. The thought was laughable; it seemed so glaringly—and painfully—obvious to him. Clearly, Emily had her doubts.

He looked forward to removing them. And a few other things, as well.

'What…' she began, her voice scratchy. Her tongue darted out to moisten her lips. Jason's gut clenched. 'What are you saying?'

Jason let his gaze rest on her, his eyes heavy-lidded, his expression thoughtful. Suggestive. He saw Emily's eyes widen, her pupils dilate. 'Things have changed,' he said finally, his voice no more than a steady, low thrum. He took a step closer to her, lifted his hand to touch her chin, his thumb grazing her jawbone. He felt her response shudder through her. 'Haven't they?' Her lips parted, but no words came out. Jason smiled and lowered his head, his lips a breath away from hers. He could feel her tremble, sway towards him. 'Not too much, though...' He waited, his mouth hovering over hers, needing her response. Her acceptance. She needed to understand what he was saying... and what he wasn't.

'Jason...'

'Emily?'

Emily jerked away from him as Stephanie's sister-in-law Lucy, terrifyingly organised and brisk, popped her head in the little lounge. 'There you are! Stephanie is about to throw her bouquet. You won't want to miss it.'

Jason watched as Emily's face flooded with colour. She turned away from him, her head clearly averted from his gaze. 'Thank you, Lucy. I'll be right there.'

Lucy disappeared and still Emily hesitated for a moment, her back to Jason, clearly waiting.

'We'll have to finish this...conversation...another time,' he said. He took a breath and let it out slowly, needing to state the obvious. Wanting her to understand. 'I want you, Emily. But I don't want you to be hurt.' He waited, willing her to agree, to say something at least, to indicate she understood. *This is just a fling. Fun. What we both want.*

She half-turned so her face was in profile, and he saw the smooth curve of her cheek, the downward sweep of her golden lashes. She looked uncertain and so very young. 'I won't get hurt,' she said, her voice low.

Yet as she slipped from the room Jason wondered if she'd spoken to convince him...or herself.

CHAPTER SEVEN

EMILY did not see Jason for a week. It was a week of anxiety and also a little anger, of tensing and turning every time someone came to her door, of wondering why he'd made such a startling confession and then disappeared without a trace.

Was he teasing her? Had he changed his mind? Or was he serious, and he was giving her time to decide what she wanted?

Emily didn't know which she preferred. Every option seemed alarming. Meanwhile, she found she was checking her mobile for messages or texts far too often. She scoured the internet's social networking pages to see if he was on any, which of course he wasn't. Jason was hardly the kind of man to update his online status. Annoyed with herself, she stayed away from her mobile and laptop except for work, determined not to think of him at all.

Unfortunately, that proved impossible. She kept going over her conversation with Jason again and again, marvelling at his words…and their meaning.

I want you, Emily. But I don't want you to be hurt.

It amazed her to think that Jason desired her now, had been intimating that he wanted there to be something between them now.

But what? A kiss? A fling? Clearly, he wasn't proposing marriage, and that was the last thing she wanted anyway. She wasn't in love with Jason; she wasn't in love with anyone. But she wanted him. And he wanted her.

It could be so very simple. She wouldn't get hurt, just as she'd told him. So why was she still mired in doubt?

Perhaps, Emily reflected, it was because it seemed so *impossible* for Jason to want her physically. And even for her to want him. They had so much history, so many shared memories and moments that were at odds with what he was feeling now. What she was feeling.

If she were honest, the thought of Jason actually desiring her terrified and excited her in equal amounts. She'd *never* thought of him that way, never dared to…and yet another part of her sly mind whispered that in reality she'd *always* thought of him that way, or wanted to. That was why that dance—and almost-kiss—seven years ago had actually devastated her… even though she'd convinced herself for so long that it hadn't. That it had been nothing.

And now? Emily didn't know what the truth was, or could be. She was afraid to find out. Maybe Jason hadn't meant that at all anyway. Perhaps he'd just been teasing her as usual, and she'd read far too much into a few throwaway remarks because her own need was suddenly so great. Maybe she was making everything up in her mind, and the next time she saw Jason he would be back to his familiar, mocking self, one eyebrow arched, a faint smile curving his mouth.

Oh, that mouth…

She really was a mess. An obsessed mess, she acknowledged as she kept checking her phone and surfing the Internet and looking for clues to the truth about Jason because he wasn't there in person. Even if he had been she knew she did not yet possess the courage to confront him about any of it.

Meanwhile November drifted into December, and the charity fund-raiser at Jason's flat loomed closer. Emily could barely hide her surprise when Gillian Bateson approached her again, for help with the organisation.

'I thought you had it well in hand?' she asked, surveying Gillian from across her desk. The older woman looked a little more subdued than usual. Her hair was not as immaculately styled and her nail varnish was chipped. Her smile seemed a bit fixed.

'Oh, I do, of course I do. But I thought you might like a peek at Jason's penthouse. It's fab, you know—or actually you don't—'

Emily gritted her teeth. 'I'm sure it is, and I'll see it at the party. I don't really need a…a peek.' Even if she was intensely curious about where Jason lived. Where Jason slept.

Gillian paused, her gaze sliding away from Emily's. 'Actually, I could use a little help,' she said, the admission drawn from her with obvious reluctance. 'It turns out my daughter is visiting that weekend, and I promised to take her out for a bit—' She glanced back at Emily, her laugh a little wobbly. 'You have no idea how demanding pre-teens are.'

'I can imagine, considering I was one myself once.' Emily smiled, surprised and gratified by this insight into Gillian's life. She knew it was practically killing her to ask for help, but Emily was glad she had. And she was honest enough to admit to herself she did want a peek at Jason's flat—badly. 'I'd be happy to help, Gillian.'

After Gillian left her office Emily stared at her computer screen, restless yet needing to work. She had not been able to concentrate on anything. Her fingers drummed on her desktop and she glanced at her to-do list scribbled on a spare piece of paper. She was meant to follow up a shortlist of applications for an assistant in the legal department, arrange the details for an expatriate hire, and draft an email regarding intra-office communications. And that was just this morning. Sighing, she reached for her empty coffee mug.

She was just about to stagger to the coffee machine when her mobile rang. She glanced at the number; it was Philip.

'Hello, sweetheart,' he practically purred. 'Heading out to any Christmas parties this weekend?'

Emily thought of the unanswered invitations scattered across her mantelpiece. 'I don't think so, Philip.'

'I've got two tickets to a new art exhibit in Soho,' Philip told her. 'Very exclusive. You free?'

A ripple of unease made its way down Emily's spine. Why was Philip inviting *her*? 'I don't think so, Philip. I'm quite busy this weekend.' She let out a little gasp, as if she'd just thought of something wonderful. 'I know. Why don't you ask Helen? You've been seeing a lot of her lately, haven't you?'

'I don't know whether I'd say a lot,' Philip replied, his tone one of bored dismissal. Emily froze, her fingers clenched around her mobile. This was not how Philip was meant to talk about Helen. Yet despite the icy feeling of dread developing in the pit of her stomach, she could not give up so easily.

'Well,' she said brightly, 'I'm sure she'd love to go to an art exhibit…and you two were certainly cosy when we all went out to the theatre…' She let out a little suggestive laugh, waiting for Philip's affirmation, but instead he just gave a rather dry chuckle.

'Only because you dragged her along.'

Emily nearly dropped her phone. 'But…but Philip!' she said, her voice rising to something between a squeak and a shriek. 'You were so…you sat next to her…you touched her hair…' She sounded ridiculous, Emily thought distantly, but surely she couldn't have been so terribly mistaken. So *wrong*.

'You thought I was interested in *Helen*?' Philip asked, and then laughed. There was nothing funny about that laugh, nothing warm or generous. It was a laugh of scorn, of mockery. It made Emily's insides shrivel. 'Come on, Emily. She's a lovely girl, of course, but…' He sounded horribly patronising.

'But?' Emily prompted coldly.

'Well, she's not our sort, is she?' Philip said, and Emily

could tell he was trying to be reasonable. 'I thought you were dragging her around as some sort of charity case, and I was nice enough to her because of that, but you couldn't actually think…' He laughed again, and Emily closed her eyes.

Oh, no. No, no, *no*. This was not how she'd imagined this conversation going at all. Philip was supposed to start gushing about Helen, and how lucky he was, and Emily had even envisioned a little teary-eyed gratitude towards the person who had pushed them together. *Push* being the operative word.

This was bad. This was very, very bad for Helen, and almost as bad for her because it meant she'd been horribly, humiliatingly wrong.

And Jason had been right.

Both realisations were equally painful. She opened her eyes and took a deep breath. 'Then I think you've been a bit unfair to Helen,' she said, her voice tight with both anger and guilt. 'You've certainly spent enough time with her so she might think—'

'You're the one who seems to think something,' Philip cut her off. 'Not Helen.'

There was too much truth in that statement for Emily to object. She *had* encouraged Helen. If she'd given her a word of caution instead, who knew how much of this mess might have been averted. And, Emily was forced to acknowledge miserably, she'd encouraged Helen at least in part because it had been a way of proving something to Jason. Of showing him he was wrong.

Except it looked like he wasn't.

'Well, I'm afraid I'm not free this weekend, Philip,' Emily said, her voice decidedly frosty. 'Goodbye.'

She disconnected the call and then with a groan buried her head in her hands. Shame and regret roiled through her. She heard Helen asking her, *Do you think he likes me?* and her own assured—smug!—response: *I'm sure of it.*

And now…now she would have to tell Helen just how awful

Philip was. She surely could not let Helen go on wondering, *hoping*...yet how could she do it? How could she admit how wrong she'd been? Wrong on one occasion, at least.

She straightened in her chair. She might have been wrong about Philip, but she was still right about Richard. He was the same, just as she'd always known.

Predictable. Steady. Cautious. And far too sensible.

Just like—

Emily stopped that train of thought immediately. It wasn't going anywhere good. And, really, she needed to focus on Helen, who deserved someone special, someone who would sweep her off her feet properly—

Already she began a mental flip through the eligible men she knew. Doug in accounting was divorced; Eric, a friend of a friend was reportedly single although there had been rumours of—

She forced herself to stop. It was too soon to set Helen up with someone else and, considering this current catastrophe, perhaps she should take a short break from matchmaking. Relationships could so clearly be disastrous.

At lunchtime Emily went reluctantly downstairs, knowing she would see Helen and somehow have to break the news.

Helen's face lit up as Emily entered the lobby. Emily forced herself to smile back. 'Are you free? I thought we could grab a bite.'

Helen nodded happily. 'Oh, yes—' Then she gave herself away by glancing towards the blank screen of her mobile; Emily had a sinking feeling she'd been waiting for Philip to ring.

'Come on, then,' she said in an attempt at brisk cheer, and hurried Helen out of the building.

In the end the only way to tell Helen was honestly, flatly, without any evasions. Emily kept it as brief as possible, not wanting Helen even to guess at Philip's awful attitude of contempt.

'I'm sorry, Helen,' she said after she'd told her, in the kindest terms possible, about Philip's decided lack of interest. 'I know it's my fault for encouraging you—I really thought he was a better man than he is. And—' she swallowed, forcing herself to meet Helen's bewildered, wide-eyed gaze '—and honestly I think you're better off without him. I just wish I'd realised that a bit sooner.'

Helen glanced down at her untouched lunch. 'You can hardly blame yourself,' she said quietly. 'I'm a grown woman, Emily, and I was the one who—' She swallowed and sniffed, making Emily's heart ache again with guilt and regret. 'And I let myself be blinded by him. He was so charming, and when he…we…' She stopped, sniffing again, and a wave of dread crashed over Emily.

'Helen…did anything actually…*happen* between the two of you?'

Miserably, Helen nodded. 'A few weeks ago, after the theatre, I…I invited him back afterwards. I didn't tell you because I didn't want you to think I was…well…' She stopped as tears began to silently leak out of the corners of her eyes. 'You're so together, Emily, and everyone likes you even if you don't need anyone. But I was lonely and he seemed so nice—'

Emily reached across the table and clasped Helen's hand tightly. She felt perilously close to tears herself. 'This is all my fault,' she said quietly, guilt lancing through her again, causing a physical pain. 'All my fault.' Damn Philip. He might have been quick to dismiss Helen to her that morning, but he'd obviously liked her enough to take her to bed. The thought made Emily's insides burn with both shame and anger. The blame could not be laid solely at Philip's feet. The man was a snake, but she'd convinced Helen he was kind and charming. She'd convinced herself, as well. The only person she hadn't convinced was Jason. 'I'm so sorry, Helen,' she said uselessly, for the damage was already done. This was why she kept

herself out of relationships. Perhaps she should start keeping
other people out of them too.

Her matchmaking days, Emily thought grimly, were
over.

The next few days passed in a blur of work and regret.
Emily could not let go of the guilt that ate at her for pushing
Helen towards Philip. She dreaded seeing Jason, knowing he'd
been right all along and would undoubtedly let her know it
too, yet he didn't make an appearance.

'He had to fly back to Africa again for a few days,' Eloise
told her when Emily broke down and asked for information.
'But he'll be back for the fund-raiser.'

The charity fund-raiser, next week at his flat. Emily would
be going early to help decorate, and yet while this thought
had filled her with a certain tense expectation just a few days
ago, now it was accompanied by a different dread. She wasn't
really looking forward to admitting he'd been right, which,
knowing Jason, she would be forced to do sooner or later. She
certainly wasn't looking forward to his response.

What did I tell you, Em? Sensible is what women need...

No, it isn't, she thought crossly. It *isn't*.

Still, curiosity and anticipation helped to staunch that deepening dread as she headed over to Jason's flat in Chelsea
Harbour that Friday afternoon. She'd invited Helen as her
guest, hoping an evening out—without Philip in attendance—
would help cheer her up. She tried not to think of what Jason
might say about that; no doubt he would accuse her of med-
dling again.

The air was sharp with cold as she and Helen climbed into
a cab and headed for the well-heeled neighbourhood just north
of the Thames.

Gillian had given her a detailed list of instructions about the
caterers, the decorators and the musicians. All Emily would
have to do was supervise. And perhaps have a *little* peek
round.

A tingle of excitement made its way up her spine as she and Helen left the cab for the sleek modern building that housed Jason's penthouse. The high-speed lift had her racing to the top floor, and the doors swished silently open directly into Jason's flat. His home.

Emily stepped gingerly onto a floor of highly polished ebony that seemed to stretch endlessly in several directions. The flat was as fabulous as Gillian had said, and also stark. And even soulless. If she'd been hoping to gain some clue into Jason's inner workings—or even his heart—from where he lived, then she was surely disappointed. The flat revealed nothing. Perhaps, Emily thought wryly, that was indicative of his inner workings. Jason was not a man given to great emotion.

Emily stepped into a soaring reception room with floor-to-ceiling windows overlooking the river. Just as Gillian had said, everything was black or white. Or black and white. Emily took in several very expensive looking black leather sofas, a coffee table of white marble that looked like a piece of modern sculpture, a canvas hanging over the black marble fireplace that was nothing more than a rectangle of white with one messy splotch of black ink in the bottom right corner. It had probably sold for thousands of pounds, Emily thought wryly, and it looked like something her niece had made by accident.

She glanced in the dining room and took in the huge ebony table and matching chairs, a thick snowy-white carpet and several more modern canvases—one black-and-white prison stripes, another like the stripes of a zebra. It was amazing. It was awful.

It revealed nothing about Jason, not the Jason she knew, the man who had always been there to bail her out and scold her afterwards, who managed to smile with both disapproval and amusement, whose eyes turned the colour of honey—

The man who had kissed her. And who had *wanted* to kiss her, maybe more than once.

The buzzer sounded and Emily jumped nearly a foot in the air. The caterers must have arrived. She and Helen exchanged guilty looks—they'd both been snooping—and Emily went to let them in.

The next hour was spent organising all the staff, checking on a thousand tiny details and dealing with the dozens of texts from Gillian, who still clearly wanted to have a hand in the operations.

'I thought you were at a film,' Emily said when Gillian rang her for the third time.

'I am,' Gillian told her. 'Some boy band thing. It's dire. Did the caterers find white asparagus?'

'Yes, and black truffles.' Even the canapés were black and white. 'Don't worry, Gillian. Just enjoy your time with your daughter.'

Gillian let out a rather trembling sigh. 'It's just so odd,' she confessed in a low voice. 'We haven't spent much time together at all.'

Emily's heart twisted in more sympathy than she'd ever had for Gillian before. 'Then go spend some,' she said, 'boy band film and all.'

Finally, by half past six, almost everything was set up. Emily glanced at the makeshift bar, the string quartet, the caterers, and let out a breathy sigh of relief. She hadn't realised how much organisation a party like this actually took.

'Everything looks wonderful,' Helen said, and Emily gave her a grateful smile.

'Gillian said we could use the guest suites to shower and change—shall we get cleaned up?'

Helen nodded and, after grabbing their bags they headed down the long corridor—stark white walls and ebony flooring—towards the bedroom wing. Gillian had told her the guest rooms were the first two doors and, after Helen had disappeared into the first room, an irrepressible curiosity made Emily tiptoe towards the third and last door. Jason's bedroom.

Her heart began to thud as she gently pushed open the door and stepped into the room. Her feet sank into the plush white carpet and she gazed at the king-sized bed with its black satin sheets. Although the sheets were drawn across the wide bed with military precision, she pictured them pulled back and rumpled, with Jason lying there—naked.

Good heavens. Where had that thought come from? It had sprung into her mind so suddenly, so vividly, that her cheeks burned and she glanced around guiltily. Still, she could imagine it all too easily and yet not at all, because nothing about this bed or room or entire flat made her think of Jason. And of course she'd never seen him naked. And most likely never would—

'I think you've wandered into the wrong bedroom.' *Oh!* Emily whirled around, one hand to her thumping heart. Jason stood in the doorway, his shoulder propped against the frame, one hand already starting to loosen his tie. His eyes glinted with humour and his mouth quirked upwards. 'Haven't you?' he added so Emily's face burned all the more and she could feel herself going scarlet. Lovely. Just the look she was going for.

She arched an eyebrow, tossing her hair over her shoulder. 'I was just checking to see if there's any colour in this place,' she said, striving to sound nonchalant. 'I have this mad urge to spill a can of red paint on your carpet.'

'That sounds interesting,' Jason said. 'Although my decorator would have a fit. I suppose I can start with this.' Emily watched in a sort of horrified fascination as Jason tugged off his tie—red silk—and tossed it onto a nearby chair. It landed on the white suede like a splash of paint. Emily swallowed.

'That's a start,' she managed with a light little laugh. 'Although this place still is rather stark.' She gave him a teasing smile, the kind of smile she'd always given him, except now it felt like flirting. And, even stranger still, it felt like Jason was flirting back, an answering smile quirking the corners of his mouth—*those lips*—as he held her gaze a second longer than necessary. A second full of heat. She hadn't imagined what he'd said at Stephanie's wedding. What he'd wanted.

Emily cleared her throat. 'I apologise for being so curious,' she said after a few seconds as Jason simply gazed at her, his eyes sweeping over her rather dishevelled state, lingering on…certain places. Making her feel hot and shivery all at once. 'Anyway,' she said, struggling for words, for air, 'I just couldn't imagine you living in a place like this.'

'I don't live here very much, to tell you the truth,' Jason replied. He dropped his attaché case by the bed and then shrugged out of his suit jacket, dropping it onto the same chair as the tie.

Emily watched his muscles ripple under the crisp white cotton. She'd never quite realised how *built* Jason was. Did he work out? Or did he just lift things when he was doing all that engineering stuff? She swallowed again and tore her gaze away from him. She had to get a grip on this conversation—or at least herself. 'Now that you're back for a bit perhaps you should invest in a new decorator.'

Jason chuckled. His fingers went to the buttons of his shirt. Was he actually undressing? Was he going to take his shirt *off*? Emily found she couldn't breathe. She was staring at his hands as they slid the first button out of its hole and she caught a glimpse of the strong brown column of his throat.

'I suppose I'll never think of this place as home,' Jason said musingly. He seemed unaware that he was undressing in front of her, or that she was staring. 'Weldon will always be that.'

Weldon, Jason's family estate, sprawling and comfortable, one of Surrey's finest homes, yet he hadn't been there properly in years. 'Do you think you'll move back there one day?' she asked.

He paused, his fingers stilling on the buttons of his shirt. Her mesmerised stare finally broken, Emily lifted her gaze to Jason's face. He was watching her with that same little knowing smile. Not so unaware, then. He knew he was unnerving her; he was teasing her. Like always. Except…not.

'Yes, eventually. I'll need to take care of the estate.' A slight frown had settled between his brows, even as he undid another button.

Emily swallowed. 'Yes…to produce that heir of yours, I suppose. Find any suitable candidates yet?' The words held a bit of an edge, but her gaze was still hopelessly drawn to Jason's shirt and how he was slowly—so slowly—unbuttoning it.

'Actually, no,' he said. 'Not yet.'

And not her. The thought really shouldn't bother her, Emily told herself almost frantically. She surely did not want to be in the running for that rather tedious role. And whatever was—or could be—between her and Jason, it certainly wasn't marriage. Or love.

Just basic, primal, overwhelming attraction.

Jason's fingers moved lower. If he undid another button, Emily thought with a lurch of panic, she'd be able to see his chest. 'But I'm not really looking at the moment,' he added. His fingers hovered over the button and Emily realised she was staring. Again. And Jason knew it. Even though her whole body felt heavy and strange, as if it belonged to someone else, she managed a step towards the door.

'Well, I suppose I should get dressed,' she said, attempting a brisk tone. Her voice wobbled instead. 'So I'll leave you to it…' She gestured towards his state of half-undress, her face reddening once more. She could *feel* the heat coming off her. And from Jason. It was all so new, so overwhelming, she felt as if her brain had been short-circuited All she could do was feel. *Want.*

'Don't rush off on my account,' Jason replied, his words laced with lazy amusement. 'You obviously wanted to be in my bedroom, Em…'

Emily froze. 'I was just looking,' she said stiffly.

'And you still are,' Jason replied softly. He'd undone that third button and once more Emily's gaze was glued to his chest. She knew it, he knew it, and yet she still couldn't move. That enticing glimpse of hard, sleek muscle and warm brown skin was making her remember how his chest had felt when she'd touched it—by accident—and how she would like to touch it again. Minus the shirt. What would his skin feel like? Warm, cool? Smooth, rough?

'Really, Jason,' she managed, finally tearing her gaze away from his chest. It took her a moment to focus on his face. 'I had no idea you were such a tease.'

'I'm not,' he told her, his voice low, and he took a step towards her.

Involuntarily, Emily took a step back. 'What are you doing?' she whispered.

Jason gazed at her for a moment, the glint of amusement gone from his eyes. His mouth thinned as he gave a little shake of his head. 'Terrifying you, apparently—'

'No—' Yet she could not deny the wild beat of her heart, the flush of her face. It wasn't terrifying, but it was something close. She certainly *felt*. A lot. And it scared her, even as desire raced through her veins, made her dizzy with need.

She wanted this. She wanted Jason. And yet she was afraid, because at least part of her knew that Jason was different, that she would be different with him. Everything would be different, deeper. Dangerous.

'Go get dressed, Em,' Jason said, turning away from her. He sounded tired. 'In another bedroom.'

Emily hesitated, wanting to say something witty and

sophisticated. Something sexy. Yet she couldn't; her brain had frozen. Why did she still have to act so gauche with him?

Because this is Jason and you still feel like you're silly and giddy and seventeen years old.

'Fine,' she whispered and left the room, but not without looking back once, her gaze arrested as she watched Jason shrug out of his shirt, the bronzed muscles of his back rippling with the simple movement. Then his hands went to his belt buckle and she fled.

CHAPTER EIGHT

EMILY watched Jason from the other side of his living room, a glass of wine clutched in her hand. He looked breathtaking in a tuxedo, the elegant cut of his clothing emphasising his powerful frame, the breadth of his shoulders and the trimness of his hips. She hadn't really noticed either of those attributes before. She took a large gulp of wine.

Yet she *had* seen him in a tuxedo before. He'd worn one at Isobel's wedding. Perhaps that was why she'd asked him to kiss her. A man in a tuxedo was hard to resist. Jason was proving hard to resist.

Now that she'd acknowledged just how attracted she was to him, it seemed to be all she could think about. It certainly was all she could feel. And she wondered what could happen—tonight, even—if she let it.

She glanced over to where he stood, leaning against one of the living room's soaring white pillars. Her gaze remained fixed on the column of his throat and she imagined him undoing that little black bow tie, just like he'd undone his shirt buttons, revealing the warm skin underneath... She had a thing about his neck, apparently. And a few other parts of his body.

And Jason seemed to be thinking the same way about her. The thought caused an icy thrill to race down her spine right out to her fingers and toes. Icy and yet warm at the same time. Hot.

Perhaps she was coming down with a cold.

No, her fever was of an entirely different sort. And if Jason desired her—if he *suggested* something, how was she going to respond? It all seemed too incredible, too impossible. Any moment he would turn to her with a little smile, a shake of his head, and cluck his tongue.

Oh, Em...you didn't actually think...

She could, quite possibly, make a complete and utter ass of herself. She had to be careful. But then she'd always been rather careful in matters of the heart. Her heart, anyway. She'd been impulsive enough with Helen's.

Although Jason hadn't indicated any interest in her heart, of course. Love was out of the question, and he'd told her he didn't see her as a suitable candidate for marriage. Not that she was interested. No, this attraction between them was purely physical.

Her gaze returned yet again to Jason; he wasn't even looking at her. He hadn't looked at her all evening, and the realisation made her just a little bit annoyed. She was quite sure he was ignoring her—teasing her—on purpose. Sighing, she glanced around the room, checking that everyone was enjoying themselves—although not too much—and her heart sank a little bit when she saw Helen standing by the window, looking lost and forlorn. Emily realised with a little pang of guilt that she'd been so caught up in her lustful thoughts of Jason that she'd completely forgotten about Helen.

'Everything all right?' Stephanie came to stand beside her, her arm around her husband's waist. As former Head of HR, Stephanie was still on the guest list for the exclusive event. She and Tim had returned from their honeymoon only a week ago, and both still had that rapturous glow that made Emily feel both happy and sad—and a bit envious—at the same time. She'd never felt like that, not even close, and although there was nothing precisely missing from her life, standing next to her friend so radiant with joy, made her feel just a little...*less than*. Like something—or someone—was missing, and she didn't know what—or who—it was.

Was it Jason?

The question popped so suddenly and slyly into her head that Emily's mind blanked. How could she have even thought such a thing? What did that even *mean*? 'Sorry...' She turned to Stephanie, blinking as if she could clear the thought from her still-spinning mind. 'What did you say?'

Stephanie laughed. 'I just asked how things were... You look a million miles away, Emily!'

'Yes,' Emily admitted. She glanced again at Helen, who still stood alone. Stephanie naturally followed her gaze.

'She looks rather lost, doesn't she?' she murmured.

'Yes.' Emily shifted uncomfortably. Perhaps inviting Helen to an event like this had been a mistake. Her friendship with Helen had seemed somewhat strained since Philip's about-face; she didn't know if it was out of her own sense of guilt or Helen's hurt. Probably both. 'I should go and talk to her,' she said, and excusing herself, started towards Helen, only to be waylaid by Gillian.

'We've run out of wine glasses,' she hissed. 'Stupid caterers didn't bring enough. I can't ask Jason—'

'I'll sort it out,' Emily soothed. Gillian had been on edge ever since she'd arrived, and Emily assumed it had to do with her daughter's visit. 'I'm sure we can borrow some.' She glanced again at Helen, who was looking more miserable by the minute.

'People are waiting for their wine...' Gillian bit her lip and Emily realised just how distressed she was. Gillian swiped angrily at her eyes. 'I'm sorry, I'm a mess. My daughter—'

'It's okay,' Emily said, squeezing her shoulder. 'I'll deal with it.'

It didn't take more than a few minutes to organise the

glasses, and the crowd by the bar gratefully dispersed with drinks in hand. Emily turned to see to Helen and froze in horror. Stephanie had taken the matter into her own hands and was attempting to introduce Helen to the people standing near her. And one of them was Philip Ellsworth.

By the way a sleek blonde was clinging to him, Emily guessed he'd come as her date. She started towards them, wanting to intercede, yet she knew she wasn't in time. She could already hear Stephanie's cheerful voice.

'This is Sylvie, who volunteered for a well-building project last year, didn't you, Sylvie?'

The blonde nodded, and Emily had to grudgingly concede that, while she clearly had awful taste in men, she did possess an admirable altruistic streak. 'And this is...' Stephanie glanced at Philip, eyebrows raised enquiringly, and Emily watched with a sinking heart as he smiled rather smugly at Helen.

'Helen knows who I am,' he said, and there was enough innuendo in his voice to make Emily cringe. Stephanie looked confused and Helen bit her lip, her eyes filling with tears. She didn't say anything.

Damn Philip Ellsworth, Emily thought with a savage bitterness. She started forward, determined to rescue Helen, but someone else got there first.

'Helen.'

Emily's head jerked around as she heard Jason speak in a tone she almost didn't recognise. It was friendly and warm and intimate, and he crossed the room in a few long strides, placing his hand firmly on Helen's elbow as he smiled down at her. 'I don't think you've seen the view from the terrace. It's really quite stunning. The lights of the marina are spectacular at night.'

Emily watched as he expertly guided Helen away from the crowd—how many people had heard Philip's remark, guessed at his sly innuendo? Too many, Emily knew. Far too many.

Yet now Helen smiled up at Jason as if he'd just charged in on his steed, and she allowed him to guide her outside.

And despite the guilt and regret that still lanced her, she felt a deep and heartfelt gratitude towards Jason for rescuing Helen. He might be a bit staid, a bit taciturn, but he was *kind*. Emily swallowed past the sudden lump of emotion in her throat. She had the uncomfortable feeling that she'd dismissed Jason all these years in a way perhaps she never should have. And it made her physical response to him all the more powerful—and alarming.

The party lasted until midnight. Emily could not focus enough to enjoy it, despite her best intentions to act as if she were. She chatted and smiled and laughed and pretended not to notice that Jason did not talk to her once the entire evening.

A month ago it wouldn't have mattered. A year ago it hadn't. Yet now everything had changed, *she* had changed, and this restless ache inside her would not go away. An ache for Jason. And though he didn't talk or even look at her the entire evening, she couldn't keep a sense of fizzy anticipation at bay, as intoxicating as the champagne she drank, filling her with bubbles of expectation. Surely Jason would seek her out before the end of the party. Surely *something* would happen.

Her mind left the details provocatively blank, although her body had no trouble remembering the slide of Jason's lips on hers, their urgent demand… and her unquestioning response.

As the guests filtered away, Emily organised the clearing up, the caterers and quartet packing up their supplies while Gillian tallied the amounts pledged towards the desalination plant. 'I think Jason will be very pleased,' she said smugly.

'Pleased about what?' Jason strolled into the living room, having seen the last of the guests off.

'Oh, Jason, you startled me.' Gillian fluttered her false eyelashes at him and all the goodwill Emily had been feeling towards her abruptly evaporated. 'We did very well tonight,' she continued, ever so slightly emphasising the *we*. 'Of course we'll have to wait until the cheques clear—'

'Wonderful,' Jason cut across her in a way Emily was quite familiar with. 'Now, Gillian, you look exhausted. I've called you a taxi,' he told her as Gillian's mouth dropped open in surprise and perhaps a little dismay. 'And I insist you take it. You've, as always, done an absolutely brilliant job with the fund-raiser. Enjoy your rest. You deserve it.' He smiled so charmingly that it didn't feel like a dismissal, although Emily was quite certain it was. He wasn't telling *her* to go take a taxi…and the thought filled her with fizzy bubbles again, the most delicious sort of anticipation.

Aimlessly, she wandered around the living room, waiting for Jason to return, her heart already starting a hectic beat. She saw a few half-drunk glasses of wine on a side table and reached for them, intending to take them to the kitchen.

'Leave that.'

Emily stilled, turned around. Jason stood in the doorway, his bow tie and the top button of his shirt undone, his hair just a little rumpled. He looked unbearably sexy. How had she ever thought he was boring? Now she felt so fizzy with anticipation and excitement she could barely breathe. 'Just trying to tidy up,' she said in a breathy, wobbly voice she barely recognised as her own.

'We can do it later.'

She swallowed down the question: *So what should we do now?* Her heart was beating so hard and fast it hurt and her palms were slick. She struggled to appear normal, as if *this* were normal, for her and Jason to be alone in his flat, the night dark all around them, his gaze steady on hers. She glanced around the stark black and white room with all of its after-party detritus. 'I think everyone had a lovely time, don't you?'

'I hope so.' He didn't sound very interested in continuing

the conversation, and as he moved towards her Emily felt a lurch of something close to alarm. This was so new, so *strange*. This was *Jason*. And she still had a lurking fear that he was suddenly going to chuckle and say, *Oh, Emily, you didn't actually think...*

'I feel terrible about Philip and Helen,' she blurted, then wished she hadn't. They were just about the last two people on earth she wanted to talk about right now. It looked as if Jason felt the same for he stilled mid-stride, his brows drawing together.

'Do you?' he said neutrally, and Emily decided she might as well come clean. Better now than...later. If there was a later.

'Philip rang me last week,' she confessed. 'And it was obvious that he...that he didn't...' She stopped, wishing she'd never started this wretched conversation. 'I had no idea he was such a...a...'

'Bastard?' Jason supplied, and Emily nodded.

'Yes,' she admitted in a small voice. 'I'm afraid I really was blinded by his charm. And so was Helen.'

'Understandable, I suppose,' Jason replied. Emily watched as he removed his bow tie and slung it on a nearby chair. He certainly was very casual about removing his clothes. 'He's quite good at all that *sweeping*.' His gaze met hers, glinting with amusement, although she sensed something deeper, something darker underneath. Philip, Emily supposed, was a case in point for Jason. Sensible won over romantic. Except Philip really hadn't been either, in the end.

And Emily wasn't sure what Jason was being now.

'Yes...thank you for rescuing her from Philip this evening. I had no idea he would be here, or I wouldn't have invited her. I thought she could use a night out, away from Philip, and then of course he showed up with that Sylvie person, who builds *wells*, would you believe—'

'Emily,' Jason said, moving towards her, 'stop talking.'

Emily shut her mouth with a snap. She *had* been babbling, but she was so nervous. And Jason looked so assured. 'Okay,' she managed, her voice wobbling slightly. Jason stood in front of her, smiling faintly even as he drew his brows together in concern.

'Why are you so nervous?'

Emily shook her head, unwilling to admit how uncertain she still was. Even now she wasn't sure what Jason intended. What he wanted. She certainly knew what she wanted. Her gaze remained fixed on the column of his throat, the skin so smooth and warm-looking. 'I'm not nervous.'

'Really?' Jason arched an eyebrow, glancing pointedly at the pulse fluttering wildly in her throat. 'I wonder,' he said softly, his gaze now sweeping over her body like a blush, 'why the thought of me being anything other than boring, stuffy Jason terrifies you so much?'

Emily straightened her shoulders, her eyes flashing. 'Do I look terrified?'

'Do you really want to know the answer to that question?'

She let out an uncertain laugh, conceding the point. She supposed it did seem fairly obvious. 'Maybe not.'

'I think we've both needed to change the way we think about each other,' Jason continued, his voice musing, his gaze sweeping over her once more, lingering, languorous. Emily knew there could be no misinterpreting or imagining a look like that. His look was like a caress, his eyes touching her body. 'Of course, we might need some practical help in that regard.'

Only Jason would use the word *practical* in a moment like this. Emily didn't feel practical at all. Her entire body was buzzing with awareness, aching with need. 'Practical…?' she repeated in a whisper.

'Yes,' Jason confirmed, and he lifted a hand to tuck a stray tendril behind her ear, his fingers lingering on her lobe, that little touch possessive and sure. 'And the practical thing for me to do now is seduce you.'

CHAPTER NINE

'SEDUCE me?' Emily repeated. The words rippled over her, dousing her in shock. 'What is that supposed to mean?'

Jason laughed softly. 'I intend to show you in vivid detail.'

Images danced before Emily's eyes, intimate, evocative, startling images. Candlelight on bared skin, clothes slithering to the floor. 'What I meant was,' she amended hastily, 'that most people don't announce their intentions to *seduce*—'

'I told you I'd always be honest with you.'

'Ah.' She managed a shaky laugh. 'Right.' She was still reeling from Jason's sudden announcement. 'So seduction is practical, is it?' she said and Jason smiled.

'Eminently. You are attracted to me, aren't you?'

Emily flinched at such a direct question. There could be no evading, no protecting herself. Still, she tried. 'I... I suppose.'

He laughed softly. 'Damned with faint praise.' Emily said nothing, not wanting to admit just how attracted she was. Even now she was nervous, afraid. Terrified. Jason was right. The thought of him being anything other than what she'd known was scary, strange.

Thrilling.

'I suppose,' Jason murmured, 'I'll just have to convince you how attracted to me you are.'

Emily realised she'd just inadvertently issued another challenge with her tentative answer. She decided, despite the wild beating of her heart, to see it through. 'And how do you intend to do that?'

'Well…' He smiled and brushed another stray tendril of hair behind her ear. His fingers didn't even linger this time. Yet still it was enough for Emily to expel a breath in a ragged rush she couldn't quite control. 'Perhaps,' Jason murmured, 'I should start by kissing you.' Emily swallowed. Audibly. 'This time,' he told her, touching her chin with his fingertips, 'you won't ask me what it was for.'

Emily let out a shaky little laugh. 'Since you've already told me your intention, I won't have to.'

'Good.' And then he did kiss her, finally, and it was as unlike the last time as anything Emily could have imagined. There was nothing tentative about this kiss, nothing tenuous or tender or hesitant. This kiss was hot, hard, a searing brand that told Emily more than anything Jason had said or done just what he wanted to do. What he would do.

That she was his.

Her mouth opened under his, and she gasped aloud as his tongue plunged inside, an erotic mimicry of what would surely come later. And even though Jason didn't move his hands or body or touch her in any other way, Emily was on fire. Liquid fire, her insides melting, her hands reaching up to grasp the lapels of his shirt, pressing closer to him, revelling in the feel of his body next to hers, hard against soft.

Jason broke the kiss with a smile; Emily felt his lips curve against hers. 'Oh, no, Emily,' he said softly. 'We're not rushing this.'

He called this rushing? Emily's face was flushed, her breathing already ragged, as if she'd just done a sprint. Or ten. Her hands were still fisted in his shirt. How could he look so unruffled? So in control?

But then Jason had always been in control. He was

certainly calling the shots now. She was at his mercy, under his command.

'Fine,' she managed, shaking her hair over her shoulders. 'Take your time.'

Jason laughed softly. 'Oh, I will,' he assured her. 'I will.' He moved around her, his head cocked as if he were studying her. Underneath that steady, assessing gaze Emily felt suddenly vulnerable, conscious of the skimpiness of her form-fitting cocktail dress, the black silk hugging her rather generous curves. What was Jason thinking? Why was he looking at her so…thoroughly?

'You're beautiful,' he said. The words were spoken with such simple sincerity that Emily quivered. She'd been told she was beautiful before; her father said it all the time. She'd accepted it, taken it for granted even, yet she hadn't really *felt* it. Believed it. But she did when Jason told her in that honest, heartfelt tone. His voice echoed through her, filled her up to overflowing.

'Thank you,' she whispered, because she didn't know what else to say. 'You're not too bad yourself.'

Jason laughed softly. 'You're rather grudging with your compliments, aren't you?' He stood behind her now, and she felt his breath tickle the back of her neck. She tried not to shiver, but she could not suppress the urge, and when Jason pressed his lips to her nape she gasped aloud. She hadn't expected that, or for his hands to span her waist, sliding over the silk of her dress so he fitted her against him, and she leaned back, yielding to his touch.

She really did feel beautiful, sexy, *wanted*. She'd never felt so desired before, and it was the most intoxicating and powerful feeling in the world.

Slowly, savouring each bit of skin, he kissed his way from her neck to the sensitive curve of her shoulder, his hands sliding upwards from her hips. The sensation was achingly exquisite, almost too much, and they'd barely started.

'Jason—' she gasped, but stopped because she didn't know what to say. What to think. She could just feel this glorious spiralling inside of her, rising upwards, needing to be sated. Slowly, Jason slid his hands down to the hem of her dress, sliding it slowly, sensuously over her thighs. His fingers snagged on the tops of her stockings and he let out a choked laugh.

'God help me, you're wearing *garters*?'

Emily could barely think with his thumbs skimming the bare flesh of her thighs. 'They're…they're sensible,' she finally managed.

Jason slid his palm along the tender, exposed skin of her upper thigh, his thumb easily unhooking her garter. 'And I thought you didn't like sensible,' he murmured. 'Although if you call this sensible…' He moved around to her front and knelt before her. Emily watched, transfixed, as he slowly unrolled her stocking, his hands sliding along her knee and then calf and ankle until the stocking was crumpled on the floor and her leg was bare.

'Very sensible,' she said breathlessly as Jason started on the other leg. His head was bent and the light caught the gold glints of his hair amidst the brown. How had she ever thought his hair was boring? *He* was boring? He was the most exciting man she'd ever met. 'I don't like the feel of tights,' she explained, the words coming in fits and starts. She was mesmerised by the sight of him, by the feel of his hands on her skin. He'd unrolled the stocking and was now slowly peeling it away from her foot. 'Garters are more comfortable.'

'Comfortable and sensible,' Jason murmured. He tossed the stocking and garter to the ground. 'You sound as if you're speaking of orthopaedic shoes, not black lace garters.' He glanced up and Emily's breath dried in her throat at the look in his eyes. They blazed. She'd never seen Jason look so ferociously intense, so amazingly passionate…about her. The thought thrilled her, shook her to her core in a way that was both wonderful and a little frightening. She felt so *much*.

She was conscious then of her bare legs splayed out before her, her dress rucked up nearly to her waist. Slowly Jason slid his hands up her bare legs. Ankles, calves, knees. Emily had had no idea how erotic a touch to the leg could be. And when his hands came to her thighs and rested there possessively, fingers spread, as if he were taking ownership of her, she felt herself sway. Jason's hands, firm and sure, steadied her.

'Jason—' she said again, because she wanted his hands to slide upwards still. She wanted it desperately.

He smiled. He knew what she wanted. 'No rushing,' he reminded her, and then, still smiling, he slid his hands upwards and let his thumbs brush the silk of her underwear. Emily's knees buckled.

He was barely touching her, but it was enough. More than enough, and yet she still wanted more. Jason knelt before her, his hands still strong on her thighs and, leaning forward, he nipped at that scrap of lace with his teeth. Her hands fisted in his hair, half to draw him to her, half to push him away. She didn't know what she wanted. She wanted more, and yet part of her felt the intense vulnerability of having Jason before her like this, touching her in a way no one else ever had. Sex had never been like this before, but then this felt like so much more than sex.

They weren't even *having* sex yet, and already her mind and body were on physical and emotional overload. She didn't know if her body could take any more. If her heart could.

For surely her heart was involved. This wasn't just sex. This was a pure form of communication, elemental, essential. They were talking with their bodies, with hands and lips, and it was a language that was far more powerful than any words they might have spoken.

Jason must have sensed something of her struggle for he reached up and took her hands in his, wrapping his fingers around hers, and then placed them on his shoulders, anchoring her, so when he leaned forward again and pressed his mouth against her, she was actually using him to steady herself. To keep her balance and pull him even closer.

Emily's eyes closed, her body filled with a hot, restless yearning that was painful in its pleasure. It needed to end. She needed release.

Then she found it, and she cried out loud, a long jagged splinter of sound that ended as her body shook with sudden spasms of pleasure and her nails dug into Jason's shoulders.

Still holding her, he stood up, his body sliding against hers. Emily sagged against him, weak with the aftermath of spent desire. Jason easily scooped her up in his arms, leading her to his bedroom and that big black satin bed.

Emily let him carry her; she could hardly protest. She felt as weak as a kitten, her body and mind both utterly sated. Then Jason released her, her body sliding along his until she landed on her feet, and he touched her chin with one finger.

'I said I was going to seduce you, but this is a two-way street, Em.'

Her eyes fluttered open. 'Wh…what?'

'Do you think I'm going to do all the work?' He arched an eyebrow, looking so much like the Jason she knew that it was hard to reconcile him with the man who had just touched her so intimately, who had brought her a fierce pleasure she had never known before.

'Work?' she said, thinking dazedly of Kingsley Engineering and her position there. Jason, following her thoughts so easily, shook his head, smiling slightly.

'Now it's your turn.'

He released her and Emily tried to get her bearings. She felt as if she could barely stand, yet she knew what Jason wanted. He wanted her to touch him as he had touched her. They were equals in this.

Emily gazed at him; he was still completely dressed. So was she save her stockings, although she felt as if she were nearly naked. She'd certainly shown more of herself than

Jason had. She swallowed, wondering what to do. What Jason wanted her to do. She'd had two relationships before this, but sex had been a messy, fumbling affair in the dark. She hadn't known it could be anything else. She hadn't been that fussed, to be honest, because it had never occurred to her that it could actually be more. She wondered if that made her woefully naive, or just inexperienced. Both, she supposed.

'Em,' Jason prompted. There was laughter lurking in his voice, kind laughter that made Emily smile. 'Don't over-analyse this.'

'Really?' She gave him one of her old teasing smiles. 'I think you'd be the king of analysis. You probably have spreadsheets dedicated to the most effective technique.'

He laughed softly. 'Well, *spread* and *sheet* certainly figure into my thinking.' He reached for her hand, threading his fingers through hers, and guided it to his chest. 'Touch me.' There was a raw note of pleading in his voice, an unexpected vulnerability that spoke to Emily's heart and she realised just how much she wanted to touch him.

She laid her palm on his chest, spreading her fingers so his heart beat under her hand. She looked up and saw the longing in his eyes, and it nearly undid her. She'd had no idea how *emotional* this would be. The connection was as intimate as anything they were doing with their bodies, and just as new. Just as terrifying.

Slowly, she drew a breath and then laid her other hand on his chest. 'No rushing,' she reminded him, because now she was the one who needed to take her time.

'No rushing,' Jason assured her and, taking a deep breath, Emily started to undo the buttons of his shirt. Her fingers snagged on the studs of his tuxedo and she fumbled with the clasps, laughing a little bit as she realised unbuttoning his shirt was not going to be as easy as she'd hoped. So much for seeming experienced or sophisticated.

'Sorry,' she mumbled and Jason stilled her hands with his own.

'Next time I won't wear a tuxedo.'

Next time. The words sizzled through Emily's body, fried her mind. There was going to be a next time.

Quickly, Jason undid the studs and then shrugged out of his shirt and cumberbund, revealing the broad brown expanse of his chest. Emily laid her hands against the warm, taut skin, revelling in the feel of it. Of him.

She risked a glance upwards, saw Jason looking at her with almost a pained expression, a frown furrowing his forehead. She snatched her hands back. 'Wh...what? Am I—'

'I've just waited a long time for this.' He reached for her hands, laughing softly. 'I'm starting to want to rush a little bit.'

The thought that her touch could inflame him so much was incredible. Incredibly powerful. Emily splayed her hands on his chest, let her fingernails scrape his skin. She heard Jason's rush of breath and smiled. 'Good things come to those who wait,' she told him softly, and Jason gave a laugh that sounded more like a shudder.

Emily let her hands drift down his chest, reached the waistband of his trousers. She felt powerful and a little shy. This was still Jason—*Jason*—and she could hardly believe any of this was happening. And might happen again.

'Emily...' Her name was a whisper, a hiss.

'Patience, remember?' Emily reminded him, her voice husky. Her heart had started to beat hard and fast again as she slid Jason's trousers down his legs. She'd felt so replete moments ago, but now desire was pooling deep inside her, causing that restless ache to surge through her body, demanding satiation.

Jason helped kick off his trousers, so all he wore was a pair of black silk boxers. Emily trailed her hands up the length of his legs, the crisp hairs tickling her palms. Taking another deep breath, she let her hand slide along the silk of his boxers, her fingers wrapping around the hard length hidden underneath before she continued to skim upwards, sliding along the hard, muscled wall of his chest, reaching for his shoulders.

Standing on her tiptoes, she kissed him. His mouth slackened under hers for an instant before he took control of the kiss, as she instinctively knew he would. She surrendered to it, to him, as his arms came around and he lifted her easily to the bed.

His hand tugged at the zip of the dress and he slid it off her easily, far more easily than she had managed with his own clothes. She lay on the bed, the satin duvet slippery under her, and felt a blush heat her body as Jason gazed at her. She wore only a skimpy black lace bra and thong, which had seemed sexy earlier but now felt indecent. She'd always liked sexy underwear, but nobody ever saw it except her. And now Jason.

'Incredible,' Jason whispered and bent his head to her breast. Emily stopped thinking. Sentences fragmented in her mind and died on her lips as sensation took over once more. Her fingers threaded in his hair as he continued his relentless onslaught, his lips moving over her skin as he undid her bra and slipped off her underwear. She felt him shrug out of his boxers and they were both finally naked.

The feel of his body against hers was another onslaught as every pressure point came into sharp and exquisite focus. Emily hooked her leg around his to draw him even closer, her arms wrapped around his shoulders, her mouth finding his again and again.

Now there was rushing, sweet wonderful rushing, as the need became too great to ignore, the desire too strong to resist.

'I've longed for this,' Jason whispered as he slid into her, and she felt her body open underneath him and accept him, and it amazed her in that instant how good it felt, how surprising and yet how right.

Nothing was strange about this moment. Nothing was embarrassing or awkward. It was all good.

It was wonderful.

And then she stopped thinking again, at least coherently. Thoughts blurred like colours and she felt her body arch in acceptance and deeper need as she pulled him closer still, matching him thrust for thrust, her face buried in the curve of his neck until the colours burst in a rainbow of sensation and they both fell back against the slippery pillows as if they were stars falling to earth, and the night exploded around them.

Neither of them spoke. Emily closed her eyes, her body replete, her heart full. From that fullness she acted, her arms coming around Jason, drawing her to him. Smiling, she kissed him, a soft, gentle kiss of both promise and gratitude.

She felt Jason tense, and then he kissed her back, gently, sweetly. Still smiling, Emily snuggled against him, fitting her body to his, and slept.

Jason felt Emily relax in his arms as her breathing evened out. She was asleep. Asleep in his bed, in his arms. He finally had what he wanted, and it was wonderful. Emily had been as sweetly generous with her body as she was in every other aspect of her life. Giving, honest and artless, and so very thrilling.

It couldn't last. He tensed again, as he had when she'd kissed him so sweetly, curling against him, utterly trusting and satisfied. He'd felt something in that kiss that he hadn't expected, wasn't sure he wanted. He couldn't want it.

This was just a fling, easy, enjoyable and with an end. Those were the terms. He'd convinced himself Emily understood that, wanted that, and yet now—with that kiss—a tendril of doubt unfurled inside him.

He really didn't want to hurt her. Yet he surely couldn't

marry her. He needed a sensible wife, someone like him who valued the practical approach to marriage.

Not someone who wanted sweeping statements, grand gestures, a big romance—all things he didn't want, couldn't give. He wasn't that kind of man, never had been. He'd known it from childhood, seen it in his own father and knew he was of the same mould. He didn't want to disappoint his wife the way his father had his mother; he couldn't live with the devastating consequences.

He *wouldn't*.

A convenient marriage—agreed on both sides—was so much simpler.

Emily sighed in her sleep and Jason pushed the thoughts away. There was still time to find a suitable wife. Plenty of time. And right now he simply wanted to enjoy being with Emily. For however long it lasted.

CHAPTER TEN

EMILY woke slowly, blinking in the sunlight that slanted through Jason's floor-to-ceiling windows...the windows of his bedroom. She stretched, felt the slippery satin sheets slide against her naked limbs. A thrill ran through her, a thrill of excitement, remembrance and just a little fear, as the memories from last night tumbled and arranged themselves in her mind.

Jason kissing her, touching her, inside her.

She turned, expecting to see him, but the bed was empty. A little splinter of disappointment needled her soul.

'Good morning.'

Emily turned to the sound of Jason's voice and saw him emerge from the en suite bathroom. He was showered and wearing a pair of faded jeans, his hair damp and his chest gloriously bare. He looked wonderful and also alarmingly energetic, while she was still lazing about in bed with her hair in rat's tails and last night's make-up caked and sticky on her face. She hiked the sheet up a little higher. 'Good morning.'

He smiled and tossed the towel he'd worn around his neck onto a bedpost. 'Coffee?'

Emily watched as he selected a shirt from a closet of frighteningly well-pressed clothes and slid it on. He sounded very brisk. 'Sure. I can make it.' She didn't move, though, because she didn't want to leave the bed naked and she didn't relish the idea of wearing last night's crumpled cocktail dress again.

'It's all right, it's already brewing.' Jason buttoned up his shirt, smiling at her, so clearly relaxed while she felt so horribly awkward.

Emily pushed a tendril of hair behind her ear, now stiff with old hairspray. 'Okay. I think I'll take a shower.'

'Great. You should fine everything you need in there.' *Except clothes.* He raked his fingers through his damp hair, so clearly relaxed, while Emily felt a little lost, a little lonely. A *lot* vulnerable. This was new territory, and she didn't know how to act or how to feel. She didn't feel strong or brave enough to manage her usual flippant tone. Giving her one last quick smile, Jason left the bedroom, whistling tunelessly as he went, and Emily slipped from the bed and hurried into the bathroom.

The hot, stinging spray of the shower felt good, healing, wiping away the traces of make-up and hairspray, everything except the ache in her heart.

Last night had been fun. A fling. She knew that. She understood it, she'd accepted the terms. The rules. Jason had spelled them out clearly enough when he'd told her she wasn't in the running to be his wife. He'd reminded her again at Stephanie's wedding: *I want you, Emily. But I don't want you to be hurt.*

She'd harboured no illusions, no fantasies. This wasn't love; it wasn't even romantic. So why did she now feel such a yawning emptiness looming inside of her, as if she could tumble into its darkness and never return? Why did she feel so…*sad*?

She closed her eyes and let the water wash over her.

Love *always* had a habit of disappointing you.

Emily opened her eyes, the shampoo suds running into them and stinging. Why on earth had *that* word slipped into her mind? She didn't love Jason. She hadn't even considered such a thing. She didn't *want* to love him, didn't want to let herself in for even more disappointment.

Yet when she'd let him into her body, she'd cracked open the door to her heart. And now life had the potential—and Jason had the power—of not just disappointing her, but something far worse.

Hurt. Pain. Heartbreak.

That was why, despite the intense pleasure, last night felt like a mistake. A regret.

And she had no idea how to act—or feel—this morning. Jason obviously wasn't suffering from the same doubts. He'd been whistling, for heaven's sake. He'd seemed energised and efficient and brisk. It terrified her; she didn't know how to respond to it. She didn't know anything.

Ten minutes later, her body near-scalded from the constant spray of hot water, Emily stepped out of the shower. She swathed herself in a towel and glanced hopelessly around Jason's bedroom for her discarded underwear. She did not feel like slipping into one of his shirts, acting cute and flirtatious. She felt dire.

She finally found the relevant garments, and did her best to smooth the wrinkles from her dress. She slipped it on, struggling with the zip in the back, and then brushed her hair and straightened her shoulders, ready—as she would ever be—to face Jason.

The sight of her discarded garters and stockings in the living room sent another pang of both pain and remembered pleasure through her, and she forced it aside as she stuffed her stockings in her bag and slipped her heels on her bare feet. Then she went to find Jason. She badly needed that cup of coffee.

Jason blinked in surprise as she came into the kitchen. 'You could have borrowed something of mine,' he said mildly, and handed her a mug of steaming coffee.

Emily wrapped her hands around the mug, grateful for its

warmth. 'I'm fine,' she said, taking a sip. Her voice sounded stiff, brittle, and Jason noticed. He raised his eyebrows in silent enquiry, his gaze skimming over her. Emily knew she looked somewhat ridiculous. Her dress was crumpled, her legs bare, her hair wet. Worse, she felt suddenly near tears. There was no way she could tease or joke her way out of this, and from the look on Jason's face, he knew it.

'Emily,' he said. 'Come here.'

'What...?'

He put down his mug and held out his arms, and Emily blinked at him in shock for several seconds before her feet acted of their own accord and she went.

Jason's arms folded around her as he drew her snugly to him so her cheek rested on his shoulder and she breathed in the comforting smells of toothpaste and coffee, aftershave and the scent that was just Jason.

'I don't know how to be,' she confessed, snuffling a little against his shirt.

'Be yourself.'

She drew back to glance up at him, took in the kindness in his eyes, the hint of a smile around his mouth. 'But I'm not sure you even like it when I'm myself.'

'Like it?' Jason's brows snapped together in a sudden frown. 'What are you talking about, Em?'

She pushed a hank of wet hair behind her ear and tried to step out of his embrace. Jason's arms tightened around her; he wouldn't let her go. 'Be honest, Jason,' she said, although she wasn't sure she wanted him to be. 'You've always disapproved of me a little bit. You think I'm hopeless and scatty and who knows what else. I'm not—' She clamped down on that thought, her lips pressed tightly together. *I'm not even in the running.* Why was she thinking like this? Why did she care?

She should have sashayed out of Jason's bedroom wearing

his shirt and her heels and tossed her hair over one shoulder, teasing him about how he wasn't *that* boring after all.

The words bubbled inside of her now but she knew they were too late because she'd already said too much. Revealed too much of how she really felt, what she was afraid of, and now she was left feeling exposed and vulnerable and *awful*.

This was why she avoided relationships, why she'd told Jason she wasn't interested in love. Love had the power to hurt you, because it never could live up to your expectations. You let someone see your weaknesses and fears and opened yourself up to all sorts of pain when they didn't feel the way you did, or they didn't act the way you wanted them to or they died…like her mother had, leaving her father to grieve these twenty years and more.

Thank God she didn't actually love Jason, she thought with a rush of relief. This was bad enough.

'I don't think you're hopeless,' Jason finally said, and Emily thought he sounded rather grudging.

'Scatty, then.'

'Emily—' He let out a little huff of breath, and Emily could only imagine how all this talk of feelings was annoying him. This was not part of their understanding. 'Let me make you some breakfast,' he said instead, and Emily knew better than to press. She didn't really want to hear Jason tell her how he agreed with everything she'd just said and then top it off with a nonplussed *'so what?'*

'Fine,' she said, and then amended that ungracious reply with, 'Thank you. I usually just have toast in the mornings.'

'Which is why you're such a lightweight by dinner time,' he said, sliding her an amused glance. Emily conceded the point with a stiff smile. 'I'll make you eggs. It's the one thing I can actually make. You want the full fry-up?'

Emily didn't know how much she'd be able to choke down but at least if they were eating they wouldn't be talking. Saying things she didn't want to hear. 'Why not?' she said, tossing her hair, but it was wet and heavy and the gesture lacked the careless insouciance she'd been going for. Jason noticed, for he frowned slightly before turning towards the stove.

Jason concentrated on cracking eggs into a pan. He didn't want to have to see the uncertainty in Emily's clear green eyes. Of course the morning after was going to be strange; they had too much shared history for it to feel normal. Natural.

And yet holding her in his arms just then had felt all too natural. Too right. He'd drawn her to him without thinking or analysing. He'd just acted. And it had felt good. He liked the way she fitted in his arms. He liked the way it made him feel.

The thought unsettled him. He didn't want to think about feelings, even if Emily seemed intent on pressing him to do so. He didn't want to think about the surprising rush of emotion he'd felt towards Emily last night, or even now.

This was just a fling. It had to be. Emily understood that; so did he. Yet right now, with the memory of last night still stirring through his body, all he knew was he didn't want to let her go.

'So do you cook for yourself when you're on these engineering projects of yours?' Emily asked. She'd hoisted herself up onto a bar stool, her dress riding up her thighs. Jason turned away, desire spiking through him once more, although he was relieved they were talking about more innocuous matters.

'Not really. When we're on site there is a catering team, but the food still is pretty basic. However, breakfast in most sub-Saharan countries is just a gruel made from cassava, and I've always been partial to a fried egg and toast.'

'So you learned to cook yourself breakfast there?'

'Actually, I learned to cook when I was younger,' Jason said. He kept his back to her, wanting to keep his voice light even though the question—and its answer—discomfited him. He wasn't sure he wanted to go into such personal territory.

'My mum died when I was eight, as you know, and my dad didn't cook at all.'

Emily was silent for a moment and Jason flipped the eggs over. He didn't particularly like to remember those lonely years, a house of taciturn silence and unspoken grief, painful memories. 'Almost everything I tried was a near disaster,' he continued lightly, 'but I did manage to make a decent fry-up.'

'That's more than I can say,' Emily replied, her voice as light as his. Still they somehow both managed to sound rather brittle. 'I can barely boil water.'

'What do you do, then?' Jason slid the fried eggs and toast onto two plates, giving her a knowing glance. 'Eat out?'

'Of course. I am *very* talented at speed-dialling.'

'A necessary skill in this day and age.' Jason passed the plate over to her. 'Dig in.'

'One of the few I have,' Emily agreed nonchalantly, and Jason had the feeling that she was trying to prove something to him. Was she actually trying to show him how scatty and hopeless she really was? He shook his head, unable—and perhaps unwilling—to understand the complicated working of the female mind. 'This is delicious,' she told him, her voice a bit more subdued. 'Thank you.'

The eggs were delicious, but Emily could barely swallow a mouthful. That moment in Jason's arms had both relieved and worried her, because it had felt too good to simply stand there, leaning against him, accepting his strength. Wanting more.

And even though she wanted to sit here and enjoy the breakfast and the time with Jason, the winter sunshine pouring through the huge windows, she couldn't. Her chest felt tight, her insides raw, and her brain was hammering home the realisation that she'd *known* this could have happened, that she'd been afraid of this all along.

She cared about him. And she couldn't allow herself to.

'So,' she said, dryly swallowing a mouthful of toast, 'how are you going to pick this paragon of yours?'

Jason looked up, his eyes narrowing. 'What are you talking about?'

Emily gave him a teasing smile. 'Your wife, Jason. You mentioned a list of candidates—'

'Actually, I didn't. You did.' He didn't look pleased by the turn in conversation.

'Only because I'm not one of them,' Emily reminded him sweetly. She smiled, even though it made her face hurt. Jason pressed his lips together in a hard line. Now he looked really annoyed, and she knew why. This was hardly morning-after conversation. She was picking a fight because it was better than bursting into tears, and she was perilously close to doing just that.

'I don't see the point to this conversation,' he said, a definite edge to his voice.

Emily arched her eyebrows. 'Does there need to be a point?'

'Emily—'

'I thought we were just making conversation. You *did* come back to London to find yourself a wife, didn't you? That's your personal business, isn't it?' Although he hadn't said as much, she could certainly put the pieces together. She might be scatty, but she wasn't stupid.

'In a manner of speaking,' Jason conceded after a moment.

'But since you're here with me, you must not be having any luck.'

'No, I'm not feeling lucky at all,' Jason snapped. 'Why are we talking about this, Emily? I think we both knew what we were getting into last night—'

'Of course. You seduced me. End of story.'

He let out an irritated breath. 'It was mutual, or so it seemed to me.'

She flashed him a quick cat-like smile. 'Absolutely.'

'Are you having regrets? Second thoughts?' he asked, the words coming out in staccato bullets, like gunfire.

Yes. And it was the last thing she'd admit to him now. She slipped off the stool. 'Of course not,' she said lightly. 'Why should I? I told you I never wanted to get married. And certainly not to you.' Emily knew how childish her words sounded, but she couldn't keep herself from saying them. Or the hurt from showing in her voice, her eyes. She hated feeling so vulnerable.

Jason's eyes narrowed to near slits, his mouth nothing more than a thin line. 'Then there's no problem,' he finally said, his voice so very neutral.

'None at all.' Except for the fact that she felt as if she might splinter apart in seconds. Still smiling, Emily turned and left the kitchen. Jason followed her out into the foyer, watched as she reached for her coat and jabbed her arms into the sleeves.

'Where are you going?'

'I have things to do,' Emily said, her back to him, her tone dismissive. 'I can't spend the whole day here, Jason.' She'd spend it huddled in bed with a box of tissues.

'All right,' Jason accepted after a moment. 'I'll see you at work on Monday.'

Emily didn't answer because she didn't know if she'd make it into work on Monday. She had a feeling she might call in sick.

Her back still to him, she jabbed the button for the lift. The silence ticked on between them, tautening with tension and unspoken words.

'Emily—' Jason said, just as the lift doors opened. She slipped quickly inside, turning only to waggle her fingers at him as they thankfully closed.

'Bye, then.'

The doors closed, but not before she saw Jason staring at

her, a hard look on his face, his eyes narrowed as if he were trying to understand just what game she was playing.

Emily sagged against the wall as the lift sped downwards. Hopefully he would never know how much the last ten minutes had cost her.

Jason stood in the foyer, sifting through the last few minutes of conversation. He felt restless and annoyed and, bizarrely, a little hurt. That last emotion was ridiculous, because surely Emily was acting true to form, as he wanted her to. This was a fling, after all. She was...flinging.

So why didn't he like it?

Why did he feel as if he'd just been dismissed? Intentionally? *He* was the one who walked away, who left after one evening. One night. Yet Emily had just left him. The thought was aggravating. Insulting. *Hurtful.* He turned away from the lift doors, determined not to think of it, or why she'd gone so suddenly. Not to care. He had plenty of things he needed to do today, including drawing up that list of candidates Emily had mentioned. He did, after all, need to find a wife.

Even if the thought now filled him with a restless, aching discontent.

Emily lay in bed, staring at the ceiling. Her body and mind both ached and she wished she could find some kind of oblivion in sleep, but it eluded her. Her mind continued to run a looping reel of just about every moment she'd ever had with Jason, from that first tender dance to last night's soul-shattering events. Tears slipped down her cheeks in silent recrimination.

What was *wrong* with her?

She shouldn't be this sad, this *shattered*. Yet that was how she felt, as if all the secure pieces of her existence, her very self, had scattered and she was left with nothing, empty and aching inside.

Last night had changed the way she thought about life, about herself. The realisation scared her. She'd been *happy* before, content and confident, satisfied with her life. Then a single night with Jason Kingsley had made her feel as if all that—all of herself—had been flimsy and false. She'd been fooling herself all along, and it had taken last night—a night of incredible, intense intimacy, as well as this morning's hard wake-up call—to make her realise it.

She *wasn't* happy. She didn't know what she wanted… from Jason, or out of life itself. This was why she didn't do relationships, Emily thought miserably. They were either disappointing or devastating. Hugging her knees to her chest, she thought she'd take the disappointment she'd felt in her last two relationships over the swamping sense of loss she felt now. Then she'd been able to walk away with simple disillusionment rather than actual pain.

Now she felt as if she teetered on the precipice of a great, yawning chasm of heartache and it was only her refusal to probe too deeply into her own inner anguish that kept her from spiralling downwards into that endless space.

She didn't think. Wouldn't remember. Instead, she slipped down under the covers, pulling them over her head, and squeezed her eyes shut tight. She didn't know how long she lay there, willing sleep to come, but it finally did, and she existed in a deep, dreamless state where memories thankfully lost their power.

Of course, she couldn't sleep all day. She tried, but after a while her body's basic needs compelled her to rise from bed. She had a cup of tea and a piece of toast as she gazed moodily out of her window at a now snow-covered Hyde Park. It was going to be a white Christmas.

Christmas. She was meant to go home for Christmas on Wednesday, but Emily absolutely knew she could not go into work on Monday. She didn't even know if Jason would be there, but just the possibility was too awful to risk or even to contemplate. She'd been able to pretend—just—that she didn't care for a morning, but she couldn't do it for a whole day. Yet that was what her whole future looked like, day after day of pretending, until her heart stopped hurting and she forgot about Jason Kingsley and the way he looked at her with those glinting eyes, the sound of his dry laughter, the feel of his mouth—

Except she couldn't forget about him because their families were related. He might even turn up in Surrey at Christmas. The thought of sitting down at the same table and passing the potatoes made her groan aloud.

How could she face any of it?

She'd ring work and say she was ill, Emily decided, and go home early. It was the coward's way out, but she felt like a coward. She was too cowardly even to face her own thoughts—or heart. She did not dare probe too much about how she felt about Jason, how deep the hurt ran. She was certainly not going to face him.

The thought of home with all of its dear familiarities, her father's welcoming arms and her sister's comforting presence, invigorated Emily and she grabbed a case from her cupboard and began to haphazardly throw clothes and cosmetics into it, desperate now to get away. To escape. Again.

Twenty miles from Highfield it had started to snow again, thick, fat flakes that drifted lazily down and completely obliterated the road in front of her. Emily tightened her grip on the steering wheel, her body tense—she'd been tense for hours, an entire day—as she willed herself and her vehicle onward.

When she finally turned into the sweeping drive of Hartington House, its lights twinkling in the distance, the wheels of her car skidded on an icy crust of snow and impatiently she braked and turned off the engine, leaving the car half in a drift. She grabbed her case and headed up the drive, her feet soon soaked through. She didn't care. She just wanted to get home.

Her father met her at the door, wearing a shabby dressing gown and slippers. He looked shocked to see her, his eyes widening, a pipe forgotten in one hand.

'Emily! What on earth! I didn't think you were coming until Wednesday, darling.'

'I wasn't.' Emily stepped into the welcoming circle of her father's arms, breathed in the familiar scents of pipe tobacco and aftershave. 'I just wanted to come home,' she said, her voice muffled against his shoulder. She felt his hands stroke her hair and she closed her eyes, the unshed tears hot against her closed lids.

'Is everything all right, mouse?' he asked, using her nickname from her childhood. Emily sniffed and smiled.

'Yes,' she managed, and couldn't say any more.

Henry Wood squeezed her shoulders and stepped back. 'Well, it's good to have you. I'm afraid Carly has left for the night or I'd ask her to make up your bedroom.'

'It's all right.' Emily smiled, knowing her father would never have dreamed of making the bed himself. He was dear, but he was also stuck in his old-fashioned ways and he depended on his housekeeper. 'I'll do it myself.'

'We'll talk at breakfast,' Henry said and Emily nodded her acceptance.

It felt a little strange to be back in her childhood bedroom, although she'd spent just about every holiday there since leaving Hartington House at the age of twenty. Yet now it felt different, because she felt different, and she wondered if life would ever be the same again.

Had she any idea what being with Jason would mean? Would cost her?

Refusing to think of it any more, she made up her bed and slipped gratefully under the sheets. Sleep, for once, came quickly.

The next morning the sun shone brightly over a world white with snow, and Emily felt her spirits lift just a little bit. Her father was already downstairs tucking into eggs and bacon when she joined him at the table.

They ate in silence for a little while; Henry had never been one to press for confidences. After a moment Emily cleared her throat and, looking at her father bent over his bacon, said, 'May I ask you something about Mum?'

Henry straightened, his expression one of surprise and, Emily thought, a little pain. Even twenty-two years after his wife's death, just the mention of her hurt. 'What do you want to know?'

He'd told her plenty of stories over the years, as had Isobel. Emily was the only one without any memories of her mother, beyond a vague, shadowy yet comforting presence. Yet the stories Henry and Isobel had told had been mostly about Elizabeth Wood as a mother. Now Emily wanted to know what she'd been like as a wife.

'You loved her very much…' she began hesitantly.

Henry's eyes widened. 'You have to ask?'

Emily shook her head, smiling a little bit. 'No. I know you did. You always told me how there wasn't another woman like her.'

'And there wasn't,' Henry said robustly. 'One in a million, your mother. One in a hundred million. She was perfect.' He shook his head, his expression fading into a sorrowful reflectiveness. 'I was a lucky sod, you know, that she loved me back. An old grump like me. She was everything to me, Emily, everything.'

Emily swallowed, her throat tight. 'You still miss her.'

'Every day,' Henry said simply. 'I'll never stop. But it's easier now than it was. Those first few years… Well, you don't remember, but they were dark days.' He shook his head. 'I wasn't sure I could go on living without her. She was my anchor, my very soul. But I had you and Izzy to look after, and thank God I did, because I couldn't ever imagine life without you.'

'And,' Emily asked, the words no more than a whisper, 'do you ever—do you ever regret loving her so much? Since you lost her?'

Henry looked at her shrewdly for a moment before answering. 'Not for one second. Not one bit.' He smiled a bit sadly, and Emily suddenly saw how white his hair was, how lined his face. Her father had married late in life and he was already well into his seventies. He looked his age, the years of grief etched on his dear face. Her throat tightened with emotion. 'Loving your mother was the best thing I ever did, Emily. Don't ever doubt it.'

Emily nodded, accepting. The risk had been worth it for her father, she knew that. The love he'd had with her mother had been rare, overwhelming, precious. And nothing like what was—or had been—between her and Jason.

Yet that, she knew now, was what she wanted. Love. Romance. To be swept off her feet.

If you're swept off your feet…you might even fall.

Recalling Jason's words, she acknowledged how true they unfortunately were. She'd fallen. Hard.

Emily spent the days before Christmas tucked away at Hartington House, grateful to avoid the rush of the holiday season. She visited her sister and Jack at their home in a neighbouring village, a relaxed sprawl of a place where children and dogs ran amok amid the cheerful chaos of family life. She watched their easy banter and their casual affection with envy, a jealousy she had never felt before but had now sunk its razor claws into her soul.

She wanted that. All of it. And she'd never realised how much until she'd experienced a tiny taste of it with Jason. Of course, she knew how appalled he'd be if she were ever to tell him. *That* was not part of his precious agenda. She was the fling, not the wife. The bit of fun before he settled down, she supposed, and she could hardly blame him. She'd presented herself as just that, blithely informing him that love and marriage were well and good for other people, but not for her. She wanted to have *fun*.

Well, she'd had her fun. And in the end it hadn't been very fun at all.

Would he announce his engagement to whatever practical paragon he chose at Christmas? Easter? Would she have to attend the wedding, smile for the photographs? It was all just too awful to think about, yet Emily spent endless hours torturing herself by doing just that.

On Christmas Eve she was finally forced out of her moody lethargy. 'I haven't even asked what we're doing for Christmas dinner tomorrow,' Emily said as she sat down to breakfast with her father. She'd bought presents, at least, but she wasn't feeling very festive.

'Oh, don't worry, it's all taken care of,' Henry assured her with a wave of his hand.

'Isobel's arranging something, I suppose?' Her sister had always been the organised one.

'No, no, Izzy's taking some time off this year,' Henry said. 'Actually, we've all been invited over to Weldon. Jason's coming home.'

CHAPTER ELEVEN

EMILY slid out of her father's car and gazed up at the ancient, imposing Weldon Manor with trepidation and foreboding. Jason was in that house. Just the thought of seeing him again sent her nerves jangling, her palms sweating and her heart beating far too hard.

'Ready, darling?' Henry smiled at her, and Emily was assailed again with how old he looked. He wasn't quite frail, but he picked his way over the uneven cobblestones of the Manor drive with care. Emily slid her arm through his, steadying him without seeming to.

'This should be fun,' she said, attempting airiness. 'A nice family gathering.' *If only.*

Henry gestured to the Land Rover already parked in the drive. 'Looks like Izzy and Jack have already arrived.'

Fortunately Isobel was the one who opened the door and even as Emily glanced furtively around the huge, soaring entrance hall Jason was nowhere in sight. She let herself be enveloped in hugs and tackled around the knees by her niece and nephew, grateful for the temporary reprieve.

Of course it couldn't last for ever. This was Jason's home, after all. His father's home. Edward Kingsley welcomed them into the front drawing room for sherry by the fire, presiding over the gathering like a king on his throne, polite yet distant, a little bit remote. A little bit like Jason. Neither man, it seemed, was given to much emotion.

Emily accepted her glass of sherry and stood by the window, half-hidden by the curtains. She looked away when Jason strolled into the room, his manner relaxed and assured. Unlike her.

'Jason!' All smiles, Isobel crossed the room to embrace her brother-in-law. 'We haven't seen you in an age. It's so good to have you back.'

'It's good to be back,' Jason replied, kissing her cheek. Emily felt his gaze move over her like a shadow even though she was pretending a deep and abiding interest in the view of the snowy front lawn outside.

She couldn't focus on her sister's cheerful chatter; every muscle and nerve was concentrated on maintaining this attitude of relaxed disinterest. She had a feeling she was failing miserably.

'And you must see if you can cheer Emily out of her blues,' Isobel continued playfully. Emily stiffened at the mention of her name.

'The blues?' Jason repeated neutrally.

'Yes, she hasn't been herself, have you, darling?' Isobel smiled at Emily, who tried to give her a quelling look without Jason noticing. It proved impossible, or her sister simply ignored it. Isobel pursed her lips knowingly. 'Is it a man, Emily?'

She felt herself flush and her fingers clenched so tightly around her sherry glass she thought she might snap its fragile stem. 'No, of course not,' she said, her voice sounding stiff and awkward. 'Why would you think that?'

'Because you've been positively moping. And it's *Christmas*.'

'Isobel—' Emily spoke warningly, not that her sister ever heeded such warnings. She was bossy in the most lovable way, yet right now Emily felt like strangling her.

'Well,' Jason said, and Emily's gaze instinctively flew to him, drinking him in despite her intentions to appear unmoved. His cheeks were still flushed with cold, his eyes bright and glinting. 'We'll have to see what we can do about that.' His gaze rested on her, so knowing, so assured, and, panicking, Emily wondered what he could possibly mean by that statement.

'I'm fine,' she said rather sharply, looking away again. 'You don't need to do anything.'

Edward Kingsley cleared his throat, surely a sign that this discussion was over. Undoubtedly it had become too personal for his taste.

Jason watched Emily walk stiffly from the room, her head held high, her body radiating tension. She'd been jumpy as a cat since he'd arrived. He'd had a lot of time to think about what had happened the morning after their night together, to consider why Emily had left so suddenly—and why he had been so aggravated by her departure.

He wasn't used to such reflection, and he didn't particularly enjoy it. He was a man of action, not thoughts. Not words. Words, he well knew, accomplished little. Meant nothing. Made no difference.

He wanted to act, to accomplish and to complete. And after almost a week of thinking about Emily, about that alleged list of wifely candidates, he'd had enough. He knew what he wanted. And he knew what he was going to do.

It was just a matter of presenting his plan to Emily.

Even with Isobel's steady chatter, Christmas dinner felt stilted. Of course, Jason was used to these heavy silences; they had defined his youth, ever since his mother's death. His father was a man of few feelings or words, and he'd moulded his oldest son to his likeness. Jack had been the rebel, not Jason.

Yet now he felt more than ever the oppressiveness of his

father's presence, his silence, the grim dourness of Weldon Manor—all the more apparent when Emily sat across from him, as beautiful and brilliant as a butterfly.

He pictured her moving among the dark, heavy rooms of the house, filling them with light and laughter. If she was willing to let go of some of her childish flights of fancy—and he thought she might be—they could have a good life together. He hoped she would, for once, see sense.

He waited until after dinner, when everyone had retired back to the drawing room. Isobel was putting the baby down for a nap and Jack was deep in conversation with his father-in-law; Edward Kingsley had retreated to his study.

Jason turned to Emily. 'Why don't we go for a walk? It's beautiful outside.'

She looked startled, and trapped, and even afraid. 'I...'

'I think that's a wonderful idea,' Isobel said, coming back into the drawing room, now child-free. 'You can get some fresh air. And I'm sure you'll cheer her up, won't you, Jason?'

'I intend to.'

Emily looked as if she still wanted to resist but, with a shrug she capitulated. 'I'll just get my coat.'

Jason waited for her by the back door, smiling easily as she joined him with obvious reluctance and they headed out into the Manor's landscaped gardens, now blanketed in snow.

It was a beautiful, brilliant day, the sky a hard, bright blue and the air clean and sharp. The trees that lined the stone walk through the garden were encased in ice, every twig and branch glittering with sunlight.

'Why didn't you come to work on Monday?' Jason asked after a few minutes of walking and Emily stiffened.

'I'm sorry if it inconvenienced you,' she said stiltedly, 'but I am entitled to several personal days—'

'Emily, I'm not asking as your boss,' Jason cut her off, keeping his voice mild. 'I'm asking as your lover.'

She stared at him, her eyes wide, her mouth slightly parted. Clearly shocked. 'I needed some time,' she said after a moment, her voice low. 'To think.'

He'd thought, too. He wondered if they'd come to the same conclusions. If they hadn't, he thought he could convince her with certain...methods. 'And did you?' he enquired. 'Think?'

'Yes.' She didn't say anything more and they kept walking, the only sound the crunch of their boots in the snow. 'I don't think this is going to work,' Emily finally said. Her voice was barely audible, her eyes on the ground. 'Whatever it is. A fling. An affair.'

'Oh?' He kept his voice neutral, waiting to hear what she said. What she thought.

'No. I've...I've realised I want something different.'

'And what is it that you want?'

'It doesn't matter,' she said quickly. 'The night we had together was pleasurable, Jason, you know that, but—' She stopped, turning to look at him with heartbreaking honesty. 'I think it's better if we just stay...friends.'

'That is an idea,' Jason allowed, stopping, as well. He gazed at her, taking in her tousled hair, her wide jade eyes, the lush fullness of her parted lips. He wanted to pull her into his arms, to kiss her until they were both breathless, but he waited. First there were things he needed to say. 'I have another idea.'

Her eyes widened, her face so open and artless. She hid nothing. 'You do?'

'Yes. I want you to marry me.'

Jason's words echoed in Emily's brain, but they didn't make sense. Surely he hadn't said—hadn't suggested—

'What did you say?' she managed, her voice no more than a thready whisper.

'I want you to marry me, Emily. I've been thinking about it all week and I've realised it makes sense.'

'Makes sense,' Emily repeated numbly. He sounded so *reasonable*.

'I told you I was looking for a wife—'

'And you also told me I wasn't in the running,' she reminded him. She heard the hurt in her voice and didn't care. She was feeling too overwhelmed, too incredulous, too *furious* to hide her emotions now.

Jason looked a tiny bit discomfited, but then he smiled easily and spread his hands wide. 'I changed my mind.'

'Oh, you did, did you?' She let out a laugh, abrupt and sharp, like a gunshot. 'So was that a proposal?'

Again she saw that annoyance flash across his features. She supposed this wasn't the conversation he'd intended on having.

'Call it what you will. We're good together, Emily. You can't deny that—'

'In bed, maybe.'

'Out of it, as well,' Jason said firmly. 'I'm not suggesting a marriage based purely on physical attraction.'

'Oh, no, I'm sure you have several other practical considerations,' Emily retorted. She was angry, perhaps unreasonably so, but it was better than bawling, which was what she felt like doing, because she hadn't, in a million years, expected this. Or how much it would hurt.

And she'd thought *making a go of it* was bad. This was infinitely worse.

'As a matter of fact, yes,' Jason said calmly. He was obviously on familiar territory now. Emily folded her arms and waited. 'We come from a similar background, our families are friendly, we're compatible physically and, I believe, emotionally.'

'Emotionally?' Emily repeated in disbelief. It wasn't a word she'd expected him to use. And as far as *compatibility* went—

'Yes. We complement each other, Em. We're different, I know that, but that can be a good thing.'

She didn't bother asking how. She wasn't sure she wanted to know. *I'll keep you from being completely irresponsible…* 'That's quite a list you've got.'

'And, most importantly,' Jason continued, as if delivering the coup de grâce, 'we're realistic about love.'

She swallowed. Her heart felt like a stone. 'We are?'

'You said so yourself,' Jason reminded her. 'You told me you weren't waiting for Prince Charming to rescue you. You agreed it was overrated. You're happy as you are.' He parroted back all the statements she'd given him with such breezy—and false—confidence. Obviously she'd been too convincing; he'd actually believed her.

'If I'm so happy, why should I get married?'

'Children, companionship, sex.' Yet another list. How could he be so sensible—so heartless—about the rest of their lives? About each other?

'So,' Emily managed through stiff lips, 'why did you change your mind? How did I suddenly become so suitable?' Jason hesitated, and for the first time he seemed truly at a loss for words. Emily shook her head. She didn't really want to hear how he'd made some kind of pro and con list. *Pros: sex. Cons: hopelessly scatty.* 'It doesn't matter. I'm not going to marry you, Jason.'

His brows snapped together. 'And do you have a reason?'

She almost laughed. Yes, she did, a great, big, obvious and awful one. 'You don't love me.' It hurt to say the words, to feel them, because she knew in that moment that she loved Jason. It had been building inside her, the pressure mounting, the knowledge inarguable and consuming. She'd done exactly what she hadn't wanted to do, and fallen in love. And she'd done it with someone who had no interest in love even as a concept. She'd found that rare, precious thing called love; unfortunately it hadn't found her.

How had she fooled herself even for a moment that she didn't love him? Of course she did. That was why she'd been so nervous about being involved with Jason in the first place, why she'd never been able to forget that dance. That kiss. Why she'd run away the morning after they'd made…had sex. Because that was all it had been. Sex. And she'd been running and hiding from the truth of her feelings, her desires, because she hadn't wanted to face this moment, when he looked at her with a blank confusion that stated so clearly the idea of loving her hadn't even crossed his mind.

Jason was silent for a long moment. 'Anyone can tell you he loves you,' he finally said.

Except you, Emily thought miserably. She blinked hard. 'Well, obviously he needs to mean it.' She dragged in a desperate breath. 'And, in any case, it's not just about words. It's about feelings and…and actions.'

Jason gazed at her levelly. 'And what actions have made you think I don't love you?'

She blinked again, trying to focus. Was he trying to trick her with that question? He was trapping her somehow, Emily could see it in his narrowed gaze, the dangerous glitter in those honeyed eyes. She struggled to frame an honest response. 'Because this conversation would have gone very differently if you did,' she finally said.

'Would it?' Jason challenged. 'You came into this conversation with some kind of preconceived notion about what love is, didn't you? You'd already decided whatever I felt—whatever I did—wasn't enough. Because you want something more.' Each word was delivered like a hammer blow, an attack on everything she felt. 'And maybe you don't even know what that is, but it's always got to be more. You want me to tell you I can't live without you, that life would be hell if you're not in it. You want roses and rings and maybe even tears. Don't you?' His voice rang out, strong and scornful, and yet underneath Emily detected a thread of hurt. And she knew that she couldn't blame Jason for not loving her; they'd both come to this sorry point. They simply wanted different things. She was asking for something he was incapable of giving.

She tried to smile and failed. Her lips moved at least. 'Maybe not the tears,' she conceded. 'A sniffle would do. But yes, I do want those things. I want the fairy tale.'

'And that's just what it is. A fairy tale.' He dug his hands into the pockets of his coat, shaking his head as he turned away from her. 'That's why I don't want a marriage based on love. It's fickle, fleeting, and it makes you unhappy. I thought you'd see sense—'

She tried to laugh, but it sounded more like a bark. 'When have I ever seen sense?'

The anger seemed to seep out of Jason, leaving him silent, even defeated. He turned to her with a small, sad smile. 'I suppose I'm the one who hasn't been sensible, convincing myself that you wanted the same thing I did, that you didn't care about love and romance and the rest.' He looked at her ruefully, trying to lighten the moment, although his eyes were still shadowed. 'If I'd really thought about it I'd know it was utter bunk. You've been pairing everyone else into happily-ever-afters. Of course you want the same for yourself.'

She sniffed. Loudly. 'Yes, I do.'

'And my idea for a happily-ever-after isn't the same as yours.' He paused, his voice quiet. 'It isn't enough.'

Emily's heart twisted. Tore. She felt as if she'd failed him somehow, as if she were being demanding and unreasonable by wanting that most elemental and ephemeral thing, *love*. And part of her wanted to tell him that it didn't matter, that maybe her love could be enough for both of them. But she knew it couldn't.

'It's better this way, I suppose, than to realise later.' He paused, his gaze turning distant. 'I've seen how different expectations from a marriage can make things miserable. A living hell, in fact.' He gave a short, rather cold laugh, and Emily stiffened, surprised by this sudden intimacy, this peek into Jason's personal life that she'd never even known about. 'My parents had that. My father has never been a very expressive man, and I don't know if he loved my mother. I know he never told her.' He paused, his throat working, and Emily knew how hard this must be for him to say. 'She certainly didn't know. She became more and more unhappy, wanting something from him that he could never give.' He glanced at her, his lips twisting in a rather grim smile. 'Words. Gestures. All these proofs of love that are meaningless—'

Plastic-wrapped bouquets and meaningless compliments. 'But they're not meaningless if you really do mean them, Jason,' Emily said quietly. 'If there's something behind the words. The gestures.' She paused, then dredged up the courage to say quietly, 'If you love me.'

He stared at her, his face like a mask, a curtain coming down over his eyes, his heart. She couldn't see in. She didn't know what he was thinking, but he certainly didn't need to say any words to confirm the awful truth: he didn't love her. Why was she torturing herself this way? 'Tell me,' she asked, her throat raw and scratchy, the tears crowding the corners of her eyes and then sliding down her face, 'have you ever told anyone you loved them?' She swiped at her wet cheeks, her tears already freezing in the winter air.

Jason did not answer for an endless, aching moment. Finally, he said in a voice Emily could barely hear, 'Once.'

He didn't elaborate and Emily stared at him sadly. 'And what happened?'

'It was my mother,' he said, the words drawn from him with deep and obvious reluctance. 'And she didn't say anything.' He pressed his lips together, clearly finished.

There had to be more to that memory than Jason seemed willing to tell, Emily thought. Perhaps it held a clue or even a key to why he was so reluctant to love anyone now. She sighed, the sound trembling with suppressed emotion. 'We're a sorry pair.'

'Aren't we just.'

They both lapsed into a silence of sorrow, an ocean of regret opening up between them. Jason let out a ragged sigh and nodded towards the Manor, looming in the distance, a darkened hulk against the violet sky. Twilight had crept over the countryside without her even realising it; darkness had come. 'You should go in. You look cold.'

'Aren't…aren't you coming?'

Jason shook his head, his gaze on the distance, his expression remote. 'I'll walk a bit longer.'

And silently, because there was really nothing more to say, Emily turned and went back inside the house.

When Jason returned an hour later, he barely looked at her. He brushed off Isobel's fussing that he must have frozen himself to death, and accepted Jack's good-natured teasing that he preferred the cold to being inside with the lot of them. When Emily sneaked glances at him, his expression was sometimes blank, sometimes brooding, and gave her no insight as to how he really felt.

Yet it shouldn't even matter, because everything had already been said. The only option now was to pick up the pieces of her broken heart and cobble them together, carrying on, just like before. Perhaps Jason's personal business would conclude sooner than he anticipated and he'd return to Africa or Asia or wherever his next engineering project would take him.

Yet even that thought gave her a weary pang. She'd miss him. She missed him already.

The hour slogging through the snow had numbed Jason's heart and mind, as well as his body. He needed that numbness because the conversation with Emily had opened up too many feelings, too many regrets. Too many memories.

Have you ever told anyone you loved them?
Once.

For a moment, in his mind's eye, Jason could see his

mother's pale face, the tears sliding silently down her waxen cheeks. He heard his stammering protest that *he* loved her at least, and watched her turn her face to the wall.

It was the last time he'd ever seen her alive.

He pushed the memory down, not wanting to deal with the swamping sense of devastation and loneliness it caused. There was a reason he never thought of it. A reason he'd decided to pursue a marriage of convenience, a marriage without the pain and disappointment of love.

Love hurt. It hurt the person loved and the person loving. It was messy, disappointing, complicated and unnecessary. He'd witnessed his parents' marriage crumble to nothing, seen his mother collapse into herself because his father could never give her what she wanted. As an adult he'd realised his mother had most likely been suffering from depression, which had contributed to her unhappiness in her marriage. He knew plenty of people fell in love, believed the fairy tale. Lived it. Yet he wasn't willing to take the risk. He was too like his father, sensible, silent, unwilling to say those three little words.

Have you ever told anyone you loved them?

Once.

And that was why—at least in part—he never planned to say—or feel—it again.

CHAPTER TWELVE

THE snow had turned to slush by the time Emily returned to work after New Year's. Her mood matched the dreary weather, as it had since that last painful conversation with Jason. She hadn't seen him since Christmas Day; he'd left Weldon that afternoon to drive back to London and work.

Now, as she dragged herself back to the office, she wondered if she'd see him. What he would say. What *she* would say. Her mind felt empty of words or even thoughts. She felt numb, although it was the kind of numbness that still allowed her to be aware of the yawning unhappiness fogging the fringes of her mind; she felt as if she were skating on very thin ice and at any time she could crash through and drown in the churning emotions below.

Helen greeted her at reception, looking bright-eyed and rosy-cheeked. She seemed, Emily thought with equal parts relief and resentment, to have recovered from Philip's put-down.

'Happy Christmas, Emily!' Helen called out. 'Or should I say Happy New Years? In any case, it's glorious out, isn't it?'

Emily glanced over her shoulder at the icy, needling drizzle and made a face. 'I don't know if glorious is the term I'd choose.'

Helen blushed, making her look lovelier than ever. 'Oh, no, I suppose…it's just…I'm so *happy*.'

'That's certainly good to hear.' Helen's obvious cheer lifted Emily's own sagging spirits a little. 'You had a nice holiday?'

'Oh, yes.' Helen leaned forward. 'I know you're going to think me so scatty, but I'm not broken up over—' she nibbled her lip '—you-know-who any more.'

'I'm glad to hear that.' Even if she still felt guilty. And miserable. 'I'm so sorr—'

'No, no, don't be sorry,' Helen said quickly. 'Really, it's fine. And—' she glanced up shyly at Emily, her face colouring a little more '—there's someone else now.'

'There is?' Emily tried to keep the note of surprise—and perhaps even censure—from her voice. 'Well, that's…that's wonderful. And I suppose by how happy you are he feels the same?'

'I think he does,' Helen said, and Emily wondered if a word of caution might be needed. Clearly there had been some mis-understanding in the past. If Helen needed advice, however, she was hardly the person to give it. 'I know he does,' Helen stated firmly, and Emily decided not to press.

'Well, who is this lucky man?'

'I don't know if you'll approve—'

'Oh, Helen, you hardly need my approval.' Emily smiled, suppressing a weary sigh. 'I've obviously proved myself to be quite useless at matchmaking, and at relationships in general, for that matter. I'm sure the two of you will be fine.'

'It's Richard,' Helen admitted in a whisper, and Emily stared at her in surprise.

'But—'

'He asked me to marry him,' Helen confessed in a rush. 'I didn't say yes yet, but he really is so kind and I know he'll treat me right—'

Emily swallowed down the words she wanted to say. She

would not offer advice. Not any more. 'And do you think that will be enough?'

'What more is there?' Helen asked simply and Emily let out a little laugh.

'Not much, I suppose.' Roses and proclamations of love and being swept off your feet. Romance. Passion. Love.

Plastic-wrapped bouquets and meaningless compliments.

Jason would quite approve of Helen's statement, Emily thought as she headed up to her office. She felt like the last person in the world who still believed in love. In something more.

Back in her office, Emily sank into her seat, her fingers rubbing her temples. She felt the beginnings of a headache coming on, but it was nothing compared to the misery swamping her soul. When did it get better? How?

She wondered if she should change jobs, just to give herself a little space from Jason. Even if he spent every second in Africa, or wherever else, this was still his company and there were reminders of him everywhere. Yet the thought of leaving Kingsley Engineering—and any chance to be near Jason, however small—was heart-wrenching.

She really was a mess, Emily thought as she switched on her computer. After years of feeling breezily confident and put together, of arranging other people's lives and being so very sure of her own, she was now coming apart at the seams. Had it all been a mirage, a *lie* all this time, and this was who she really was—and how she really felt?

Grimly, Emily had to acknowledge that this overwhelming love for Jason had not sprung suddenly over the course of a single night. It had been there all along, quietly growing, from the moment he'd taken her into his arms at her sister's wedding—or perhaps before then. Who even knew how long she'd loved Jason? He'd been so much a part of her life, and yet now he was the most important part, and he wasn't even in it any more.

Emily pushed the thoughts away, knowing these painful reflections would only become maudlin if she continued to indulge herself in useless recriminations. Reaching for her coffee mug, she straightened her shoulders and prepared for a long day of work.

The days passed slowly, marked by their mundanity. And the absence of Jason. Once again he remained out of the office, and Emily couldn't bring herself to ask his assistant or anyone else where he might be. It was, so very clearly, none of her business.

So when Jason's PA telephoned her a week later, she received the urgent summons to his office with surprise, trepidation and even a little terror.

'You mean...now?'

'Yes, Mr Kingsley's waiting.'

'I'll be right there.' Emily hung up the phone, trying to quiet the swarm of butterflies that had just taken residence in her stomach and now threatened to crawl up her throat. She'd never been so urgently summoned to Jason's office. She hadn't even been in his office in years.

What did he want?

Already her mind—and heart—leapt ahead, imagining a most unlikely scenario. He'd changed his mind. He realised he loved her.

Forget what I said before, Em. I was crazy to think I could last a day without you...

Somehow Emily knew that was not what Jason intended to say. Anyway, he'd already lasted well over a week. After checking her reflection in the mirror—she looked pale, but composed—she headed upstairs to the CEO's office.

Eloise, his PA, nodded briskly as Emily stepped into the reception area in front of a pair of closed mahogany doors.

'Go right in, Emily. He's waiting.'

Good heavens, was she in trouble? Was she going to be *fired*? Was this Jason's way of excising her from his life? He didn't need to leave; she would.

Swallowing down her nerves, Emily turned the handle of one of the doors and slipped into Jason's huge, sumptuous office.

He stood at the far end, behind his desk, his back to her as he surveyed the panoramic view of the city. Emily took a few hesitant steps inside. Her heart beat wildly and she didn't trust herself to speak, or at least to sound normal.

After a long, torturous moment Jason turned around. His dark eyes swept over her and there was no glint of amusement, no welcoming smile. No dimple. His expression looked frighteningly sober. 'Hello, Emily.'

Emily nodded her own greeting. She still didn't think she could speak. A huge lump had risen in her throat and it was making everything inside her ache.

Jason surveyed her quietly, his gaze seeming not just to take her in but to *memorise* her, and Emily suddenly had an awful feeling about why she'd been summoned to his office. The last faint flicker of hope that he'd changed his mind crumbled to ash. Stupid of her to have even entertained such an idea for a second. The only reason Jason would look at her like that was because he was going to say goodbye.

'You wanted to speak to me?' she finally managed to ask in a husky whisper.

'I wanted to say goodbye,' Jason said. 'I'm leaving. To Brazil this time. There's a dam being built on the Parana River and they've asked me to come in as a consultant.'

'Oh.' Emily cleared her throat, trying to ignore the searing pain of loss this announcement caused her. It shouldn't matter, yet it did. It hurt, unbearably. 'I thought you were staying in London for a while.'

'Well—' Jason smiled crookedly '—I've concluded my personal business for the moment.'

'You mean finding a wife,' she said flatly. *Business*. He shrugged his assent and Emily forced the words out. 'So who did you decide on, in the end?'

He stared at her, unspeaking, as if he were trying to make sense of her words. 'You think I found someone else to marry in the last ten days?' He shook his head in disbelief. 'I may be a bit sensible for your liking, Emily, but I'm not completely heartless. No, I've decided not to pursue marriage at this time.'

He sounded as if he were talking about a corporate merger. *At this time*. Well, he would eventually. He'd find someone who agreed with his plan, who liked his lists. It just wasn't—couldn't be—her. Even if at this moment she wanted it to be.

'Well,' she said when she trusted her voice, 'I don't think there's any pressing business in HR you need to—'

'*Emily*—' Jason's voice sounded a raw note of pain she hadn't expected '—do you think I called you up here to talk about HR?'

'Considering the kind of summons I received, I assumed it was *business*,' Emily replied stiffly.

Jason rubbed a hand over his face. He suddenly looked incredibly weary. 'I'm sorry if that's the way it seemed. I simply wanted to say goodbye. My plane leaves this afternoon.'

'Oh.' Emily swallowed. 'Well…' She tried to smile. She did, but instead she found the corners of her mouth turning down. 'Have a good—' She couldn't finish the sentence because her voice wobbled all too revealingly. Before she could even feel the wash of humiliation this caused, Jason strode towards her and in one swift, sure movement he took her by the shoulders and pulled her towards him.

Shock and then pleasure raced through her as his lips came down hard on hers and he kissed her with all the pent-up sorrow and ferocity she'd thought only she felt. And, as her body kicked into its overwhelming physical response, her breasts colliding with his chest, her fingers threading through his hair, her mind insisted on dismissing whatever didn't work between them. She wanted love? Forget it. She needed romance? It didn't matter. She could live without them as long as they had *this...*

Yet, even as her body was clamouring for him and her mind was insisting it was enough, her heart knew better. And when Jason released her so abruptly that she took a stumbling step backwards, she didn't speak. Jason did.

'Goodbye,' he said and turned away from her.

Emily stood there for a moment, bereft, humiliated, *aching* as the tears crowded her eyes and stung her lids. She blinked hard, swallowed down the restless churn of emotions Jason's kiss had caused and left his office without another word.

It wasn't supposed to hurt this much. Jason kept his gaze fixed on the window as he heard the soft click of the door closing. He'd hoped that saying goodbye to Emily would kick-start his body and mind into forgetting her.

Forget that.

He ached all over, ached with the knowledge that he'd lost her, that he loved her.

No. He did not love Emily Wood. He would not indulge himself in that useless emotion, that recipe for unhappiness—

His childhood had been marked by his mother's sorrow, his adolescence by his father's silence. He'd seen what love did to people. How it disappointed them. And involving himself with Emily when that was what she so clearly wanted would be a very grave error. He couldn't take that risk.

Have you ever told anyone you loved them?

He wasn't going to do it again.

She stayed numb. January dragged into February, and Emily went to work and home again like an automaton, performing the necessary functions of survival without ever really engaging in anything. Somehow she managed to smile and talk and even laugh. She thought she was giving a pretty convincing performance that she was fine. And maybe, eventually, her mind and heart would be convinced as well and she'd really start living—and feeling—again.

Other people had recovered from their setbacks, Emily told herself. Helen was now happy with Richard, even though he'd gone to Brazil with Jason. Skype and email worked wonders, and her brief infatuation with Philip was clearly a thing of the past. Even Gillian Bateson was doing better; she had gained partial custody of her daughter and she'd dropped some of the lofty smugness that Emily knew had just been a way of protecting herself. Everyone had armour of some kind.

So why did she feel so stripped bare?

Why couldn't she feel *better*?

As February limped towards March and her heart continued its awful ache, Emily wondered if she ever would.

She was considering this rather dire possibility when the lights in her office flicked off. She looked up in surprise to see Isobel standing in the doorway.

'Work's over for the day,' she announced. 'I'm taking you out.'

'It's not even lunchtime—'

'Doesn't matter,' Isobel replied breezily. 'You need a break. Even your boss agreed.'

'*Jason?* He's in Brazil—'

'I emailed him and asked his permission because I knew you'd resist. He said of course.'

Just the thought that Jason had been thinking about her in some small way sent a fierce bolt of longing through her. She really was pathetic. She hadn't seen or spoken to him in over six weeks. 'Why would I ever resist an afternoon out?' Emily finally said, smiling. 'I've never been a workaholic, Izzy.'

'Because,' Isobel said, reaching for Emily's coat and thrusting it at her, 'I intend to give you the full sisterly interrogation.

And by the end of the day you won't have a single secret from me.'

Emily sank back into her chair, eyeing her sister with increasing alarm. 'On second thoughts—'

'Consider yourself warned,' Isobel cut her off, holding up a finger in warning. 'I've booked the babysitter already, so no backing out, Emily. We have a reservation at one. And it's Jason's treat.'

'Jason's?' Emily repeated in incredulity. Another bolt of pain rocketed through her.

'Yes, he said to make sure to lunch in style.'

Emily silently digested this little bit of information, wondering why on earth Jason would offer such a thing. Was it to show how much he didn't care, or how much he did? And why would she even think he cared, when he'd made it so painfully clear that he didn't? Was she still living in pointless, impossible hope?

'I'm coming,' she said and, still rather reluctant, followed her sister out of her darkened office.

They ate at the Ivy and, while Emily toyed with her chicken, Isobel leaned over the table, her expression rather fierce and said, 'So you did love him.'

Startled, Emily looked up. For a shocked second she thought Isobel knew about Jason, but then she realised her sister was just speaking in generalities. 'Yes,' she admitted quietly. 'Did you think I didn't?'

Isobel shrugged and poured them both more wine. 'Well, you haven't had all that many relationships, have you? And the ones you have had haven't been spectacular. No one you even wanted to bring back to us.'

'No,' Emily agreed slowly, 'they weren't.' The two boyfriends she'd had seemed mere shadows compared to Jason; she could barely remember them now.

'Do you think that was on purpose?'

'Them not being spectacular?' Emily asked in surprise and

then, after a moment's quiet reflection, she nodded. 'I suppose…it was safer that way. I didn't get hurt.' Disappointed,
but not destroyed. Not like now.

'And now?' Isobel asked quietly.

Emily let out a small, sad sigh. 'Now I feel completely
wrecked…but I'll get over it. I will.' She smiled, a gesture
with more will than actual feeling behind it. 'I'll have to,
won't I?'

'I'd bash his head in if I knew who it was…or I'd tell Jason
to! It's someone from work, isn't it? I asked Jason if he knew
who it was, but—'

'Oh, Izzy.' Emily let out a trembling laugh. 'I don't suppose
he told you, did he?'

'No. He said it was your business and to butt out, actually.
Typical Jason.'

'It *is* Jason.'

The look of shock on her sister's face would have been
comical if Emily still didn't feel so awful. *'Jason?'* Isobel
finally repeated in a hushed whisper. Emily nodded miserably
and Isobel sat back in her chair. 'But…of course. That's why
you were so miserable all holiday! And that's why Jason left…'
Emily could practically see the wheels spinning in her sister's
brain. 'But why did he break your heart?' she demanded. 'And
how dare—'

'Don't.' Emily held up a hand. 'Don't drag the family into
this, Izzy. This is about Jason and me. And the simple truth
is we want different things out of life.'

Isobel arched an eyebrow, clearly sceptical. 'That different?'

'Different enough.' Emily drew in a shaky breath. 'He's
not interested in love, Izzy. Not the way I am.'

Isobel cocked her head. 'And how are you interested in
love?'

Emily didn't want to go over the agonising details of her
conversation with Jason; it had been hard enough the first

time. She shook her head, meaning it as a dismissal. 'I want what Mum and Dad had. The real thing. True love.'

'How do you even remember what they had?' Isobel asked reasonably. 'You were three when Mum died, Emily.'

'I know, but you can tell how much they loved each other when Dad talks about Mum. He adored her, Isobel. He told me she was perfect—'

'And you want someone to think you're perfect?' Although her tone was gentle, the question felt like a rebuke…and all too similar to what Jason had told her.

'No, of course not—'

'In any case, it was twenty years ago, Emily. Don't you think Dad's memories might have become a bit rosier over time?'

Emily stared at her sister in shock. 'Are you saying they didn't love—'

'No, I am saying what they had was *real*. They disagreed. They argued. I can remember. Mum was a good deal more emotional than Dad. He did love her, but he didn't think she was perfect. Not when she was alive, anyway. And it wasn't roses and romance all the time either. It isn't for anyone.'

Roses and romance. It was far too close to what she'd said, what she'd felt. And maybe she had held a few naive dreams about what love really meant, but it still came down to the hard truth that Jason didn't love her. He didn't even want her to love him. No love, full stop.

'I understand what you're saying, Izzy. But I still want someone to love me and be able to say it at least, and Jason wasn't capable of that.'

'But if he shows you—'

'He didn't.' Emily spoke sharply. 'It's over, okay? Let me just recover in peace.' She placed her napkin on the table. 'Now, how about a bit of retail therapy? And you can thank Jason for me for the lunch.'

* * *

March dragged on and Emily found herself recalling her conversation with Isobel, as well as just about every moment she'd shared with Jason. She remembered little things, things she'd dismissed or forgotten that suddenly seemed important now. The way he smiled, and how sweet his touch had been. His gentle teasing, which she'd always enjoyed until her heart had got tangled up in it. She thought of how she'd always trusted him, always known he would keep her safe.

The memories ran through her head in an endless reel and left her restless and wanting, wishing she could at least see him again. Ask him…what?

What could she possibly say? *I don't care if you only love me a little bit. I don't need any grand gestures…*

But she didn't even know if he loved her at all. She was quite sure he didn't, and gestures didn't even come into it. They had no relationship. No future.

Nothing.

Jason ran his hands through his hair, every muscle in his body aching. He'd been working twelve- and fourteen-hour days in an effort to wrap up the consulting work in Brazil…and in a useless attempt to forget Emily.

It wasn't working. Even in the middle of the most complicated, mind-consuming work, she slipped into his thoughts. He could hear her laughter, picture the way her eyes glittered jade with amusement. He imagined he could smell her strawberry shampoo. And at night she came to him in his dreams. He woke up restless and painfully unfulfilled. Four months of celibacy had taken their toll on his temper to boot. His staff tiptoed around him; the only one whose mood hadn't soured was Richard, who had celebrated his engagement last night.

At least *someone* had seen sense.

The trill of his mobile had him turning away from his laptop screen, as irritable as ever. He glanced at the telephone's little screen, intending not to take the call, when he saw who it was. Isobel.

'Izzy?'

'Oh, Jason, I'm so glad I reached you.' Isobel sniffed, and with a lurch of alarm, Jason realised she must have been crying.

'What's happened? What's wrong?'

'Oh, Jason, it's…'

'Emily?' Alarm turned to panic and he felt as if his heart had stopped, suspended in his chest, refusing to beat. 'Is Emily all right?' Already he pictured her lying pale and life-less on a stretcher, broken on a road. *Something* must have happened—

'No, no, Emily's all right. It's our father. He's had a stroke. They don't think…' Isobel swallowed. 'They don't think he'll recover. I thought you'd want to know.'

'Of course. Oh, Isobel, I'm so sorry.' He thought of Henry's kindly face, his ready smile and ever-present good humour. And then he thought of Emily, her father's spoiled darling, and he realised how agonising this must be for her. And, as he listened to Isobel give more details about Henry Wood's condition, he knew what he needed to do. What he wanted to do.

Emily stared at her father's still form on the hospital bed. He suddenly seemed so *small,* barely making a hump under the bed covers. She swallowed past the lump in her throat, her body aching with fatigue. Ever since Isobel had rung her yesterday, she'd maintained this vigil by her father's bed, pray-ing that it might make a difference. That he might come back to them. She couldn't lose another person she loved, not like this. She rested her hand on top of his, felt the thin, papery texture of his skin. 'Oh, Daddy,' she whispered. 'Don't leave me, not yet. I love you so much.'

A nurse came in, pausing in the doorway. 'There's a visitor

here, miss, but as he's not immediate family I didn't know whether—'

Emily turned to her with an audible sniff. 'Is he outside? I'll talk to him.' There had been a steady stream of well-wishers coming to visit Henry, old work colleagues and family friends, and the thought of greeting another one made her spirits dip even lower. She was tired of answering the same questions over and over when her own grief still threatened to overwhelm her.

She headed out into the fluorescent-lit hallway, blinking in the bright light. And then she thought she must be seeing things. She was tired enough to start hallucinating, and perhaps her exhausted mind had manufactured the one person she wanted to see more than anyone.

Jason stood in the hallway.

CHAPTER THIRTEEN

SHE stared at him, half-expecting him to disappear or dissolve, the product of an overtired mind—and a still-broken heart. But he didn't vanish; he was real. He came towards her, his expression serious, his arms outstretched.

'Emily, I'm so sorry about your father. I came as soon as I heard.'

And naturally, without even questioning what she was doing, Emily walked into Jason's outstretched arms. It was the only place she wanted to be. He held her, his chin resting on top of her head, his arms around her and Emily closed her eyes. It felt so good to be held like this. By Jason. 'Has there been any change?'

She shook her head, her eyes still closed. 'No…but they say there's still a chance he might recover.' Belatedly, Emily realised it was probably not a good idea to be held by Jason like this. It made too many longings rise up inside her, caused her heart to hurt with fresh, raw wounds, when it had numbed to a steady ache over the last four months.

'I thought you were in Brazil,' she said, stepping out of his arms.

'I was. I flew directly from there.'

Emily saw the shadows under his eyes, the lines of fatigue etched onto his face. 'You didn't have—'

'I know I didn't have to. I wanted to.'

She stared at him, trying to make sense of his words. And her own feelings. She'd needed him, and he'd come. She hadn't even admitted to herself that she needed him, yet somehow Jason had known. And that was better than any words he could—or couldn't—say.

'Thank you,' she said simply, because her heart was too full and fearful to say—or think—anything more.

'How is Henry?'

Jason jerked his gaze away from the darkened windows of the drawing room to gaze at his father. He'd come to Weldon directly from the hospital, but his mind was still with Emily. She'd looked so tired, so pale, so *sad*. He hated seeing her that way. 'The same. He hasn't been responsive since the stroke.'

'Will he recover, do you think?'

Jason suppressed the stab of irritation he felt at his father's dispassionate tone. Henry Wood was one of Edward Kingsley's oldest friends, yet you'd hardly know it to hear his father talk. His face was expressionless, his gaze on the fire.

'I don't know. They said it could go either way at this point, although any recovery he has will be limited.'

Edward rubbed his jaw, his expression still inscrutable. 'Hard to believe,' he finally said. 'Makes you think.'

'Oh, does it?' Jason couldn't quite keep the sarcasm from his tone. Emily's haggard face flashed across his mind.

'Yes, it does,' Edward said. He turned to look at his son, and Jason saw a surprising bleakness in his eyes. 'Makes you look at your own life a bit, when you realise how the clock is winding down for us all. My health hasn't been good. You know that.'

Jason didn't think he'd ever heard his father speak so many words in one go. He almost sounded maudlin. 'And have you come to any conclusions?' he asked, his tone diffident.

'Not as such.' Edward glanced back at the fire. 'I suppose I have a few regrets. Things I should have said. Never did.' Each sentence was said in staccato, with clear reluctance.

Jason's body tensed, and he realised he wanted to know what his father thought he should have said over the years. He wanted to know very much, more than he'd ever realised. 'You could say them now,' he said after a moment.

Edward gave him a fleeting smile, no more than a grim twisting of his lips. 'No, I can't. The person I should have said them to is dead.'

Jason's fists clenched of their own accord. He strove to keep his voice neutral. 'You mean my mother?'

'Yes.' Edward was silent for a long moment, gazing into the fire. 'I loved her, you know. I never said it.'

Jason made himself unclench his fists. 'Why not?'

Edward shrugged. 'I don't know. No one ever said it much to me. Wasn't the thing. And I suppose I didn't like the thought of admitting something that seemed like weakness.' He let out a long, slow breath. 'Perhaps it's weaker not to say it at all.' He faced Jason again, his expression more open and vulnerable than Jason had ever seen it. 'I can say it to you though, can't I? I never did.' Edward smiled again, even let out a little laugh. 'God knows it's still damned difficult. I love you though, Jason. I'm sorry I've never said.' He spoke gruffly, averting his head quickly, yet the words still flooded through Jason. Just words.

Powerful words. A powerful *feeling*, one that completely swept him off his feet.

Not meaningless sentiments. Not just grand gestures.

Hearing his father's simple, heartfelt statement made Jason realise the truth of his own feelings. The truth about love.

It was powerful, strong, real.

And he needed to tell Emily.

It had been a long, exhausting week. Emily cradled her mug of coffee in the kitchen of Hartington House, fatigue making her whole body ache. Yet even amidst the exhaustion she felt a sweet, sweet relief; last night her father had finally regained consciousness. It was going to be a long, arduous road, and he would never see a complete recovery. Emily knew that, had heard the specialists talk about limited speech and mobility, the use of a walker or a wheelchair. It was hard to accept that, but it was better than the alternative. It was something.

And something was enough.

Jason had visited Henry every day this week, commuting from London, and Emily had welcomed and appreciated his presence more than she could say.

She *hadn't* said, because part of her wanted to tell Jason how much he meant to her, how much she loved him. Yet surely there was no point. Jason had shown up as a family friend, nothing more. It didn't change things between them.

Except *she* felt changed. The last week—the last four months—had made her realise just how childish and naive her dreams about love had been. Love wasn't about words or gestures, it was about action. Connection.

Anyone can tell you he loves you.

But not everyone would travel thousands of miles to be with her in her moment of need. Not everyone would be so trustworthy, so solid and steady and safe… The exact thing she needed. Wanted.

Jason.

She still loved him, would always love him. Yet, even so, it didn't change how he felt. He didn't love her, and even if she could have accepted that, lived with it, she knew Jason would not accept what she had to offer.

He didn't want love. He didn't want her.

A knock on the front door jolted her out of her gloomy thoughts. Sighing, Emily prepared to accept another casserole from one of the village's well-meaning widows. She'd had no idea her father was so popular.

Yet when she opened the door, there were no widows in sight. Jason stood there, smiling. Looking wonderful.

Emily stared at him in shock. 'I thought you'd returned to London—'

'I came back.'

'Why?'

'I have something to say to you.' He suddenly looked so serious that Emily felt as if her heart had frozen in her chest. Cold and lifeless. Was he going to tell her he'd found his sensible wife at last? Was she going to have to pretend to be pleased? It had been four months, after all. Plenty of time.

Reluctantly, she moved from the doorway. 'Come in, then,' she said, knowing she sounded ungracious.

'Actually, I want you to come with me.'

Emily blinked. 'Where?'

'It's a surprise.'

A surprise? She eyed him warily. Jason didn't generally do surprises. 'I'm not sure I'm up to going anywhere, Jason. I'm expecting a call from the hospital—'

'I just checked in with the nursing station. Your father's sleeping. And we can visit him afterwards, if you like.'

'Afterwards?'

'Come on.' He smiled and tugged her hand and, still uncertain, a little suspicious and even afraid, Emily let him lead her to his Porsche.

She sneaked a glance at him as he drove; his jaw was tense, his gaze fixed straight ahead. He looked determined, fiercely so, and the thought gave her a little lurch of alarm.

They drove in silence towards London, skirting the south side of the city before heading towards Greenwich. Emily only just kept herself from asking where they were going. She wasn't sure she wanted to know.

Jason finally turned into a small park next to the Thames; the water glinted silver under the fragile spring sunlight.

'So where have you brought me?' Emily asked as she got

out of the car. The wind breezing off the river blew her hair into tangles and she pushed the unruly mass back from her face.

'One of my favourite places in England,' Jason said ruefully, 'although it might not seem like very much. Walk with me.'

Obediently, Emily fell into step alongside him, her curiosity rising like a tide inside her. Why had Jason taken her to one of his favourite places? And *why* was this one of his favourite places? She glanced around; it looked like a rather bland park, nothing more than a couple of picnic tables and benches on a bit of green.

Jason stopped on the pavement that ran alongside the river and, bracing his forearms on the rails, he gestured out towards the flat expanse of water. 'There.' Emily glanced at the river; there were a few large bulky silver things positioned across the water. 'Do you know what that is?'

'Er...' She had a feeling she *should* know, considering she worked for the foremost firm in hydraulic engineering. 'Some flood...thing?'

Jason smiled faintly. 'The Thames Flood Barrier. The largest in the world. My father brought me here when it opened, when I was about ten.' Emily nodded, wondering why he'd brought *her* here, what he was going to say. 'I was fascinated by its strength,' Jason said slowly. 'Water is one of the most powerful forces in the world, and yet when these gates go up this barrier is able to stop it. Control it. I thought that was what drew me to engineering—the ability to control a powerful force. But I realise there's another side to it—the sheer power and beauty and even unpredictability of water.' He must have seen Emily's rather blank look for he laughed softly and said, 'I'm not making much sense, am I? And here I was, trying to say something romantic about love and how it overwhelmed me, a far more powerful force than any river.'

'*Love?*' Emily echoed in both disbelief and dawning hope. 'I'm afraid I didn't get that at all.'

'I told you I wasn't good at this.'

'Good at what?'

'Grand gestures. Words. Three words in particular.'

Emily's heart seemed to stop right in her chest, as if a huge fist had clenched around it. 'And here I thought you were wittering on about flood barriers,' she managed weakly.

'Waxing poetically, actually.' He glanced at his watch. 'Ah, just about time.'

'Time for what?'

He pointed upwards and Emily looked uncomprehendingly at the pale blue sky, a few fleecy clouds scudding across its surface. 'What…?' And then she saw the plane cutting across the blue, making recognisable loops. Spelling letters.

'Sky writing?' she exclaimed, and Jason smiled self-consciously.

'To be honest, I didn't know if you'd go for it. But I wanted to make a statement.'

She watched in silence as the plane spelled the words, words she'd longed to hear. *I. Love. You.* She turned to him, hope and disbelief warring within her. 'Jason—'

'Of course I can't take the easy way out and let that do the talking for me,' he said, pointing to the words emblazoned in smoke across the sky. 'I need to say it myself. I want to, because God knows I feel it. And that's what I *didn't* want, what I've been fighting against for a long time now.' Emily waited, her heart seeming to squeeze inside her chest, as Jason turned to her, smiling although his eyes were dark and serious. 'I love you, Emily. And loving you means loving all of you, including the part of you that wanted more from me than I was willing to give.'

She stared at him, her mind dazed and body rocked by this admission. 'But all I wanted was you to love me, Jason,' she whispered. 'And I didn't think you did—'

'I didn't want to,' Jason admitted. 'Loving someone is, I've discovered, scary. You open yourself up to all sorts of risk and hurt.'

'I know.' Did she ever. She'd felt the same way…even if she'd expressed it differently.

'I'd convinced myself for so long that I didn't want it, wasn't capable of it,' Jason continued. 'Just like my father.'

'What made you change your mind?' Emily whispered.

'You did. Wanting you, just being with you. I still fought it, of course. I'm stubborn.' He smiled wryly before his expression grew serious again. 'But you gave me a wake-up call when you asked me if I'd ever told someone I loved them, and I was going to tell you I hadn't. Of course I hadn't.' He shook his head in memory. 'And then I suddenly remembered telling my mother I loved her. She'd been crying because she was so unhappy with my father, feeling he never loved her, always wanting more. She was depressed, I realise that now, but as a child…I just wanted to make her feel better.' He let out a shaky breath. 'So I told her I loved her, and that night she killed herself.'

Emily let out a little gasp of shock. She'd had no idea Jason lived with a memory like that, felt its terrible pain through the years. 'I'm sorry—'

'So am I. Sorry for my mother, who was so desperately unhappy, and sorry that her experience—and mine as a child—made me doubt the power of love and only acknowledge its pain. I convinced myself that loving someone was a bad idea. That words and gestures could never be enough, just like my father's love wasn't enough for my mother. Like my words—my love—hadn't been enough.'

'Oh, Jason—'

'So I convinced myself I wanted a convenient marriage on both sides because I didn't want anyone to be disappointed, but I see now I was just protecting myself from being hurt. But it didn't work, of course, because love is like that water

out there.' He gestured to the river. 'An unstoppable force.'
He reached for her, his arms coming around her, drawing her
to him. Emily went into the embrace, dazed, still disbelieving. 'My heart has no flood barrier,' Jason said softly. 'And
love—*you*—overwhelmed me.'

'I did?'

'Yes, with your warmth and your openness and your sexy
shoes.'

Emily let out a laugh of incredulity. 'I thought you hated
my shoes.'

'They drove me crazy. You drove me crazy. I couldn't keep
away from you. I still can't. I can't believe I waited this long
to finally admit how much I love you.'

Emily let out a trembling laugh. 'And I was just trying to
convince myself I didn't need you to love me.'

'What?' Jason stared at her in surprise. 'Why not?'

'Because I love you so much. And when you showed up at
the hospital, and I knew you'd come all that way because you
knew I needed you…well, that meant more to me than any…
any plastic-wrapped bouquets or meaningless sentiments!'

Jason laughed wryly. 'I really have been an awful cynic.'

'And I've been a bit silly about what I thought love needed
to be,' Emily said, reaching up to caress his cheek, needing to
touch him. 'Thinking it was all about the roses and romance.
And there I was, trying to tell you I was an expert.'

'I think love has a habit of knocking you for six.' He drew
her to him, tilting her face up to his. 'Sweeping you off your
feet, as a matter of fact.' He kissed her then, the feel of his
lips so sweet and warm and *perfect*. 'I love you, Emily,' Jason
said as he gazed down at her. 'You are warm and generous
and impulsive and emotional—'

'Even though I've been a bit of an idiot?' Emily said. 'I
didn't even know what love really meant—'

'I've been an idiot for four months. I could have solved

all this a lot sooner if I hadn't fought against the thought of loving you so much.'

'You love me,' Emily said slowly, wonderingly, for she still felt as if she ought to pinch herself.

'Yes. I love you, Emily Wood. I think I've loved you for years. I certainly couldn't forget that dance.'

'I felt such a fool—'

'And I was the bigger fool. I thought I knew what I needed, but all I've ever needed is you. And now it's time for my grand gesture.' Smiling, his eyes alight with both mischief and love, Jason dropped to one knee. Emily's heart seemed to freeze in her chest before it did a complete somersault. She watched him take a small black velvet box out of his pocket and flip it open to reveal the most exquisite antique ring, a diamond nestled amidst a cluster of sapphires. 'Emily Wood, I love you madly, deeply, completely. Will you be my wife and make a go of it with me?'

Emily burst out laughing, the sound one of utter joy. 'Yes, I will,' she said, pulling on his hands to get him to rise. Jason slid the ring on her finger, the diamond sparkling in the sunlight. 'I will be overjoyed to make a go of it with you.'

'Music to my ears,' Jason murmured, and pulled her closer for a kiss that made Emily's head spin and her heart overflow.

She pulled him closer, her fingers threading through his hair, her body pressed to his as joy filled and overwhelmed her. Beside them, the waters of the river flowed past the flood barrier, sparkling and silver, a beautiful, powerful force, forever surging onwards.

The Darkest
of Secrets

KATE HEWITT

CHAPTER ONE

'OPEN it up.'

It had taken the better part of two days to reach this moment. Khalis Tannous stood back as the two highly skilled engineers he'd employed to open his father's steel vault finally eased the door off its hinges. They had used all their knowledge and skill trying to unlock the thing, but his father was too paranoid and the security too advanced. In the end they'd had to use the newest laser technology to cut straight through the steel.

Khalis had no idea what lay inside this vault; he hadn't even known the vault had existed, on the lowest floor of the compound on his father's private island. He'd already been through the rest of the facility and found enough evidence to see his father put in prison for life, if he were still alive.

'It's dark,' one of the engineers said. They'd propped the sawn-off door against a wall and the opening to the vault was black and formless.

Khalis gave a grim smile. 'Somehow I doubt there are windows in there.' What *was* in there he couldn't even guess. Treasure or trouble? His father had had a penchant for both. 'Give me a torch,' he said, and one was passed into his hand.

He flicked it on, took a step towards the darkness. He

could feel his hand slick on the torch, his heart beating far too hard. He was scared, which annoyed him, but then he knew enough about his father to brace himself for yet another tragic testament to the man's power and cruelty.

Another step, and the darkness enveloped him like velvet. He felt a thick carpet under his feet, breathed in the surprising scents of wood and furniture polish, and felt a flicker of relief—and curiosity. He lifted the torch and shone it around the vault. It was a surprisingly large space and fashioned like a gentleman's study, with elegant sofas and chairs, even a drinks table.

Yet somehow Khalis didn't think his father came down to a sealed underground vault just to relax with a tumbler of his best single malt. He saw a switch on the wall and flicked it on, bathing the room in electric light. His torch lay forgotten in his hand as he slowly turned in a circle, gazing first at the furniture and then at the walls.

And what they held…frame after frame, canvas after canvas. Some he recognised, others he didn't but he could guess. Khalis gazed at them all, felt a heaviness settle on him like a shroud. Yet another complication. Another testament to his father's many illegal activities.

'Mr Tannous?' one of the engineers asked uneasily from the outside hallway. Khalis knew his silence had gone on too long.

'It's fine,' he called back, even though it wasn't fine at all. It was amazing…and terrible. He stepped further into the room and saw another wood-panelled door in the back. With a flicker of foreboding, he went to it. It opened easily and he entered another smaller room. Only two paintings were in this tiny chamber, two paintings that made Khalis squint and step closer. If they were what he thought they were…

'Khalis?' his assistant, Eric, called, and Khalis came

out of the little room and closed the door. He switched off the light and stepped out of the vault. The two engineers and Eric all waited, their expressions both curious and concerned.

'Leave it,' he told the engineers, who had propped the enormous steel door against the wall. He felt the beginnings of a headache and gave a brisk nod. 'I'll deal with all this later.'

No one asked any questions, which was good since he had no intention of spreading the news of what was in that vault. He didn't yet trust the skeleton staff left on the compound since his father's death, all of them now in his employ. Anyone who had worked for his father had to be either desperate or completely without scruples. Neither option inspired trust. He nodded towards the engineers. 'You can go now. The helicopter will take you to Taormina.'

They nodded, and after Khalis disarmed the security system everyone headed into the lift that led to the floors above ground. Khalis felt tension snap through his body, but then he'd been tense for a week, ever since he'd left San Francisco for this godforsaken island, when he'd learned his father and brother had both died in a helicopter crash.

He hadn't seen either of them in fifteen years, hadn't had anything to do with Tannous Enterprises, his father's dynastic business empire. It was huge, powerful and corrupt to its core…and it was now in Khalis's possession. Considering his father had disowned him quite publicly when he'd walked away from it all at the age of twenty-one, his inheritance had come as a bit of a surprise.

Back in his father's office, which he'd now taken for his own, he let out a long, slow breath and raked his hands through his hair as he considered that vault. He'd spent the last week trying to familiarise himself with his father's many assets, and then attempt to determine just how illegal they were. The vault and its contents was yet another complication in this sprawling mess.

Outside, the Mediterranean Sea sparkled jewel-bright under a lemon sun, but the island felt far from a paradise to Khalis. It had been his childhood home, but it now felt like a prison. It wasn't the high walls topped with barbed wire and broken glass that entrapped him, but his memories. The disillusionment and despair he'd felt corroding his own soul, forcing him to leave. If he closed his eyes, he could picture Jamilah on the beach, her dark hair whipping around her face as she watched him leave for the last time, her aching heart reflected in her dark eyes.

Don't leave me here, Khalis.

I'll come back. I'll come back and save you from this place, Jamilah. I promise.

He pushed the memory away, as he had been doing for the last fifteen years. *Don't look back. Don't regret or even remember.* He'd made the only choice he could; he just hadn't foreseen the consequences.

'Khalis?'

Eric shut the door and waited for instructions. In his board shorts and T-shirt, he looked every inch the California beach bum, even here on Alhaja. His relaxed outfit and attitude hid a razor-sharp mind and an expertise in computers that rivalled Khalis's own.

'We need to fly an art appraiser out here as soon as possible,' Khalis said. 'Only the best, preferably someone with a specialisation in Renaissance paintings.'

Eric raised his eyebrows, looking both intrigued and impressed. 'What are you saying? The vault had *paintings*?'

'Yes. A lot of paintings. Paintings I think could be worth millions.' He sank into the chair behind his father's desk, gazed unseeingly at the list of assets he'd been going through. Real estate, technology, finance, politics. Tannous Enterprises had a dirty finger in every pie. How, Khalis wondered, not for the first time, did you take the reins of a company that was more feared than revered, and turn it into something honest? Something good?

You couldn't. He didn't even want to.

'Khalis?' Eric prompted.

'Contact an appraiser, fly him out here. Discreetly.'

'No problem. What are you going to do with the paintings once they're appraised?'

Khalis smiled grimly. 'Get rid of them.' He didn't want anything of his father's, and certainly not some priceless artwork that was undoubtedly stolen. 'And inform the law once we know what we're dealing with,' he added. 'Before we have Interpol crawling all over this place.'

Eric whistled softly. 'This is one hell of a mess, isn't it?'

Khalis pulled a sheaf of papers towards him. 'That,' he told his assistant and best friend, 'is a complete understatement.'

'I'll get on to the appraiser.'

'Good. The sooner the better—that open vault presents too much risk.'

'You don't actually think someone is going to steal something?' Eric asked, eyebrows raised. 'Where would they go?'

Khalis shrugged. 'People can be sly and deceptive. And I don't trust anyone.'

Eric gazed at him for a moment, his blue eyes narrowed shrewdly. 'This place really did a number on you, didn't it?'

Khalis just shrugged again. 'It was home,' he said, and turned back to his work. A few seconds later he heard the door click shut.

* * *

'Special project for La Gioconda.'

'So amusing,' Grace Turner said dryly. She swivelled in her chair to glance at David Sparling, her colleague at Axis Art Insurers and one of the world's top experts on Picasso forgeries. 'What is it?' she asked as he dangled a piece of paper in front of her eyes. She refused to attempt to snatch it. She smiled coolly instead, eyebrows raised.

'Ah, there's the smile,' David said, grinning himself. Grace had been dubbed La Gioconda—the Mona Lisa— when she'd first started at Axis, both for her cool smile and her expertise in Renaissance art. 'Urgent request came in to appraise a private collection. They want a specialist in Renaissance.'

'Really?' Her curiosity was piqued in spite of her determination to remain unmoved, or at least appear so.

'Really,' David said. He dangled the paper a bit closer. 'Aren't you just a teeny bit curious, Grace?'

Grace swivelled back to her computer and stared at the appraisal she'd been working on for a client's seventeenth century copy of a Caravaggio. It was good, but not that good. It wouldn't sell for as much as he'd hoped. 'No.'

David chuckled. 'Even when I tell you they'll fly the appraiser out to some private island in the Mediterranean, all expenses paid?'

'Naturally.' Private collections couldn't be moved easily. And most people were very private about their art. She paused, her fingers hovering over the keys of her computer. 'Do you know the collector?' There were only a handful of people in the entire world who owned significant collections of Renaissance paintings of real value, and most of them were extremely discreet...so discreet they didn't want appraisers or insurers looking in and seeing just what kind of art they had on their walls.

David shook his head. 'Too top secret for me. The boss wants to see you about it ASAP.'

'Why didn't you tell me?' she asked, and David just grinned. Pressing her lips together, she grabbed the printout he'd been teasing her with and strode towards the office of Michel Latour, the CEO of Axis Art Insurers, her father's oldest friend and one of the most powerful men in the art world.

'You wanted to see me?'

Michel turned from the window that overlooked the Rue St Honoré in the 1st arrondissement of Paris. 'Close the door.' Grace obeyed and waited. 'You received the message?'

'A private collection with significant art from the Renaissance period to be appraised.' She shook her head slowly. 'I can think of less than half a dozen collectors who fit that description.'

'This is different.'

'How?'

Michel gave her a thin-lipped smile. 'Tannous.'

'Tannous?' She stared at him, disbelieving, her jaw dropping before she thought to snap it shut. 'Balkri Tannous?' Immoral—or perhaps amoral—businessman, and thought to be an obsessive art collector. No one knew what his art collection contained, or if it even existed. No one had ever seen it or even spoke of it. And yet the rumours flew every time a museum experienced a theft: a Klimt disappeared from a gallery in Boston, a Monet from the Louvre. Shocking, inexplicable, and yet the name Tannous was always darkly whispered around such heists. 'Wait,' Grace said slowly. 'Isn't he dead?'

'He died last week in a helicopter crash,' Michel confirmed. 'Suspicious, apparently. His son is making the enquiry.'

'I thought his son died in the crash.'

'His other son.'

Grace was silent. She had not known there was another son. 'Do you think he wants to sell the collection?' she finally asked.

'I'm not sure what he wants.' Michel moved to his desk, where a file folder lay open. He flipped through a few papers; Grace saw some scrawled notes about various heists. Tannous suspected behind every one, though no one could prove it.

'If he wanted to sell on the black market, he wouldn't have come to us.' There were plenty of shady appraisers who dealt in stolen goods and Axis was most assuredly not one of them.

'No,' Michel agreed thoughtfully. 'I do not think he intends to sell the collection on the black market.'

'You think he's going to donate it?' Grace heard the disbelief in her voice. 'The whole collection could be worth millions. Maybe even a billion dollars.'

'I don't think he needs money.'

'It doesn't have to be about need.' Michel just cocked his head, his lips curving in a half-smile. 'Who is he? I didn't even know Tannous had a second son.'

'You wouldn't. He left the Tannous fold when he was only twenty-one, after graduating from Cambridge with a First in mathematics. Started his own IT business in the States, and never looked back.'

'And his business in the U.S.? It's legitimate?'

'It appears to be.' He paused. 'The request is fairly urgent. He wishes the collection to be dealt with as soon as possible.'

'Why?'

'I can certainly appreciate why an honest businessman

would want to legally off-load a whole lot of stolen art quite quickly.'

'If he is honest.'

Michel shook his head, although there was a flicker of sympathy in his shrewd grey eyes. 'Cynicism doesn't suit you, Grace.'

'Neither did innocence.' She turned away, her mind roiling from Michel's revelations.

'You know you want to see what's in that vault,' Michel said softly.

Grace didn't answer for a moment. She couldn't deny the fact that she was curious, but she'd experienced and suffered too much not to hesitate. Resist. Temptation came in too many forms. 'He could just turn it all over to the police.'

'He might do so, after it's been appraised.'

'If it's a large collection, an appraisal could take months.'

'A proper one,' Michel agreed. 'But I believe he simply wants an experienced eye cast over the collection. It will have to be moved eventually.'

She shook her head. 'I don't like it. You don't know anything about this man.'

'I trust him,' Michel said simply. 'And I trust the fact that he went to the most legitimate source he could for appraisal.'

Grace said nothing. She didn't trust this Tannous man; of course she didn't. She didn't trust men full stop, and especially not wealthy and possibly corrupt tycoons. 'In any case,' Michel continued in that same mild tone, 'he wants the appraiser to fly to Alhaja Island—tonight.'

'Tonight?' Grace stared at her boss, mentor and one-time saviour. 'Why the rush?'

'Why not? I told you, holding onto all that art has to be an unappealing prospect. People are easily tempted.'

'I know,' Grace said softly, and regret flashed briefly in Michel's eyes.

'I didn't mean—'

'I know,' she said again, then shook her head. That brief flare of curiosity died out by decision. 'It's not something I can be involved with, Michel.' She took a deep breath, felt it sear her lungs. 'You know how careful I have to be.'

His eyes narrowed, mouth thinning. 'How long are you going to live your life enslaved to that—?'

'As long as I have to.' She turned away, not wanting Michel to see her expression, the pain she still couldn't hide, not even after four years. She was known by her colleagues to be cool, emotionless even, but it was no more than a carefully managed mask. Just thinking about Katerina made tears rise to her eyes and her soul twist inside her.

'Oh, *chérie*.' Michel sighed and glanced again at the file. 'I think this could be good for you.'

'*Good* for me—'

'Yes. You've been living your life like a church mouse, or a nun, I don't know which. Perhaps both.'

'Interesting analogies,' Grace said with a small smile. 'But I need to live a quiet life. You know that.'

'I know that you are my most experienced appraiser of Renaissance art, and I need you to fly to Alhaja Island— tonight.'

She turned to stare at him, saw the iron in his eyes. He wasn't going to back down. 'I can't—'

'You can, and you will. I might have been your father's oldest friend, but I am also your employer. I don't do favours, Grace. Not for you. Not for anyone.'

She knew that wasn't true. He'd done her a huge favour four years ago, when she'd been desperate and dying inside. When he'd offered her a job at Axis he had, in his own way, given her life again—or as much life as she could have, given her circumstances. 'You could go yourself,' she pointed out.

'I don't have the knowledge of that period that you do.'

'Michel—'

'I mean it, Grace.'

She swallowed. She could feel her heart beating inside her far too hard. 'If Loukas finds out—'

'What? You're just doing your job. Even he allows you that.'

'Still.' Nervously, she pleated her fingers together. She knew how high-octane the art world could be. Dealing with some of the finest and most expensive art in the world ignited people's passions—and possessiveness. She'd seen how a beautiful picture could poison desire, turn love into hate and beauty into ugliness. She'd lived it, and never wanted to again.

'It will all be very discreet, very safe. There's no reason for anyone even to know you are there.'

Alone on an island with the forgotten son of a corrupt and hated business tycoon? She didn't know much about Balkri Tannous, but she knew his type. She knew how ruthless, cruel and downright dangerous such a man could be. And she had no reason—yet—to believe his son would be any different.

'There will be a staff,' Michel reminded her. 'It's not as if you'd be completely alone.'

'I know that.' She took a deep breath and let it out slowly. 'How long would it take?'

'A week? It depends on what is required.'

'A *week*—'

'Enough.' Michel held up one hand. 'Enough. You will go. I insist on it, Grace. Your plane leaves in three hours.'

'Three hours? But I haven't even packed—'

'You have time.' He smiled, although his expression remained iron-like and shrewd. 'Don't forget a swimming costume. I hear the Mediterranean's nice this time of year. Khalis Tannous might give you some time off to swim.'

Khalis Tannous. The name sent a shiver of something—curiosity? Fear?—through her. What kind of man was he, the son of an undoubtedly unscrupulous or even evil man, yet who had chosen—either out of defiance or desperation—to go his own way at only twenty-one years old? And now that he was back, in control of an empire, what kind of man would he become?

'I don't intend to swim,' she said shortly. 'I intend to do the job as quickly as possible.'

'Well,' Michel said, smiling, 'you could try to enjoy yourself—for once.'

Grace just shook her head. She knew where that led, and she had no intention of *enjoying herself* ever again.

CHAPTER TWO

'THERE it is.'

Grace craned her neck to look out of the window of the helicopter that had picked her up in Sicily and was now taking her to Alhaja Island, no more than a rocky crescent-shaped speck in the distance, off the coast of Tunisia. She swallowed, discreetly wiped her hands along the sides of her beige silk trench coat and tried to staunch the flutter of nerves in her middle.

'Another ten minutes,' the pilot told her, and Grace leaned back in her seat, the whine of the propeller blades loud in her ears. She was uncomfortably aware that two of Khalis Tannous's family members had died in a helicopter crash just a little over a week ago, over these very waters. She did not wish to experience the same fate.

The pilot must have sensed something of her disquiet, for he glanced over at her and gave her what Grace supposed was meant to be a reassuring smile. 'Don't worry. It is very safe.'

'Right.' Grace closed her eyes as she felt the helicopter start to dip down. She might be one of the foremost appraisers of Renaissance art in Europe, but this was still far out of her professional experience. She mostly dealt with museums, inspecting and insuring paintings that hung on revered walls around the world. Her job took her to quiet back rooms and sterile laboratories, out of the public eye and away from scandal. Michel himself handled many private collections, dealt with the tricky and often tempestuous personalities that accompanied so much priceless art.

Yet this time he'd sent her. She opened her eyes, saw the ground seeming to swoop towards them. A strip of white sand beach, a rocky cove, a tangle of trees and, most noticeably of all, a high chain-link fence topped with two spiky strands of barbed wire and bits of broken glass. And Grace suspected that was the least of Tannous's security.

The helicopter touched down on the landing pad, where a black Jeep was already waiting. Her heart still thudding, Grace stepped out onto the tarmac. A slim man in a tie-dyed T-shirt and cut-off jeans stood there, his fair hair blowing in the sea breeze.

'Ms Turner? I'm Eric Poulson, assistant to Khalis Tannous. Welcome to Alhaja.'

Grace just nodded. He didn't look like what she'd expected, although she hadn't really thought of what a Tannous employee would look like. Certainly not a beach bum. He led her to the waiting Jeep, tossing her case in the back.

'Mr Tannous is expecting me?'

'Yes, you can refresh yourself and relax for a bit and he'll join you shortly.'

She prickled instinctively. She hated being told what to do. 'I thought this was urgent.'

He gave her a laughing glance. 'We're on a Mediterranean island, Ms Turner. What does urgent even mean?'

Grace frowned and said nothing. She didn't like the man's attitude. It was far from professional, and that was what she needed to be—always. Professional. Discreet.

Eric drove the Jeep down a pebbly road to the compound's main gates, a pair of armoured doors that looked incredibly forbidding. They opened seamlessly and silently and swung just as quietly shut behind the Jeep, yet Grace still felt them clang through her. Eric seemed relaxed, but then he obviously knew the security codes to those gates. She didn't. She had just become a prisoner. *Again.* Her heart raced and her palms dampened as nausea churned along with the memories inside her. Memories of feeling like a prisoner. *Being* a prisoner.

Why had she agreed to this?

Not just because Michel had insisted, she knew. Despite his tough talk, she could have refused. She didn't think Michel would actually fire her. No, she'd agreed because the desire to see Tannous's art collection—and see it, God willing, restored to museums—had been too strong to ignore. A temptation too great to resist.

And temptation was, unfortunately, something she knew all about.

As Grace slid out of the Jeep, she looked around slowly. The compound was an ugly thing of concrete, like a huge bunker, but the gardens surrounding it were lovely and lush, and she inhaled the scent of bougainvillea on the balmy air.

Eric led her towards the front doors of the building and disarmed yet another fingerprint-activated security system. Grace followed him into a huge foyer tiled in terracotta, a soaring skylight above, and then into a living room decorated with casual elegance, sofas and chairs in soothing neutral shades, a few well placed antiques and a view through the one-way window of the startling sweep of sea.

'May I offer you something to drink?' Eric asked, his hands dug into the pockets of his cut-off jeans. 'Juice, wine, a pina colada?'

Grace wondered if he was amused by her buttoned-up attitude. Well, she had no intention of relaxing. 'A glass of sparkling water, please.'

'Sure thing.' He left her alone, and Grace slowly circled the room. She summed up the antiques and artwork with a practised eye: all good copies, but essentially fakes. Eric returned with her water and withdrew again, promising that Tannous would be with her in a few minutes and she could just 'go ahead and relax'. *No, thanks.* Grace took a sip, frowning as the minutes ticked on. If Tannous's request really was urgent, why was he keeping her waiting like this? Was it on purpose?

She didn't like it, but then she didn't like anything about being here. Not the walls, not the armoured gates, not the man she was meant to meet. All of it brought back too many painful memories, like knives digging into her skull. What didn't kill you was meant to make you stronger, wasn't it? Grace smiled grimly. Then she must be awfully strong. Except she didn't feel strong right now. She felt vulnerable and even exposed, and that made her tense. She worked hard to cultivate a cool, professional demeanour, and just the nature of this place was causing it to crack.

She could not allow that to happen. Quickly she went to the door and tried the handle. With a shuddering rush of relief she felt it open easily. Clearly she was acting a little paranoid. She stepped out into the empty entry hall and saw a pair of French windows at the back that led to an enclosed courtyard, and an infinity pool shaded by palms shimmering in the dusky light.

Grace slipped outside, breathing in the scents of lavender and rosemary as a dry breeze rustled the hair at the nape of her neck. She brushed a tendril away from her face, tucking it back into her professional chignon, and headed towards the pool, her heels clicking on the tiles. She could hear the water in the pool slapping against the sides, the steady sound of limbs cutting through water. Someone was swimming out here in the twilight, and she thought she knew who it was.

She came around a palm tree into the pool area and saw a man cutting through the water with sinuous ease. Even swimming he looked assured. Arrogant and utterly confident in his domain.

Khalis Tannous.

A dart of irritation—no, anger—shot through her. While she was cooling her heels, anxious and tense, he was *swimming*? It felt like the most obvious kind of power play. Deliberately Grace walked to the chaise where a towel had been tossed. She picked it up, then crossed over to where Khalis Tannous was finishing his lap, her four-inch heels surely in his line of vision.

He came to the edge, long lean fingers curling around the slick tile as he glanced upwards. Grace was not prepared for the jolt of—what? Alarm? Awareness? She could not even say, but something in her sizzled to life as she gazed down into those grey-green eyes, long dark lashes spiky with water. It terrified her, and she instantly suppressed it as she coolly handed him the towel.

'Mr Tannous?'

His mouth twisted in bemusement but she took in the narrowing of his eyes, the flickering of suspicion. He was on his guard, just as she was. He hoisted himself up onto the tiles in one fluid movement and took the towel from her. 'Thank you.' He dried himself off with deliberate ease, and Grace could not keep her gaze from flicking downwards to the lean chest and lithe torso, muscled yet trim, his golden-brown skin now flecked with droplets of water. Tannous had a Tunisian father and a French mother, Grace knew, and his mixed ethnicity was evident in his unique colouring. He was beautiful, all burnished skin and sleek, powerful muscle. He gave off an aura of power, not from size, although he was tall, but from the whipcord strength and energy he exuded in every easy yet precise movement.

'And you are?' he finally said, and Grace jerked her gaze upwards.

'Grace Turner of Axis Art Insurers.' She reached in the pocket of her coat for her business card and handed it to him. He took it without looking. 'I believe you were expecting me.'

'So I was.' He slung the towel around his hips, his shrewd gaze flicking over her in one quick yet thorough assessment.

'I thought,' Grace said, keeping her voice professionally level, 'this appraisal was urgent?'

'Fairly urgent,' Tannous agreed. She said nothing, but something of her censure must have been evident for he smiled and said, 'I must apologise for what appears to have been discourtesy. I assumed the appraiser would wish to refresh himself before meeting me, and I would have time to finish my swim.'

'Herself,' Grace corrected coolly, 'and, I assure you, I am ready to work.'

'Glad to hear it, Miss—' he glanced down at her card, his eyebrows arching as he corrected himself '—*Ms* Turner.' He looked up, his gaze assessing once more, although whether he was measuring her as a woman or a professional Grace couldn't tell. She kept her gaze level. 'If you care to follow me, I'll take you to my office and we can discuss what you've come here for.'

Nodding her acceptance, Grace followed him through the pool area to a discreet door in the corner. They walked down another long hallway, the windows' shutters open to the fading sunlight still bathing the courtyard in gold, and then into a large masculine office with tinted windows overlooking the landscaped gardens on the other side of the compound.

Unthinkingly Grace walked to the window, pressed one hand against the cool glass as she gazed at all that managed beauty kept behind those high walls, the jagged bits of glass on top glinting in the last of the sun's rays. The feeling of being trapped clutched at her, made her throat close up. She forced herself to breathe evenly.

Khalis Tannous came to stand behind her and she was uncomfortably aware of his presence, and the fact that all he wore was a pair of swimming trunks and a towel. She could hear the soft sound of his breathing, feel the heat of him, and she tensed, every nerve on high alert and singing with an awareness she definitely did not want to feel.

'Very beautiful, don't you think?' he murmured and Grace forced herself not to move, not to respond in any way to his nearness.

'I find the wall quite ruins the view,' she replied and turned away from the window. Her shoulder brushed against his chest, a few water droplets clinging to the silk of her blouse. Tension twanged through her again so she felt as if she might snap. She could not deny the physical response she had to this man, but she could suppress it. Completely. Her body stiff, her head held high, she moved past him into the centre of the room.

Tannous gazed at her, his expression turning thoughtful. 'I quite agree with your assessment,' he said softly. She did not reply. 'I'll just get dressed,' he told her, and disappeared through another door tucked in the corner of the room.

Grace took a deep breath and let it out slowly. She could handle this. She was a professional. She'd concentrate on her job and forget about the man, the memories. For being in this glorified prison certainly brought back the memories of another island, another wall. And all the heartbreak that had followed—of her own making.

'Ms Turner.'

Grace turned and saw Tannous standing in the doorway. He had changed into a pewter-grey silk shirt, open at the throat, and a pair of black trousers. He'd looked amazing in nothing but a towel, but he looked even better in these casually elegant clothes, his lean strength powerfully apparent in every restrained movement, the silk rippling over his muscled body. She took a slight step backwards.

'Mr Tannous.'

'Please, call me Khalis.' Grace said nothing. He smiled faintly. 'Tell me about yourself, Ms Turner. You are, I take it, experienced in the appraisal of Renaissance art?'

'It is my speciality, Mr Tannous.'

'Khalis.' He sat behind the huge oak desk, steepling his fingers under his chin, clearly waiting for her to continue.

'I have a PhD in seventeenth century da Vinci copies.'

'Forgeries.'

'Yes.'

'I don't think you will be dealing with forgeries here.'

A leap of excitement pulsed through her. Despite her alarm and anxiety about being in this place, she really did want to see what was in that vault. 'If you'd like to show me what you wish to be appraised—'

'How long have you been with Axis Art Insurers?'

'Four years.'

'You are, I must confess, very young to be so experienced.'

Grace stifled a surge of annoyance. She was, unfortunately, used to clients—mainly men—casting doubt upon her abilities. Clearly Khalis Tannous was no different. 'Monsieur Latour can vouch for my abilities, Mr Tannous—'

'Khalis,' he said softly.

Awareness rippled over her in a shiver, like droplets of water on bare skin. She didn't want to call him by his first name, as ridiculous as that seemed. Keeping formal would be one way of maintaining a necessary and professional distance. 'If you'd prefer another appraiser, please simply say so. I will be happy to oblige you.' Leaving this island—and all the memories it churned up—would be a personal relief, if a professional disappointment.

He smiled, seeming so very relaxed. 'Not at all, Ms Turner. I was simply making an observation.'

'I see.' She waited, wary, tense, trying to look as unconcerned as he did. He didn't speak, and impatience bit at her. 'So the collection...?' she finally prompted.

'Ah, yes. The collection.' He turned to stare out of the window, his easy expression suddenly turning guarded, hooded. He seemed so urbane and assured, yet for just a moment he looked like a man in the grip of some terrible force, in the cast of an awful shadow. Then his face cleared and he turned back to her with a small smile. 'My father had a private collection of art in the basement of this compound. A collection I knew nothing about.' Grace refrained from comment. Tannous arched one eyebrow in gentle mockery. 'You doubt me.'

Of course she did. 'I am not here to make judgements, Mr Tannous.'

'Are you ever,' he mused, 'going to call me Khalis?'

Not if she could help it. 'I prefer work relationships to remain professional.'

'And calling me by my first name is too intimate?' There was a soft, seductive lilt to his voice that made that alarming awareness creep along Grace's spine and curl her toes. The effect this man had on her—his voice, his smile, his body—was annoying. Unwanted. She smiled tightly.

'*Intimate* is not the word I would use. But if you feel as strongly about it as you seem to, then I'm happy to oblige you and call you Khalis.' Her tongue seemed to tangle itself on his name, and her voice turned breathy. Grace inwardly flinched. She was making a fool of herself and yet, even so, she'd seen something flare in his eyes, like silver fire, when she said his name. Whatever she was feeling—this attraction, this magnetism—he felt it, too.

Not that it mattered. Attraction, to her, was as suicidal as a moth to a flame. 'May I see the paintings?' she asked.

'Of course. Perhaps that will explain things.'

In one fluid movement Khalis rose from the desk and walked out of the study, clearly expecting Grace to follow him. She suppressed the bite of irritation she felt at his arrogant attitude—he didn't even look back—only to skid to a surprised halt when she saw him holding the door open for her.

He smiled down at her, and Grace had the uncomfortable feeling that he knew exactly what she'd been feeling. 'After you,' he murmured and, fighting a flush, she walked past him down the same corridor they had used earlier. 'Where am I going?' she asked tersely. She could *feel* Khalis walking behind her, heard the whisper of his clothes as he moved. Everything about him was elegant, graceful and sinuous. Sexy.

No. She could not—would not—think that way. She hadn't looked at a man in a sexual or romantic way in four years. She'd trained herself not to, suppressed those longings because she'd had to. One misstep would cost her if not her life, then her very soul. It was insane to feel anything now—and especially for a man like Khalis Tannous, a man who was now the CEO of a terrible and corrupt empire, a man she could never trust.

Instinctively she walked a little faster, as if she could distance herself from him, but he kept pace with ease.

'Turn right,' he murmured, and she heard humour in his voice. 'You are amazingly adept in those very high heels, Ms Turner. But it's not a race.'

Grace didn't answer, but she forced herself to slow down. A little. She turned and walked down another long corridor, the shutters open to a different side of the villa's interior courtyard.

'And now left,' he said, his voice a soft caress, raising the tiny hairs on the back of Grace's neck. He'd come close again, too close. She turned left and came to a forbidding-looking lift with steel doors and a complex security pad.

Khalis activated the security with a fingerprint and a numbered code while Grace averted her eyes. 'I'll have to give you access,' he said, 'as all the art will need to stay on the basement level.'

'To be honest, Mr Tannous—'

'Khalis.'

'I'm not sure how much can be accomplished here,' Grace continued, undeterred. 'Most appraisals need to be done in a laboratory, with the proper equipment—'

Khalis flashed her a quick and rather grim smile. 'It appears my father had the same concerns you do, Ms Turner. I think you will find all the equipment and tools you need.'

The lift doors opened and Khalis ushered her inside before stepping into the lift himself. The doors swooshed closed, and Grace fought a sudden sense of claustrophobia. The lift was spacious enough, and there were only two of them in there, but she still felt as if she couldn't breathe. Couldn't think. She was conscious of Khalis next to her, seeming so loose-limbed and relaxed, and the lift plunging downwards, deep below the earth, to the evil heart of this awful compound. She felt both trapped and tempted—two things she hated feeling.

'Just a few more seconds,' Khalis said softly, and she knew he was aware of how she felt. She was used to hiding her emotions, and being good at it, and it amazed and alarmed her that this stranger seemed to read her so quickly and easily. No one else ever had.

The doors opened and he swept out one arm, indicating she could go first. Cautiously Grace stepped out into a nondescript hallway, the concrete floor and walls the same as those in any basement. To the right she saw a thick steel door, sawn off its hinges and now propped to the side. Balkri Tannous's vault. Her heart began to beat with heavy thuds of anticipation and a little fear.

'Here we are.' Khalis moved past her to switch on the light. Grace saw the interior of the vault was fashioned like a living room or study and, with her heart still beating hard, she stepped into that secret room.

It was almost too much to take in at once. Paintings jostled for space on every wall, frames nearly touching each other. She recognised at least a dozen stolen paintings right off the bat—Klimt, Monet, Picasso. Millions and millions of dollars' worth of stolen art.

Her breath came out in a shudder and Khalis laughed softly, the sound somehow bleak. 'I'm no expert, but even I could tell this was something else.'

She stopped in front of a Picasso that hadn't been seen in a museum in over twenty years. She wasn't that experienced with contemporary art, but she doubted it was a forgery. 'Why,' she asked, studying the painting's clean geometric shape and different shades of blue, 'did you ask for a Renaissance expert? There's art from every period here.'

'True,' Khalis said. He came to stand by her shoulder, gazing at the Picasso as well. 'Although, frankly, that looks like something my five-year-old god-daughter might paint in Nursery.'

'That's enough to make Picasso roll in his grave.'

'Well, she is very clever.'

Grace gave a little laugh, surprising herself. She rarely laughed. She rarely let a man make her laugh. 'Is your god-daughter in California?'

'Yes, she's the daughter of one of my shareholders.'

Grace gazed at the painting. 'Clever she may be, but most art historians would shudder to compare Picasso with a child and a box of finger paints.'

'Oh, she has a paintbrush.'

Grace laughed again, softly, a little breath of sound. 'Maybe she'll be famous one day.' She half-turned and, with a somersault of her heart, realised just how close he had come. His face—his *lips*—were mere inches away. She could see their mobile fullness, amazed at how such a masculine man could have such lush, kissable, *sexy* lips. She felt a shaft of longing pierce her and quickly she moved onto the next painting. 'So why me? Why a Renaissance specialist?'

'Because of these.'

He took her hand in his own and shock jolted through her with the force of an electric current, short-circuiting her senses. Grace jerked her hand away from his too hard, her breath coming out in an outraged gasp.

Khalis stopped, an eyebrow arched. Grace knew her reaction had been ridiculously extreme. How could she explain it? She could not, not easily at any rate. She decided to ignore the whole sorry little episode and raised her chin a notch. 'Show me, please.'

'Very well.' With one last considering look he led her

to a door she hadn't noticed in the back of the room. He opened it and switched on an electric light before ushering her inside.

The room was small and round, and it felt like being inside a tower, or perhaps a shrine. Grace saw only two artworks on the walls, and they stole the breath right from her lungs.

'What—' She stepped closer, stared hard at the wood panels with their thick brushstrokes of oil paint. 'Do you know what these are?' she whispered.

'Not precisely,' Khalis told her, 'but they definitely aren't something my god-daughter could paint.'

Grace smiled and shook her head. 'No, indeed.' She stepped closer, her gaze roving over the painted wood panels. 'Leonardo da Vinci.'

'Yes, he's quite famous, isn't he?'

Her smile widened, to her own amazement. She hadn't expected Khalis Tannous to *amuse* her. 'He is, rather. But they could be forgeries, you know.'

'I doubt they are,' Khalis answered. 'Simply by the fact they're in their own little room.' He paused, his tone turning grim. 'And I know my father. He didn't like to be tricked.'

'Forgeries can be of exceptional quality,' Grace told him. 'And they even have their own value—'

'My father—' Khalis cut her off '—liked the best.'

She turned back to the paintings, drinking them in. If these were real…how many people had seen these *ever*? 'How on earth did he find them?'

'I have no idea. I don't really want to know.'

'They weren't stolen, at least not from a museum.'

'No?'

'These have never been in a museum.'

'Then they are rather special, aren't they?'

She gave a little laugh. 'You could say that.' She shook her head slowly, still trying to take it in. Two original Leonardo paintings never seen in a museum. Never known to exist, beyond rumours. 'If these are real, they would comprise the most significant find of the art world in the last century.'

Khalis sighed heavily, almost as if he were disappointed by such news. 'I suspected as much,' he said, and flicked out the lights. 'You can examine them at length later. But right now I think we both deserve some refreshment.'

Her mind still spinning, Grace barely took in his words. 'Refreshment?'

'Dinner, Ms Turner. I'm starving.' And with an almost wolfish smile he led her out of the vault.

CHAPTER THREE

GRACE paced the sumptuous bedroom Eric had shown her to, her mind still racing from the revelations found in that vault. She longed to ring Michel, but she'd discovered her mobile phone didn't get reception on this godforsaken island. She wondered if that was intentional; somehow she didn't think Balkri Tannous wanted his guests having free contact with the outside world. But what about Khalis?

It occurred to her, not for the first time but with more force, that she really knew nothing about this man. Michel had given her the barest details: he was Balkri Tannous's younger son; he'd gone to Cambridge; he'd left his family at twenty-one and made his own way in America. But beyond that?

She knew he was handsome and charismatic and arrogantly assured. She knew his closeness made her heart skip a beat. She knew the scent and heat of him had made her dizzy. He'd made her laugh.

Appalled by the nature of her thoughts, Grace shook her head as if the mere action could erase her thinking. She could not be attracted to this man. And even if her body insisted on betraying her, her mind wouldn't. Her heart wouldn't.

Not again.

She took a deep, shuddering breath and strove for calm.

Control. What she didn't know about Khalis Tannous was whether the reality of a huge billion dollar empire would make him power hungry. Whether the sight of millions of dollars' worth of art made him greedy. Whether he could be trusted.

She'd seen how wealth and power had turned a man into someone she barely recognised. Charming on the outside—and Khalis *was* charming—but also selfish and cruel. Would Khalis be like that? Like her ex-husband?

And why, Grace wondered with a lurch of panic, was she thinking about Khalis and her ex-husband in the same breath? Khalis was her client, no more. Her client with a great deal of expensive art.

Another breath. She needed to think rationally rather than react with emotion, with her memories and fears. This was a different island, a different man. And she was different now, too. Stronger. Harder. Wiser. She had no intention of getting involved with anyone…even if she could.

Deliberately she sat down and pulled a pad of paper towards her. She'd make notes, handle this like any other assignment. She wouldn't think of the way Khalis looked in his swimming trunks, the clean, sculpted lines of his chest and shoulders. She wouldn't remember how he'd made her smile, lightened her heart—something that hardly seemed possible. And she certainly wouldn't wonder if he might end up like his father—or her ex-husband. Corrupted by power, ruined with wealth. It didn't matter. In a few days she would be leaving this wretched island, as well as its owner.

Grace Turner. Khalis stared at the small white card she'd given him. It listed only her qualifications, the name of her company and her phone number. He balanced the card on his knuckles, turning his hand quickly to catch it before he brought it unthinkingly to his lips, almost as if he could catch the scent of her from that little bit of paper.

Grace Turner intrigued him, on many levels. Of course he'd first been struck by her looks; she was an uncommonly beautiful woman. A bit unconventional, perhaps, with her honey-blond hair and chocolate eyes, an unusual and yet beguiling combination. Her lashes were thick and sooty, sweeping down all too often to hide the emotions he thought he saw in her eyes.

And her figure…generous curves and endless legs, all showcased in business attire that was no doubt meant to look professional but managed to be ridiculously alluring. Khalis had never seen a white silk blouse and houndstooth pencil skirt look so sexy. Yet, despite the skyscraper heels, he doubted she intended to look sexy. She was as prickly as a sea urchin, and might as well have had *do not touch* emblazoned on her forehead.

Yet he *did* want to touch her, had wanted it from the moment those gorgeous legs had entered his vision when he'd completed his lap in the pool. He hadn't been able to resist when they'd been in the vault, and her reaction to his taking her hand had surprised, he thought, both of them.

She was certainly a woman of secrets. He sensed her coiled tension, even her fear. Something about this island—about him—made her nervous. Of course, on the most basic level he could hardly blame her. From the outside, Alhaja Island looked like a prison. And he was a stranger, the son of a man whose ruthless exploits had been whispered about if not proved. Even so, he didn't think her fear was directed simply at him, but something greater. Something, Khalis suspected, that had held her in its thrall for a while.

Or was he simply projecting his own emotions onto this mysterious and intriguing woman? For he recognised his own fear. He hated being back on Alhaja, hated the memories that rose to the forefront of his mind like scum on the surface of a pond.

Get used to it, Khalis. This is how it is done.

Don't leave me here, Khalis.

I'll come back…I promise.

Abruptly he rose from his chair, prowled the length of his study with an edgy restlessness. He'd resolutely banished those voices for fifteen years, yet they'd all come rushing back, taunting and tormenting him from the moment he'd stepped on this wretched shore. Despite Eric's tactful suggestion that he set up a base of operations in any number of cities where his father had had offices, Khalis had refused.

He'd run from this island once. He wasn't going to do it again.

And at least the enigmatic and attractive Grace Turner provided a welcome distraction from the agony of his own thoughts.

'Khalis?' He glanced up and saw Eric standing in the doorway. 'Dinner is served.'

'Thank you.' Khalis slid Grace's business card into the inside pocket of the dark grey blazer he'd put on. He felt a pleasurable tingle of anticipation at the thought of seeing the all too fascinating Ms Turner again, and firmly pushed away his dark thoughts once and for all. There was, he'd long ago decided, never any point in looking back.

He'd ordered dinner to be served on a private terrace of the compound's interior courtyard, and the intimate space flickered with torchlight as Khalis strolled up to the table. Grace had not yet arrived and he took the liberty of pouring a glass of wine for each of them. He'd just finished when he heard the click of her heels, felt a prickle of awareness at her nearness. Smiling, he turned.

'Ms Turner.'

'If you insist on my calling you Khalis, then you must call me Grace.'

He inclined his head, more gratified than he should be at her concession. 'Thank you…Grace.'

She stepped into the courtyard, the torchlight casting her into flickering light and wraith-like shadow. She looked magnificent. She'd kept her hair up in its businesslike coil, but had exchanged her work day attire for a simple sheath dress in chocolate-brown silk. On another woman the dress might have looked like a paper sack but on Grace it clung to her curves and shimmered when she moved. He suspected she'd chosen the dress for its supposed modesty, and the fact that she had little idea how stunning she looked only added to her allure. He realised he was staring and reached for one of the glasses on the table. 'Wine?'

A hesitation, her body tensing for a fraction of a second before she held out one slender arm. 'Thank you.'

They sipped the wine in silence for a moment, the night soft all around them. In the distance Khalis heard the whisper of the waves, the wind rustling the palm trees overhead. 'I'd offer a toast, but the occasion doesn't seem quite appropriate.'

'No.' Grace lowered her glass, her slim fingers wrapped tightly around the fragile stem. 'You must realise, Mr Tannous—'

'Khalis.'

She laughed softly, no more than a breath of sound. She did not seem like a woman used to laughing. 'I keep forgetting.'

'I think you want to forget.'

She didn't deny it. 'I told you before, I prefer to keep things professional.'

'It's the twenty-first century, Grace. Calling someone by a first name is hardly inviting untoward intimacies.' Even if such a prospect attracted him all too much.

She lifted her gaze to his, her dark eyes wide and clear with a sudden sobriety. 'In most circles,' she allowed, intriguing him further. 'In any case, what I meant to tell you was that I'm sure you realise most of the art in that vault downstairs has been stolen from various museums around the world.'

'I do realise,' he answered, 'which is why I wished to have it assessed, and assured there are no forgeries.'

'And then?'

He took a sip of wine, giving her a deliberately amused look over the rim of his glass. 'Then I intend to sell it on the black market, of course. And quietly get rid of you.'

Her eyes narrowed, lips compressed. 'If that is a joke, it is a poor one.'

'*If?*' He stared at her, saw her slender body nearly vibrating with tension. 'My God, do you actually think there is any possibility of such a thing? What kind of man do you think I am?'

A faint blush touched her pale cheeks with pink. 'I don't know you, Mr Tannous. All I know is what I've heard of your father—'

'I am nothing like my father.' He hated the implication she was making, the accusation. He'd been trying to prove he was different his whole life, had made every choice deliberately as a way to prove he was not like his father in the smallest degree. The price he'd paid was high, maybe even too high, but he'd paid it and he wouldn't look back. And he wouldn't defend himself to this slip of a woman either. He forced himself to smile. 'Trust me, such a thing is not in the remotest realm of possibility.'

'I didn't think it was,' she answered sharply. 'But it is something, perhaps, your father might have done.'

Something snapped to life inside him, but Khalis could not say what it was. Anger? Regret? *Guilt?* 'My father was not a murderer,' he said levelly, 'as far as I am aware.'

'But he was a thief,' Grace said quietly. 'A thief many times over.'

'And he is dead. He cannot pay for his crimes, alas, but I can set things to rights.'

'Is that what you are doing with Tannous Enterprises?'

Tension tautened through his body. 'Attempting. It is, I fear, a Herculean task.'

'Why did he leave it to you?'

'It is a question I have asked myself many times already,' he said lightly, 'and one for which I have yet to find an answer. My older brother should have inherited, but he died in the crash.'

'And what about the other shareholders?'

'There are very few, and they hold a relatively small percentage of the shares. They're not best pleased, though, that my father left control of the company to me.'

'What do you think they'll do?'

He shrugged. 'What can they do? They're waiting now, to see which way I turn.'

'Whether you'll be like your father.' This time she did not speak with accusation, but something that sounded surprisingly like sympathy.

'I won't.'

'A fortune such as the one contained in that vault has tempted a lesser man, Mr...Khalis.' She spoke softly, almost as if she had some kind of personal experience of such temptation. His name on her lips sent a sudden thrill through him. Perhaps using first names did invite an intimacy...or at least create one.

'I have my own fortune, Grace. But I thank you for the compliment.'

'It wasn't meant to be one,' she said quietly. 'Just an observation, really.' She turned away and he watched her cross to the edge of the private alcove as if looking for exits. The little nook was enclosed by thick foliage on every side but one that led back into the villa. Did she feel trapped?

'You seem a bit tense,' he told her mildly. 'Granted, this island has a similar effect on me, but I wish I could put you at ease in regard to my intentions.'

'Why didn't you simply hand the collection over to the police?'

He gave a short laugh. 'In this part of the world? My father may have been corrupt, but he wasn't alone. Half of the local police force were in his pocket already.'

She nodded, her back still to him, though he saw the tension radiating along her spine, her slender back taut with it. 'Of course,' she murmured.

'Let me be plain about my intentions, Grace. After you've assessed the art—the da Vincis, mainly—and assured me they are not forgeries, I intend to hand the entire collection over to Axis to see it disposed of properly, whether that is the Louvre, the Met, or a poky little museum in Oklahoma. I don't care.'

'There are legal procedures—'

He waved a hand in dismissal. 'I'm sure of it. And I'm sure your company can handle such things and make sure each masterpiece gets back to its proper museum.'

She turned suddenly, looking at him over her shoulder, her eyes wide and dark, her lips parted. It was an incredibly alluring pose, though he doubted she realised it. Or perhaps he'd just been too long without a lover. Either way, Grace Turner fascinated and attracted him more than any woman had in a long time. He wanted to kiss those soft parted lips as much as he wanted to see them smile, and the realisation jarred him. He felt more for this woman than mere physical attraction. 'I told you before,' she said, 'those Leonardos have never been in a museum.'

He pushed away that unwanted realisation with relief. 'Why not?'

'No one has ever been sure they even existed.'

'What do you mean?'

'Did you recognise the subject of the paintings?'

'Something in Greek mythology, I thought.' He racked his brain for a moment. 'Leda and the Swan, wasn't it?'

'Yes. Do you know the story?'

'Vaguely. The Swan was Zeus, wasn't it? And he had his way with Leda.'

'Yes, he raped her. It was a popular subject of paintings during the Renaissance, and depicted quite erotically.' She'd turned to face him and in the flickering torchlight her face looked pale and sorrowful. 'Leonardo da Vinci was known to have done the first painting downstairs, of Leda and the Swan. A romantic depiction, similar in style to others of the period, yet of course by a master.'

'And yet this painting was never in a museum?'

'No, it was last seen at Fontainebleau in 1625. Historians think it was deliberately destroyed. It was definitely known to be damaged, so if it is genuine your father or a previous owner must have had it restored.'

'If it hasn't been seen in four hundred years, how does anyone even know what it looked like?'

'Copies, all based on the first copy done by one of Leonardo's students. You could probably buy a poster of it on the street for ten pounds.'

'That's no poster downstairs.'

'No.' She met his gaze frankly, her eyes wide and a soft,

deep brown. Pansy eyes, Khalis thought, alarmed again at how sentimental he was being. *Feeling.* The guarded sorrow in her eyes aroused a protective instinct in him he hadn't felt in years. Hadn't wanted to feel. Yet one look from Grace and it came rushing back, overwhelming him. He wanted, inexplicably, to take care of this woman. 'In fact,' Grace continued, 'I would have assumed the painting downstairs is a copy, except for the second painting.'

'The second painting,' Khalis repeated. He was having trouble keeping track of the conversation, due to the rush of his own emotions and the effect Grace was having on him. A faint flush now coloured her cheekbones, making her look more beautiful and alluring than ever. He felt his libido stir insistently to life and took a sip of wine to distract himself. What was it about this woman that affected him so much—in so many ways?

'Yes, you see the second painting is one art historians thought Leonardo never completed. It's been no more than a rumour or even a dream.' She shook her head slowly, as if she couldn't believe what she'd seen with her own eyes. 'Leda not with her lover the Swan, but with her children of that tragic union. Helen and Polydeuces, Castor and Clytemnestra.' Abruptly she turned away from him, and with the sudden sweep of those sooty lashes Khalis knew she was hiding some deep and powerful emotion.

'If he never completed it,' he asked after a moment, 'how do art historians even know about its possibility?'

'He did several studies. He was fascinated by the myth of Leda.' Her back was still to him, radiating tension once more. Khalis fought the urge to put his hand on her shoulders, draw her to him, although for a kiss or a hug of comfort he wasn't even sure. He felt a powerful desire to do both. 'He's one of the few artists ever to have thought of painting Leda that way. As a mother, rather than a lover.'

'You seem rather moved by the idea,' he said quietly, and he felt the increase of tension in her lithe body like a jolt of electricity that wired them both.

She drew in a breath that sounded only a little ragged and after a second's pause, turned to him with a cool smile. 'Of course I am. As I told you before, this is a major discovery.'

Khalis said nothing, merely observed her. Her gaze was level, her face carefully expressionless. It was a look, he imagined, she cultivated often. A mask to hide the turbulent emotions seething beneath that placid surface. He recognised it because he had a similar technique himself. Except his mask went deeper than Grace's, soul-deep. He felt nothing while her emotions remained close to the surface, reflected in her eyes, visible in the soft, trembling line of her mouth.

'I didn't mean the discovery,' he said, 'but rather the painting itself. This Leda.'

'I can't help but feel sorry for her, I suppose.' She shrugged, one slender shoulder lifting, and Khalis's gaze was irresistibly drawn to the movement, the shimmery fabric of her dress clinging lovingly to the swell of her breast. She noticed the direction of his gaze and, her eyes narrowed and mouth compressed, pushed past him. 'You mentioned earlier you were starving. Shall we eat?'

'Of course.' He moved to the table and pulled out her chair. Grace hesitated, then walked swiftly towards him and sat down. Khalis inhaled the scent of her perfume or perhaps her shampoo; it smelled sweet and clean, like almonds. He gently pushed her chair in and moved to the other side of the table. Nothing Grace had said or done so far had deterred him or dampened his attraction; in fact, he found the enigmatic mix of strength and vulnerability she showed all the more intriguing—and alluring. And as for the emotions she stirred up in him… Khalis pushed these aside. The events of the last week had left him a little raw, that was all. It should come as no surprise that he was feeling a bit stupidly emotional. It would pass…even as his attraction to Grace Turner became stronger.

Grace laid her napkin in her lap with trembling fingers. She could not believe how unnerved she was. She didn't know if it was being on this wretched island, seeing those amazing paintings, or the proximity to Khalis Tannous. Probably—and unfortunately—all three.

She could not deny this man played havoc with her peace of mind by the way he seemed to sense what she was thinking and feeling. The way his gaze lingered made her achingly aware of her own body, created a response in her she didn't want or like.

Desire. *Need.*

She'd schooled herself not to feel either for so long. How could this one man shatter her defences so quickly and completely? How could she let him? She knew what happened when you let a man close. When you trusted him. Despair. Heartbreak. *Betrayal.*

'So tell me about yourself, Grace Turner,' Khalis said, his voice low and lazy. It slid over her like silk, made her want to luxuriate in its soft, seductive promise. He poured her more wine, which Grace knew she should refuse. The few sips she'd taken had already gone to her head—or was that just the effect Khalis was having on her?

'What do you want to know?' she asked.

'Everything.' He sat back, smiling, the glass of wine cradled between his long brown fingers. Grace could not keep her gaze from wandering over him. Wavy ink-black hair, left just a little long, and those surprising grey-green eyes, the colour of agate. He lifted his brows, clearly wait-

ing, and, startled from her humiliatingly obvious perusal
of his attractions, Grace reached for her wine.

'That's rather comprehensive. I told you I did my PhD
in—'

'I'm not referring to your professional qualifications.'
Grace said nothing. She wanted—had to—keep this professional. 'Where are you from?' he asked mildly, and she
let out the breath she hadn't realised she'd been holding.

'Cambridge.'

'And you went to Cambridge for your doctorate?'

'Yes, and undergraduate.'

'You must have done one after the other,' he mused.
'You can't be more than thirty.'

'I'm thirty-two,' Grace told him. 'And, as a matter of
fact, yes, I did do one after the other.'

'You know I went to Cambridge?' She inclined her head
in acknowledgement; she'd read the file Michel had com-
piled on him on the plane. 'We almost overlapped. I'm a
few years older than you, but it's possible.'

'An amazing coincidence.'

'You don't seem particularly amazed.'

She just shrugged. She had a feeling that if Khalis
Tannous had been within fifty miles of her she would
have known it. Or maybe she wouldn't have, because then
she'd been dazzled by another Cambridge student—her ex-
husband. Dazzled and blinded. She felt a sudden cold steal
inside her at the thought that Khalis and Loukas might
have been acquaintances, or even friends. What if Loukas
found out she was here? Even though this trip was business, Grace knew how her ex-husband thought. He'd be
suspicious, and he might deny her access to Katerina. *Why*
had she let Michel bully her into coming?

'Grace?' She refocused, saw him looking at with obvious concern. 'You've gone deathly white in the space of about six seconds.'

'Sorry.' She fumbled for an excuse. 'I'm a bit tired from the flight, and I haven't eaten since breakfast.'

'Then let me serve you,' Khalis said and, as if on cue, a young woman came in with a platter of food.

Grace watched as Khalis ladled couscous, stewed lamb and a cucumber yogurt salad onto her plate. She told herself it was unlikely Khalis knew Loukas; he'd been living in the States, after all. And, even if he did, he'd surely be discreet about his father's art collection. She was, as usual, being paranoid. Yet she *had* to be paranoid, on her guard always, because access to her daughter was so limited and so precious…and in her ex-husband's complete control.

'Bon appétit,' Khalis said, and Grace forced a smile.

'It looks delicious.'

'Really? Because you're looking at your plate as if it's your last meal.'

Grace pressed two fingers to her forehead; she felt the beginnings of one of her headaches. 'A delicious last meal, in any case.' She tried to smile. 'I'm sorry. I'm just tired, really.'

'Would you prefer to eat in your room?'

Grace shook her head, not wanting to admit to such weakness. 'I'm fine,' she said firmly, as if she could make it so. 'And this really does look delicious.' She took a bite of couscous and somehow managed to choke it down. She could feel Khalis's gaze on her, heavy and speculative. Knowing.

'You grew up in Cambridge, you said?' he finally asked, and Grace felt relief that he wasn't going to press.

'Yes, my father was a fellow at Trinity College.'

'Was?'

'He died six years ago.'

'I'm sorry.'

'And I should say the same to you. I'm sorry for the loss of your father and brother.'

'Thank you, although it's hardly necessary.'

Grace paused, her fork in mid-air. 'Even if you were estranged from them, it's surely a loss.'

'I left my family fifteen years ago, Grace. They were dead to me. I did my grieving then.' He spoke neutrally enough, yet underneath that easy affability Grace sensed an icy hardness. There would be no second chances with a man like Khalis.

'Didn't you miss them? At the time?'

'No.' He spoke flatly, the one word discouraging any more questions.

'Do you enjoy living in the States?' she tried instead, keeping her tone light.

'I do.'

'What made you choose to live there?'

'It was far away.'

It seemed no question was innocuous. They ate in silence for a few moments, the only sound the whisper of the waves and wind. When she couldn't see those high walls she could almost appreciate the beauty of this island paradise in the middle of the Mediterranean. Yet she could still *feel* them, knew that the only way out of here was by another person's say-so. At this thought another bolt of pain lanced through her skull and her hand clenched around her fork. Khalis noticed.

'Grace?'

'Did you grow up here?' she asked abruptly. 'Behind these walls?'

He didn't answer for a moment, and his narrowed gaze rested on her thoughtfully. 'Holidays mostly,' he finally said. 'I went to boarding school when I was seven, in England.'

'Seven,' she murmured. 'That must have been hard.'

Khalis just shrugged. 'I suppose I missed my parents, but then I didn't know as much about them as I should have, being only a child.'

'What do you mean?'

'You are most certainly aware that my father was not the most admirable of men.'

'I'm aware.'

'As a child, I did not realise that. And so I missed him.' He said it simply, bluntly, as if it were no more than an obvious fact. Yet Grace was both curious and saddened by his statement. When, she wondered, had Khalis become disillusioned with his father? When he left university? And did learning of a loved one's flaws make you stop loving them? In Khalis's view, it certainly seemed so.

'What about your mother?'

'She died when I was ten,' Khalis told her. 'I don't remember much about her.'

'You don't?' Grace didn't hide her surprise. 'My mother died when I was thirteen, and I remember so much.' The scent of her hand lotion, the softness of her hair, the lullabies she used to sing. She also remembered how dusty and empty their house on Grange Road had seemed after her death, with her father immersed in his books and antiques.

'It was a long time ago,' Khalis said, and although his tone was pleasant enough Grace could still tell the topic of conversation was closed. It almost sounded as if he didn't *want* to remember his mother…or anyone in his past.

She felt an entirely unreasonable flash of curiosity to *know* this man, for she felt with a deep and surprising certainty that he hid secrets. Sorrow. Despite his often light tone, the easy smile, Grace knew there was a darkness and a hardness in him that both repelled and attracted her. She had no business being attracted to any man, much less a man like Khalis. Yet here she was, seeing the sleepy, veiled look in his grey-green eyes, feeling that slow spiral of honeyed desire uncurl in the pit of her belly, even as pain continued to lance her skull. How appropriate. Pain and pleasure. Temptation and torture. They always went together, didn't they?

With effort she returned the conversation to work. 'Tomorrow morning I should like to see the equipment you mentioned,' she told him, keeping her voice brisk. 'The sooner I am able to assess whether the Leonardos are genuine, the better.'

'Do you really doubt it?'

'My job is to doubt it,' Grace told him. 'I need to prove they're real rather than prove they're forgeries.'

'Fascinating,' Khalis murmured. 'A quest for truth. What drew you to such a profession?'

'My father was a professor of ancient history. I grew up around antiques, spent most of my childhood in museums, except for a brief horse-mad phase when all I wanted to do was ride.' She gave him a small smile. 'The Fitzwilliam in Cambridge was practically a second home.'

'Like father like daughter?'

'Sometimes,' Grace said, her gaze locking with his, 'you are your father's child in more than just blood.'

His grey-green gaze felt like a vice on her soul, for she could not look away. It called to something deep within her, something she had suppressed for so long she barely remembered she still possessed it. The longing to be understood, the desire to be known or even revealed. And reflected back in those agate eyes she saw a strange and surprising torment of emotions: sorrow, anger, maybe even despair. Or was she simply looking into a mirror? Her head pounded with the knowledge of what she'd seen and felt, the ache increasing so she longed to close her eyes. Then he broke their gaze, averting his face, his mouth hardening as he looked out at the gardens now cloaked in darkness.

'You must have some dessert,' he finally said, and his voice was as light as ever. 'A Tunisian speciality, almond sesame pastries.' The young woman entered with a plate of pastries as well as a silver tray with a coffee pot and porcelain cups.

Grace took a bite of the sticky sweet pastry, but she could not manage the coffee. Her head ached unbearably now, and she knew if she did not lie down in the dark she would be incapacitated for hours or even days. She'd had these migraines with depressing regularity, ever since her divorce. With an unsteady clatter she returned her coffee cup to its saucer. 'I'm sorry, but I am very tired. I think I'll go to bed.'

Khalis rose from the table, concern darkening his eyes. 'Of course. You look unwell. Do you have a headache?'

Tightly Grace nodded. Spots swam in her vision and she rose from the table carefully, as if she might break. Every movement sent shafts of lightning pain through her skull.

'Come.' Khalis took her by the hand, draping his other arm around her shoulder as he led her from the table.

'I'm sorry,' she murmured, but he brushed aside her apologies.

'You should have told me.'

'It came on suddenly.'

'What do you need?'

'To lie down…in the dark…'

'Of course.'

Then, to Grace's surprise, he pulled her up into his

arms, cradling her easily. 'I apologise for the familiarity, but it is simpler and quicker this way.' Grace said nothing, shock as well as pain rendering her speechless. In her weakened state she didn't have the strength to draw away, nor, she realised, the will. It felt far too good to be held, her cheek pressed against the warm strength of his chest. It had been so very long since she'd been this physically close to someone, since she'd felt taken care of. And even though she knew better than to want it, knew where letting someone take care of you led, she did not even attempt to draw away. Worse, she instinctively, irresistibly nestled closer, her head tucked in the curve of his shoulder. 'You should have told me sooner,' he murmured, brushing a tendril of hair from her cheek, and Grace just closed her eyes. The pain in her head overwhelmed her now, making speech or even thought impossible.

Eventually she heard a door open, felt Khalis lay her gently on a silk duvet. He left, making her feel suddenly, ridiculously bereft, only to return moments later with a cool damp cloth he laid over her forehead. Grace could not keep from groaning in relief.

'Can you manage these?' he said, pressing two tablets in her hand.

She gave the barest of nods. 'What are they?'

'Just paracetamol, I'm afraid. I don't have anything stronger.' He handed her a glass of water and, despite the dagger points of pain thrusting into her skull, she managed to choke the tablets down. She lay back on the bed, utterly spent, in too much pain even to feel humiliated that Khalis was seeing her so weak and vulnerable, and on her very first day.

She felt him slip off her heels, and then he took her feet in his hands and began massaging her soles with his thumbs. Grace lay on the bed in supine surrender as he ministered to her, rubbing his thumbs in deep, slow circles. It felt unbelievably, unbearably good and she felt her headache start to recede, her body relax. She would not have moved even if she possessed the strength to do so.

She must have fallen asleep, for the last thing she remembered until morning was Khalis still rubbing her feet, his touch sure, knowing and so achingly gentle.

CHAPTER FOUR

GRACE woke to sunlight streaming through the crack in the curtains and her head feeling much better. She opened her eyes and stretched, felt a surge of relief mingled with an absurd disappointment that Khalis was gone.

Of course he was gone, she told herself. It was morning. She *wanted* him to be gone. The thought that he might have spent the entire night in her bedroom made her squirm with humiliation. And yet he'd seen enough; she still recalled the gentle way he'd rubbed her feet, how tenderly he'd cared for her. She squirmed some more. She hated feeling weak or vulnerable. Hated the thought of Khalis seeing that and using it to his advantage somehow, even if last night he'd made her feel cherished and cared for.

Forget it, she told herself. *Forget Khalis, forget how he made you feel.* Quickly she rose from the bed, even though it made her head swim a bit. She took a deep breath and staggered to the shower, determined to forget the events of last night and put today on an even and professional keel. She felt better when she'd showered and dressed in work clothes, a pair of slim black trousers and a fitted white T-shirt. She applied the minimum of neutral make-up, pulled her hair back into a ponytail and reached for her attaché case, her professional armour now firmly in place. This was how she needed to be with Khalis, with any man. Professional, strong and completely in control. Not weak or needy. Not wanting.

Khalis's assistant Eric met her at the bottom of the main staircase. He wore a pair of board shorts and a T-shirt with a logo that read 'I work at Silicon Valley. But if I told you more I'd have to kill you'.

Grace thought of her admonition last night. *If that is a joke...* She must have seemed completely ridiculous.

'Ms Turner,' Eric greeted her with an easy smile, 'may I show you to the breakfast room?'

'Thank you.' He led her down a tiled hallway and, curious, she asked, 'Did you meet Mr Tannous in California?'

He turned back to give her a smiling glance. 'How did you know?'

'Oh, I don't know, maybe the hair,' she replied with a small smile. He had light blond hair, bleached by the sun in rather artful streaks. 'Have you known him long?'

'Since he moved out there fifteen years ago. I've been with his gig from the start. He had big ideas and, while I don't have any of those, I'm pretty decent with the admin side.'

'Did you know about his family?'

Eric hesitated for only a second. 'Everyone in California is starting over, more or less,' he said and, although his tone was relaxed, it was also final. He had the same kind of affability Khalis possessed, Grace thought wryly, although rather less of the unyielding hardness she sensed underneath. 'Here you go,' he said, and ushered her into a pleasant room at the back of the building. Khalis was already seated at the table, drinking coffee and reading the newspaper on his tablet computer. He glanced up as she entered, his easy and rather familiar smile making her flush and remember how he'd held her last night. How she'd pressed her cheek against his chest, how he'd rubbed her feet. How much she'd savoured it all. Judging by that smile, he'd probably been able to tell.

'You look like you're feeling better.'

She sat down and poured herself coffee, her gaze firmly on the cup. 'Yes, thank you. I apologise for last night.'

'What is there to be sorry for?'

She added milk. 'I was incapacitated—'

'You were in pain.'

He spoke so quietly and firmly that Grace was startled into looking up, her gaze locking on his green-grey one that was full of far too much understanding. It almost made her want to tell him things. She stirred her coffee and took a sip. 'Still, I am here to perform a set task—'

'And I'm sure you will perform it admirably today. What exactly is on the agenda?'

Relief surged through her as she realised he was going to graciously drop the subject of last night. Today she could talk about. 'First I'll need to catalogue all the works in the vault and check them against the Art Loss Register. Those that appear to have been stolen can be, for the moment, set to one side. Experts from the museums concerned will need to be contacted along with—'

'I'd prefer,' Khalis said, 'not to contact anyone until we know just what we're dealing with.'

Unease crept along her spine with cold fingers. Ridiculous it might be, but she couldn't keep from feeling it. She didn't think Khalis intended to keep the art for himself, but she still didn't trust him. Not on either a professional or personal level. 'And why is that?'

'Because the media storm that will erupt when it is discovered my father had however many stolen paintings in his possession is one I want to control, at least somewhat,' he replied mildly. 'I don't particularly like publicity.'

'Nor do I.'

'And yet,' he said musingly, 'you will certainly be mentioned in any of the articles that will undoubtedly appear.'

'Axis Art Insurers will,' Grace replied swiftly. 'My name will be kept out of it. That has always been our agreement.'

He gazed at her over the rim of his coffee cup. 'You really don't like publicity.'

'No.'

'Then my decision to wait to contact any outside source should meet with your approval.'

'I don't like being managed,' Grace said flatly.

Khalis arched an eyebrow. 'I'd hardly call a request to wait on calling the police being *managed*.'

'It potentially compromises my position.'

'You have a moral objection?'

She bit her lip. She didn't, not really, not if she trusted him to inform the proper legal authority and dispose of the art as necessary. And, logically, she knew she should. She had no real reason to think otherwise, and yet…

And yet she'd once believed a man's assurances. Trusted his promises. Let herself be led into captivity and despair. Every muscle coiled and tightened at the memory. Pain snapped at the edges of her mind, the remnants of her migraine mocking her. *Khalis Tannous is not your ex-husband. Not even close. All you have is a professional relationship.*

'You still don't trust me,' Khalis said quietly. 'Do you? To handle my father's collection properly.'

Grace was not about to admit this wasn't really about the art. It went deeper, darker, and she didn't even understand why. She barely knew this man. She met his gaze as levelly as she could. 'I don't even know you.'

'And yet,' Khalis observed, 'if I intended to keep the paintings or sell them on the black market, contacting your company would be just about the most idiotic thing I could do. Your lack of trust borders on ridiculous, Grace.'

She knew that. She knew his intentions towards the art had to be legitimate. And yet she couldn't keep her frightened instinct from kicking in, from remembering how it felt to be like one of those paintings in that vault, adored and hidden away, for no one else to see. It had been a miserable life for her, just as it was for Leda. And it coloured her response to this man, in shades too dark for her to admit.

And as for what was ridiculous... When he said her name, in really, a completely normal tone of voice...why did it make her insides unfurl, like a seedling seeking sunlight? *That* was absurd. 'It might seem ridiculous to you,' she said stiffly, 'but I've experienced enough to be justified in my lack of trust.'

'Experienced professionally? Or personally?'

'Both,' she said flatly, and began to butter her toast. Khalis was silent for a long moment, but she could still feel his speculation as he sipped his coffee. She'd said too much. Just one word, but it had been too much. Not that it mattered. All it would take was one internet search for Khalis to learn her history, or at least some of it. Not the most painful parts, but still enough to hurt. Perhaps he'd learned it already, although his air of unconcern suggested otherwise.

'So,' he finally said, 'what will you do after you catalogue the paintings and check them against this register?'

'Run preliminary tests on the ones that do not appear to come from any museum. I don't suppose your father kept any files on his artwork?'

'I don't think so.'

'Most paintings of any real value have certificates of

authentication. It's virtually impossible to sell a valuable painting without one.'

'You're saying my father should have these certificates?'

'Of the ones that are not stolen, yes. Obviously the stolen works' certificates would remain with the museums they were taken from. Really, some legal authority should be contacted. Interpol, or the FBI's Art Crimes department—'

'No.' He still spoke evenly enough, but his voice made Grace go cold. It reminded her of Loukas's implacable tone when she'd asked to go to Athens for a shopping trip. One miserable little shopping trip, for things for Katerina. She'd said nothing then, and she said nothing now. Perhaps she hadn't changed as much as she'd hoped. 'I'm not ready to have law enforcement of any kind swarming over this compound and investigating everything.'

'You're hiding something,' she said, the words seeming to scrape her throat.

'My father hid plenty of things,' he corrected. 'And I intend to find out what they all were before I invite the law in.'

'So you can decide which ones to reveal and which ones to keep hiding?'

Ice flashed in his eyes and he leaned forward, his hand encircling her wrist, his movements precise and controlled, yet radiating a leashed and lethal power. 'Let me be very clear. I am not corrupt. I am not a criminal. I do not intend to allow Tannous Enterprises to continue to engage in any illegal activity. But neither do I intend to hand the reins over to a bunch of bureaucratic, bumbling policemen who might be as interested in lining their pockets as my father was. Understood?'

'Let go of my wrist,' she said coldly, and Khalis looked

down as if surprised he was touching her. He hadn't grabbed her, hadn't hurt her at all, yet she felt as if he had.

'I'm sorry.' He released her, then let out a gusty sigh as he raked a hand through his hair. 'I'm sorry if I scared you.' Grace said nothing. She wasn't about to explain that she had been scared, or why. Khalis gave her a thoughtful look from under his lashes, his mouth pursed. 'You've been hurt, haven't you? By a man.'

Shock caused her to freeze, her nerveless fingers almost dropping her coffee cup before she replaced it on its saucer. 'That,' she said, 'is none of your business.'

'You're right. Again, I apologise.' He looked away; the silence in the room felt electric. 'So these preliminary tests. What are they?'

'I need to see what facilities are in the basement. Artwork, especially older artwork, needs to be handled very carefully. A few minutes' exposure to sunlight can cause irreparable damage. But I would expect to analyse the pigments used, as well as use infrared photography to determine what preliminary sketches are underneath the paintings. If I have the right equipment, I can test for the age of the wood of the panels used. This is an especially good way of dating European masters, since they almost always painted on wood.'

'The two in the back room are on wood.'

'Yes.'

'Interesting.' He shook his head slowly. 'Really quite fascinating.'

'I certainly think so.'

He shot her a quick smile and she realised how invigorating it was to have a man actually interested in her work. During their marriage, Loukas had preferred for her never to discuss it, much less practise her chosen profession.

She'd gone along for the sake of marital accord, but it had tried her terribly. Too terribly.

'I'd better let you get to it,' Khalis said, and Grace nodded, pushing away her plate. She'd only eaten half a piece of toast, but she had little appetite.

'Eric will escort you to the basement. Let me know if there is anything you require.' And, with another parting smile, Khalis took his computer and left the room. Grace watched him go, hating that she suddenly felt so lonely.

The rest of the day was spent in the laborious yet ultimately rewarding work of checking all the artworks against the international Art Loss Register. The results were dispiriting. Many of the paintings, as Grace had suspected, were stolen. It made her job of authentication and appraisal easier, yet it saddened her to think of how many paintings had been lost to the public, in some cases for generations.

At noon the young woman who had served her meals earlier brought down a plate of sandwiches and a carafe of coffee. 'Mr Tannous said you needed to eat,' she murmured in hesitant English, and Grace felt a curious mingling of gratitude for his thoughtfulness and disappointment that she wouldn't see him.

Stupid. She hadn't really expected to share another meal with him, had she? Last night had been both an introduction and an aberration. Even so, she could not deny the little sinking feeling she had at the thought of an afternoon working alone. It had never bothered her before; she was certainly used to solitude. It wouldn't bother her now. Frowning, she turned back to her laptop with grim concentration.

Immersed in her work, she wasn't really aware of time passing until she heard a light tap-tap at the door of the lab across from the vault where she'd set up her temporary office. She looked up to see Khalis standing in the doorway. He had changed from his dark trousers and silk shirt of this morning into board shorts and a T-shirt that hugged the lean sculpted muscles of his chest. His hair was a little rumpled.

'You've been at it for eight hours.'

She blinked, surprised even as she felt the muscles in her neck cramp. 'I have?'

'Yes. It's six o'clock in the evening.'

She shook her head, smiling a little, unable to staunch the ripple of pleasure she felt at seeing him. 'I was completely absorbed.'

He smiled back. 'So it would appear. I didn't realise art appraisal was *that* fascinating.'

'I've checked all the works against—'

'No, no talk about art and theft or work. It's time to relax.'

'Relax?' she repeated warily. Both Eric and Khalis seemed big on relaxing, yet she had no intention of letting down her guard, and especially not with this man. Last night's headache episode had been bad enough. She didn't intend to give him another chance to get close, to *affect* her.

'Yes, relax,' Khalis said. 'The sun will set in another hour, and before it does I want to go for a swim.'

'Please, don't let me stop you.'

His mouth quirked in another smile. 'I want you to go with me.'

Her heart seemed to fling itself against her ribs at the thought. 'I don't—'

'Swim? I could teach you. We'll start with the dog paddle.' He mimed a child's paddling stroke and Grace found herself smiling. Again.

'I think I can manage to keep myself afloat, thanks very

much.' Strange, how light he made her feel. How *happy*. It was as dangerous and addictive as the physical response her body had to him. She shook her head. 'I really should get this done—'

Khalis dropped his arms to his sides. 'It's not good to work without taking a break, especially considering the strength of your migraine last night. I let you work through lunch, but you really need to take some time off.'

'Most employers don't insist on their staff taking time off.'

'I'm not most employers. Besides, you're not actually my employee. I'm your client.'

'Still—'

'Anyone with sense knows that people work more effectively when they're rested and relaxed. At least they know that in California.' He held out one hand, his long lean fingers stretching so enticingly towards her. 'Come on.'

She absolutely shouldn't take his hand. *Touch* him. And she shouldn't go for a swim. She shouldn't even *want* to go for a swim, because she didn't want to want anyone ever again. As for love, trust, desire...? Forget it. Forget them all.

And yet... And yet she remained motionless, hesitating, suspended with suppressed longing, because no matter what her brain told her about staying safe, strong and in control, her body and maybe even her heart said differently. They said, *Yes. Please.*

'Do you have a swimming costume?'

Reluctantly she nodded. She had brought one, despite what she'd told Michel.

'Well, then? What's stopping you?'

You. Me. The physical temptation that the very idea of

a swim with Khalis presented. The two of them, in the water and wearing very little.

And then there was the far more alarming emotional temptation…to draw closer to this man, to care about him when she couldn't care about anyone. Never mind what restrictions her ex-husband had placed on her, her heart had far more stringent ones.

'Grace.' He said her name not as a question or a command, but as a statement. As if he knew her. And when he did that Grace felt as though she had no choice, and it both aggravated and amazed her. How could she fight this?

She reached out and took his hand. His fingers closed around hers with both strength and gentleness, and he glanced at her carefully, as if he needed to check she was OK. And, after the way she had yanked her hand away from his last night, he probably did.

Taking a breath, Grace met his questioning gaze—and nodded her assent.

Khalis felt an entirely triumphant thrill as he led her from the basement, up into the sunshine and fresh air. He felt as if he'd won a major victory, not against her, but for her. Something about Grace's hidden vulnerability called out to him, made him want to offer her both protection and pleasure. He'd spent the better part of the day thinking about her, wondering what she was doing, thinking, feeling. Wondering about the man who had hurt her and how soft her lips would be if—*when*—he kissed her.

It had been a long time since he'd been in a relationship, even longer since a woman had aroused these kinds of protective feelings in him. Never before, if he were honest, at least not on a romantic, sexual level. The last woman who he'd been emotionally close to had been his sister. Jamilah.

And look what happened then.

Khalis resolutely pushed the thought away. It was just this island, these memories that were temporarily awakening his emotions.

This woman.

It would pass, Khalis told himself. He'd leave Alhaja and get back to his normal life soon enough. And in the meantime Grace provided a welcome distraction.

Except to think of her as a distraction was to think of her dismissively, as something disposable, and he knew he didn't. Couldn't. Already it had become something more, and he didn't know whether to be alarmed, annoyed or amazed. Perhaps he was all three. But, for right now, all he wanted was a simple swim.

Up in the foyer, she stopped, pulled her hand away from his with firm purpose. 'I need to change.'

'Why don't I meet you at the pool?'

'All right.'

Fifteen minutes later a stiff and self-conscious Grace approached the pool area. He was sitting on the edge of the pool waiting for her, dangling his legs in the water, enjoying the last golden rays of sunshine. He took in her appearance in one swift and silent glance. Her swimming costume was appalling. Well, appalling might be too strong a word. It fitted, at least. But it was black and very modest, with a high neckline and a little skirt that covered her thighs. She looked like a grandmother. A very sexy grandmother, but still. Clearly she meant to hide her attractions. He smiled. Even a ridiculous swimming costume couldn't make Grace Turner unattractive. Her long, slim legs remained on elegant display, and a swimming costume was, after all, a swimming costume. Her generous curves were also on enticing view.

She stiffened under his rather thorough inspection and then tilted her chin in that proud, defensive way he was coming to know so well. He stretched out his hand, which she ignored, instead moving gingerly to the steps that led into the shallow end.

'The water's warm,' he offered.

'Lovely.' She dipped a toe in, then stood on the first step, up to her ankles, looking as if she were being tortured.

'Lovely, you said?' he teased, his voice rich with amusement, and she looked startled before giving him a very small smile.

'I'm sorry. I'm not used to this.'

'And here you told me you could swim.'

Impatiently, she shook her head, gesturing between them with one hand. *'This.'*

And he knew—of course he knew—that she felt it, too. This connection, this energy between them. And, while it alarmed him, he had a feeling it *terrified* her. He saw that, felt it and, without thinking too much about what he was doing—or why—he slipped waist-deep into the water and strode towards her. She watched him approach with wide, wary eyes. He stopped a few feet away and gave her a little splash. She blinked, bewildered.

'What are you doing?'

'Having fun?' Her mouth tightened and she looked quickly away. Intrigued, he asked softly, 'Is there something wrong with that?'

'No,' she said, but she didn't sound convinced. He splashed her again, gently, and to his relief he got a little smile, a sudden flash of fire in her eyes.

'You're asking for it, aren't you?'

Desperately. He waited, watched as she trailed her fingers in the water. She had beautiful fingers, long and slim with elegant rounded nails. His gaze was still fixed on them when she suddenly lifted her hand and hit the water hard with the flat of her palm, sending a wave of water crashing over him, leaving him blinking and spluttering. And laughing, because it was just about the last thing he'd expected.

He sluiced the water from his face and grinned at her. She smiled back, almost tremulously, as if her lips weren't used to it. 'Got you.'

'Yes,' he said, and his voice came out in a husky murmur. 'You did.' Even in that awful swimming costume, she was incredibly, infinitely desirable. And when she smiled he was lost. He felt his fears fall away when he looked at her, any alarm that this was all going too fast and too deep seemed ridiculous. He wanted this. He wanted her. He took a step towards her and she stilled, and then another step so he was close enough to feel her breath feather his face, see the pulse beating in her throat. Then he leaned down and kissed her.

It was the gentlest kind of kiss, his mouth barely brushing over hers. She didn't move away, but she trembled. Her lips parted, but it didn't feel like surrender. It felt like surprise. He reached with one hand to cradle her face, his palm cupping the curve of her cheek, revelling in the satiny softness of her skin. It didn't last more than a few seconds, but it felt endless and yet no time at all. And then it was over.

With a ragged gasp she tore away, stared at him with eyes wide with shock and even anger.

'Grace—'

He didn't get the chance to say any more. As if she had the devil himself on her heels, she scrambled out of the pool, slipping on the wet tiles and landing hard on one knee before lurching upright and running back into the villa.

CHAPTER FIVE

STUPID. Stupid, stupid, stupid idiot—

The litany of self-recrimination echoed remorselessly through her as Grace ran through the villa, pounded up the stairs and then into her room, slamming and locking the door behind her as if Khalis were actually chasing her.

She let out a shuddering breath and then turned from the door, tearing the swimming costume from her body before she went to the en suite bathroom and started the shower.

What had possessed her to go swimming? To splash him? *Flirt?* When he'd moved closer to her in the water she'd known—of course she'd known—what he intended to do. In that moment she'd wanted him to kiss her. And the feel of his lips on hers, his hand on her cheek, had been so unbearably, achingly wonderful—until realisation slammed into her and Katerina's face swam in her vision, reminding her just how much she had to lose.

And not just Katerina, Grace thought with a surge of self-recrimination. What about herself? Her freedom? Her *soul*? Marriage to Loukas had nearly destroyed her. He'd levelled her identity, his words and actions a veritable emotional earthquake, and for years afterwards she'd felt blank, a cipher of a person. Working at Axis had helped restore some of her sense of self, yet she still felt as if she drifted through parts of life, had empty spaces and yawning silences where other people had companionship and joy. And perhaps she always would feel that way, as long as she didn't have her daughter. But she'd at least keep herself, Grace thought fiercely. She'd keep her identity, her independence, her strength. She wouldn't give those away to the first man who kissed her, even if his gentleness nearly undid her.

Grace stepped into the shower and let the hot water rush over her, wash away the memory of Khalis's gentle touch. She felt that endless ache of loneliness deep inside, a well of emptiness she'd convinced herself she'd got used to. Preferred, even. Yet it had only taken one man—one touch—for her to realise just how lonely she really was. She might be strong and safe and independent, but a single kiss had made her achingly aware of the depths of her own unhappiness.

Swallowing hard, she turned off the taps and stepped out of the shower. Work. Work would help. It always did. Quickly she dressed, pulled her damp hair into another serviceable ponytail and then headed downstairs.

Eric had given her a temporary password for the lift's security system and Grace used it, glancing around quickly in search of Khalis. He was nowhere to be found.

Squaring her shoulders, she entered the laboratory that Balkri Tannous had had built to verify the authenticity of the artworks, stolen or otherwise, he acquired on the black market. Grace had been reluctantly impressed by his thoroughness; the laboratory held all the necessary equipment for infrared photography, pigment analysis, dendrochronology and many of the other tests necessary to authenticate a work of art.

She opened her laptop, stared blankly at the catalogue she'd made of the vault's inventory; she'd already checked

most of it against the Art Loss Register. It would take another hour or two to finish, yet now she couldn't summon
the energy to do it. Instead she slipped off her stool and
went back into the vault, past all the canvases in the main
room, to the tiny little shrine in the back. She flicked on
the lights and sat on the room's one chair; clearly this
room had been meant only for Balkri Tannous. She let
out a shuddering breath as she stared at the painted wood
panels.

The first one, of Leda and the Swan, she'd seen many
times before. Not the original, of course, but very good
copies. The original, for she didn't really doubt this was
the original, had been painted on three wooden panels.
The panels had split apart—that had been documented
four hundred years ago—but someone had very carefully
repaired them. The damaged sections of the painting had
been restored, although Grace could still see where the
damage had occurred. Still, the painting was incredibly
arresting. Leda stood naked and voluptuous, yet with her
head bowed in virginal modesty. Her face was turned away
as if she were resisting the advances of the sinuous swan,
but she had a sensual little half-smile on her face, remi-
niscent of the Mona Lisa. Did she welcome Zeus's attentions? Had she any idea of the heartbreak that lay ahead
of her?

'There you are.'

Grace tensed, even though she wasn't really surprised
that Khalis had found her. The overwhelming emotional
response she'd felt when he kissed her had receded to a
weary resignation that felt far more familiar. Safer, too.
'Do you think she looks happy?' she asked, nodding towards Leda.

Khalis studied the painting. 'I think she's not sure what
she feels, or what she wants.'

Grace's gaze remained fixed on Leda's little half-smile, her face turned away from the swan. 'I can't become involved with you, in any way,' she said quietly. 'Not even a kiss.'

Khalis propped one shoulder against the doorway to the little room. 'Can't,' he asked, 'or won't?'

'Both.'

'Why not?'

Another deep breath. 'It's unprofessional to be involved with a client—'

'You didn't sprint from the pool because it was unprofessional.' Khalis cut her off affably enough, although she sensed the steel underneath. 'How's your knee?'

It ached abominably, but Grace had no intention of saying that, or explaining any more. 'There's no point in pressing the matter.'

'You're attracted to me, Grace.'

'It doesn't matter.'

'Do you still not trust me?' he asked quietly. 'Is that it? Are you afraid—of me?'

She let out a little sigh and turned to face him. He looked so achingly beautiful just standing there, wearing faded jeans and a grey T-shirt that hugged the sculpted muscles of his chest. His ink-black hair was rumpled, his eyes narrowed even though he was smiling, a half-smile like Leda's.

'I'm not afraid of you,' she said, and meant it. She might not trust him, but she didn't fear him, either. She simply didn't want to let him have the kind of power opening your body or heart to someone would give. And then, of course, there was Katerina. So many reasons not to get involved.

'What, then?' She just shook her head. 'I know you've been hurt,' he said quietly and she let out a sad little laugh. He was painting his own picture of her, she knew then, a happy little painting like one his god-daughter might make. Too bad he had the wrong paintbox.

'And how do you know that?' she asked.

'It's evident in everything you do and say—'

'No, it isn't.' She rose from the chair, half-inclined to disabuse him of his fanciful notion that she'd been hurt. She *had* been hurt, but not the way he thought. She'd never been an innocent victim, as much as she wished things could be that simple. And she knew, to her own shame and weakness, that she wouldn't say anything. She didn't want him to look at her differently. With judgement rather than compassion, scorn instead of sympathy.

'Why can't you get involved then, Grace?' Khalis asked. 'It was just a kiss, after all.' He'd moved to block the doorway, even though Grace hadn't yet attempted to leave. His face looked harsh now, all hard angles and narrowed eyes, even though his body remained relaxed. A man of contradictions—or was it simply deception? Which was the real man, Grace wondered—the smiling man who'd rubbed her feet so gently, or the angry son who refused to grieve for the family he'd just lost? Or was he both, showing one face to the world and hiding another, just as she was?

It didn't matter. She could not have anything more to do with Khalis Tannous except the barest of professional acquaintances. 'It's complicated, and I don't feel like explaining it to you,' she said shortly. 'But if you've done any digging on the internet, you'll be aware of the details.'

'Is that an invitation?'

She shrugged. 'Just a fact.'

'I'm not some internet stalker,' Khalis told her flatly. 'I'd prefer to hear the truth from you, rather than some gossip website.' She said nothing and he sighed, raking a hand through his hair. Grace nodded towards the exit he was still blocking.

'I should get back to work.'

'It's after seven.'

'Still. If I start running the preliminary tests now, you should have enough information to contact a legal authority in a day or two.'

'Is that what you want?' He gazed at her almost fiercely, and she felt a spasm of longing to walk into his arms, to tell him everything. To feel safe and desired all at once.

Ridiculous. *Dangerous*. To do such a thing would be to open herself up to all kinds of shame and pain, and it would certainly put an end to feeling safe or desired.

'Of course it is,' she said and made to walk past him. He didn't move, so she had to squeeze past in the narrow doorway, her breasts brushing his chest, every point of contact seeming to sizzle and snap her nerve endings to life. She looked up at him, which was a mistake. His eyes blazed need and for an endless charged moment she thought he would kiss her again. He'd grab her and take her right there, with Leda watching with her half-smile. She wouldn't resist, not in that moment. She wouldn't be able to. But instead he stepped back and as she moved past he let out a shuddering breath. She kept walking.

Half an hour later he sent a dinner tray down to the lab. He'd included a snowy-white linen napkin, sterling silver cutlery, and even a carafe of wine and a crystal wine glass. His thoughtfulness made her ache. Did he realise how he was taking apart her defences with these little gestures? Could he possibly know how much they hurt, because they made her afraid and needy all at once?

She picked at the meal, alone in the sterile, windowless lab, feeling lonelier than ever and hating that she did.

Then she determinedly pushed the tray away and turned back to her work.

She didn't see him all the next day, although she felt his presence. At breakfast he'd left a newspaper by her plate, already turned to the Arts section. He'd even written a funny little comment next to one of the editorials, making her smile. She pushed the paper away and drank her coffee and ate her toast alone before heading back downstairs.

Work kept her from thinking too much about him, although he remained on the fringes of her mind, haunting her thoughts like a gentle ghost. She'd had Eric help her move the panels into the lab, and she started running a basic dendrochronology test on the wood. At noon the young woman—her name, Grace had learned, was Shayma—brought her sandwiches and coffee. The tray also held a narrow vase with a single calla lily. After Shayma had left Grace reached for the lily and brushed the fragrant petals against her lips. She closed her eyes, remembering how Loukas had sent her roses. She'd been so touched at the time, grieving her father's death, needing someone's attention and love. Only later did she wonder if the flowers had been a genuine expression of his affection, or just a rote seduction. Did it even matter when things had broken down, or what had been real? She'd learned her lesson. She'd learned it the hard way, which was why this had to stop.

She shoved the tray away and turned back to her work. She worked the rest of the day, through dinner, and went directly up to her room. Both exhausted and restless, she fell into an uneasy sleep.

The next day followed the same pattern. She analysed the pigments used in both the Leonardos, and ate from trays brought down by Shayma. And thought about Khalis.

She could feel his presence in every thoughtful touch, from the different flowers on her tray to the newspaper left on the breakfast table, to the subtle changes in the lab: better lighting, a more comfortable chair. How did he even know? She didn't see him at all, though, and she realised she missed him.

An emotion, she knew, she didn't want and couldn't afford to feel. Over the last four years loneliness was a price she'd always been willing to pay for her freedom. Yet in just the space of a few days Khalis had opened up a sweet yearning inside her, a longing for a closeness she'd denied herself and half-forgotten. A longing that terrified her on so many levels.

That night she left the lab craving fresh air, and slipped out of the doors in the back of the entrance hall that led to the interior courtyard of the villa. She stopped by the pool, now still and empty, and realised by the flash of disappointment she felt that she'd been hoping to see him there. Amazing, how deceptive her own heart could be. She'd convinced herself she simply wanted some air but, really, she wanted Khalis.

She pressed her hands to her temples, as if she could will the want away. *Think what you have to lose. Your daughter. The precious moments you have with her. One Saturday a month. Just twelve days a year.*

She started walking down one of the twisting garden paths as fast as she could, as if she could outrun her thoughts. But they chased her, relentless in their power. *Let a man close and not only will you lose your daughter, you'll lose yourself. Khalis can't be that different. And, even if he is...you aren't.*

Yet right now she wanted to be different. She craved the possibility of a loving, generous, equal relationship.

Impossible. Even if it existed, she couldn't have it. She

couldn't risk it, and yet, for the sake of one man, one unbearably kind and gentle man, she was tempted to try. To throw it all away—and for what? A kiss? An affair? She could not believe she could be so weak…again.

Suddenly a pair of strong hands clamped around her shoulders and she let out a shocked yelp.

'It's just me.' Khalis loomed in front of her, his smile gleaming in the moonlight. She could feel the heat radiating from his lithe body.

'You startled me.'

'So I see.' He released her and stepped back. 'I was out here walking as well, and you almost crashed into me.'

'I'm sorry.'

'It's OK.'

They stood there, a foot or so separating them, yet, considering the nature of her recent thoughts, it felt like an endless chasm. She wanted to walk into his arms and run away both at the same time. She was, Grace thought, an emotional schizophrenic. The sooner she got off this island the better.

'Do you want to walk with me?' Khalis asked and, after a charged pause, she nodded. *Compromise.* There was not room on the narrow little paths to walk side by side, so Khalis let her go first, wending her way among the fragrant foliage, the silver swathe the moon cut through the gardens their only guide.

'Did you play out here?' Grace asked. 'When you were a child?'

Khalis shrugged. 'Sometimes.'

'With your brother?'

'Not really. With my…' A second's pause. 'With my sister.'

'I didn't realise you had a sister.'

'She died.'

'Oh!' Grace turned around. Even in the darkness she saw how hooded his expression seemed. 'So your whole family has died,' she said quietly. 'I'm sorry.'

'So has yours.'

'Yes…' She felt a shudder run through her. 'But it must be harder for you, to lose siblings—'

'I do miss my sister,' Khalis said, the words seeming to be drawn reluctantly from him, although he spoke with a quiet evenness. 'I never had a chance to say goodbye to her.'

'How did she die?'

'A boating accident, right off the coast here. She was nineteen.' He sighed, digging his hands into his pockets. 'She was about to be married. My father had arranged it, but she didn't like the chosen groom.'

Grace frowned, connecting the pieces, threaded together by the darkness of Khalis's tone. 'Do you think it…it wasn't an accident?'

He didn't answer for a long moment. 'I don't know. I hate to think that, but she was determined in her own way, and it would have been a way to escape the marriage.'

'A terrible way.'

'Sometimes life is terrible,' Khalis said, and his voice was bleak. 'Sometimes there are only terrible choices.'

'Yes,' Grace said quietly. 'I think that's true.'

He gave her a wryly sorrowful smile, his teeth gleaming in the darkness. 'I never speak of my sister. Not to anyone. What is it about you, Grace, that makes me say things I wouldn't say to another soul? And *want* to say them?'

She shook her head, her heart thudding treacherously. 'I don't know.'

'Do you feel it?' he asked in a low voice, and in the soft darkness of the garden she couldn't deny or pretend.

'Yes,' she said, the word no more than a thread of sound.

'It scares you.'

Of course it does. She took a deep breath. 'I told you before, I can't—'

'Don't give me that,' Khalis said almost roughly. 'You think this is easy for me and hard for you?'

'No—' Yet she realised she had thought that. He seemed so relaxed and assured, so comfortable with what stretched and strengthened between them, and she was the only one quaking with nerves and memories and fear. She let out a wobbly laugh. 'Maybe it's just the island.'

'The island?'

She gestured to the dense fragrant foliage around them. 'It's like a place and time apart, separate from reality. We can say what we want here. Feel what we want.'

'Except,' Khalis said quietly, 'I don't think you know what you want to feel.'

She felt a sudden spark of anger. 'Don't patronise me.'

'Am I wrong?'

She swallowed and looked away. 'I already explained to you—'

'You didn't explain anything,' Khalis said, cutting her off. He sighed, stepping towards her, his hand resting on her shoulder. 'Life hasn't been very fair to you, has it, Grace?'

She tensed under his touch, as well as his assumption. 'Life isn't very fair,' she said in a low voice.

'No,' Khalis agreed. His hand was warm and heavy on her shoulder, a comforting weight she longed to lean into. 'Life isn't very fair at all. I think we've both learned that the hard way.'

Her whole body tensed, fighting the desire to lean into him. It was like trying to resist a magnetic force. 'Maybe,' she said, the word half-strangled.

'And here we are,' he mused softly, 'two people completely alone in this world.'

Her throat tightened with emotion. This man made her feel so much. 'I feel alone,' she whispered, the words drawn from her painfully. She almost choked on them. 'I feel alone all the time.'

His hand still rested on one shoulder, and he laid his other hand on her shoulder and drew her gently to him. 'I know you do,' he said quietly. 'So do I.' She rested in the circle of his arms for a moment, savouring the closeness as she breathed in the woodsy scent of his aftershave, felt the comforting heat of his body. It felt so good, so safe, and it would be so easy to stay here, or even to tilt her head up for him to kiss her. So easy, and so dangerous.

Think what you have to lose.

Resolutely she turned away from him, jerking away from his grasp, not wanting him to see the storm of unwilling need she knew would be apparent on her face. She plunged down the twisting path, only to stop abruptly when it ended against a stone wall. The wall that surrounded the villa, the moon illuminating the evil shards of broken glass on its top, reminding her that she was a prisoner. Always a prisoner.

In a sudden burst of fury, Grace slapped her hands against the stone, her palms stinging, as if she could topple it over. 'I hate walls,' she cried in frustration, knowing it was a ridiculous thing to say, to *think*, yet feeling it with every breath and bone.

'Then let's leave them behind,' Khalis said and reached for her hand. Too surprised to resist, she let him lead her away from the wall and down another dark path.

Khalis kept hold of her hand as he guided her down several paths and then finally to a door. The high, forbidding wall had a door, and Khalis possessed the key. Grace watched as he activated the security system, first with his fingerprint and then a number code, before swinging the door open and leading her out to freedom.

The air felt cooler, fresher and more pure without the walls. Khalis led her away from the compound and down a rocky little path towards the shore.

He still held her hand, his fingers wrapped warm and sure around hers as he guided her down the path to the silky sweep of sand. She heard the roar of the waves crashing onto the shore and saw the beach nestled in a rocky cove, now washed in silver.

'This feels better,' she said, as if she'd just had a little dizzy spell.

'Why do you hate walls so much?'

She tugged her hand out of his. 'Who likes them?'

'Nobody really, I suppose, but it seems personal to you.'

Grace kept her gaze on the silvered sea. 'It is. I used to live on an island like this. Private, remote, with high walls. I didn't like it.'

'Couldn't you leave?'

'Not easily.'

She could feel him staring at her, trying to figure her out, even though her back was to him. 'Are you saying,' he asked finally, 'you were some kind of prisoner?'

She sighed. 'Not really. Not literally. But other things can imprison you besides walls.' She turned so she was half-facing him. 'Hopes. Fears.' She paused, her gaze sliding to and then locking with his. 'Mistakes. Memories.'

She felt tension snake through him, even though he kept his voice light. 'That sounds like psychobabble.'

'It probably is,' she admitted with a shrug. 'But can you really deny this island has an effect on you?'

Khalis didn't answer for a moment. 'No,' he said finally, 'I can't.'

Neither of them spoke for a moment, the truth of what he'd said seeming to reverberate through them. 'What will you do with this place?' Grace asked eventually. 'Will you live here?'

He gave a harsh laugh. 'After what you just observed? No, never. Once I've finished going through my father's assets, I'll sell it.'

'Will you manage Tannous Enterprises from the States, then?'

'I don't intend to manage Tannous Enterprises at all. I'm going to dismantle it and sell it off piece by piece, so no one has that kind of power again.'

'Sell it?' Even in the moonlit darkness she could make out the hard set of his jaw, the flintiness in his eyes. 'I thought you were going to turn it around. Redeem it.'

He looked away from her, out to the sea. 'Some things can't be redeemed.'

'Do you really think so?' She felt a sudden sorrowful twist of disappointment inside her. 'I like to think they can. I like to think any…mistake can be forgiven, if not rectified.'

'My father is not alive for me to forgive him,' Khalis said flatly. 'If I even wanted to.'

'You don't?'

'Why should I? Do you know what kind of man my father was?'

'Sort of, but—'

'Shh.' Smiling now, Khalis drew her to him and pressed one finger to her lips. His touch was soft and yet electric, the press of his skin against her lips making the bottom of her stomach seem to drop right out. 'I didn't bring you to this moonlit cove to talk about my father.'

'I could tell you about what I've discovered about the panels—' Grace began. Her heart beat hard in her chest for she could not mistake the look of intent in Khalis's eyes. Or the answering pulse of longing she felt in herself.

He laughed softly. 'I didn't bring you here for that, either.'

Her heart thudded harder. 'Why, then?'

'To have you kiss me.'

Shock made her mouth drop right open and he traced the curve of her parted lips with the tip of his finger. A soft sigh escaped her before she could suppress it. 'Kiss you—'

'The reaction when I kissed you was not quite what I was hoping for,' Khalis explained, a hint of humour in his voice although his gaze blazed into hers. 'So I thought perhaps we'd try it the other way.'

His finger still rested on her mouth, making her dizzy. 'How do you know I even want to kiss you?' she challenged.

'Do you?'

How could she lie? His gaze was hungry and open; he hid nothing. And she hid so much. From him, and even from herself. For even if she didn't want to want him, she knew she did. And she wouldn't hide it. 'Yes,' she whispered, and Khalis waited.

Grace took a shuddering breath. Just one kiss. One kiss no one would ever know about. And then she'd walk away, go back to being safe and strong and independent. Slowly she reached out and touched his cheek, his own hand falling away from her mouth. She took a step towards him so her breasts brushed his chest. He gazed down at her, still, steady. Trustworthy.

Her palm cradled his cheek, the tips of her fingers brushing the softness of his hair. She leaned closer, so her body pressed fully against his and she could feel the hard thrust of his arousal. And then she kissed him.

CHAPTER SIX

Her lips barely brushed his, but Khalis held himself still, and Grace knew he was purposely letting her control the kiss. She closed her eyes, luxuriating in the feel and taste of him. He tasted like mint and whisky, a sensual combination. His lips were soft and yet his yielding touch was firm, so that even though she was in charge she knew it was only because he allowed it. And somehow that made her feel safe rather than threatened or repressed.

Gently she touched her tongue to his lips, exploring the seam of his mouth, the caress a question. She felt a shudder go through him but he didn't move. She pulled away, blinking up at him with a new shyness. She saw his eyes were closed, his body rigid. He looked almost as if he were in pain, but surely he couldn't be…unless it was costing him to remain so still.

'A kiss involves a bit of give and take, you know,' she told him.

He opened his eyes, giving her a wry smile. 'I didn't want to scare you off.'

'I don't scare quite that easily.' At least she hoped she didn't.

'No?' His arms came around her, gently, slowly, giving her time to pull away. She didn't. She'd allow herself this one moment, that was all. In a minute she'd step away.

'Good,' Khalis murmured, and Grace slid her hands up along the hard wall of his chest, lacing her fingers around his neck as she pulled his mouth down towards her. And then she kissed him again, deeply this time, a plunging sensation in her stomach as he responded in kind, their tongues tangling in a blaze of exquisite sensation. When had she last kissed like this? Felt like this?

You know when.

A shudder ran through her, a shudder of both longing and loss. It felt so wonderful and it had been so long, and yet just the memory of a man holding her made the memories rise up, the shame rushing through her in a hot, fast river, along with the desire and the hope. She closed her eyes and kissed Khalis more deeply, pressing herself against him, wanting desperately to banish the memories that taunted her even now.

You kissed a man like this. You wanted a man like this. And it cost you your daughter.

She felt Khalis's hands span her waist, then slide under her T-shirt. The warmth of his palm against her skin made her shudder again and he stilled, waiting. He was so careful, so *caring*, yet she could not halt the relentless encroaching of her memories and that cold hard logic that swamped even her desire, and she knew he felt it, too.

'Grace…?'

She pulled away from him, her head bowed, her hair falling in front of her face. 'I'm sorry.'

'No need to be sorry.' He took her chin in his hand so he could study her face. See her blush. 'We don't need to rush this, do we?'

Yes, she wanted to say, *we do. Because this is all we have.*

'I shouldn't have kissed you.'

'It's a little late for regrets,' he said wryly and Grace jerked her chin from his hand.

'I know that.'

'Why shouldn't you have kissed me, Grace?'

'Because—' Her breath came out in a rush. *Because I'm scared. Of so many things. Of losing myself in you, and losing my daughter as well.* How could she explain all that? She couldn't, didn't want to, because to explain was to open herself up to all kinds of vulnerability and pain. She just shook her head.

Khalis let out a slow breath, the sound of controlled impatience. 'Are you married or something?'

She forced herself to meet his gaze levelly. 'No. But I was.'

He stilled, his eyes narrowing. 'You're divorced?'

'Yes.'

'I still don't understand.'

'It's…complicated.'

'That much I could guess.'

She turned away, wrapping her arms around herself. Now the wind felt cold. 'I just can't be involved with you,' she said quietly. 'My marriage wasn't… It wasn't happy. And I'm not…' She let out a little weary sigh. 'I can't…' She stopped again, her throat too tight for any more words.

'What,' he asked, 'would it take for you to trust me?'

Grace turned back to him, and she saw a man who had only been gentle and patient and kind. 'I don't know,' she whispered. 'But it doesn't matter, Khalis. I wish it did matter, in a way. But, even if I wanted to, I couldn't be in a relationship with you.' Belatedly she realised he'd never actually said that word. *Relationship.* It implied not just intimacy, but commitment. 'Or anything,' she added hurriedly. 'There can't be anything between us.' And, before he could answer, she walked quickly down the beach, back towards the door and that high, high wall.

That night she slept terribly. Memories came in fragments, as dreams, bizarre and yet making too much sense. Khalis kissing her. Her kissing Khalis. The sweet yearning of it, suddenly obliterated by the shame and guilt as she stared into Loukas's face so taut with anger, his lips compressed into an accusing line.

How could you do this to me, Grace? How could you betray me so?

With a cry she sat up in bed, the memory roiling through her mind, racking her body with shudders. Knowing she would not be able to get back to sleep, she rose from the bed and pulled on a pair of jeans and a light cotton jumper. She piled her hair up with a clip and slipped out of her room, along the cool, dark corridors and downstairs.

The basement felt eerily still in the middle of the night, even though Grace knew it should make no difference. The place had no windows. She switched on the lights and gazed down at the panels laid out on a stainless steel table.

She'd spent most of her time so far authenticating the first painting of Leda and the Swan, but now she let her gaze turn to the second painting, the one that caused a fresh shaft of pain to lance through her. Leda and her children.

Over the centuries there had been speculation about this painting; Leonardo had done several studies, a few sketches of Leda sitting, her face downcast, her children by her side. Yet the reality of the actual painting was far more powerful than any sketch. Unlike the other painting, in this one Leda was seated and clothed, the voluptuous temptress hidden or perhaps forgotten. Two children, Castor and Polydeuces, stood behind her, sturdy toddlers, their hands on her shoulders as if they were anchoring them-selves, or perhaps protecting their mother. Clytemnestra and Helen were rotund babies, lolling in Leda's lap, their angelic faces upturned towards their mother.

And Leda… What was the expression on her face? Was it sorrow, or wistfulness, or even a wary joy? Was there knowledge in those lowered eyes, knowledge of the terri-ble things to come? Helen would start a war. Castor would die in it. And Clytemnestra would lose a daughter.

Abruptly Grace turned away from the painting. If she worked for a few hours, she could present Khalis with a file of her findings tomorrow, enough for him to go on with, and for her to leave Alhaja. Leave Khalis. And they could both get on with their lives.

Khalis watched as a wan and fragile-looking Grace entered the breakfast room the next morning. She looked as if she'd barely slept, although her pale face was composed and as lovely as ever. She was dressed in a slim-fitting black skirt and white silk blouse and carried a file, and Khalis knew exactly what she was about. After last night's frustrating and half-finished kiss, he'd expected something like this. He sat back in his chair and sipped his coffee, waiting for her to begin.

'I've completed most of the preliminary tests on the Leonardos.'

'You have?'

She placed the file on the table, her lips pressed together in determination. 'Yes. The analyses of the pigments and the wood panels are consistent with the time period that he would have completed these paintings. There are also several—'

'Grace.'

She stopped, startled, and Khalis smiled at her. 'You don't need to give me a lecture. I'll read the file.'

Her lips thinned even more. 'All right, then.'

Khalis took a sip of his coffee. 'So you feel you've finished?'

'I've done all that I can do on my own. You really need to call a legal authority to—'

'Yes, I'll take care of that.'

She stopped, her eyes narrowing, and Khalis felt a sliver of hurt needle his soul. Did she *still* not trust him about the damn art? Then slowly, resolutely, she nodded. Acceptance, and he felt a blaze of gratified triumph.

'Very well.' She straightened, pressed her hands down the sides of her skirt. 'Then my work here is done. If you could arrange—'

'Done? Good.' Khalis smiled, saw the flash of hurt in her chocolate eyes that was quickly veiled. Suppressed, but he'd seen it and it gave fire to his purpose. No matter what she'd said last night, no matter how her ex-husband had hurt her so badly she trembled at the thought of a kiss, she still wanted to be with him. 'Then you can take the day off.'

'What…what do you mean?'

'A day of leisure, to enjoy yourself. With me.'

'I don't—'

'Your work was expected to take a week. It's been three days. I think you can take a day off.'

'I told you before—'

'One day. That's all. Surely you can allow yourself that?'

She hesitated, and he saw the longing in her eyes. What, he wondered yet again, kept her from enjoying herself? From *living*? 'You want to.' He leaned forward, not bothering to hide the need he was sure she could see in his eyes. The need he was sure she felt, too. '*I* want to. Please, Grace.'

Still she hesitated. Khalis waited. 'All right,' she said at last. She offered him a rather tentative smile. 'All right.'

Khalis couldn't keep himself from grinning. 'Wonderful. You'd better change into something a bit more serviceable, and I'll meet you in the foyer in five minutes.'

'That's rather quick.'

'I want to take advantage of every moment with you.'

A flush tinted her cheeks rose-pink and she turned away. 'One day,' she murmured, and he couldn't tell if she was warning him—or herself.

Grace hadn't brought too many serviceable clothes with her, at least not the kind she thought Khalis had in mind. While working she dressed with discreet professionalism, clothes that were flattering without being obvious. After a few moments' consideration she chose the slim black trousers and white fitted T-shirt she'd worn earlier in the week, and threw a cardigan in charcoal-grey cashmere over her shoulders, in case the breeze from the sea was strong.

Where could he be taking her? Alhaja Island hadn't looked that large from the air. Besides the enclosed compound, there were only a few stretches of beach and a tangle of trees. Yet Grace knew it didn't even matter where he might be taking her, because she simply wanted to be with him—for one day. One day that posed no risk to her heart or her time with Katerina. One day out of time and reality, a memory she would carry with her in all the lonely days and nights ahead.

Khalis was already waiting in the foyer when she came down the stairs, wearing jeans and a white button-down shirt, open at the throat, so Grace's gaze was inexorably drawn to that column of golden-brown skin, the pulse beating strongly. She jerked her gaze upwards and gave him a tentative smile.

'Where are we going?'

'Just to the beach,' he said, but there was a glint in his eye that told her he had something planned. Grace followed him outside to an open-topped Jeep waiting in the drive. She climbed in and fastened her seat belt as Khalis drove through the forbidding-looking gates and then out along a rutted dirt road that looked to circumnavigate the island.

Grace pushed her hair from her face and shaded her eyes as she glanced at the rocky outcrops and the stretch of golden beach, the sea jewel-bright and winking under the sun in every direction. 'This island's not very big, is it?'

'Two miles long and half a mile wide. Not large at all.'

'Did you ever feel…trapped? Living here?'

Khalis slid her a speculative glance and Grace pretended not to notice. 'Yes,' he answered after a moment, his hands tightening reflexively on the steering wheel, 'but not because of the island's size.'

'Why, then?'

His mouth curved grimly. 'Because of the island's inhabitants.'

'Your father?'

'Mainly. My brother and I didn't get along very well, either.'

'Why not?'

He shrugged. 'Ammar was my father's heir, and my father poured everything into him. He was tough with him, too tough, and I suppose Ammar needed to take it out on someone.'

'He was a bully? Your brother?'

Khalis just shrugged again. 'Boarding school was a bit of a relief.'

'What about your sister?'

He didn't answer for a moment, and Grace felt the tension in his body. 'I missed her,' he finally said. 'I'm sure she felt more trapped here than I did. My father didn't believe in educating daughters. He employed a useless governess for a while, but Jamilah never had the opportunities Ammar and I did. Opportunities she would have had if—' He stopped suddenly, shaking his head. His expression, Grace saw, had become shuttered. Closed. 'Old memories,' he said finally. 'Pointless.'

'Do you think,' she asked after a moment, 'the helicopter crash was an accident?'

'It's not outside the realm of possibility that one of his enemies—or even his allies—tinkered with the engine. I don't know what they would have hoped to gain. Perhaps it was an act of revenge—my father did business with the dregs of every society. People like that tend not to die in their beds.'

Grace felt a chill of trepidation at how indifferent Khalis sounded, as if the way his father and brother had died was a matter of little concern. His attitude towards his family was so different from the affable man she'd come to know and even to trust. Again she glimpsed a core of hard, unyielding iron underneath all that easygoing friendliness. 'You sound rather heartless,' she told him quietly.

'*I* sound heartless?' Khalis gave a short laugh. 'Good thing you never met my father.'

Grace knew she could not explain to Khalis why his opinion of his father disquieted her so much. She had heard rumours of Balkri Tannous, the bribes he took, the kind of shady business he conducted. Why was she, in her own twisted way, trying to defend him?

Because you still feel guilty. In need of forgiveness. Just like him.

'How did you find out?' she asked and Khalis did not pretend to misunderstand.

'I was sixteen,' he said quietly. 'Home from school for the summer holidays. I went looking for my father, to tell him I'd won the mathematics prize that year.' He lapsed into a silence and Grace knew he was remembering, saw the pain of that memory in the tautness of his face. 'I found him in his study. He was on the telephone, and he waved for me to sit down. I couldn't help but overhear him—not that he was trying to hide it. At first I didn't understand. He said something about money, and asking for more, and I thought he was just talking about business. Then he said, "You know what to do if he resists. Make sure he feels it this time." It sounded like something a school bully would say. I'd certainly heard such talk at school. But coming from my father—I couldn't credit it. So much so that when he got off the telephone I asked him about it, almost as if it were a joke. "Papa," I said, "it almost sounded like you were ordering someone to be beaten up!" My father gave me one hard look and then he said, "I was."'

Khalis said nothing more. He'd pulled the Jeep onto a flat stretch of beach and killed the engine, so the only sound was the crash of waves onto the shore and the distant raucous cry of gulls. 'And what then?' Grace asked, for she knew there was more.

He lifted one shoulder in something close to a shrug. 'I was shocked, of course. I don't remember what I said— something stupid about it being wrong. My father came over to me and slapped my face. Hard.' With a small smile he gestured to a tiny white scar on the corner of his mouth. 'His ring.'

'That's terrible,' Grace said quietly.

'Oh, it's not that terrible. I was sixteen, after all, almost a man. And he didn't hit me again. But it was shocking to me because he'd never hit me before. I'd adored him, and he loved to be adored. Ammar had it much worse. My father didn't pay much attention to me, although I always wanted him to. Until that day, when I realised just what kind of man he was.'

'But you didn't leave until you were twenty-one.'

Khalis's mouth tightened before he gave a hard smile. 'No. I made justifications for his activities, you see. Excuses. It was only the one time. The person he was dealing with was difficult or corrupt. So many absurd excuses because I didn't have the courage to just leave.'

'You were young,' Grace said softly. 'And that's easy to do.'

'For a while, perhaps, but then it's just wilful blindness. Even when I didn't want to, I started noticing things. The way the servants shrank from him, the telephone conversations he had. And then I started doing a bit of digging—I went through his desk once when he was away on business. He hadn't even locked his office—too arrogant to think his family would nose about. I probably saw enough in that one afternoon to put him in prison.' He shook his head. 'He helped rig an election in an island country that was desperately poor. My father lined his pockets and the people got poorer.'

'What did you do then?'

'Nothing.' Khalis practically spat the word. 'I was nineteen, about to start Cambridge, and I knew I couldn't manage on my own. So I just put it all back and tried to forget about it—for a little while at least. But I couldn't forget. I'll never forget.' Khalis shook his head, his eyes narrowed against the harsh glare of the sun, or perhaps just in memory.

Grace swallowed. 'And so you left.'

'Finally.' The one word was harsh with self-recrimination. 'I took his money to go to university first. I didn't work up the courage to leave until I knew I could make a go of it on my own.' His mouth twisted in condemnation of his own actions. 'So I wasn't really much better than he was.'

'That's rather harsh,' Grace protested. 'You weren't responsible for your father's actions.'

'No. But doing nothing can be as damaging as the action itself.'

'You were young—'

'Not that young.' He turned to her with a quick smile, his expression clearing although Grace still saw the storm clouds lurking in the depths of his agate eyes. 'You're very forgiving, much more forgiving than I am.' Grace looked away. Yes, she tried to be forgiving because she knew how easy it was to fall. The only person she couldn't forgive was herself. 'We've talked about this enough,' Khalis said. 'I didn't intend to spend the day with you raking up bitter memories. What is done, is done.'

'Is it?' Grace asked, her voice hoarse as she stared out to sea. 'Or does it just go on and on?'

Khalis gazed at her for a moment. 'It is done,' he said quietly. 'Whatever it is, Grace, it is done.'

She knew he didn't know what he was talking about, what secrets she still hid, and yet even so she wanted to believe him. She wanted to believe that things could really be finished, sins truly forgiven. His father's…and hers. She wanted to believe in a second chance even if she never got one. Silently she took his hand and let him lead her out of the Jeep.

They walked down the beach, Khalis's hand still loosely linked with her own, until they came to a sheltered spot, the rocks providing protection from the relentless wind.

Grace stopped in surprise at the sight of two gorgeous horses, a bay mare and a chestnut stallion, saddled and waiting, a groom holding their reins.

'What—?'

'I thought you might like to go riding.'

She shot him a sideways glance. 'How do you even know if I ride?'

'You mentioned a horse-mad phase,' Khalis said with a smile. 'That first night.'

'So I did.' She'd forgotten. She'd almost forgotten how to ride. She stared at the horses, reached out to stroke the bay's satiny coat. 'And I suppose you've been riding since the day you were born?'

'Only since I was two. But it's been a while.'

'For me, too.'

'We can take it slowly.'

Were they talking about riding, Grace wondered, or something else? It didn't really matter. She was touched Khalis had thought of this, had remembered her offhand comment. And she wanted to ride. With a smiling nod she let the groom help her to mount. She was glad Khalis had told her to wear serviceable clothing.

Khalis mounted his own horse and smiled at Grace. 'Ready?'

She nodded again, surprised and gratified by how much she enjoyed the feel of riding again, the wind at her back, the sun shining down. She nudged the horse into a canter and Khalis followed suit, the horses happy to trot down the length of the beach.

The breeze ruffled her hair and gulls cried raucously overhead. Grace felt a grin bloom all over her face. She'd forgotten how free she felt when she rode, how everything seemed to shrink to a point of a pin, the cares and fears and even the memories. Nothing mattered but this moment. Without even realising she was doing so, she urged her mount into a gallop. She heard Khalis laugh as he matched her pace.

'Are we racing?' he shouted to her, his words torn away on the wind.

'I think we are,' she called back and leaned low over her horse, her heart singing. It felt so good to be free.

The horses' hooves churned up damp sand and her hair streamed out behind her as they raced down the beach. Grace saw a rocky inlet ahead and knew instinctively that it would be their finish line. Khalis pulled ahead and she urged her own mount onwards so they were neck and neck, both of them laughing. In the last moment Grace pulled ahead by half a length and the mare jumped neatly over the scattering of rocks that had comprised their impromptu finish line.

Laughing, she wheeled her mount around and brushed her hair from her eyes. 'I hope you didn't let me win.'

'Never.'

Khalis looked so utterly at ease on his mount, his eyes flashing humour, his skin like burnished gold in the sunlight, that Grace suddenly felt quite dizzy with longing. She knew there was no way she'd won on her own merit, not when she hadn't ridden in over a decade, and Khalis probably having grown up on a horse. Again it didn't matter. Nothing mattered but this day, this one perfect golden day Khalis was giving her, a gift. 'Liar,' she said, smiling, and slipped off the horse. 'But I'll still take the victory. It felt so good to race like that. I'd forgotten how much I like riding.'

'I'm glad you rediscovered it,' Khalis said. He smiled as he brushed a tendril of hair away from her face and her stomach dipped in response to that casual touch. She stood there, blinking up at him, unable to move away. She might as well ask him out loud to touch her again. To kiss her.

He didn't, though, just led their horses up the beach to where the groom was waiting; he must have driven there to meet them. The groom took control of the horses and Khalis reached for Grace's hand. She let him lace his fingers with hers, reminded herself that just for today it was allowed. Today was separate from the rest of her life, alone on this island with a man she could so easily fall in love with.

The thought jolted her, made her hand tense in Khalis's. She couldn't fall in love, not with Khalis, not with anyone. She'd half-convinced herself that she could have this day—just one day—and she would walk away with no one the wiser, her heart intact. But to fall in love? That surely could only mean heartbreak...and discovery.

'Come,' Khalis said. 'Our picnic is waiting.'

He led her to a secluded little cove surrounded by rocks, a blanket already spread across the sand and a basket waiting. Grace gave a soft laugh. 'This took some planning.'

'A little,' he allowed. 'It's easy when you have staff.'

'I can only imagine.'

He drew her down to the blanket and Grace tucked her legs underneath her. Khalis opened the basket and withdrew a bottle of champagne and two glasses. 'A toast,' he said, and popped the cork.

Grace accepted the glass, pushing away the reservations and regrets that still crouched in the corners of her mind. She wasn't falling in love; she was stronger than that. She just wanted to enjoy this moment. This brief and fragile happiness.

'What are we toasting?' she asked.

'To a perfect day,' Khalis suggested.

'To a perfect day,' she echoed, and drank. As she lowered her glass she felt Khalis's gaze rest heavily upon her. 'One perfect day,' she said, and she knew she was reminding herself as well as him.

Khalis watched Grace drink, enjoyed the sight of her looking happy and relaxed, her hair tousled and free, her face flushed with pleasure. He still saw the fear and sadness lurking in her eyes, and he longed to banish those shadows—not just for one day, but for ever. The fervent nature of his own thoughts didn't alarm him any more, which surprised him. He was ready for this. Over the years he'd had a couple of serious relationships, yet he'd never found a woman who really reached him before. Who touched him and made him say and feel things he hadn't to anyone else. Not until Grace.

From the moment he'd met her he'd been intrigued by her. But he felt more for her than a mere fascination... He admired her dedication to her career, her strength of purpose. He sensed, like him, she was a survivor. And he ached not just to touch her—although he certainly felt that—but to see her smile and hear her laugh.

Smiling, he reached over and plucked the glass from her fingers. 'Ready to eat?'

'OK.'

He fed her strawberries and slices of succulent melon, ripe juicy figs and the softest bread dipped in nutty olive oil. He loved watching her eat, loved to see her finally enjoying herself, the lines of strain around her mouth and eyes relaxing at last. He loved the sensuality of feeding her, of watching her lips part, her eyes widen, her pupils dilate. It felt quite unbearably erotic.

She finally shook her head, refusing the last lone strawberry, her lips still red from the juice. 'You're spoiling me.'

'You deserve to be spoiled.'

The very air around them seemed to tense, freeze. Grace shook her head, her gaze sliding from his. 'No, I don't.'

Khalis had stretched out beside her on the blanket, one arm pillowing his head, and with the other he wound a tendril of soft blond hair around his finger. 'Why do you say that?' he asked quietly.

She shook her head, hard enough for that silky tendril to slip from his finger. 'It doesn't matter.'

He wanted to tell her that it did matter, that everything about her mattered to him, but he swallowed down the words. She wasn't ready to hear them, and perhaps he wasn't ready to say them. Whatever existed between them now was too new and fragile to test it with brash proclamations. Like her, he wanted to enjoy this day. They had plenty of time to learn about each other—learn to trust and maybe even to love—after today. Today—this perfect day—was just the beginning.

Grace watched as Khalis reached for her hair again, winding one silky strand around his finger. He did it almost without thinking, the gesture so relaxed and sure, and yet that simple little touch rocked her to her very core. She shouldn't even feel it—hair, after all, was made up of dead cells, with no nerves. Yet while the scientific part of her brain was reciting these dusty facts, her body blazed to life.

She felt it. Forget science, forget reality, she felt it. She gazed up at him, her eyes wide as she drank him in, his bronzed skin and grey-green eyes now crinkled at the corners as his sensual mouth curled into a knowing smile. Grace's whole body tingled as awareness stole through her, a certain and lovely knowledge that he was going to kiss her.

He lowered his lips to hers slowly, one hand still fisted in her hair as his mouth came down on hers. Her hands slid along his sun-warmed shoulders to clench in the softness of his hair. He lifted his mouth from hers a fraction and his smile deepened; she could *feel* that smile. 'You taste like strawberries.'

She smiled back. 'So do you.'

He let out a little huff of laughter and lowered his head so his mouth claimed hers once more. Grace revelled in that kiss, in this moment, for surely nothing had never been so pure or perfect. Khalis kissed his way slowly along her jawline to the nape of her neck; she let out a sound that was something between a shudder and a laugh as his lips tickled that sensitive spot. He moved lower, to the neckline of her T-shirt, his tongue flicking along her skin, and he tugged it down to press a kiss against the vee between her breasts. Grace arched upwards, her body unfurling like a flower in the sun.

Khalis slid a hand along her waist, his seeking fingers lifting the hem of her T-shirt to touch the sensitized skin beneath. He kissed her again, deeply, and Grace pressed against him. Her own hands sought his skin, tugged up his shirt, slid along the warm, silky stretch of his bare back. She felt his hand slide down along her middle, his palm caressing the tender skin of her tummy.

Behind them a bird suddenly cawed raucously and Grace lurched upright, panic replacing desire. With her clothes in disarray, her hair mussed and her mouth swollen, she felt as if she'd been caught out. Trapped and shamed.

Khalis still reclined on one elbow, looking relaxed. He'd obviously noticed her overreaction, though he said nothing, just let his gaze sweep lazily over her.

'I'm sorry—' she began.

'There's no need to be sorry.'

She let out a shuddering breath. 'I'm not...I haven't...'

'I know.'

He sounded so *sure*, and it made Grace flinch. He didn't know. The assumptions he was making so easily and arrogantly were wrong. Completely, utterly wrong. 'Actually,' she told him, her voice low, 'you don't know.'

'Then tell me.'

No. She tried for a smile. 'We've spent enough time today talking about old memories.'

'That's a brush-off if I've ever heard one.' He didn't sound annoyed, just accepting or perhaps amused. He rolled to a sitting position and began packing the remains of their picnic. Was their perfect day over already?

'We don't have to go yet—'

He touched her heated cheek. 'You're getting sunburn. We're very close to the coast of Africa, you know. The sun is incredibly hot.'

Silently Grace helped him pack up their things. She felt a confused welter of emotions: frustration that the afternoon had ended, as well as relief that it hadn't gone too far. And over it all like a smothering blanket whose weight she'd become so unbearably used to, guilt. Always the guilt.

'Cheer up.' Chuckling softly, Khalis touched her cheek again, his fingers lingering on her skin. 'Don't look so disappointed, Grace. It's only one day.'

Exactly, she wanted to say. Shout. One day—that was all she had. All she'd allow herself, and Khalis knew that. He'd said so himself—hadn't he? Doubt suddenly pricked her. Had she assumed he understood because it was easier to do so? Easier to be blinded by your own desires, to justify and excuse and ignore. But if he didn't understand… if he hadn't accepted her silent, implied terms that today was all they would ever share…what did he want? What did he expect?

Whatever it was, she couldn't give it to him, and a poignant sorrow swept over her as she realised for the first time she wanted to.

CHAPTER SEVEN

WHEN Grace returned to her room she was surprised to find Shayma in attendance, along with an impressive array of clothes and beauty products. Grace stared at a tray of make-up and nail varnish in bewilderment.

'What is all this…?'

Shayma smiled shyly. 'Mr Tannous, he wishes me to help you prepare.'

'Prepare?' Grace turned to gaze at the half-dozen gowns spread out on the bed in bewilderment. 'For what?'

'He is taking you somewhere, I think?'

'Taking me…' Where on earth could he take her to? Not that it mattered; she couldn't go anywhere. She couldn't be seen in public with Khalis, or with any man. Not on a proper date, at least.

'Are they not beautiful?' Shayma said, lifting one of the gowns from the bed. Grace swallowed as she looked at it.

'Gorgeous,' she admitted. The dress was a body-hugging sheath in ivory silk, encrusted with seed pearls. It looked like a very sexy wedding gown.

'And this one as well.' Shayma lifted a dress in a blue so deep it looked black, the satin shimmering like moon-light on water.

'Amazing.' The dresses were all incredible, and she

could not suppress the purely feminine longing to wear one. To have Khalis see her in one.

'And shoes and jewels to match each one,' Shayma told her happily.

Grace shook her head helplessly. She could not believe the trouble and expense Khalis had gone to. She could not believe how much she wanted to wear one of the gowns, and go on a date—a proper date—with him.

See how it happens? her conscience mocked her. *Temptation creeps in, slithers and stalks. And before you know it you're doing things you never, ever thought you'd do. And telling yourself it's OK.*

She knew the rules of her agreement with Loukas. No inappropriate behaviour. No dating. No men. It wasn't fair or really even legal, but in the four years since her divorce she hadn't really cared about the restrictions Loukas had placed upon her. Her heart had its own restrictions. Don't trust. Don't love. *Don't lose yourself.* She hadn't wanted any of it—until Khalis. Khalis made her long to feel close to someone again, to feel the fire of physical desire and the sweetness of shared joy. For the first time in four years she was tempted to let someone in. To trust him with her secrets.

Grace turned away from the sight of those tempting dresses. It was impossible, she reminded herself. Even if her contrary heart had changed, the conditions of her custody arrangement had not.

'Miss...?' Shayma asked hesitantly, and Grace turned back with an apologetic smile.

'I'm sorry, Shayma. I can't wear any of these dresses.'

Shayma stared at her in confused dismay. 'You do not like them?'

'No, I love them all. But I'm not... I can't go out with Mr Tannous.' Shayma looked more confused, and even worried. Grace patted her hand. 'Don't worry. I'll explain to him myself.'

She took a moment to brush her hair and steel herself before heading towards the part of the compound that housed Khalis's study.

Khalis sat behind his desk, and he smiled as she came in. 'I need to tell you—'

He held up one hand. 'You'd like to thank me for the dresses, but you won't go out with me tonight.'

Grace stopped short. 'How did you know?'

'I'd expect nothing less from you, Grace. Nothing about you is easy.'

She bristled; she couldn't help it. 'I'm not sure why you bother, then.'

'I think you do. We share something unusual, something profound—don't we?' He didn't sound remotely uncertain. Grace said nothing, but her silence didn't seem to faze Khalis in the least. 'I've never felt that before with any woman, Grace. And I don't think you've felt it with any man.' He paused, his gaze intent and serious. 'Not even your ex-husband.'

She swallowed. Audibly. And still didn't speak.

'You fascinate me, Grace. You make me feel alive and open and *happy*.'

Grace shook her head slowly. Did he know what his heartfelt confessions did to her? How hungry and heartbroken they made her feel? 'I'm really not that fascinating.'

He smiled wryly. 'Perhaps I'm easily fascinated, then.'

'Perhaps you're easily misguided.'

He arched an eyebrow, clearly surprised by this turn in the conversation. 'Misguided? How?'

Her throat tightened around the words she couldn't say. 'You don't really know me,' she said softly.

'I'm getting to know you. I want to know you.' She shook her head again, unwilling to explain that she didn't want him to get to know her. She didn't want him to know. 'Why won't you go out with me tonight?'

'As I've told you before, I can't.'

'Can't,' Khalis repeated musingly. His body remained relaxed, but his gaze was hard now, unyielding, and Grace knew she would bend beneath that assessing stare. She would break. 'Are you afraid of your ex-husband?'

'Not exactly.'

'Stop talking in riddles.'

Grace knew she'd prevaricated long enough. Khalis had been gentle, patient, kind. He deserved a little honesty. Just a little.

'I have a daughter,' she said quietly. 'Katerina. She's five years old.'

Khalis's expression didn't change, not really, beyond the slight flare of realisation in his eyes, turning them darker, more grey than green, like the ice that covered a lake. You had no idea how hard or thick it was until you stepped on it, let it take your full weight. And then heard the resounding crack in the air as it broke beneath you.

'And?' he finally asked softly.

'My ex-husband has custody of her. I get to see her once a month.'

She could almost hear the creak of the ice, the cracks like spiderwebs splintering the solid ground beneath them. What Khalis had *thought* was solid ground. 'Why is that?' he asked, his tone carefully neutral.

She swallowed, words sticking in her throat, jagged shards of truth she could not dislodge. 'It's complicated,' she whispered.

'How complicated?'

'He's a very powerful and wealthy man,' she explained,

choosing each word with agonised care. 'Our marriage was…troubled and…and our divorce acrimonious. He used his influence to win complete custody.' Her throat closed up over those unsaid jagged shards so they cut her up inside, although surely they'd already done all their damage? She'd lived with the loss of her daughter and her own painful part in it for four years already. Yet it hurt more to tell Khalis now because she never spoke of it. Never to anyone she cared about. And she cared about Khalis. She'd tried not to, still wished she didn't, but she couldn't deny the truth he'd spoken. They did share something. She felt her mouth wobble and tried to look away.

Khalis walked towards her, his expression softening, a sad smile tipping the corners of his mouth. 'Oh, Grace.' She closed her eyes, not wanting to see the undeserved compassion in his gaze. He put his arms around her though she didn't lean into his embrace as she longed to. 'I'm sorry.'

'It was my fault…partly…' A big part.

Khalis brushed this aside, his arms tightening around her. 'Why didn't you fight the custody arrangement? Most judges are inclined favourably towards the mother—'

Except when the mother was thought to be unfit. 'I… couldn't,' she said. At least that was true. She hadn't possessed the strength or courage to fight a judgement her heart had felt was what she deserved.

Khalis tipped her chin up so she had to face him. He looked so tender it made her want to cry. To blurt out the truth—that she didn't deserve his compassion or his trust, and certainly not his love. 'What does this have to do with you and me?'

You and me. How she wanted to believe in that idea. 'Loukas—my ex-husband monitors my behaviour. He's made it a requirement that I don't become…romantically involved with any man. If I do, I lose that month's visit with Katerina.'

Khalis drew back and stared at her in complete bafflement. 'But that…that has to be completely illegal. And outrageous. How can he control your behaviour to such an absurd degree?'

'He has the trump card,' Grace said. 'My daughter.'

'Grace, surely you could fight this. With a *pro bono* solicitor if money is an issue. There's no way he should be able to—'

'No.' She spoke flatly, although her heart raced and her stomach churned. What on earth had possessed her to tell him so much—and yet so little? Now he'd paint her as even more of a victim. 'No, don't, please, Khalis. Leave it. Let's not discuss this any more.'

He frowned, shaking his head. 'I don't understand—'

'Please.' She laid a hand on his arm, felt the corded muscles leap beneath her fingers. 'Please,' she said again, her voice wobbling, and his frown deepened. She thought he'd resist, keep arguing and insisting she fight a battle she knew she'd already lost, but then he sighed and nodded.

'All right. But I'd still like you to go out with me.'

'After what I just told you?'

Smiling, although his eyes still looked dark and troubled, he reached for her hand and kissed her fingers. 'I understand you can't be seen in public with me—yet. But we can still go out.'

She felt the brush of his lips against her fingers like an electric current, jolting right through her and short-circuiting her resolve. She longed to open her hand and press it against his mouth, feel the warmth of his breath against her flattened palm. Step closer so her breasts brushed his chest. With the last vestiges of her willpower she drew her hand back and dredged up a response. 'Go out where?'

'Out there.' He gestured towards the window, the wall. 'Away from this wretched compound.'

'But where—?'

'Grace.' He cut her off, stepping closer so she could feel the intoxicating heat of his nearness and knew her resolve was melting clean away. 'Do you trust me,' he asked, 'to take you somewhere your ex-husband could never discover? A place where you'll be completely safe—with me?'

She stared at him, fear and longing clutching at her chest. One day. One date. It had been four long years and she'd never, *never* known a man like Khalis—a man so gentle he made her ache, so kind he made her cry. A man who made her burn with need. She nodded slowly. 'All right. Yes. I trust you.'

His mouth curled in a smile of sensual triumph and he reached for her hand, kissed her fingers again. 'Good. Because I really would like to take you out to dinner. I'd like to see you in one of those dresses, and I'd like to peel it slowly from your body as I make love to you tonight.' He gave her a wry smile even as his gaze seared straight into her soul. 'But I'll settle for dinner.'

The images he'd conjured brought her whole body tingling to life. 'I can't imagine a place where we can go to dinner that's not—'

'Leave that to me.' He released her hand. 'You can spend some time being spoiled by Shayma.' He pressed a quick, firm kiss against her mouth. 'We'll have a wonderful evening. I'm looking forward to seeing which gown you pick.'

Two hours later, having been massaged and made-up and completely pampered, Grace was dressed in the dress of deep blue satin. She'd wanted to wear the ivory gown, but it had looked too bridal for her to feel comfortable wearing it. She wasn't innocent enough for that dress.

In any case, the blue satin was stunning, with its halter top and figure-hugging silhouette before it flared out in a spray of paler blue at her ankles. Shayma had fastened a diamond-encrusted sapphire pendant around her neck and given her matching earrings as well. She felt like a movie star.

'You look beautiful, miss,' Shayma whispered as she handed Grace her gauzy wrap and Grace smiled her thanks.

'You've been wonderful to me, Shayma. It's been one of the most relaxing afternoons I've had in a long time.'

Khalis was waiting for her at the bottom of the staircase, and he blinked up at her for a moment before he gave her a wide, slow smile of pure masculine appreciation. 'You look,' he told her, reaching for her hand, 'utterly amazing.'

'You look rather nice yourself.' He wore a suit in charcoal-grey silk, but Grace knew he'd look magnificent in anything. He was, simply and utterly, an incredibly attractive man. The suit emphasised the lean, whipcord strength of his body, its restrained power. 'So where are we going?'

'You'll see.'

He led her by the hand out of the compound, through the forbidding gates and then towards the beach. Night was already settling softly on the island, leaving deep violet shadows and turning the placid surface of the sea to an inky stretch of darkness.

Khalis led her to a launch where an elegant speedboat bobbed gracefully in the water. 'We're going by boat?' Grace asked a bit doubtfully, glancing down at her floor-length evening gown. 'I hate to tell you, but I'm feeling a bit overdressed.'

'Well, you look magnificent.' He helped her into the boat, taking care to keep the hem of her gown from trailing in the water. 'I will confess, I had an elegant little hotel in Taormina in mind when I originally had those gowns brought over. But it doesn't really matter where we go, does it? I just want to be with you.' He smiled at her, and Grace's heart twisted.

You're saying all the right things, she wanted to cry. *All the sweet, lovely things any woman wants to hear, and the worst part is I think you mean them.* That was what hurt.

'I am curious,' she murmured, 'where this secret place of yours is.' And nervous. And even afraid. In the four years since her divorce, she'd lost her monthly visits with Katerina twice. Once for going out for a coffee with a colleague, and another time for being asked to dance at a charity function she'd attended for work. She'd refused, but it hadn't mattered. Loukas just liked to punish her.

Khalis headed towards the helm and within a few minutes he was guiding the boat through the sea, the engine purring to life and thrumming beneath them. Grace sat behind a Plexiglas shield, but even so her careful chignon began to fall into unruly tendrils, whipped by the wind.

'Oh, dear.' She held her hands up to her hair, but Khalis just grinned.

'I like seeing you with your hair down.'

She arched her eyebrows. 'Is that a euphemism?'

His grin turned wicked. 'Maybe.'

Laughing a little, feeling far too reckless, she took the remaining pins out of her hair and tossed them aside. Her hair streamed out behind her in a windblown tangle. She probably looked a fright but she didn't care. It felt good. She felt free.

'Excellent,' Khalis said, and the boat shot forward as he accelerated.

Grace still had no idea where they could be going. All around them was an endless stretch of sea, and as far as she knew there were no islands between Alhaja and Sicily. And he couldn't be taking her to Sicily, could he? He'd said somewhere private; he'd asked her to trust him. And she did, even if her stomach still churned with nerves.

'Don't worry,' Khalis told her. 'Where we're going is completely private. And it won't take long to get there.'

'How,' she asked ruefully, 'do you always seem to know what I'm thinking?'

He paused, considering. 'I'd say your every emotion is reflected in your face, but it isn't. It just feels that way.'

Her heart seemed to turn right over. She knew what he meant. Even at his most carefully expressionless, she felt as if she knew what Khalis was feeling, as if she could feel it, too, as if they were somehow joined. Yet they weren't, and in twenty-four hours it would be over. The connection would be severed.

Unless...

For a brief blissful moment she imagined how it could go on. How she'd tell Khalis everything and somehow they'd find a way to fight the custody arrangement. Was this connection they shared strong enough for that?

She glanced at Khalis, her gaze taking in his narrowed eyes, the hard line of his cheek and jaw as he steered the boat. She thought of how he refused to grieve for his family. Forgive his father. Under all the grace and kindness he'd shown her she knew there was an inflexible hardness that had carried him as far as he'd got. A man like that might love, but he wouldn't forgive.

She swallowed, those brief hopes blown away on the breeze like so much ash. They'd been silly dreams, of course. Happy endings. Fairy tales.

'You look rather deep in thought,' Khalis said. He'd

throttled back so the noise of the engine was no more than a steady purr, and Grace could hear the sound of the waves slapping against the sides of the boat.

'Just thinking how beautiful the sea is.' *And how, now that I want to live and love again, I can't.* Khalis had been right. Life wasn't fair, and it was her own fault.

'It is, isn't it?' Khalis agreed, but Grace had the distinct feeling that she hadn't fooled him, and he knew she'd been thinking about something else. About him.

'So are we almost there yet?' she asked, peering out into the unrelieved darkness. A sudden thought occurred to her. 'Are we…are we going to stay on the boat?'

Khalis chuckled. 'You think that's my big surprise? Sausages over a propane stove on a motorboat? I'm almost offended.'

'Well, it is a rather nice boat,' Grace offered.

'Not that nice. And I don't fancy eating my dinner on my lap, bobbing in the water. Come on.' He held out his hand and, surprised, Grace took it. She couldn't see much in the darkness, the only light from the moon cutting a pale swathe of silver across the water. She had no idea where Khalis might be taking her.

He led her to the front of the boat and, even more surprised, Grace realised they had come up next to a small and seemingly deserted island. A slender curve of pale beach nestled against a tangle of foliage, palm fronds drooping low into the water.

'What is this place?'

'A very small, very secluded island my father happened to own. It's not very big at all—a couple of hundred metres across. But my father valued his privacy, and so he bought all the land near Alhaja, even if it wasn't much bigger than a postage stamp.' He vaulted out of the boat easily and then held out his hand to her. 'Come on.'

Grace reached for his hand, teetering a bit in her high heels and long dress, until Khalis put both of his hands firmly on her waist and swung her down off the boat onto the beach. Her heels sunk a good two inches into the damp sand and, ruefully, she slipped them off.

'I think these are designer. I don't want to get them ruined.'

'Much more sensible,' Khalis agreed and kicked his own shoes off. Grace looked at the empty stretch of dark, silent beach, the jungle dense and impenetrable behind it. Everything was very still, and it almost felt as if they were the only two people in the entire world, or at least the Mediterranean.

She turned to Khalis with a little laugh. 'Now I really feel overdressed.'

'Feel free to take your clothes off if you'd be more comfortable.'

Her heart rate skittered. 'Maybe later.'

'Is that a promise?'

Grace gave a little smile. She couldn't believe she was actually *flirting*. And it felt good. 'Definitely not.'

She picked up her dress and held it about her knees as she picked her way across the sand. She hadn't felt so relaxed and even happy in a long, long time. 'So we're not having sausages on the boat. A barbecue on the beach?'

'Wrong again, Ms Turner.' Grinning, Khalis reached for her hand. 'Come this way.' He led her down the darkened beach, towards a sheltered inlet. Grace stopped in surprise at the sight that awaited her there. A tent, its sides rippling in the breeze, had been set up, its elegant interior flickering with torchlight.

It was a tent, but it was as far from propane stoves and camping gear as could be possible. With the teakwood table, silken pillows and elegant china and crystal, it looked like something out of an *Arabian Nights* fantasy.

'How,' Grace asked, 'did you arrange this in the space of a few hours?'

'It was easy.'

'Not that easy.'

'It did take some doing,' Khalis allowed as he reached for the bottle of white wine chilling in a silver bucket. 'But it was worth it.'

Grace accepted a glass of wine and glanced around at the darkness stretching endlessly all about them, cocooned as they were in the tent with the flickering light casting friendly shadows. Safe. She was safe. And Khalis had made it happen. 'Thank you,' she said softly.

Khalis gazed at her over the rim of his wine glass, his gaze heavy-lidded with sensual intent and yet also so very sincere. 'Thank you,' he said, 'for trusting me.'

'Finally,' she said, and he smiled.

'It didn't take as long as all that.' He started to serve them both hummus and triangles of pitta bread. 'So you must live a very quiet life, with these restrictions your ex-husband has placed on you.'

'Fairly quiet. I don't mind.'

He gave her a swift, searching glance. 'Don't you? I would.'

'You can get used to things.' She'd rather talk about anything else. 'And sometimes,' she half-joked, 'I think I prefer paintings to people.'

'I suppose paintings never let you down.'

'Oh, I don't know,' she said lightly, 'a few paintings have let me down. I once found what I thought was a genuine Giotto in someone's attic, only to discover it was a very good forgery.'

'Isn't it interesting,' Khalis mused, 'how a painting that

looks exactly like the original is worth so much less? Both are beautiful, yet only one has value.'

'I suppose it depends on what you value. The painter or the painting.'

'Truth or beauty.'

Truth. It always came back to truth. The weight of what she wasn't telling him felt as if it would flatten her. Grace took a sip of her wine, tried to swallow it all down. 'Some forgeries,' she said after a moment, 'are worth a fair amount.'

'But nothing like the original.'

'No.'

She felt her heart race, her palms slick, even though they were having an innocuous conversation about art. Except it didn't feel innocuous because what Khalis didn't know—or maybe he already suspected—was that Grace herself was the most worthless forgery of all.

An innocent woman. A maligned wife. Both false, no matter what he thought or how she appeared. No matter what he seemed determined to believe.

'Come and eat,' he said, gesturing to the seat across from him, and Grace went forward with relief. Perhaps now they could talk about something else.

'Had you ever been to this island before?' she asked, dipping a triangle of pitta bread into the creamy hummus. 'As a boy?'

'My brother and I sailed out here once.'

'Once?'

He shrugged. 'We didn't do much together. Everything was a competition to Ammar, one he had to win. And I started not to like losing.' He smiled wryly, but there was something hard about the twist of his lips, a darker emotion that hinted at more than the average sibling rivalry.

'Do you miss him?' Grace asked quietly. 'Your brother, at least, if not your father?'

Khalis's face tensed, his body stilling. 'I already told you I don't.'

'I just find it hard to understand.' Why she felt the need to press, she couldn't say. It was the same kind of compulsion as picking a scab or probing a sore tooth. To see how much it hurt, how much pain you could endure. 'I miss my parents even now—'

'My family was very different from yours.'

'What about your sister? You must miss her.'

'Yes,' Khalis said after a moment. 'I do. But there's no point in going on about it. She's been dead fourteen years.'

He spoke so flatly, so coldly, that Grace could not keep from blurting out, 'How can you… How can you just draw a line across your whole family?'

For a second Khalis's face hardened, his eyes narrowing, lips thinning, and Grace had to look away. This was the man of unrelenting, iron control. The man who never looked back. Never forgave.

'I haven't drawn a line, as you say,' he said evenly, 'across my whole family. I simply see no point in endlessly looking back. They're dead. I've moved on. From mourning them and from this conversation.' He leaned forward, his tone softening. 'My father and brother don't deserve your consideration. You are innocent, Grace, but if you knew the kinds of things they'd done—'

'I'm not as innocent as you seem to think I am.'

'I'm sorry, I don't mean to sound patronising. And I did not intend to talk about my family tonight. Surely there are better ways for us to spend our time.'

'I'm sure there are,' Grace agreed quietly. Why had she pressed Khalis when she had not wanted to talk about her own past? She'd wanted to enjoy herself tonight, and losing themselves in dark memories was not the way to do it.

Khalis served her the next course and she watched the firelight flicker over his golden skin, saw the strength of the corded muscles in his wrist as he ladled fragrant pieces of chicken and cardamom onto her plate. Suddenly the memory of this afternoon, of Khalis's lingering kiss, his hand sliding along her skin, rose up so Grace's whole body broke out into a prickly heat, every muscle and nerve and sinew remembering how heartbreakingly wonderful it had felt when he'd touched her.

She felt her face heat and she reached for her glass. Khalis smiled, his eyes glinting knowingly. 'I think we are both thinking of one way in particular we could spend our time.'

'Probably,' Grace managed, nearly choking on her wine. She could imagine it all too well.

'Let us eat.' The food was delicious, the evening air warm and sultry, the only sound the whisper of the waves against the sand and the rattle of the wind in the palms. Khalis moved the conversation to more innocuous subjects, and Grace enjoyed hearing about how he had built up his business, his life in San Francisco. Khalis asked her about her own life, too, and she was happy to describe her job and some of her more interesting projects. It felt wondrously simple to sit and chat and laugh, to enjoy herself without worry or fear. She'd been living too long under a cloud, Grace thought. She'd needed this brief foray into the light.

All too soon they'd finished their main course and were lingering over thick Turkish-style coffee Khalis had boiled in a brass pot and dessert—a sinful tiramisu—as the stars winked above them and were reflected below upon a placid sea. Grace didn't want the night to end, the magic to stop, for it surely felt like a fantasy, wearing this gown, gazing at the sea, being with Khalis on this enchanted island.

Yet it didn't have to end…not yet, anyway. Her body both tingled in anticipation and shivered with trepidation as she imagined how this magical night could continue. How Khalis could fulfil his promise and slip this gown from her shoulders. Make love to her…as she wanted him to.

Her fingers trembled and she returned her coffee cup to its saucer with a clatter. It had been so long since she'd been with a man. So long since she'd allowed herself the intimacy and vulnerability of being desired. Loved. It scared her still, but she also wanted it. More than she ever had before.

'Why do you look afraid?' Khalis asked quietly. 'We're safe here.' Grace heard both tender amusement and gentle concern in his voice and he reached over to cover her hand with his own.

'I'm not afraid.' She lifted her head to meet his gaze directly, even boldly. She was not afraid, not of him anyway, and not even of Loukas. There was no way he could discover her here. No, she was afraid of herself, and this intense longing that had seized her body and mind and maybe even her heart. Tomorrow she would have to walk away from it.

'Do you wish to return to Alhaja now?'

'Not unless we have to.' She smiled, her eyebrows arched even as her heart thudded. 'Do we?'

'No,' Khalis said in a low thrum of a voice. 'We could stay here.'

Grace didn't know if he meant a little longer or all night. She glanced at a large pillow of crimson and cream striped silk, the torchlight shimmering off the rich material. It looked incredibly soft and inviting, and she could imagine sleeping on it. She could also imagine *not* sleeping on it.

'More coffee?'

She shook her head. 'No, thank you.' Impulsively she leaned forward. 'Let's dance.'

Khalis raised his eyebrows. 'Dance?'

'Yes, dance. On the beach.' The idea had come to her suddenly; this was a date, the only date she'd ever have, and she wanted to enjoy it. She wanted to do all the things she was never able to do because of Loukas and his restrictions. She wanted to dance with Khalis.

A small smile quirked the corner of Khalis's mouth. 'But there's no music.'

Grace held out her arms, gesturing to the rich blue satin of her dress. 'I'm wearing an evening gown on a deserted island. Do we really need music?' She smiled, longing to grab this fragile happiness with both hands. 'Does it really matter?' she echoed his own words back to him.

'Not at all.' In one swift movement Khalis rose from the table and led her out to the beach. The sand was cool and silky beneath her bare feet and the darkness swirled around them, the moon shimmering on the surface of the sea, giving it a fine pearl-like sheen. Khalis turned to her. 'Since there's no music, we can pick the kind we like.'

Grace could hardly see him out here on the dark beach, but she felt the heat and intensity of him, the desire pulsing between them, a sustaining and life-giving force. Impossible to resist. Necessary for life. 'Which kind?' she asked in a voice that sounded a little hoarse.

'Something slow and lazy,' Khalis said. He reached out and pulled her towards him so her hips collided gently with his and heat pooled in her pelvis. She let her hands slide up his shoulders, lace around his neck as he started to sway. 'A saxophone, maybe. Do you like sax?'

'Sax,' Grace repeated dazedly. Khalis had slid his hands from her shoulders to her waist to her hips, and now his fingers were splayed along her bottom as he pulled her even closer, against the full thrust of his arousal. 'I... Yes, I think so.'

'Good,' he murmured, and they swayed silently together. Grace could have sworn she heard music, the lonely wail of a saxophone as they danced on the empty beach, their bare feet leaving damp footprints in the sand.

Above them the sky was scattered with stars, a hundred thousand glittering pin-pricks in an inky, endless sky. Grace laid her head on Khalis's shoulder, felt the steady thud of his heart against her own chest. After a moment she lifted her head and tilted back so she could look up into his eyes. His lips were a whisper away. The sleepy sensuality of the dance was replaced by something far more primal and urgent, something whose force was overwhelming and irresistible.

'Grace,' Khalis said and it almost sounded like a warning.

But Grace didn't want warnings. She didn't want memories or guilt or fear. She just wanted this. 'Khalis,' she whispered and his fingers brushed her cheek.

'I love it when you say my name.'

'I was amazingly resistant to saying it.' She turned her head so her lips brushed his fingers. She felt carefree to the point of wantonness, and after four years of being completely buttoned-up it felt good. Khalis let out a little shudder as her tongue darted out and touched his fingers, tasted the salt of his skin. He took her chin in his hand and gazed down at her with a ferocity that would have frightened her if she hadn't felt it herself.

Then he kissed her hard, so different from the gentle caresses of this afternoon, and yet so right. The very air seemed to ignite around them, the stars exploded in the sky as Grace kissed him back and Khalis pulled her even closer, his mouth moving from her lips to her jaw to her throat and she heard the primal sound of her own desperate moan of longing.

He pressed another kiss in the curve of her neck and she tilted her head back, allowing him access. The feel of his lips against her skin gave her a plunging sensation deep inside, turned her mind into a whirlpool of need.

'This dress is going to get very sandy,' Khalis murmured against her throat and Grace gave a shaky laugh.

'I don't care. Although I suppose you might.' She had to find the words from somewhere deep inside her, for thought of any kind was proving virtually impossible. Khalis had undone the halter top of the dress and was slowly peeling it away from her, just as he'd promised.

'I find,' he murmured as he slid the gown down her body, 'I don't care about this dress at all.'

'It is beautiful,' Grace gasped as he finished removing it and tossed it onto the sand. 'Was,' she amended, and Khalis let out a hoarse laugh as his gaze roved over her.

'Grace, *you* are beautiful. Utterly and shockingly beautiful.'

She should have felt embarrassed, standing in her knickers in the middle of a beach, but she didn't. She wasn't even wearing a bra because she hadn't brought one that fitted the halter-style top of the dress. The cool breeze puckered her bare skin into gooseflesh.

'Shockingly?' she repeated. 'That sounds rather alarming.'

'It is alarming,' Khalis told her. He stepped closer to her, ran his hands lightly over her shoulders before cupping her breasts. His palms were warm and dry and still

Grace shivered under his touch. 'It's alarming to me, what I feel for you,' he said in a low voice.

Grace's heart lurched. Yes, it was alarming to her, too. Terrifying and wonderful at the same time. 'Kiss me,' she murmured, and as Khalis brushed his lips against her own she closed her eyes.

He deepened the kiss, but only for a moment, pulling away from her to brush her lids with his fingers. 'Open your eyes.'

'Wh-what?' Her eyes fluttered open and she stared at him, the mobile curve of his mouth hardening just a little bit as he gazed back at her.

'Don't turn your mind off, Grace. I'm making love to you, body and mind and soul.'

'You don't ask for much, do you?'

'Just everything.' And then he claimed her mouth in a kiss that was as hard and unrelenting as she knew the core of him to be, reminding her that no matter how gentle this man was, how tender and even loving, he was still a dangerous proposition. 'Kiss me back,' he muttered against her mouth, and she did, returning the demand, answering it.

He pulled her closer, her breasts crushed against his chest as his hands slid down the bare expanse of her back and tugged off her knickers. Then, his gaze still locked on hers, he stepped back and reached for the buttons of his own shirt. Mesmerised, Grace watched as he began to undress, her own nakedness almost forgotten as he slid his shirt off and revealed the lean, muscled chest underneath. His skin was golden with a satiny sheen, a light sprinkling of hair veeing down to his waistband. Her breath hitched. Khalis undid his belt.

Seconds later, they were both naked. Grace tried not to shiver. Khalis's heated gaze was enough to fire her body, yet she could not shake the feeling of vulnerability that stole over her and made her cold. She'd forgotten how *intimate* this all was. How revealing. She'd been on her own for so long, buttoned-up and barricaded, protected. Now there was nothing. Now she was bare.

At least physically. Emotionally, Grace knew, she was still as guarded as ever. And now more than ever, as Khalis led her back to the tent and drew her down to the pillows' opulent softness, she wanted to tell the last of her secrets. She wanted to bare her soul. She wanted, Grace knew, to be understood and accepted. Forgiven. *Loved.*

Yet she didn't know how to begin. Her thoughts were a ferment of uncertainty, even as pleasure began to take over.

Khalis trailed kisses from her throat to her tummy and desire dazed her senses, scattering her thoughts. His mouth moved lower, his tongue flicking against her skin, and then, thankfully, she had no more thoughts at all.

Something was missing. Even as he heard Grace's little gasps and mews, even as his own libido ran rampant, Khalis knew it wasn't enough. He wanted more from Grace, more than this physical response, overwhelming as it was. He wanted to destroy the defences she'd put around herself. He wanted her completely open to him, body and mind, heart and soul.

You don't ask for much, do you?

He'd never wanted so much from a woman before, but then he'd never felt so much for a woman before. And yet, even as her body lay naked to him, even as she parted her legs and arched up towards his caress, Khalis knew she was closing off her mind. Her heart.

'Look at me, Grace.'

Her eyes fluttered open, unfocused and dazed with passion. 'What—' He braced himself on his elbows, poised over her as her breath came in little pants. *'Please—'*

He knew what she wanted. God knew he wanted it, too. In one stroke he could be embedded deep inside her and satisfy them both. He stayed still. 'Say my name.'

Confusion clouded her eyes. Her lips parted. 'Why—?'

'Say my name.'

It wasn't much, but it was, at least, a beginning. She would acknowledge him, own this connection between them. He wouldn't let her memories or fears crowd him out. He wouldn't let her try to banish him along with her ghosts. She didn't speak and sweat beaded on his brow. He could not hold himself back much longer. *'Please.'*

Her expression softened and the sudden tears that shimmered in her eyes nearly broke him. 'Khalis,' she whispered, and with a primal groan of satisfaction he drove inside her, felt her welcoming warmth wrap around him. 'Khalis,' she said again, her nails digging into his shoulders, her body arching upwards, and triumph tore through him as they surged towards a climax. Grace cried aloud, her head thrown back as her legs wrapped around him. His name sounded like both a supplication and a blessing as her body convulsed around his. *'Khalis.'*

CHAPTER EIGHT

GRACE lay in the cradle of Khalis's arms and could not keep the tears from silently slipping down her face. She closed her eyes, but still they came, one after the other, tears of poignant joy and bitter regret. She'd never felt so close to a man before…and yet so unbearably far away. She'd been so afraid to open her heart and body and soul to him, afraid of the strength of her own feelings. Right to the end she'd resisted, and then…

Then her heart had cracked right open and instead of feeling like the end it had been a beginning. Life instead of death. Hope instead of fear. How could she not have realised how different it would be with Khalis, how wonderful?

And yet how could it last?

She thought she was crying silently, so Khalis, his arms wrapped around her as he drew her back against his chest, wouldn't hear, but he did. Or perhaps he just sensed it, as he had so many other things. Gently his hands came up towards her face and his thumbs wiped away her tears. Neither of them spoke. After a long moment Grace drew in a shuddering breath, her face still damp although at least the tears had stopped.

Khalis pressed a kiss against her shoulder, his arms still wrapped around her. 'Tell me,' he said quietly.

Grace closed her eyes. Another tear leaked out. She wanted to tell him, tell him everything about her disastrous marriage, her own stupid, selfish folly, her painful divorce, the endless aftermath. She'd given him the barest of details, made herself look far more of a victim than she was. Now she imagined telling him all of it, having every sordid secret spill out of her, and while it would be a relief, like a blood-letting, it would also be messy and painful. And it would change the way Khalis looked at her. Why that should even matter since she didn't intend to see him again after tonight, Grace couldn't say. It just did.

She drew a deep breath and rolled over onto her back, Khalis's arm heavy across her. 'It's just been a long time,' she said, attempting a smile. 'I'm kind of emotional.'

Khalis studied the tracks Grace knew her tears had made down her face. 'You're sad.'

'And happy.' She pressed a kiss against his palm. 'Very happy.'

Khalis didn't look convinced but, to Grace's relief, he let it go. He pulled her more securely against him and she lay there for a long time, his arms wrapped around her as she stared into the darkness, savouring the steady warmth of him next to her, the reassuring rise and fall of his chest. Eventually she slept.

When she woke the tent was washed in sunlight and Khalis was gone. She knew he couldn't have gone far—they were on a deserted island, after all—and so for a few seconds she just lay there against the pillows, recalling the sweet memories, enjoying this brief happiness. Then she rose, wrapping a cashmere throw around her, for her gown— the only clothes she'd brought—was lying discarded and damp on the sand some metres away.

Khalis appeared, coming from the beach, looking energised and alert, a towel slung low round his hips. His hair was damp and spiky, and when he smiled Grace started to melt.

'Good morning.'

'Good morning. You had a dip in the sea?'

'A very refreshing way to start the day,' he confirmed. 'Sleep well?'

'Yes.'

'It took you a long time to go to sleep.'

Surprised, her grip loosened and the throw slid down revealingly. She hitched it up again. 'How did you know that?'

'I just sensed it, I suppose.'

'It felt strange to sleep next to someone,' Grace admitted. 'But nice.'

'Good.' Without a modicum of self-consciousness, Khalis dropped his towel and began to dress. Grace watched as he pulled on a pair of faded jeans, his legs long, lean and sprinkled with dark hair. 'Where did you get those clothes?' she asked, more to distract herself from the sight of his naked body than any real sense of curiosity.

'I brought a bag with a change of clothes for both of us.' He gave her a quick grin. 'Just in case.'

'Rather confident, weren't you?' she said, smiling and blushing at the same time.

'I like to be prepared.' He reached for a T-shirt and Grace leaned back against the pillows and watched him dress. It was a glorious sight. 'I thought we could have a look round the island this morning,' he said as he fastened his jeans. 'Not that there's much to see.'

'That sounds nice.' Anything to extend their time together.

Khalis sat down next to her on the pillow, his expression turning serious. He rested one hand on her knee. 'And tonight I want to fly back to Paris with you.'

Shock rendered her momentarily speechless. 'You... what?'

'I put a call in to the head of my legal team,' Khalis continued, 'and asked him a few questions. There's no way this custody arrangement is legal, Grace. We can fight it. We might even be able to dig something up on Christofides. I don't think he's squeaky clean. My team is researching it now—'

Grace just stared at him, her mind frozen. 'How did you know his last name?' she asked. 'I never told you.'

'I did some research.'

'I thought you didn't like internet stalking.'

His expression hardened. 'Sometimes it's justified.'

She let out a short laugh. 'Is it?'

'What's wrong, Grace? I thought you'd be happy to hear this. I want to fight for you. And your daughter.'

She shook her head, wanting to deny the fierce hope his words caused to blaze within her. 'You should have told me you were doing those things.'

'I wanted to have some information before I said anything—'

'I don't like being bossed around.' Her words came out sharply—sharper than she intended. 'I *really* don't like it.'

Khalis was silent for a moment. 'Is that what he did to you?' he asked quietly. 'Ordered you around? Kept you imprisoned on some island?'

Grace stared at him, the fierce light in his eyes, the hard line of his mouth. 'Something like that.'

'I'm not your ex-husband.'

'I know,' she snapped. This conversation was scraping her emotions raw, making her feel more exposed than ever. Exposed and hidden at the same time, for everything about their relationship was a mess of contradictions. A paradox of pleasure and pain. Secrets and honesty. Hope and despair. She took a deep breath. 'I know,' she said again, more quietly. 'But, Khalis—it's not that simple. You should have told me what you were doing before you interfered.'

'Interfered? I thought I was *helping* you.'

'There are things—' She stopped, bit the inside of her cheek hard enough to taste blood. 'Things I haven't told you.'

'Then tell me. Whatever it is, *tell* me.'

She stared at him, trying to find the words. Form them. A few simple sentences, that was all, but it could change everything. And even now, when she'd lain sated in Khalis's arms and he'd wiped away her tears, she was desperately afraid.

'Grace,' he said quietly and reached for her hand. His hand was warm and dry and strong, and hers felt small and icy in it. Still she didn't speak. 'Whatever it is, whatever happened between you and your husband, I can handle it. I've seen a lot of things in this world. Terrible things.'

'You're talking about your father.'

'Yes—'

'But you walked away from him. From all that.'

'Of course I did.' He was silent for a moment, struggling for words. 'I don't know what your husband did to you,' he said quietly, stroking her fingers, 'but I hate him for it. I'll never forgive him for hurting you.'

Slowly Grace lifted her gaze to his. He looked intent and utterly sincere. He'd meant his words as some kind of comfort, an assurance that he was on her side. He didn't realise just how cold that comfort was. *I'll never forgive him for hurting you. I'll never forgive. Never forgive.* She heard the relentless echo of that hard promise in her mind, and she pulled her hand from his.

'There's no point in discussing this,' she said, and struggled up from the bed of pillows, wished she was wearing more than a cashmere throw. 'Did you say you brought me some clothes?'

Khalis had gone very still, his grey-green stare tracking her movements as she hunted for the bag of clothes. 'Why is there no point?'

With relief Grace pulled a pair of trousers and a T-shirt from a duffel bag. She straightened and turned to face him, the clothes clutched to her hard-beating heart. 'Because I don't want you to fly to Paris with me. I don't want you to call your legal team and tell me what to do. I don't want *you*.' She stared at him, each word a hammer blow to her heart—and his. They were lies, and yet she meant them. This, Grace thought numbly, was the worst contradiction of all: she was breaking the heart of a heartless man. She loved someone who couldn't love her back, even if he thought he did.

He didn't know her.

Khalis didn't answer for a moment. His face was devoid of expression, although the corners of his mouth had whitened. 'I don't believe you,' he said finally.

'Do I have to spell it out for you?'

'You're afraid.'

'Stop telling me what I feel,' Grace snapped. 'Stop deciding just what it is between us. You keep telling me what I feel, as if you know. Well, you don't. You don't know anything.'

'If I don't know something,' Khalis answered, his voice so very even, 'it's because you haven't told me.'

'And maybe I haven't told you because I don't want to,' Grace retorted. How could she feel heartbroken and furious at the same time? She was afraid he'd reject her if she told him the truth, and yet at that moment she was angry enough to reject him. Nothing made sense. 'Just take me back to Alhaja,' she said. 'And then I'll find my way back to Paris myself.'

Anger sparked in Khalis's eyes, turning them golden-green. 'And how will you do that? Swim?'

'If I have to,' Grace flashed back. 'If you think you can keep me on that damned island—'

'I told you before,' he cut her off icily, 'I am *not* your ex-husband.'

'There's a startling resemblance at the moment.' As soon as she said the words Grace knew she didn't mean them. Khalis was nothing like Loukas. He'd been so gentle and kind and *loving*, and she was the one pushing him away. Pushing him away because she didn't want to be pushed away first. *Coward.*

The silence between them felt taut with suppressed fury. Khalis stared at her for a long moment, his face unreadable, his chest heaving. He drew a deep breath, and Grace watched as he focused his anger into something cold and hard. 'I thought,' he said, staring into the distance, his body now angled away from her, 'we had something special. That sounds ridiculously sentimental, I know. I didn't really believe in *special* until I felt it with you.' He turned to face her and Grace flinched from the bleakness in his eyes. 'But all that *we sense each other's emotions* stuff, this connection between us—that was just crap, wasn't it? Complete rubbish.'

Grace didn't answer. She couldn't. She didn't have the strength to deny it, and yet she could not tell him the truth. She wasn't even sure what the truth was any more. How could she fall in love with someone who was so hard and unyielding? How could she truly believe in his gentleness and all the good things he'd shown her? 'There's no point to this conversation,' she finally said flatly. 'We could drag it all out, and do a post-mortem on everything we've ever said, but since we're not going to *have* a relationship—' she drew in a ragged breath '—why bother?'

'Why bother,' he repeated softly. 'I see.'

She forced herself to meet his icy stare. 'Yes,' she said, 'I think you do.'

He stared at her, his face so blank and pitiless. Slowly he shook his head. 'I thought I knew you, or was at least coming to know you, but you're really a stranger, aren't you? A complete and utter stranger.' He might as well have said *bitch* instead. 'I don't know you at all.'

'No,' Grace agreed softly, 'you don't.' She drew in a deep, shuddering breath. 'Now I think you should take me back to Alhaja, and then I'll go home.'

He stared at her, and for a moment he looked like a different man, everything about him hard and unyielding and angry. The core revealed. Grace had known it was there, had known he possessed it, yet that cold, hard fury hadn't been directed at her…until now.

'Fine,' he said shortly. 'I'll get the boat ready.' And in two swift strides he'd left the tent, disappearing down towards the beach.

Khalis didn't speak to her again except for a few terse commands when she boarded the boat. She glanced at him, his jaw bunched as he stared out at the endless blue horizon, and again she felt that ridiculous, desperate longing for things to be different. To tell him everything, to take a chance. Maybe it wouldn't matter. Maybe he'd accept and understand and—

She watched as his eyes narrowed against the now-blazing sun and all the things he'd said tumbled back into her mind. He didn't forgive. He didn't want to forgive. He was a man with high and exacting standards for himself as well as everyone else. She fell far short of them and nothing could change that. Nothing could change the fact that she didn't deserve his love.

Tears thickened in her throat and stung her eyes and, furious with herself, Grace blinked them away. Was she really going to have a pity party *now*? The notion was ludicrous, idiotic. And far too late.

Alhaja Island loomed in the distance, a green crescent-shaped speck, and then the walls with their barbed wire and broken glass became visible, the ugly concrete compound behind.

Khalis docked the boat and cut the engine and in the sudden silence they both sat there, neither speaking or even looking at each other.

'Get your things,' he finally said. 'I'll have someone take you back to Paris.'

'I can get transport from Taormina. If someone could just—'

'I'll get you home,' he told her brusquely. He paused, and as he turned to her Grace saw a welter of emotion in his agate-coloured eyes and its answer rose up in her chest, a silent howl of anguish and loss. If only things could be different. If only *they* were different. His lips twisted in something close to a smile and he lifted his hand, almost as if he were going to touch her. Grace tensed in anticipation and longing, but he didn't, just dropped it back to his side. 'Goodbye, Grace,' he said, and then he vaulted out of the boat and strode down the dock.

Fury drove Khalis to the pool. He needed to work off his frustration…and his pain. Stupid, to feel so hurt, like a kicked puppy. And it was his own damn fault.

He dived in and cut through the water with sure, swift strokes, his emotions driving him forward. Even as he swam he winced. He'd been so sentimental, so stupidly romantic, and she'd been the one to spell it out. *I don't want you.* He felt pathetic. Pathetic and bruised.

He'd blinded himself all along, he knew, turned deaf ears to what she was saying. *I couldn't be in a relationship with you.* He'd thought she was just afraid, wounded by her ex-husband, and maybe she was. Maybe it was fear that had made her reject him, but the fact still remained, hard and heartless. She didn't want him. He'd wanted to rescue her as if she were some princess in a tower, but she didn't want to be rescued. Or loved. And, really, did he even know her at all? How could you fall in love with someone so quickly and suddenly? Wasn't it supposed to grow over months and years, not a mere matter of days?

Khalis completed another lap and hauled himself, dripping, onto the side of the pool. Even now, his chest heaving and his lungs burning, he couldn't get her out of his mind. Those chocolate eyes, dark with pain or softened with humour. Her mouth, swollen and rosy from being kissed. The pure, clear sound of her rare laughter, and the way she looked at him, her attention so focused and complete it made him feel a hundred feet tall. The pliant softness of her body against his, and the way he'd felt when he'd been inside her, as if he'd finally found the home he'd long been looking for.

With a groan of frustration Khalis pushed off the side of the pool and started swimming again, harder and faster than ever, as if exercise could obliterate thought. In the distance he heard the sound of the helicopter taking off.

An hour later, showered and dressed, he strode into his office. His frustration and hurt had hardened into something cold and steely that lodged inside him like a ball of iron.

Eric was waiting for him with a sheaf of papers as he

sat behind his desk. 'You look,' Eric remarked mildly, 'like you want to rip someone's head off. I hope it's not mine.'

'Not at all.' He held out one hand for the papers. Eric handed them to him with his eyebrows arched.

'If not me, then who?' He rolled his eyes. 'Wait, I think I can guess.'

'Don't,' Khalis said, cutting him off. 'It's not up for discussion.'

'This island is really doing a number on you, isn't it?'

Khalis suppressed his irritation with effort. Eric was one of his oldest and most trusted friends, and he generally appreciated his levity. Yet, since coming to this island, tension had been wrapping itself around him like a steel band, choking all the life and hope from the air. Grace had distracted him, he realised. She'd *helped* him. And her rejection had made everything worse, the memories darker, the pain more intense.

'It's not the island,' he said shortly. 'I'd just like to wrap up this whole business quickly and get back to my real life.' Except he wasn't sure he could do that any more, or at least not easily. Not since Grace.

'I wouldn't mind a few more weeks lounging in the sun,' Eric said, although Khalis knew his assistant had done precious little lounging since arriving on Alhaja. 'Is there anything else for now?'

'No—' Khalis dropped the papers on his desk and raked a hand through his hair. 'Yes,' he amended. 'I want you to find everything you can on Grace Turner.'

'Everything?' Eric asked dubiously. 'You sure you want to go there?'

He gritted his teeth. 'Yes.'

Eric gave him a considering look, then shrugged. 'It's your party,' he said, and left the room. Resolutely, Khalis pulled the papers towards him. Grace had told him he could find out what he needed to know with one simple internet search. Well, he thought grimly, maybe now he'd take her up on that.

By the time Grace arrived back at her apartment in Paris's Latin Quarter, she felt exhausted, both emotionally and physically. Khalis's helicopter had taken her to Taormina, and then he'd arranged a private jet to take her directly to Paris. Even at the end, when he must have hated her, he was considerate. She almost wished he wasn't. When he'd been arrogant and controlling it had been far easier to stay angry and to let that carry her. Then he softened into gentleness and she felt all tangled up inside, yearning and fear tying her heart into knots. Why couldn't he make it easy for her to let go? Simple not to care? Yet nothing about her time with Khalis had been simple or easy.

Yes, it had, she corrected herself. It had been all too easy to fall in love with him.

Resolutely, Grace pushed the useless thought away. She had no space or freedom in her life for love. Khalis might have cracked open her heart, but she could close it again. Love led to pain. She knew that. She'd seen it with Loukas, when he'd left her alone on his island, trapped and miserable, half-mad with loneliness.

And as for Andrew…

No, she wouldn't think about Andrew.

Slowly, each movement aching, she dropped her bag and kicked off her heels. She curled up on the sofa, wishing she could blank out her mind. Stop thinking, stop remembering. Not Loukas or Andrew, but Khalis. Khalis smiling at her, teasing her, making her laugh.

Frankly, that looks like something my five-year-old goddaughter might paint in Nursery.

Even now Grace's mouth curved into a smile as tears

stung her eyes. Khalis looking at her, heavy-lidded with
sensual intent. Kissing her so softly, so sweetly. Finding
ways to make her feel safe and treasured.

Now the tears spilled over and Grace buried her face
in her hands. Had she made a mistake, not trusting him?
If she'd told him what she'd done, would he have forgiven
her? And wasn't loving someone worth that risk?

She drew in a shuddering breath and other memories
came to her. Khalis's eyes narrowed, his mouth a hard,
compressed line.

You're very forgiving, much more forgiving than I am.

No, he wasn't forgiving. And he wouldn't forgive her.
And even if she'd fallen in love with him, it didn't change
who he was. And who she couldn't be.

CHAPTER NINE

GRACE transferred her untouched glass of champagne to her other hand and tried to focus on what the ageing socialite across from her was droning on about. She caught a word here and there and she thought she was making the appropriate noises of interest, but her entire body and brain were buzzing with the knowledge that Khalis would be here tonight. After two months, she would see him again.

Tension coiled through her body, twanging like a wire. She had had no contact with Khalis these last few months, although she'd exchanged a few emails with Eric, arranging for the art collection to be transferred. Khalis had, of course, obeyed all the legal procedures in authenticating the artwork in his father's vault and turning it over to the proper authorities. Tonight was a gala celebrating the return of several important paintings to the Louvre, as well as Khalis's generous donation of a Monet that had been one of the few paintings in his father's collection that had not been stolen.

The party was being held in the Louvre's impressive courtyard, the distinctive glass pyramids glinting in the last rays of the setting sun. It was early summer and the air was sun-warmed and fragrant. Grace took a sip of champagne to ease the dryness in her throat and glanced around the milling crowd for Khalis. He hadn't arrived. She would know it if he had.

And when he did arrive, Grace asked herself yet again, what would she say to him? How would she act? Prudence required that she keep a professional distance, yet two months had only intensified her longing and regret and she was afraid she'd betray herself when she saw him again.

She attempted to turn her attention back to the socialite, yet within seconds it felt as if someone had suddenly turned a spotlight on her, even though nothing had noticeably changed. She felt a prickling between her shoulder blades, a tingling awareness creep through her entire body. He was here.

Barely aware of what she was saying, she excused herself from the conversation and turned away, trying to search the crowds discreetly. It didn't take long; it was as if he were equipped with a tracking device to her heart, for she saw and felt him right away. He stood alone, his figure tall and proud, his gaze sweeping over the crowd. Then that cold gaze fastened on her and Grace's breath hitched. For an endless moment they stared at one another, and from across the crowded courtyard Grace could not discern his expression. She didn't even know what the expression on her own face was, for both body and brain seemed to have frozen.

Then Khalis looked away, his gaze moving on without any real acknowledgement of her presence. Head held high, she turned away and walked towards another knot of guests, forced herself to listen to their idle chatter. What had she expected? That Khalis would run over and greet her? Kiss her? She wouldn't even have wanted that. She *couldn't* want that. Yet it still hurt, not the pain of disappointment, for Grace hadn't really expected anything from him tonight, but the agony of remembered loss.

Somehow she made it through the next hour, listening and nodding, murmuring platitudes although she barely knew what she was saying. Her body ached with the knowledge of Khalis's nearness and, even without looking, she was certain she knew exactly where he was. Amazing, and still alarming, to share this connection that they'd both acknowledged…and then she'd denied.

The evening dragged, every moment painfully slow as Grace instinctively tracked Khalis's progress around the courtyard. He looked amazing in a dark suit and silver-grey tie, as lean and powerful and darkly attractive as ever, and just glimpsing him out of the corner of her eye reminded her how warm and satiny his skin had been, how complete she'd felt in his arms.

By the end of the social hour, and then another half hour of speeches, she felt ready for bed. Tension knotted in her shoulders and her head pulsed with the beginnings of one of the stress-related headaches she'd been getting ever since her divorce. The party had moved inside to the Pavillon Denon, and Grace stayed near the back of the gallery as the director of the museum praised Khalis's civic service in restoring so many famous works of art to their rightful places. Her heart twisted like a wrung rag inside her when Khalis stepped to the podium and spoke eloquently about his duty 'to redeem what has been forsaken, and find what has been lost'.

Pretty words, Grace thought with a sudden spike of spite, but he hadn't been much interested in redemption when she'd been talking to him. When it came to his father, he'd been cold, hard and unforgiving.

And you were so afraid he'd be the same with you. That's why you ran away like a frightened child.

Not that it mattered. The only child she could think of was Katerina. Just the thought of her daughter's apple-round cheeks, her dark plaits and her gap-toothed smile made Grace blink fiercely. She had to forget about Khalis, for Katerina's sake as well as her own.

The speeches over, Grace excused herself from the party. She saw Michel give her a sharp glance from across the room; she didn't think she'd fooled him since she'd returned from Alhaja.

The rest of the museum was quiet and dark, and it felt strange to be wandering alone among all this priceless art. Of course, everything was wired to a central security system and there were guards at every exit, but Grace at least had the illusion of solitude.

She headed down the stairs, past the ancient statue of Winged Victory of Samothrace, when a voice caused her to still.

'Leaving already?'

She half-turned, saw Khalis coming down the stairs to meet her. 'I wanted some air.' She needed some now, for the sight of him had stolen the breath right from her lungs.

He stopped a foot or so in front of her and in the dim lighting Grace could not quite read his expression. His eyes were narrowed, but whether in concern or anger or mere indifference she could not say. 'Are you getting one of your headaches?'

She shrugged. 'It's been a long day.'

'You look tired.'

'I am.' She wondered why he cared, knew she wanted him to. 'I should go.' Still she didn't move.

'I haven't forgotten you, Grace.' His voice was pitched low, assured and so very sincere. She angled her head away from him, another wave of loss sweeping through her, nearly bringing her to her knees.

'You should have.'

'Have you forgotten me?'

'No, of course not.' She took a step away from him. They shouldn't be here, having this conversation alone.

'Of course not?' Khalis repeated. He'd stepped closer to her, blocking her escape route down the stairs. She glanced back at the statue of Nike, armless and headless yet still magnificent, the only witness to this encounter. 'That surprises me.' She said nothing, unwilling to continue the conversation even as her gaze roved over him, drinking him in, memorising his features. God, she'd missed him. Even now, when he looked so intent and angry, she missed him. Wanted him. 'The last time I saw you,' he said, 'you gave the distinct impression you wanted to forget me.'

'I did want to,' Grace answered. She couldn't be anything but honest now; the sheer closeness and reality of him was too much for her to be able to prevaricate. *Lie.* 'But I couldn't.' He'd stepped closer, so close she could breathe the achingly familiar scent of him, feel his intoxicating heat. She closed her eyes. 'Don't—'

'Don't what? Don't make you remember how good it was between us?' Slowly, deliberately, he reached out one hand and traced the line of her cheek. His thumb touched the fullness of her mouth and Grace shuddered.

'Please—'

'We still have it, Grace. That connection between us. It's still there.'

She opened her eyes, furious and afraid and despairing all at once. 'Yes, it is, but it doesn't matter.'

'You keep saying that, but I don't believe it.'

'I told you—'

'You didn't tell me anything. I'm still waiting for that, Grace. Waiting—and wanting to understand.' She just shook her head, unable to speak. 'I want,' he said, his teeth gritted, 'to give you a second chance—'

And she'd wanted to believe in second chances, even if she couldn't have one. 'Don't, Khalis.'

'You still want me—'

'Of course I do!' she shouted, her nerves well and truly shattered. 'I'm not denying it. So are you happy now? Satisfied?'

'Not in the least.' And, before she could protest or even think, he'd pulled her to him and his mouth came down hard and relentless and yet so very sweet on hers.

Grace gave in to the kiss for a blissful fraction of a second, her hands coming up to grip his shoulders, her body pressed so wonderfully against his, before she jerked away, her chest heaving. *'Don't!'*

Khalis was breathing as hard as she was, his face flushed, his eyes flashing fire. 'Why did you walk away from me?'

Tears pricked her eyes and her head blazed with pain. Truth spilled from her lips. 'Because I was afraid you'd hate me if I stayed.' A sound of someone on the stair above her made Grace's insides lurch in panic. She shook her head, unable to look at him. 'Just leave me alone,' she whispered. *'Please.'*

And then she fled down the stairs.

Back in her apartment, Grace peeled off her cocktail dress and took a long, hot shower, tried to banish the imprint of Khalis's mouth on hers, the blaze of desire his touch had caused her. She couldn't believe he'd still pursued her, still wanted her. She thought he'd hate her by now, and the fact that he didn't made it so much harder to forget him.

After her shower, dressed in her most comfortable worn pyjamas, Grace pulled out the photo album from the top shelf of the bookcase in her bedroom. She tried not to look at this album too often because it hurt too much. Yet tonight she needed to look at the beloved pictures, remind herself just what she had lost—and still had to lose.

Katerina at birth, her face tiny and wrinkled and red. Six weeks old, fast asleep in her pram. Six months, one chubby fist in her mouth, her eyes the same brown as Grace's own. A year, taking her first toddling steps. After that there were no photos except the ones Grace took when she saw her daughter once a month, in Athens. She gazed at these hungrily, as if she could fill in the many missing pieces of her daughter's last four years. Loukas had arranged it perfectly, she thought not for the first time, too weary now to be bitter. She saw Katerina enough for the girl to remember her, but not enough to love her as a child loved her mother. As Grace loved her daughter.

A sharp, purposeful knock on the front door startled her out of her thoughts and quickly she closed the album and slid it back on its shelf. Her heart had begun beating with hard, heavy thuds for she knew who was knocking at her door.

'Hello, Khalis.' Colour slashed his cheekbones and he held his body tensely, like a predator waiting to spring. He looked, Grace thought with a spasm of hopeless longing, as wonderful as always.

'May I come in?'

Wordlessly she nodded and stepped aside so he could enter. Khalis came into her little sitting room with its slanted ceilings and rather shabby antique furniture, seeming to dominate the small space.

To her surprise, he took a pile of folded papers from his inside pocket and dropped them on the coffee table with a thud.

'What is that?'

'Your file.'

'My *file*?'

His mouth tightened. 'After you left, I had Eric research your background.' He gestured to the thick pile of papers. 'He gave me that.'

Grace took in his hard expression, the narrowed eyes and tightened mouth, and she swallowed dryly. She knew what kind of articles the online gossip sites and tabloids had run. Sordid speculation about why Loukas Christofides, Greek shipping tycoon, had divorced his wife so abruptly and denied her custody of their daughter. 'It must have made some interesting reading,' she managed.

'No, it didn't, actually.'

She stared at him in confusion. 'What do you mean?'

'I didn't read it.'

'Why…why not?'

'Because even now I believe we shared something on that island, something important and different. I don't know why you ran from me, but I want to understand.' He stopped, his chest heaving, his gaze blazing into hers. 'Help me understand, Grace.'

How could she refuse when he asked her so rawly? And maybe…maybe he did understand. He *could.* She swallowed, her heart beating so hard it hurt. 'It's a long story,' she whispered.

'I have all the time in the world.' He sat down on her sofa, his body seeming relaxed although she still felt his tension. 'Why did you say I might hate you?' he asked quietly when the silence had ticked on for several minutes.

Grace knew he'd painted her as a victim, the most innocent of portraits. Now she would have to tell him the truth, in bold, stark colours. He would know, and he might leave here hating her more than ever before.

Or he might understand, forgive and love you more than ever before.

Did she dare hope?

Swallowing, she sat down across from him, her hands tucked between her knees. 'I've told you a bit about my marriage. About Loukas.'

'A little,' Khalis agreed neutrally. She hadn't said anything yet, and still it was so hard. Every explanation felt like an excuse.

'And that our marriage was troubled.'

'Yes, I'm aware of that, Grace.'

'I know.' She closed her eyes. He knew a little of how unhappy she'd been, trapped on that wretched island. Yet to go into detail now, to try to explain how desperate and lonely and scared she'd felt—wouldn't it all just sound as if she were justifying her actions? Khalis would certainly think so. He had given himself no excuses for accepting his father's help even after he'd realised the extent of his corruption. She wouldn't give herself any, either.

'Grace,' he prompted, and impatience edged his voice. Grace sighed and opened her eyes. There was, she knew, only one way to tell him the truth. Without any explanations, reasons or excuses. Just the stark, sordid facts. And see what he did with them.

'You've probably wondered how Loukas managed to gain complete custody of Katerina.'

'I assumed he worked the system, bribed a judge.' He paused, his voice carefully even. 'You implied as much.'

'Yes, but there was more to it than that. The truth is, he painted me as an unfit mother.' She gestured to the packet of papers he'd thrown onto her table. 'If you'd read those articles, you'd see. He made me seem completely irresponsible, negligent—' She swallowed and forced herself to go on. 'By the time he'd finished, anyone would think I hadn't cared about my daughter at all.'

Khalis's gaze remained steady on hers. 'But they would be wrong, wouldn't they?'

'They'd be wrong in thinking I didn't care,' Grace said in a low voice, brushing impatiently at the corners of her eyes. 'But they wouldn't be wrong in thinking I'd been negligent.' She drew in a shuddering breath. 'I was.'

Khalis said nothing for a moment. Grace forced herself to hold his gaze, but she couldn't tell a thing from his shuttered eyes, his expressionless face. The tears that had threatened were gone now, replaced with a deep and bone-weary resignation.

'Negligent,' he finally repeated. 'How?'

Again Grace hesitated. She wanted to rush to her own defence, to explain she'd never meant to be negligent, she'd never actually put Katerina in danger—but what was the point? The fact remained that she had betrayed her husband. Her family. Herself. She took a breath, let it out slowly. 'I had an affair.'

All Khalis did was blink, but Grace still felt his recoil. He was surprised, of course. Shocked. He'd been expecting something sympathetic, something perhaps about post-partum depression or her abusive husband or who knew what. All along he'd been thinking that she'd been hurt, not that she'd done the hurting. Not an affair. Not a sordid, sexual, adulterous affair.

'An affair,' he said without any expression at all.

'Yes,' she confirmed, tonelessly now. 'With the man who managed the island property. Gardening, house repairs—'

'I don't care what he *did*.'

'I know. I just…' She shook her head. 'I told you I didn't want to tell you,' she said in a low voice.

Khalis didn't speak, and neither did Grace. The silence that yawned between them now was worse than any words could have been. Finally he asked, 'And while you had this affair…you were negligent of your daughter?'

'I never put her in danger or anything like that,' she whispered. 'I loved her. I still love her.' Her voice wavered and she strove for control. Khalis needed to hear the facts without tears or sentiment. 'That whole time is a blur. I was so unhappy—I didn't knowingly neglect her, of course not. I just…I just wasn't the mother I wanted to be.'

'Or the wife, apparently.'

His cool observation was like a dagger thrust straight to the heart. Grace blinked hard. 'I know what it sounds like. Maybe it's a blur because I don't want to remember.' Yet she'd never been able to truly forget. How could you not remember and not forget at the same time? More contradictions. 'I'm not trying to make excuses,' she said. 'How can I? I'm just trying to explain—'

'Why you had this affair.'

'How I don't really remember.'

Khalis let out a rush of breath that sounded almost like a laugh, yet without any humour in it at all. 'How convenient,' he said, 'for you not to remember.'

'I'm not lying, Khalis.'

'You virtually lied to me from the moment I met you—'

'That is *not* fair.' Her voice rose, surprising her. 'Why should I have told you such a thing when I barely knew you?' She stuck out her hand in a mockery of an introduction. 'Hello, my name is Grace Turner, I'm an art appraiser and an adulteress?'

Khalis rose from the sofa, prowling around the room with a restless, angry energy. 'There were plenty of times after that,' he said, his words almost a growl. 'When you knew how I felt about you—'

'I know—' she cut him off with a whisper '—I know. And I was afraid, I admit that. I didn't want you to look at me…the way you're looking at me now.' With his face so terribly expressionless, as if he could not decide if she were a stranger or someone he knew, never mind loved.

And she loved him. She'd fallen in love with him on the island, with his tenderness and gentleness and understanding. She'd fallen in love with him despite that hardness inside him that she was seeing and feeling now. And she didn't know if her love was enough. She said nothing, simply waited for his verdict. Would he walk away from her just as he had from his family, no second chances, no regrets?

'How long?' he finally asked.

'How long…?'

'How long did you have this affair?'

She hesitated, the words drawn reluctantly from her. 'About six weeks.'

'And how long were you married?'

'Nearly two years.'

Khalis said nothing. Grace knew how awful it all sounded. How could she, with a little baby and a new husband, have gone and sought out another man? How could she have deceived her husband and lost her daughter? What kind of woman did that?

She did. Had. And if she hadn't been able to forget or forgive her actions, how could a man like Khalis?

Khalis stopped by the window, his back to her as he stared out at the darkness. 'And I suppose,' he said in a detached voice, 'your husband found out about the affair. And was furious.'

'Yes. He didn't want anyone to know he'd been… That I'd…' She stopped miserably. 'So in the courts he painted me as a negligent mother instead.'

'But you weren't.'

His observation, even when delivered in such a cold

voice, gave her the thinnest thread of hope. 'I don't *think*... I don't know what I was.'

Khalis didn't answer. His back was still to her. 'How?' he finally asked.

Grace blinked. 'How...?'

'How did he find out?'

'Do you really need to know all these details?' she asked rawly. 'How does it help anything—?'

'He walked in on you, didn't he?' Khalis said. He turned around and Grace quelled at his icy expression. This was the man who had faced down his father, who had walked away from his family. 'On you and your lover.'

Her scorching blush, she knew, was all the answer he needed. Khalis said nothing and Grace gazed blindly down at her lap. She couldn't bear the look of condemnation she knew she'd see on his face.

He let out a shuddering breath. 'I thought you'd been abused,' he said quietly. 'Emotionally or physically— something. Something terrible. I hated your ex-husband for hurting you.'

Grace blinked hard, her gaze still on her lap. 'I know,' she said softly.

'And all along...' He stopped and then, through her blurred vision, from the corner of her eye, she saw him pick up his coat.

Her throat was so tight she could barely choke out the words. 'I'm sorry.'

The only answer was the click of the door as Khalis shut it behind him.

CHAPTER TEN

'You look,' Michel told Grace a week later, 'like a plate of warmed-up rice pudding.'

'That doesn't sound very attractive.' She closed the door to her employer's office, eyebrows raised. 'You wanted to see me?'

Michel stared at her hard. 'I mean it, Grace. You look terrible.'

'Clearly you're full of compliments today.'

He sighed and moved around to his desk. Grace waited, trying to keep her expression enquiring and friendly even as her body tensed and another headache began its relentless pounding. This last week had been horrible. She had not seen or heard from Khalis since he'd walked out of her apartment without a word, leaving her too empty and aching even to cry. She'd drifted through the days, feeling numb and yet possessing a terrible awareness of what lay beneath that nothingness—an awful, yawning expanse of grief and despair. Just knowing it was there, like the deep and frigid waters beneath a thin layer of black ice, kept her awake at night, staring into the darkness, memories dancing through her mind like ghosts.

Memories of her marriage, the deep unhappiness she'd felt, the terrible mistakes she'd made. Memories of holding Katerina for the first time, the joy so deep it almost felt like pain as she'd kissed her wrinkled, downy head. Memories of the court hearing that had left her as close to longing for death as she'd ever been.

Memories of Khalis.

She'd taken her one night knowing she would only have the memories to sustain her, but they did not. They tormented her with their tenderness and sweetness, and she lay in bed with her eyes closed, imagining she could feel his arms around her, his body pressed against her, his thumb brushing the tear from her cheek.

Sometimes sleep came, and always dawn, and she stumbled through another day alone.

'Is there something you wanted?' Grace asked, keeping her smile in place with effort. Michel sighed and steepled his fingers under his chin.

'Not precisely. Khalis Tannous has donated the last two works in his father's collection.'

'The Leonardos?'

'Yes.'

Grace affected a look of merely professional interest. She had no idea if she succeeded or not. 'And where is he donating them?'

'The Fitzwilliam in Cambridge.'

The Fitzwilliam in Cambridge was practically a second home.

Grace angled her face away from Michel's narrowed gaze. 'A rather odd choice,' she said.

'Is it? I thought it quite spectacularly appropriate.'

'What do you mean?'

'Come now, Grace. It's quite obvious to anyone with eyes in his head that something happened between you and Tannous on that island.'

'I see,' Grace said after a second's pause.

'And that it made you more miserable than ever,' Michel

continued. 'I had hopes that Tannous might bring you back to life—'

'I wasn't *dead*,' Grace interjected and Michel gave her a mirthless smile.

'As good as. I'm your employer, Grace, but I've also known you since you were a child, and I care about you. I never liked seeing you so unhappy, and I like it even less now. I thought Tannous might help you—'

'Is that why you insisted I go to that island?'

Michel gave a dismissive and completely Gallic shrug. 'I sent you there because you are my best appraiser of Renaissance art. But I must confess I don't like the result.' He stared at her rather beadily from behind his desk. 'You're enough to make the Mona Lisa lose her smile.'

Grace thought of Leda's sorrowful half-smile and shook her head. 'I'm sorry. I'll try to—'

'Don't be *sorry*,' Michel cut her off impatiently. 'I didn't bring you in here to ask for an apology.'

'Then why?'

Michel was silent for a long moment. 'What did he do to you?' he finally asked.

'Nothing, Michel. He didn't do anything to me.' *Except make me fall in love with him.*

'Then why are you looking—?'

'Like a bowl of warmed-up rice pudding?' She gave him a small sad smile. 'Because he found out,' she said simply. 'He found out about me.'

Khalis gazed down at the financial report he was reading and tried to make sense of the numbers for the third time. In disgust at his own lack of focus, he pushed them away and stared out of the window of his father's office in Rome's EUR business district. Below him tourists and office workers bustled about their business, whether it was snapping photos or grabbing their lunch.

He should have forgotten her by now. Or at least stopped thinking of her. He'd been able to do that for his own family; why couldn't he do the same for a slip of a woman who had virtually lied to him and betrayed her own marriage vows?

Instead he kept remembering everything about her. How her eyes had lightened with sudden humour and her lips had curved as if she wasn't used to smiling. Her passion and strength of purpose for her work, her focus which matched his own. The softness of her breasts pressed against his chest, her body so wonderfully yielding against his.

And how she had deceived and duped him into thinking she was innocent, a victim like Leda. She should have told him. At some point during their time together, she should have told him. No, he realised with sudden savagery, it wasn't the telling that mattered. It was the doing. He wanted her not to have had the affair at all. After such a huge betrayal...how could he trust her? *Love* her?

His intercom buzzed, disrupting his pointless recriminations. 'A phone call for you, Mr Tannous, on line one.'

'Who from?'

'He didn't say, sir. But he said it was urgent.'

Khalis felt a flicker of irritation. He paid a receptionist to field his calls, not just pass them on. 'Very well,' he said tersely and picked up his phone.

'Yes?'

'Hello, Khalis.'

Khalis's fingers froze around the phone as his mind blanked with shock even as he registered that familiar voice. A voice he hadn't heard in fifteen years. His brother.

His brother who was supposed to be dead. Khalis's

mind raced in circles. Was his father alive as well? What the hell had happened? Swallowing, he finally managed to speak.

'Ammar,' he said without expression. 'You're alive.'

His brother let out a dry, humourless laugh. 'You don't sound pleased I am back from the dead.'

'You died to me fifteen years ago.'

'I need to talk to you.'

Khalis fought down the tide of emotion hearing his brother's voice had caused to sweep over him. Shock, anger, pain, and both a joy and regret he didn't want to acknowledge. 'We have nothing to say to each other.'

'Please, Khalis,' he said, but it still sounded like a command, the older brother bullying him into submission once more, and his resolve hardened.

'No.'

'I've changed—'

'People don't change, Ammar. Not that much.' Khalis wondered distantly why he didn't just hang up.

'Do you really believe that?' Ammar asked quietly, and for the first time in Khalis's memory he sounded sad rather than angry.

'I...' *Did* he believe that? He'd been living that truth for the last fifteen years. His father wouldn't change. Couldn't. Because if he had...if he could...then maybe Khalis wouldn't have had to leave in the dramatic fashion that he did. Maybe he could have stayed, or returned, or worked something out. Maybe Jamilah wouldn't have died.

Khalis swallowed, forced the agonising thoughts back. 'Yes,' he said stonily. 'I do believe that.' And then, his hand trembling, he hung up the phone.

The ensuing silence seemed to reverberate through the room. Khalis stabbed at his intercom. 'Please block any calls from that number,' he told the receptionist, who bumbled through an apology before Khalis severed the connection. He rose from the desk and paced the office restlessly, feeling caged not by the four walls but by his thoughts. His memories.

Had Ammar changed? He'd changed once before. Khalis had a sudden sharp memory of when his brother had turned eight. Their father had called him out of the nursery where they'd been playing with Lego together, neither of them knowing it was to be the last day of boyish pleasures. Khalis didn't know what Balkri had said or done to his oldest son that day, but when Ammar returned his lip was bleeding and the light had gone out of his eyes. He never had a kind word or action for Khalis again.

As the years had passed the rivalry between them had hardened into something unforgiving and cruel. Ammar always had to win, and not just win but humiliate Khalis. He was older, stronger, tougher and he let his little brother know it at every opportunity. Grace had asked him if Ammar was a bully, but it hadn't been a simple case of sibling rivalry. Ammar had been driven by something darker, and sometimes Khalis thought he'd seen a torment of emotion in his brother's eyes he knew he didn't understand. If he tried to, Ammar just turned away or hit him. There was no going back to those simple days of childhood. There was no going back at all.

Do people change?

Ammar might not have changed, but could he make that kind of assumption about everyone? About Grace?

Khalis halted his restless prowling and stared unseeingly out of the office window. He pictured Grace as he'd last seen her, her head bowed in regret, tears starting in her eyes. Did he believe she'd changed, or was he going to freeze her in her weakest moment, refuse to allow her to move past it? How much was his experience of his father and brother colouring his perception of Grace?

She was different, he realised with a shaft of self-recrimination. Of course she was. He still didn't like the stark reality of it, he knew. He wished things could be different. But he'd told Grace there was no point in looking back, no point in useless regrets. He wanted to look forward.

He turned away from the window, a new resolve hardening inside him. He needed to see Grace again. Speak to her. *Help me understand*, he'd asked. But he hadn't understood, not then. Maybe they both needed a second chance.

Grace straightened her simple grey sheath dress and glanced round the crowd of art enthusiasts and academics that comprised the guest list for tonight's reception at the Fitzwilliam Museum. Khalis was once again being hailed a hero for donating his father's works of art, in this case the two Leonardos of Leda.

'You must be thrilled,' one of her old professors told her as she plucked a glass of champagne from one of the circulating trays. 'Such important works of art being exhibited so close to home!'

'Yes, it's wonderful news for the museum,' Grace answered dutifully. Cambridge didn't really feel like home although she did still possess the house on Grange Road where she'd grown up. She let it out to visiting academics. And as for Khalis donating the works to the Fitzwilliam... *why* had he done that? Grace had wrestled with that question for many sleepless nights. It almost seemed like the kind of tender, thoughtful gesture that had made her fall in love with him—but he hated her now. So what kind of message was he trying to send?

She continued her progression around the grand entrance hall of the museum, chatting to guests, keeping an eye on the door. Even though she knew there was no real point, she still could not keep herself from looking for him and wanting to know when he was here.

Even if she hadn't felt it—that curious prickling between her shoulder blades—she would have known he'd arrived by the speculative murmurs that rippled through the crowd. Tall, imposing in an immaculate navy suit and utterly gorgeous, Khalis would draw admiration wherever he went. Grace stepped back against the wall, holding her untouched glass of champagne in front of her like some kind of shield. She saw Khalis's grey-green gaze search the crowd and knew he was looking for her. And then he found her, his unwavering stare like a laser that pierced all of her defences. She stood there, still clutching her glass, unable to move or even think.

Khalis's face was neutral yet his eyes seemed to blaze right into her, searing her soul. He really did hate her. With effort Grace turned away, walked on wobbly legs towards the next knot of people and tried desperately to seem unconcerned as their chatter washed over her in an incomprehensible wave.

Regret lashed him as Khalis watched Grace walk away. Her back was straight, her figure lithe and slender in the simple silk sheath she wore. Had she lost weight? Her face had been so pale, her eyes huge as they'd gazed at each other.

He'd had plenty of time to acknowledge how his past had coloured his perception of the present, of Grace. He'd duped himself, just as he had with his own father. He'd wanted to believe only the best of her and so he'd refused to heed her warnings, insisted on painting his own rosy picture.

And when she'd finally worked up the courage to give him the truth, he'd walked away. He'd wanted her trust—demanded it, even—only to abuse it at the first opportunity.

Why, he wondered bleakly, should she ever trust him again?

CHAPTER ELEVEN

GRACE felt her nerves tauten throughout the evening, so by the time the reception came to an end she felt as if they were overstretched threads, ready to snap. Her body ached with the effort of appearing interested and unconcerned, as well as thrilled that Khalis had donated such magnificent works of art to the museum.

Khalis, she'd observed, had circulated around the room in distinct counterpoint to her rotation; there could be no question he was avoiding her—or at least that she was avoiding him. Perhaps he was simply indifferent to her now. Yet, despite the distance between them, she remained constantly and agonisingly aware of him. Even as she chatted with guests she strained to hear his low, husky voice, felt every one of his easy movements reverberate through her own body.

At least she wouldn't see him again. The Leonardos had been the last two works from the Tannous collection. There would be no more receptions or galas, no need to encounter him at all. No risk, no danger. The thought should have brought blessed relief, not the wave of devastation Grace felt instead.

Finally the guests were trickling out into Trumpington Street and Grace found an opportunity to slip away. Khalis, she'd seen, was still chatting with a few hangers-on. She hurried out of the entrance hall, grabbing her coat, and into the damp night. It was midsummer, but the weather was wet and chilly and she wrapped her coat more firmly around herself as she headed down the street, her heels clicking on the slick pavement.

So that was that, she thought dully as she walked towards the hotel in the centre of town where she'd booked a room for the night. She'd probably never see him again. Talk to him again. *Touch* him again…

'Grace.'

For a second Grace thought she must be imagining things. Fantasising that she'd heard Khalis because she missed him so much, even though she knew she shouldn't—

'Grace.'

Slowly, stunned, she turned around. Khalis stood there, his hair damp and spiky with rain. He'd forgotten his coat.

Grace simply stared, her mind empty of thoughts. Why had he sought her out? He didn't look as if he was angry but she could not think of a single reason why he would come and find her. Surely everything had been said that awful night at her apartment?

'Are you staying at your father's house?' he finally asked after they'd simply stared at each other for an endless moment.

Grace shook her head. 'I've let it out. I booked into a hotel, just for the one night.'

'Tomorrow you go back to Paris?'

She nodded. 'Thank you for donating the Leonardos to the Fitzwilliam,' she said awkwardly. 'The museum is thrilled, of course.'

'Well,' Khalis answered with a crooked smile, 'the Louvre has the Mona Lisa, after all. And I know how much you care about these paintings. I thought they should go to your second home.'

Sudden tears stung Grace's eyes as she slowly shook her head. 'Thank you,' she said. 'It was kind of you, especially considering—' Her throat closed up and all she could do was stare at him, knowing her heart was in her eyes. Her heartbreak.

'Oh, Grace.'

In one fluid movement Khalis strode forward and pulled her into his arms, wrapping her in a gentle yet fierce hug. Grace felt the damp wool of his suit against her cheek, her mind frozen on the fact that he was here, hugging her, and it felt unbelievably, unbearably wonderful.

With effort she pulled away. 'Someone will see—'

'To hell with that.'

'I don't understand you,' Grace whispered. 'Why are you here? Why are you—?' *Hugging me. Looking at me as if... Almost as if you love me.*

'Because I'm sorry, Grace. I messed up. A lot.' His voice wavered on the last word and she stared.

'*You* messed up?'

'I shouldn't have walked out on you. I was shocked, I admit that, but I...I wanted you to trust me and then I threw that trust away with both hands.'

She blinked, taking in his words, the self-recrimination that lanced each one. 'You judge yourself pretty harshly.'

'I had no right to judge you.'

'I know what I did, Khalis—'

'I know you do. Everything you said and did is marked by guilt, Grace. I couldn't believe I didn't see that before.'

She angled her face away from him, knowing he was right. Wishing he wasn't. 'I don't know how to let go of it,' she whispered.

'I asked you to help me understand,' Khalis said quietly. 'And you told me the truth, but I don't think you told me all of it.'

She nearly choked. 'What more do you want me to say—?'

'Help me understand,' Khalis said as he drew her to him, his arms enfolding her and holding her close. Accepting her, even now. Especially now. 'Not just the things you regret or wish were different. Help me understand *you*.'

'I don't know how—'

'Tell me. Tell me everything.'

It wasn't until she was lying in his arms that she started to speak. Khalis knew he had to be patient. Gentler than he ever had been before. He'd thought it had been hard to get her to trust him before, when she hadn't told him anything and he'd thought she was perfect. Now he knew there were things he wouldn't want to hear, facts he would be reluctant to accept. And still he needed to hold her close and justify this fragile trust she'd placed in him.

She stirred, her hair brushing against his bare chest. He'd brought her to the luxury hotel he'd booked in town, the windows of the penthouse suite overlooking the River Cam. She'd come into the room warily, her eyes wide as she took in the huge four-poster bed piled high with pillows and a silken duvet.

He'd been about to reassure her that they could just talk, that all he wanted was to talk—well, sort of. After nearly three months apart, he wanted *her* desperately.

'Grace—' he began, and then she turned to him suddenly and wrapped her arms around him. He pulled her close, buried his face in her hair, inhaling its sweet fragrance.

'I missed you,' she said in a whisper. 'I missed me with you.' And he knew what she meant. He'd missed her, too, missed the sense of rightness he felt when he was with her. He kissed her then and, though he meant to keep it gentle, neither of them could control the tide of desire that swept over them as their lips met and met again. They'd missed each other too much to go slowly. In one fluid movement Khalis undid the zip of Grace's dress and she wriggled out of it, laughing a little as it snagged round her ankles.

'Another dress bites the dust,' Khalis said with a grin as he tossed it aside. Grace kicked off her heels. He pulled her towards the bed, his breathing turned harsh and ragged as they both fell upon its softness and each other, hands roving over skin with an urgent need to remember, to feel, to know.

Grace arched upwards as Khalis slid his hand between her thighs, his own voice coming out in a moan of longing. 'Oh, Grace. I missed this. I missed you.'

'Yes,' she panted, her head thrown back, her fingers digging into his shoulders as she urged him closer. And then he was filling her, making her gasp and his heart fill with the wonder of it, with the knowledge that the connection they'd both experienced was finally, joyously restored.

Afterwards she lay in his arms, her heart thundering against his as he brushed her dry cheek. 'No tears,' he said softly, his hand cupping her face, and she smiled against his palm.

'No tears,' she answered, and then neither of them spoke for a long moment. The weight of the words she hadn't said lay between them, but as Khalis held her he knew they bore it together. And then she stirred, settled herself against him and began.

'I first met Loukas when I was just fourteen,' she said softly. She ran her hand down his arms, her fingers curling around his bicep, holding onto him like an anchor. Khalis pulled her closer and waited. 'My mother had died the year before and I suppose I was lonely. My father was wonderful, but he was also easily distracted, absorbed by his books. And Loukas was so kind then. He was full of important plans about how he'd make his fortune, but he still made time for me.' She sighed and her hair whispered against his chest once more. 'The next time I saw him was at my father's funeral. I was twenty-six, and I'd just finished my doctorate. I was about to join an auction house in London, and before he died I felt like I had everything before me. But then...' She paused, shaking her head. 'I felt so alone. I realised I had no one left, and when Loukas invited me out, listened to me...well, it felt wonderful. I hadn't had any really serious relationships; I'd been too involved in my studies. And at that moment...' She paused. 'Sometimes I wonder if we'd met at a different point, if I would have noticed him at all. Maybe that's just...wishful thinking, I don't know. I don't think my head would have been quite so turned.'

'You were vulnerable.'

She shook her head. 'That's just an excuse.'

'We're not talking about excuses,' Khalis reminded her. 'Just understanding.'

'We were married within six weeks. It was far too fast, I see that now. I barely knew what I was doing. I was still grieving, really. I still thought of him as the university student with a kind word for me and a friendly smile, but he'd changed. He was wealthy now, terribly wealthy, and I think...I think he saw me as a possession. A prized one, but...' She stopped, swallowing, before she continued in a voice heavy with remembrance. 'He took me to his island for what I thought was a honeymoon. I thought we'd go back, live in London, have a normal life.' She stopped again, and he felt her body tense. He ran his hand down her shoulder and arm, pulled her closer to him. 'He left me there,' Grace confessed in a whisper. 'He informed the auction house that I wasn't taking up the post, and told me he wanted to keep me safe. He made it sound like he was trying to take care of me, but I felt—' She drew in a ragged breath. 'I felt like Leda, trapped in that little room with no one to see her or even know she was there.' She gave something that Khalis supposed was meant to be a laugh, but it wobbled too much. 'It sounds so ridiculous because I wasn't really a prisoner. I mean, I was a grown woman—I could have arranged transport or something. I wasn't *trapped*.'

'But?' Khalis prompted when it seemed as if she wouldn't go on.

'But I was afraid. Loukas felt like the only person I had in the world and, even though he wasn't there most of the time, I didn't want to lose him. And sometimes I convinced myself that it was all reasonable, that living on an island paradise was no hardship.'

'No wonder you hated Alhaja with all of its security and walls.'

'I don't like feeling trapped. Or managed. Loukas was always telling me what to do, even what to think.' She sighed, shaking her head. 'I think I was working up the courage to leave when I found out I was pregnant. I knew I couldn't leave him then. He wouldn't let me, and I still wanted our family to work.' She rolled over to face him now, her eyes clouded with sadness and yet so heartbreakingly clear. She hid nothing from him now. 'After Katerina was born, I thought it would be enough. It should have been enough. But she didn't sleep or nurse well and I was tired. Loukas had hired a nanny to help me but she was awful, as bossy and controlling as he was. At times I felt like I was going out of my mind.'

Khalis said nothing, just kept stroking her back, her shoulder, her arm. Touches to show he was listening. He understood. 'And then,' she whispered and stopped. She rolled back onto her side, tucked her knees up into her chest. The silence ticked on. 'Loukas hired him, you know,' she whispered. 'To tend the property. Sometimes I wonder... I think maybe...maybe he was testing me, and I failed.'

'That's not how a marriage is meant to work.'

'No,' Grace said after a moment, her voice no more than a scratch of sound. 'None of it was meant to work that way.' Her shoulders shook then and he knew she was crying, not just tears trickling down her face, but sobs that wrenched her whole body.

Khalis didn't say anything. He just held her, rubbing her back, his cheek pressed against her hair. The sound of her sorrow made his own eyes sting. How could he have ever doubted this woman? Thought he couldn't love her?

He loved her now more than ever.

Finally her sobs abated and she gave a loud sniff, a trembling laugh. 'I'm sorry. I haven't cried like that since... well, since forever.'

'I thought as much.'

She rolled over to face him again. Her eyes were red and puffy from weeping, her face completely blotchy. Khalis smiled and pressed a gentle kiss to her lips.

'You're beautiful,' he told her. 'And I love you.'

Her mouth curved in a trembling smile. 'I love you, too.' She laid her palm against his cheek. 'You know,' she said softly, 'for the first time I feel like the past isn't hanging over me. Suffocating me. I almost feel...free.' She stroked his cheek and another tear slid down her cheek. 'Thank you,' she whispered.

* * *

When Grace awoke the bed was empty and sunlight flooded the room. She lay there, the memories of last night washing over her in a healing tide. She never would have thought telling Khalis everything would feel so good, so restorative. Surely there were no secrets between them now.

What about your daughter?

Grace rolled over onto her side. Loukas would have found out about last night. Somehow, some way, he would know she'd been indiscreet. And even as her heart ached at this knowledge, she realised she no longer lived in the kind of terror he'd kept her in for four long years. With Khalis's help, she could fight the custody arrangement. She didn't know how long it would take or how they would do it, but for the first time in four years she had hope. It was as powerful and heady a feeling as the love she felt for Khalis. Smiling, she rose from the bed. She heard the sound of the shower from the bathroom and saw a tray with a carafe of coffee, a couple of cups and a newspaper. She poured herself a cup and reached for the paper.

Ammar Tannous survives helicopter crash.

It wasn't even on the front page, just a corner of the second page, hardly noticeable, and yet the words seemed to jump out and grab her by the throat. Khalis's brother was alive.

She'd barely processed this information when the bathroom door opened and Khalis emerged, dressed only in boxers, a towel draped over his shoulders.

'Good morning.'

She looked up, the paper still in her hands. 'Khalis… Khalis, I've just read…'

'Something amazing, it would seem.' He smiled as he reached for the carafe of coffee.

'Look at this.' She thrust the paper at him, pointing to the article about Ammar. And in the second it took Khalis to read the headline, his mouth compressing, she felt her hope and joy being doused by the icy chill of foreboding.

He glanced away from the paper and finished pouring his coffee. 'What about it?'

'*What about it?* Khalis, that's your brother. Isn't it?' For a second she thought she must have got it wrong. Surely he couldn't be so cold about *this*.

'It appears to be.' He sat across from her and sipped his coffee. Grace would have thought he was completely indifferent except for the tension radiating from his body. The bone china cup looked as if it might snap between his fingers. 'I went to file a custody appeal this morning.'

Grace blinked, trying to keep up. 'A custody—'

'My legal team thinks the trial judge abused his wide discretion,' Khalis explained. 'And because there was so little finding to support the court order, it's manifestly in error. I think you could have complete custody.'

Even as that thought caused new hope to leap within her, Grace shook her head. 'You're just changing the subject.'

'I'm talking about your daughter.'

'And I'm talking about your brother. You don't even seem surprised that he's alive.' She saw a wariness enter his eyes, felt his hesitation. 'You knew, didn't you?' she said slowly. 'You already knew.'

Khalis glanced away. 'He phoned me a few days ago.'

'And what…what did he say?'

'I didn't really talk to him.'

'Why not?'

He snapped his gaze back to her. 'Because he was up to

his neck in the same illegal activities as my father. I don't trust him, don't even know him any more. As far as I'm concerned, he's my enemy.'

She stared at him, saw the taut, angry energy of his body, and knew there was more to this than Khalis was saying. More darkness and pain and fear. He'd helped her look into the abyss of her own past regrets and mistakes last night; maybe it was her turn to help him.

'Couldn't you at least talk to him?' she asked.

'I don't see any point.'

'Maybe he's changed—'

Khalis gave a short, hard laugh. 'He suggested the same thing. People don't change, Grace. Not that much.'

She felt a sudden shaft of pain pierce her. 'Don't they?'

Khalis glanced at her, his lips pressed in a thin line. 'You know I didn't mean you.'

'I don't really see the difference.'

'You don't see the difference between you and my brother? Come on, Grace.'

'What *is* the difference, Khalis? It sounds like we're two people who made mistakes and regret them.'

'You think Ammar regrets—'

'You said he told you he'd changed.'

Khalis looked away. 'This is ridiculous. You made one single mistake which you regret bitterly, and Ammar made dozens—'

Grace felt herself go cold. 'Oh, I see,' she said. 'There's a maximum on how many mistakes you can make? I'm all right because I just made the one?'

'You're twisting my words.'

'I don't understand why you can't just talk to him at least.'

'Because I don't *want* to,' Khalis snapped. Colour

slashed his cheekbones. He looked angry, Grace thought, but he also looked afraid.

'You don't *want* to forgive him,' she said slowly. 'Do you?' Khalis didn't answer, but she saw the truth in his eyes. 'Why not?' she asked, her voice soft with sorrow. 'Why do you want to hold onto all that anger and pain? I know how it can cripple you—'

'You *don't* know,' Khalis said shortly. He rose from the table and moved to the window, his back to her. 'I don't want to talk about this any more.'

'So I'm meant to tell you everything,' she said, her voice rising. 'I'm meant to completely open my heart and soul but you get to have certain parts of your life be off-limits. Well, *that* seems fair.'

The very air seemed to shiver with the sudden suppressed tension, tension Grace hadn't even really known existed between them. She'd thought they'd both been laid bare and healed last night, but only she had. Khalis was still living in the torment of his past, holding onto his hard heart. How could she not have seen that? She'd seen that unyielding iron core the very first day they'd met. It didn't just magically melt or disappear. She'd been dreaming of happy endings, but now she saw that as long as Khalis held onto this anger they were just fairy tales.

'Khalis,' she said quietly, 'if you aren't willing to forgive your brother, if you can't believe that he might have changed, how can I believe you think I have?'

Khalis let out a ragged breath. 'It's completely different—'

'No, it isn't. It really isn't.' She shook her head sadly. She wanted to help him, but she didn't know if she could. If he'd let her. 'I almost wish it was. But don't you see how this—this coldness in you will affect anything we have together?'

He turned back to her, his eyes flashing a warning. 'You don't know my family, Grace.'

'Then tell me. Tell me what they did that's so bad you can't give your brother—your brother whom you thought was dead—a second chance.'

Khalis swung away from her and raked a hand through his hair. 'You are trying to equate two very different situations. And it simply doesn't work.'

'But the principles are the same.' Grace rose and took a step closer to him. 'The heart involved in the relationships is the same—yours.'

Khalis let out a sound that was close to a laugh, but filled with disbelief and disgust. 'Are you saying I can't love you if I don't forgive my brother?'

Grace hesitated. She didn't want to make ultimatums or force Khalis to do something he wasn't ready for or capable of. Yet she also knew that they could have no real, secure future as long as he harboured this coldness towards his family. 'Ever since we first met,' she began, choosing her words with care, 'I sensed a darkness—a hardness in you that scares me.'

He turned around, eyebrows arched in cynical incredulity. 'I *scared* you? I thought you loved me.'

'I do, Khalis. That's why I'm saying this.'

'Cruel to be kind?' he jeered, and Grace knew she was getting closer to the heart of it. The heart of him, and the thing—whatever it was—he was afraid of.

'I'm not trying to be cruel,' she said. 'But I don't understand, Khalis. Why won't you even talk to your brother? Why do you refuse to mourn or even think of your family? Why are you so determined never to look back?'

'I told you, the past is past—'

'But it *isn't*—' Grace cut him off '—as long as it controls your actions.'

He stared at her long and hard and she ached to cross the room and hold him in her arms. 'You helped me face my demons,' she said softly. 'Maybe now you need to face yours.'

His features twisted and, with a lurch of mingled hope and sorrow, Grace thought she'd won. *They* had. Then he turned away and said tonelessly, 'That's just a lot of psychobabble.'

Her eyes stung. 'Do you really believe that?'

'Don't make this into something it isn't, Grace. This isn't about us. We can be perfectly happy without me ever seeing my brother again.'

'No. We can't.' Her words fell slowly into the stillness, as if from a great height. Grace imagined she could almost see the irrevocable ripples they created, like pebbles in a pond, disturbing the calm surface for ever.

He turned back to face her, shock replacing anger. 'What are you saying?'

'I'm saying,' Grace said, each word a knife-twist in her heart, 'that if you can't even talk to your brother—your brother whom you thought was dead—then I can't be with you.' He looked as if she'd just punched him. Maybe she had. 'I'm not trying to give you some kind of ultimatum—'

'Really?' he practically snarled. 'Because it looks that way from here.'

'I'm just stating facts, Khalis. Our relationship has been a mess of contradictions from the beginning. Keeping secrets even as we had this incredible connection. Amazing intimacy and terrible pain. Well, I don't want a relationship—a love—that is a contradiction. I want the real thing. Whole. Pure. Good. I want that with you.'

He let out a shuddering breath. 'When we first met, I put you on a pedestal. I thought you were perfect, and I was disappointed when you showed me your feet of clay.

But I accepted you, Grace. I accepted you and loved you just as you are. Yet now you can't do the same for me? I've got to be perfect?'

'No, Khalis.' She shook her head, blinked back tears. 'I don't want you to be perfect. I just want you to try.'

His mouth curved in a disbelieving and humourless smile. 'Try to be perfect.'

'No,' she said, her heart breaking now, 'just try to forgive.'

Khalis didn't answer, and that was answer enough. He couldn't do it, she realised. He couldn't even try to let go. And they couldn't have a future together—a secure, trusting future—as long as he didn't.

Slowly Grace walked over to the bed, where her clothes from last night still lay discarded on the floor. She reached for her dress. 'I think,' she said, 'I have a flight to catch.'

Khalis stared at the nondescript door of the hotel room where his brother was staying. It had taken two days to work up the courage to call Ammar, and then fly to Tunis where he was staying. Now he was here, standing in the hallway of a nameless hotel, the cries and clangs from the busy medina of metalwork and craft shops audible on the hot, dusty air.

Even now he was tempted to walk away. Grace had demanded answers, yet how could he explain his reasoning for refusing simply to speak to his brother? What kind of man could be so hard-hearted?

Apparently he could.

Yet the feeling—the *need*—to keep himself distant from his family was so instinctive it felt like a knee-jerk reflex. And when he'd heard Ammar's voice on the telephone, sounding so ragged and even broken, that deep-seated instinct had only grown stronger. Grace was right. He didn't want to forgive Ammar. He was afraid of what might happen if he did.

It had taken her leaving him—*devastating* him—for him to finally face his brother. His past.

Khalis raised one trembling fist and knocked on the door. He heard footsteps, and then the door opened and he was staring at his brother. Ammar still stood tall and imposing, reminding Khalis that his brother had always been older, stronger, tougher. Ammar's face looked gaunt, though, and there was a long scar snaking down the side of his face. He stared long and hard at Khalis, and then he stepped aside to let him in.

Khalis walked in slowly, his body almost vibrating with tension. The last time he'd seen Ammar he'd been twenty-one years old and leaving Alhaja. Ammar had laughed. *Good riddance*, he'd called. And then he'd turned away as if he couldn't care less.

'Thank you for coming,' Ammar said. He sounded the same, surly and impatient. Maybe he hadn't changed after all. Khalis realised he would be glad, and felt a spurt of shame.

'I'm not sure why I did,' Khalis answered. He couldn't manage any more. Raw emotion had grabbed him by the throat and had him in a stranglehold, making further speech impossible. He hadn't seen his brother in fifteen years. Hadn't spoken to him or even looked at a photograph of him. Hadn't *thought* of him, because to think of Ammar was to remember the happy days of their childhood, when they had been friends and comrades-in-arms. Not competitors. Not enemies.

To think of Ammar, Khalis knew with a sudden flash of pain, was to think of Jamilah and to regret. To wonder if he might have made a mistake in leaving all those years ago. And that was a thought he could not bear to consider for a moment.

'So,' he finally said, and his voice sounded rusty, 'you're alive.' As far as observations went, it was asinine. Yet Khalis felt robbed of intelligent thought as well as speech. Part of him wanted to reach forward and hug the brother he'd lost so long ago. The other part—the greater part, perhaps—still had a heart like a stone.

The heart involved in the relationships is the same— yours.

And he wanted that heart to belong to Grace. For her— for them—he had to try. 'Why did you want to talk to me?' he asked.

Ammar's face twisted in a grimace. 'You're my brother.'

'I haven't been your brother for fifteen years.'

'You'll always be my brother, Khalis.'

'What are you saying?' Khalis tried to keep his voice even. It was hard with so many contrary emotions running through him. Hope and fear. Anger and joy. *I don't want a relationship...that is a contradiction.* He swallowed. He had to see this through.

Ammar released a shuddering breath. 'God knows I have made many mistakes in this life, even as a boy. But I've changed—'

Khalis let out a disbelieving laugh, the sound harsh and cold. Grace was right. There was a coldness inside him, a hard darkness he did not know how to dispel. *She only wanted you to try.* 'How have you changed?' he managed.

'The helicopter crash—'

'A brush with death made you realise the error of your ways?' Khalis heard the sneer in his own voice.

'Something like that.' He gazed levelly at Khalis. 'Do you want to know what happened?'

He shrugged. 'Very well.'

'The engine failed. I think it was a genuine accident, although God knows our father always suspected someone of trying to kill him.'

'When you deal with the dregs of society, that tends to happen.'

'I know,' Ammar said quietly.

Khalis gave another hard laugh. 'As well you should.'

'I was piloting the helicopter,' Ammar continued. 'When we realised we were going to crash, Father gave the one parachute to me.'

For a second Khalis was stunned into silence. He had not thought his father capable of any generosity of spirit. 'Why was there only one parachute?' he asked after a moment.

Ammar shrugged. 'Who knows? Maybe the old man only wanted there to be one so he could be sure to take it in case of an accident. I always thought he'd be the last one standing.'

'But he changed his mind?'

'He *changed*,' Ammar said quietly, and Khalis heard a note of sorrow in his brother's usually strident voice. 'He was dying. He'd been diagnosed with terminal cancer six months ago. It made him start to really think about things.'

'*Think* about things?'

'I know he had a lot to answer for. I think that's why he decided to hand the company over to you. He only did that a month or so before he died, you know. He talked about you, said he regretted being so harsh with you.' Ammar gave him a bleak smile. 'Admired what you'd done with yourself.'

It seemed so hard to believe. Painful to believe. The last time he'd seen his father, Balkri Tannous had spat in his face. Tried to hit him. And recklessly Khalis had told him he was taking Jamilah with him.

Over my dead body, Balkri Tannous had said. Except in the end it had been Jamilah's.

And still Khalis had left. Without her.

Pain stabbed at him, both at his head and his heart. This was why he never thought about the past. This was why he'd cut himself off from his family so utterly, had insisted his father or brother could not be redeemed. So he wouldn't wonder if he should have stayed. Or returned sooner. Or taken her anyway. Anything to have kept his sister alive.

'You're thinking of Jamilah,' Ammar said quietly and Khalis swung away, braced one hand against the door. He wanted to leave. He was *desperate* to leave, and yet the thought of Grace—the warmth of her smile, the *strength* of her—made him stay. 'It was an accident, you know,' Ammar said. 'Her death. She didn't mean to kill herself.' He paused, and Khalis closed his eyes. 'I knew you'd wonder.'

'How do you know it was an accident?'

'She was determined, Khalis. Determined to live. She told me so.'

Khalis let out a strangled sound, choking off the cry of anguish that howled inside him. 'If I'd come back for her—'

'You could not have prevented an accident.'

'If I'd stayed—'

'You couldn't have stayed.'

His hand clenched into a fist. 'Maybe I should have,' he said in a low voice. 'Maybe if I'd stayed, I could have changed things for the better.'

His back to Ammar, Khalis didn't hear his brother move. He just felt his hand heavy on his shoulder. 'Khalis, it took an act of God and my own father's death for me to want to change. It took Father's diagnosis for him to even think about changing. Do not attempt to carry the world on your shoulders. We were grown men. We were not your responsibility, and neither was Jamilah.'

Khalis didn't speak for a long moment. He couldn't. 'So what happened next?' he finally asked.

'I parachuted into the sea and managed to get to land. A small island south of here, closer to the coast. It had fresh water, so I knew I could survive for a few days at least. I dislocated my shoulder when I landed, but I managed to fix it.' Ammar spoke neutrally enough, but Khalis was humbled anyway. He could not imagine enduring such a catastrophe.

'And?' he asked after a pause.

'After six days I managed to flag down a fishing boat, and they brought me to a small village on the coast of Tunisia. I'd developed a fever by that point and I was out of my mind for several days. By the time I knew who I was and I remembered everything, weeks had passed since the crash. I knew I needed to speak with you, so I flew to San Francisco to find out where you were, and then to Rome.'

'How did you even know about my company?'

'I've kept track of what you've been doing,' Ammar said. 'All along.'

And meanwhile Khalis had deliberately refused to read or listen to anything about Tannous Enterprises. Again he felt that hot rush of guilt. He couldn't bear the thought of his brother or father regretting his departure, watching him from afar. He couldn't bear the thought he'd been wrong.

'I know I wasn't a good brother to you,' Ammar said.

Khalis just shrugged. 'Sibling rivalry.'

'It was worse than that.' He didn't answer. He knew it was. 'Please forgive me, Khalis.'

Ammar couldn't say it plainer than that. Khalis registered the heartfelt sincerity in his brother's gaunt face, and said nothing. The words he knew his brother wanted to hear stuck in his throat.

If I forgive you then the past can't be the past any more and I'll have to live with the guilt and regret of knowing I should have stayed and saved Jamilah. And I don't think I can survive that. I'm not strong enough.

But Grace was strong. Grace made him strong. And he knew, just as Grace had known, it wasn't only Ammar he needed to forgive. It was himself.

You helped me face my demons. Maybe now you need to face yours.

His throat worked. His eyes stung. And somehow he found the words, raw and rusty, scraping his throat and tearing open his heart. 'I forgive you, Ammar.' *And I forgive myself.*

Ammar broke into a smile and started forward. Clumsily, because it had been so long, he reached to embrace Khalis. Khalis put his arms around Ammar, awkwardly, yet with a new and hesitant hope.

He couldn't have done it, he knew, without Grace. Without her strength. She'd been strong enough to walk away from him. And now he prayed she would come back to him when he found her.

Ammar stepped back, his smile as awkward as Khalis's hug. This was new and uncomfortable territory for both of them. 'It is good,' he said, and Khalis nodded.

'What will you do now?' he asked after a moment. 'Tannous Enterprises should by rights be yours.'

Ammar shook his head. 'Father wanted you to have it—'

'But I don't want it. And your whole life has been dedicated to the company, Ammar. Perhaps now you can make something of it. Something good.'

'Maybe.' Ammar looked away. 'If it is possible.'

'I'll sign my shares over to you—'

'I need to do something first.'

Surprised, Khalis blinked. 'What?'

'I need to find my wife.'

'Your *wife*?' He had not known his brother had married. But of course he had not known anything about these last fifteen years.

'Former wife, I should say,' Ammar corrected grimly. 'The marriage was annulled ten years ago.'

Curiosity sharpened inside him, but the hard set of his brother's features kept Khalis from asking any more probing questions. 'Still,' he said, 'you should take control of Tannous Enterprises. Turn it around, if you will.' Perhaps then the company could be redeemed, as Grace had suggested. Redeemed rather than dismantled and destroyed.

'There is time to discuss these matters,' Ammar said, and Khalis nodded.

'You must come to Alhaja. We can celebrate there.'

Ammar's mouth twisted. 'I've always hated that place.'

'As did I. But perhaps we can redeem even that wretched island.'

'You are full of hope,' Ammar observed wryly. He did not sound particularly hopeful himself. His brother might have changed, but he still looked haunted.

'I am,' Khalis answered. His heart felt light, lighter than ever before. He felt as if he could float. And he needed to find Grace. 'And while you need to find your wife, I need to find my—' He paused. 'My love.' Smiling, he embraced his brother once more. 'And tell her so.'

Six hours later, Khalis strode into the head office of Axis Art Insurers. A receptionist flapped at him, saying she'd have to check if Ms Turner was available, but Khalis just flashed her a quick smile and kept walking. Nothing was going to keep him from Grace now.

He'd wandered down several wrong corridors before he finally found her in one of the labs. She was standing in front of a canvas—he couldn't see what it was and, frankly, he didn't care—and his heart swelled with love at the sight of her. She wore a crisp white blouse and navy pencil skirt, reminding him of when he'd first seen her. Her hair was up in its classic chignon, but a few tendrils had escaped and curled around her neck. She gestured to the unseen canvas with one slender arm, and he felt pride swell along with overwhelming love. She was so strong. So amazing, to have come so far and done so much on her own. To have not just survived, but triumphed.

Khalis opened the door.

Grace heard the door open, felt that prickling along the nape of her neck that had alerted her to Khalis's presence before. Her body was wired to his in some elemental way, and yet...

Surely he couldn't be here.

He was. She turned and saw him looking as mouthdryingly gorgeous as ever, his expression intent and serious as he gazed at her. And Grace gazed back, drinking him in, knowing that even though it had only been a few days she'd missed him. Terribly.

He nodded towards the canvas on the stainless steel table. 'Forgery?'

'No, it appears to be genuine so far.'

Khalis gave her a crooked smile. 'I don't know much about art, but thank God I know the real thing when I see it.' He closed the space between them in two long strides and swept her into his arms. 'You.'

Grace's arms came around him as a matter of instinct even as she searched his face. 'Khalis—'

'I found my brother. I talked to him.'

Her arms tightened around him. 'I'm glad.'

'So am I. Mainly because losing you over something like that would have killed me. But also because you were right. I did need to face my past. Face my family, and that darkness in myself.' His throat worked as his voice choked just a little. 'I needed to forgive myself.'

She laid one hand against his cheek. 'Sometimes that's the most difficult part.'

'But worth it. Most definitely worth it.' He bent his head and, smiling, Grace tilted her own back as he kissed her softly, a promise. 'Now,' Khalis said as he lifted his head, 'we really can look towards the future. Our future.'

'That sounds like a wonderful idea.' Grace's gaze widened when she saw him retrieve a small velvet box from his pocket.

'And I think,' Khalis said with a smile, 'it can begin with this. Grace Turner, will you marry me?'

She let out a shocked and joyous laugh. 'Yes. Yes, I will.'

'Then,' Khalis said, sliding a gorgeous diamond and sapphire ring onto her finger, 'the future looks very bright indeed.'

EPILOGUE

GRACE stared at the imposing villa in one of Athens's best neighbourhoods and felt a flutter of nerves so strong it was more like a kick in the gut.

'What if she's forgotten me?' she whispered. 'What if she doesn't want to go with me?'

Khalis slipped his hand into hers and squeezed. 'We'll take it together, one step at a time. One second at a time, if need be.'

Grace let out a slow breath and nodded. It had taken six months to get to this moment. Her ex-husband had been brought to court in a custody appeal, and after a lengthy trial Grace had been awarded main custody of Katerina, with Loukas having her every other weekend. Furious that he'd been thwarted, her ex-husband had relinquished all claims on his daughter. Even though Grace was saddened that he'd rejected Katerina, she was thrilled to have her daughter back. Thrilled and terrified. After years of stilted and unsatisfactory visits, she'd finally tuck her in at night. Sing her songs. Hold her close.

If Katerina would let her.

'I'm so scared,' she whispered and Khalis put his arm around her as he guided her up the front steps.

'The past really is the past,' he reminded her. 'We're looking towards the future now—as a family.'

A family. What a wonderful, amazing, humbling thought. Gulping a little, Grace nodded and pressed the doorbell.

Katerina's nanny answered the door; she had remained on as the child's carer while the trial went on. Now, with trepidation, Grace introduced herself and then waited as the nanny went to bring her Katerina.

The first sight of her daughter in several months nearly brought her to her knees. She'd grown several inches and, at nearly six years old, she was starting to lose some of that toddler roundness. Her eyes were wide and dark as she stared at Grace.

'Hello, Katerina,' Grace said, her voice only just steady. Khalis squeezed her hand in silent, loving encouragement. 'Hello, darling.'

Katerina gazed at her for a long moment, and then glanced at Khalis curiously before turning back to Grace. She offered a shy, hesitant smile. 'Hello, Mama,' she said.

* * * * *

The Undoing
of de Luca

KATE HEWITT

CHAPTER ONE

HER eyes, he decided, were the most amazing shade of lavender. The colour of a bruise.

'Larenz, did you hear a word I was saying?'

Reluctantly, Larenz de Luca pulled his fascinated gaze from the face of the waitress and turned back to his dining partner. Despite his growing interest in the lovely young woman who had served him his soup, he couldn't fathom why his head of PR had brought him to this manor house. The place was a wreck.

Amelie Weyton drummed her glossy French-manicured nails on the polished surface of the antique dining table, which looked as if it could serve at least twenty, although there were only the two of them seated there now. 'Really, I think this place is perfect.'

Amused, Larenz let his gaze slide back to the waitress. 'Yes,' he murmured, 'I quite agree.' He glanced down at the bowl of soup she had placed in front of him. It was the colour of fresh cream with just a hint of gold and a faint scent of rosemary. He dipped in his spoon. Cream of parsnip. Delicious.

Amelie drummed her fingernails again; Larenz saw a tiny crescent-shaped divot appear on the glossy surface of the table. From the corner of his eye, he saw the waitress flinch but when he looked up her face was carefully expressionless, just as it had been since he'd arrived at Maddock Manor an hour ago. Larenz could tell she didn't like him.

He'd seen it the moment he had crossed the threshold. Lady Maddock's eyes had narrowed and her nostrils had flared even as she'd smiled in welcome. Now her violet gaze swept over him in one quick and quelling glance, and Larenz could tell she was not impressed. The thought amused him.

He was used to assessing people, sizing them up and deciding whether they were useful or not. It was how he'd fought his way up to run his own highly successful business; it was how he stayed on top. And while Lady Maddock may have decided he was an untitled, moneyed nobody, he was beginning to think she was very interesting indeed. And possibly very...useful...as well.

In bed.

'You haven't even seen the grounds yet,' Amelie continued. She took a tiny sip of soup; Larenz knew she wouldn't eat more than a bite or two of the three-course meal Lady Maddock had prepared for them. Ellery Dunant was cook, waitress *and* chatelaine of Maddock Manor. It must gall her terribly to wait on them, Larenz thought with cynical amusement. Or, perhaps, on anyone. Both he and Amelie had acquired plenty of polish but they were still untitled, the dreaded nouveau riche, and, no matter how much money you had, nothing could quite clean the stink of the slum from you. He knew it well.

'The grounds?' he repeated, arching an eyebrow. 'Are they really so spectacular?' He heard the mocking incredulity in his own voice and, from the way he saw Ellery flinch out of the corner of his eye, he knew she had heard it, too.

Amelie gave a sharp little laugh. 'I don't know if *spectacular* is really the word. But it will be perfect—' Her soup forgotten, she'd propped her elbows on the table—Amelie had never quite learned her manners—and now gestured wildly with her hands, knocking her wine glass onto the ancient and rather threadbare Oriental carpet.

Larenz gazed down impassively at the fallen glass—at least it hadn't broken—and the spreading, scarlet stain. He heard Ellery's sharply sucked-in breath and she dropped to her knees in front of him, reaching for the tea towel she'd kept tucked into her waist to blot rather hopelessly at the stain.

He gazed at her bent head, her white-blonde hair scraped up into a sorry little bun. It was an unflattering hairstyle, although at this angle it revealed the pale tender skin at the back of her neck; Larenz had a sudden impulse to press his fingers there and see if her fresh and creamy skin was as soft as it looked. 'I believe a little diluted vinegar gets red wine out of fabric,' he commented politely.

Ellery glanced up swiftly, her eyes narrowing. They were no longer lavender, Larenz observed, but dark violet. The colour of storm clouds, which was rather appropriate as she was obviously furious.

'Thank you,' she said in a voice of arctic politeness. She had the cut-glass tones of the English upper crust; you couldn't fake that accent. God knew, Larenz had once tried, briefly, when he'd been sent to Eton for one hellish year. He'd been scorned and laughed at, easily labelled as a pretender, a poser. He'd walked out before he'd sat his exams—before they could expel him. He'd never gone back to another school of any kind. Life had provided the best education.

Ellery rose from the floor and, as she did so, Larenz caught a faint whiff of her perfume—except it wasn't perfume, he decided, but rather the scent of the kitchen. A kitchen garden, perhaps, for she smelled like wild herbs: rosemary and a faint hint of something else, maybe thyme.

Delicious.

'And, while you're at it,' Amelie drawled in a bored voice, 'perhaps you could bring me another glass of wine?' She arched one perfectly plucked eyebrow, her generous collagen-inflated lips curving in a smile that did not bother to disguise her malice. Larenz suppressed a sigh. Sometimes Amelie could be rather…obvious. He'd known her since his first days starting out in London, sixteen years old and an errand boy at a department store. She'd been working in the shop where Larenz bought sandwiches for the businessmen to eat at their board meetings. She'd cleaned up quite nicely, but she hadn't really changed. Larenz doubted if anyone ever did.

'You don't,' he commented after Ellery had walked swiftly out of the dining room, the green baize-covered door swinging shut behind her, 'have to be quite so rude.'

Amelie shrugged. 'She's been arsey with me since I arrived. Looking down that prim little nose at me. Lady Muck thinks she's better than anyone, but look at this hovel.' She glanced contemptuously around the dining room with its tattered curtains and discoloured patches on the wall where there had surely once been original paintings. 'Her father may have been a baron, but this place is a wreck.'

'And yet you said it was spectacular,' Larenz commented dryly. He took a sip of wine; despite the wreck of a house this manor appeared to be, the wine was a decidedly good vintage. 'Why did you bring me here, Amelie?'

'Spectacular was your word, not mine,' Amelie returned swiftly. 'It's a mouldering wreck, there's no denying it.' She leaned forward. 'That's the point, Larenz. The *contrast*. It will be perfect for the launch of Marina.'

Larenz merely arched an eyebrow. He couldn't quite see how a decrepit manor house was the appropriate place to launch the new line of haute couture that De Luca's, his upmarket department store, had commissioned. But then perhaps this was why Amelie was his head of PR; she had vision.

He simply had determination.

'Imagine it, Larenz, gorgeous gowns in jewel tones—
they'll stand out amazingly against all the musty gloom—a
perfect backdrop, the juxtaposition of old and new, past and
future, where fashion has *been* and where it's going—'

'It all sounds rather artistic,' Larenz murmured. He had no
real interest in the artistry of a photo shoot; he simply wanted
the line to succeed. And, since he was backing it, it would.

'It'll be amazing,' Amelie promised, her Botoxed face
actually showing signs of animation. 'Trust me.'

'I suppose I'll have to,' Larenz replied lightly. 'But did
we have to *sleep* here?'

Amelie laughed lightly. 'Poor Larenz, having to rough it
for a night.' She clucked. 'How will you manage?' Her smile
turned coy. 'Of course, I know a way we could both be more
comfortable—'

'Not a chance, Amelie,' he replied dryly. Every once in
a while, Amelie attempted to get him into bed. Larenz knew
better than to ever mix business and pleasure, and he could
tell Amelie's attempt was half-hearted at best. Amelie was
one of the few people who had known him when he was a
young nobody; it was one of the reasons he allowed her so
much licence. Yet even she knew not to get too close, not to
push too hard. No one—and in particular no woman—was
allowed those kinds of privileges. Ever. A night, a week,
sometimes a little more, was all he allowed his lovers.

Yet, Larenz acknowledged with some amusement,
here was Amelie thinking they might get up to something
amidst all this mould and rot. The thought was appalling,
although…

Larenz's glance slid back to Lady Maddock. She'd returned to the dining room, her lovely face devoid of any
make-up or expression, a glass of wine in one hand and a
litre of vinegar in the other. She carefully placed the glass in
front of Amelie and then, with a murmur of apology, knelt
on the floor again and began to dab at the stain. The stinging

smell of vinegar wafted up towards Larenz, destroying any possible enjoyment of the remainder of his soup.

Amelie hissed in annoyance. 'Can't you do that a bit later?' she asked, making a big show of having to move her legs out of the way while Ellery scrubbed at the stain. 'We're trying to eat.'

Ellery looked up; the vigorous scrubbing had pinkened her cheeks and her eyes now had a definite steely glint.

'I'm sorry, Miss Weyton,' she said evenly, not sounding apologetic at all, 'but if the stain sets in I'll never get it out.'

Amelie made a show of inspecting the worn carpet. 'I hardly think this old thing is worth saving,' she commented dryly. 'It's practically rags already.'

Ellery's flush deepened. 'This carpet,' she returned with icy politeness, 'is a nearly three-hundred-year-old original Aubusson. I have to disagree with you. It's most certainly worth saving.'

'Not like some of the other things in this place, I suppose?' Amelie returned, her gaze moving rather pointedly to the empty patches on the wall, the wallpaper several shades darker there than anywhere else.

If it was possible, Ellery's flush deepened even more. She looked, Larenz thought, magnificent. He'd first thought her a timid little mouse but now he saw she had courage and pride. His lips curved. Not that she had much to be proud about, but she certainly was beautiful.

She rose from her place at their feet in one graceful movement, retrieving the bottle of vinegar and tucking the dirty cloth back into the pocket of her apron.

'Excuse me,' she said stiffly and walked quickly from the room.

'Bitch,' Amelie said, almost idly, and Larenz felt a little flash of disappointment that she had gone.

* * *

Ellery's hands shook as she rinsed out the rag and returned the vinegar to the larder. Rage coursed through her, and she clenched her hands into fists at her sides, pacing the huge kitchen several times as she took in great cleansing breaths in an attempt to calm her fury.

She'd handled that badly; those two were her *guests*. It was so hard to remember that, to accept their snide jibes and careless remarks. They thought paying a few hundred pounds gave them the right, yet Ellery knew it did not. They gave mere money while she gave her life, her very blood, to this place. And she couldn't bear to have it talked about the way that callous crane of a woman had, wrinkling her nose at the carpets and curtains; Ellery knew they were threadbare but that didn't make them any less precious to her.

She'd disliked Amelie Weyton from the moment she'd driven up the Manor's long sweeping drive that afternoon. She'd been at the wheel of a tiny toy of a convertible and had gone too fast so the gravel had sprayed all over the grass and deep ruts had been left in the soft rain-dampened ground. Ellery had said nothing, knowing she couldn't risk losing Amelie as her customer; she'd rented out the manor house for the weekend and the five hundred pounds was desperately needed.

Only that morning the repair man had told her the kitchen boiler was on its very last legs and a new one would cost three thousand pounds.

Ellery had swayed in horror. Three *thousand* pounds? She hadn't earned that kind of money, even with several months at her part-time teaching job in the nearby village. Yet the news should hardly surprise her for, from the moment she'd taken over the running of her ancestral home six months ago, there had been one calamity after another. Maddock Manor was no more than a wreck on its way to near certain ruin.

The best Ellery could do was slow its inevitable decline. Yet she didn't like thinking like this, couldn't think like this, not when holding on to the Manor sometimes felt akin to holding on to herself, the only way she could, even if only for a little while.

Most of the time she was able to push such fears away. She focused on the pressing practical concerns, which were certainly enough to keep both her mind and body occupied.

And so Ellery had kept her focus on that much-needed boiler as Amelie had strolled through the house as if she owned the place.

'This place really is a disaster,' she'd said, dropping her expensive faux-fur coat on one chair; it slithered to the floor and she glanced pointedly at Ellery to pick it up. Biting down hard on the inside of her cheek, Ellery had done so. 'Larenz is going to have a *fit*,' Amelie added, half to herself. Ellery didn't miss the way the woman's mouth caressed the single word: Larenz. An Italian toy boy, she surmised with disgust. 'This is a step—or ten—down for him.' Her eyes glinted with malicious humour as she glanced at Ellery. 'However, I suppose we can rough it for a night or two. It's not like there's anything else around here, is it?'

Ellery forced a polite smile. 'Is your companion arriving soon?' she asked, still holding the wretched woman's coat. When Amelie had emailed the reservation, she'd simply said 'and guest'. Ellery presumed this guest was the aforementioned Larenz.

'Yes, he'll be here for dinner,' Amelie informed her idly. She turned around in a slow circle, taking in the drawing room in all of its shabbiness. 'Good heavens, it's even worse than the photos on the website, isn't it?' she drawled, and Ellery forced herself not to say anything.

She'd chosen photographs of the best rooms for her website, Maddock Holiday Lettings. The conservatory, with throw pillows carefully covering the threadbare patches on the sofa and the sunlight pouring in, bathing the room in mellow gold; the best bedroom, which she'd had redecorated with new linens and curtains.

It had set her back a thousand pounds but she'd been realistic. You couldn't charge people to sleep on tattered sheets.

Still, Amelie's contempt of her home rankled. This venture, letting the Manor out to holidaymakers, was new, and Amelie, in fact, was only the second guest to actually come and stay. The other had been a kindly elderly couple who had been endearingly delighted with everything. They'd appreciated the beauty and history of a house that had stayed in the same family for nearly five hundred years.

Amelie and her Italian lover just saw the stains and the tears.

'And they're making a few more while they're at it,' Ellery muttered under her breath now. She pictured the scarlet splash of red wine on the Aubusson once more and she groaned aloud.

'Are you quite all right?'

Ellery whirled around; she'd been so lost in her thoughts that she hadn't heard the man—Larenz—enter the kitchen. He'd arrived only a few minutes before dinner had been served and Ellery hadn't really had time to greet or even look at him properly. Yet she'd seen enough to form an opinion: Larenz de Luca was not the toy boy she'd expected. He was much worse.

From the moment he'd arrived, Amelie had flirted and fawned over him, yet Larenz had been impervious and even indifferent to the attentions of the gorgeous, if rather emaciated, Amelie, and every careless or callous remark or look had grated on Ellery's nerves, which was ridiculous because she didn't even like Amelie.

Yet she *hated* men who treated women like playthings just to be enjoyed and then discarded. Men like her father.

Ellery forced such negative thoughts away and nodded

stiffly at Larenz. He lounged in the doorway of the kitchen, one shoulder propped against the frame, his deep blue eyes alight with amusement.

He was laughing at her. Ellery had sensed it before, when she'd been scrubbing at the stain. He'd enjoyed seeing her on her knees, working like a skivvy in front of him. She'd seen the smile curl the corner of his mouth—his lips were as perfectly sculpted as a Renaissance statue's—and the same smile was quirking them now as he watched her pace the kitchen.

'I'm perfectly fine, thank you,' she said. 'May I help?'

'Yes, you may, actually,' he returned, his voice a drawl with only a hint of an Italian accent. 'We've finished the soup and we're waiting for the next course.'

'Of course.' She felt colour flare in her face. How long had she been wool-gathering in the kitchen while they waited for their meal? 'I'll be right out.'

Larenz nodded but he didn't move, his eyes lazily sweeping over her, assessing and dismissing all in one bored glance. Ellery could hardly blame him for it; she was dressed in a serviceable black skirt and a white blouse with a sauce stain on the shoulder, and the heat from the kitchen was making her sweaty. Still, his obvious contempt aggravated her, and was so typical of a man like him.

'Good,' he finally said and pushed off from the doorframe, disappearing back into the dining room without another word.

Ellery hurried to check on the chicken simmering on the stove. Fortunately, the tarragon cream sauce hadn't curdled.

Back in the dining room, Amelie and Larenz sat unspeaking. Larenz looked relaxed, sprawled in his seat, while Amelie seemed tense, drumming her nails once more, the little clicks seeming to echo through the silent room. She had, Ellery saw, caused another divot in the ancient tabletop.

Amelie had barely touched her soup but Ellery saw, to her satisfaction, that Larenz had completely cleaned his bowl. As she reached for the empty dish, he laid a hand on her wrist, shocking her with the unexpected touch. His skin was warm and dry and it sent a strange, not unpleasant, jolt right down to her plimsoll-encased toes.

'The soup was delicious,' he murmured, and Ellery jerked her head in the semblance of a nod.

'Thank you. Your main course will be out shortly.' Nerves caused her hands to tremble and the bowl clanked against his wine glass as she took it, making her flush and Larenz smile lazily.

'Careful. You don't want to spill another glass of wine.'

'Your glass is empty,' Ellery returned tartly. She hated that he'd seen how he affected her—and why should he affect her? He was incredibly attractive, yes, but he was also an arrogant ass. 'I'll refill it in a moment,' she added, and turned back to the kitchen.

Dumping the dishes in the sink, Ellery hurried to serve the plates of chicken, sauce and the roasted new potatoes she'd left crisping in the oven. Quite suddenly, she felt utterly exhausted. She had an entire weekend of catering meals—and enduring Amelie's snide remarks and Larenz's speculative looks—ahead of her, yet all she wanted was to go upstairs and hide under the covers.

Behind her, the boiler clanked mournfully and Ellery gritted her teeth. She had to bear it. The only other option was to sell Maddock Manor, and that was no option at all. Not yet, at least. The Manor was the only thing she had left of her family, her father. Sometimes, as impossible and irrational as she knew it was, the Manor felt like the only thing that validated who she was and where she had come from.

She was keeping it.

* * *

Two hours later, Larenz and Amelie had finally retired upstairs. Ellery scraped the remains of their meal—Larenz had finished both his main course and a generous slice of chocolate gâteau, while Amelie had barely touched any of it—into the bin and tried to ease the persistent ache in her lower back. What she really wanted was a long soak in a very hot bath, but the repair man had already told her that such a venture would push the boiler past its limited endurance. She'd have to settle for a hot-water bottle instead, which had been her companion most nights anyway. Now that it was late October, the cold stole into the Manor and crouched in corners, especially in the draughty, unheated room where Ellery slept.

Sighing, she stacked the rinsed plates in the dishwasher and mentally ran through her to-do list for breakfast. Part of the weekend package was a full English fry-up, yet she was quite sure Amelie Weyton ran only to black coffee in the mornings.

Larenz, on the other hand, probably required a hearty breakfast that he'd tuck into with relish while never putting on an ounce. Quite suddenly, Ellery found her mind wandering upstairs, to the best bedroom with its antique four-poster—the new silk hangings had eaten up most of her budget for the room's redecoration—and the birch logs she'd laid in the hearth that morning. Would Larenz light a fire so he and Amelie could be cosy in bed together, the flames casting dancing shadows over the bed and their entangled bodies?

Or perhaps they would have another source of heat—she imagined them there, among the pillows and blankets, Amelie's limbs twined around Larenz, and felt a sudden dart of completely unreasonable jealousy.

She could not possibly be jealous. What was there to be jealous of? She despised the pair of them. Yet even as she asked herself this, Ellery already knew the answer. She was jealous of Amelie having someone—anyone—but especially someone as attractive and, face it, as sexy as Larenz de Luca. She was jealous of them both, and the fact that neither of them would be alone tonight. Like she would.

Ellery sighed. She'd been living at Maddock Manor, attempting to make ends if not meet, at least glimpse each other, for six long, lonely months. She'd made a few friends in the village, but nothing like the life she'd once had. Nothing like the life she wanted.

Her university friends were all in London, living the young urban lifestyle that she'd once, ridiculously, enjoyed. Even after only half a year it seemed as faded and foggy as a dream, the kind where you could only remember hazy fragments and surreal snatches. Her best friend, Lil, was constantly urging her to come back to London, even if just for a visit, and Ellery had managed it once.

Yet one weekend in the city didn't completely combat the loneliness of living alone in an abandoned manor house, day after day after day. Ellery shook her head in an attempt to rid herself of such useless thoughts. She was acting maudlin and pathetic and it annoyed her. She couldn't visit London right now, but she could at least ring her friend. She imagined telling Lil all about the horrible Amelie and Larenz and knew her friend would relish the gossip.

Smiling at the thought, Ellery resumed stacking the dishwasher and wiping the worktops. She had just finished and was about to switch off the lights when a voice made her jump nearly a foot in the air.

'Excuse me—'

Ellery whirled around, one hand to her chest. Larenz de Luca stood in the kitchen doorway, leaning against the door. How had she not heard him come in again? He must, she thought resentfully, be as quiet as a cat. He smiled sleepily, and Ellery noticed how deliciously rumpled he looked. His hair, glinting darkly in the light, curled over his forehead and was just a little ruffled. He'd shed his suit jacket and tie from earlier and had unbuttoned the top two buttons of his shirt; Ellery could glimpse a stretch of golden skin there, at the base of his throat, that made her suddenly swallow rather dryly.

'Did I frighten you?' he asked, and she thought his accent sounded more pronounced. It was probably intentional, Ellery thought with a twinge of cynical amusement. He did the sexy Italian thing rather well, and he knew it.

'You startled me,' she corrected, sounding as crisp and buttoned-up as the spinster schoolteacher she was for the children in the village. She gave him her best teacher's glare and was satisfied to see him inadvertently straighten. 'Is there something you need, Mr de Luca?'

Larenz cocked his head, his heavy-lidded gaze sweeping over her as it had earlier that night. 'Yes, there is,' he finally said, still in that sleepy yet speculative voice. 'I wondered if I could have a glass of water.'

'There are glasses and a pitcher in your room,' Ellery replied, and heard the implied rebuke in her voice. Larenz heard it too, for he arched his eyebrows, his mouth quirking—Ellery couldn't tear her gaze away from those amazing lips—and said, 'Perhaps, but I prefer ice.'

Somehow she managed to drag her gaze upwards, to those blue, blue eyes that were so clearly laughing at her. She managed a stiff nod. 'Of course. Just a moment.'

She felt Larenz's eyes on her as she went to the chest freezer and rifled through the economy-sized bags of peas and chicken cutlets.

'Do you live here alone?' he asked, his tone now one of scrupulous politeness.

Ellery finally located a bag of ice and pulled it out, slamming the lid of the freezer down with a bit more force than necessary. 'Yes.'

She saw his glance move around the huge empty kitchen. 'You don't have any help?'

Surely that was obvious, considering how she'd cooked and waited on them tonight. 'A boy from the village mows the lawns every now and then.' She didn't want to admit just how alone she really was, how sometimes the house seemed to stretch in endless emptiness all around her so she felt as tiny and insignificant as one of the many dust motes filtering through the stale air. She *really* needed to ring Lil and get some perspective.

Larenz raised his brows again and Ellery knew what he was thinking. The lawns were bedraggled and rather overgrown; she hadn't had the money to pay Darren to mow recently. So what? she wanted to demand. It was nearly winter anyway. No one mowed their lawns in winter, did they?

She dumped the ice into two glasses and thrust them at Larenz, her chin lifted. 'Will that be all?'

His mouth quirked again as he glanced at the glasses—Ellery realized she'd assumed Amelie wanted ice too—and then he took the glasses, his fingers sliding across hers. The simple touch of skin on skin made Ellery jerk back as if she'd been scalded. She felt as if she had; she could still feel the warmth of his hand even though he was no longer touching her.

She hated that she reacted so obviously to his little touches—his intentional little touches, for there could be no doubting that he did it on purpose, just to see her jump. To enjoy how he affected her, for wasn't that the basic source of power of a man over a woman? And here she was, hating Larenz de Luca yet still in his thrall. The thought made Ellery's face flame with humiliated aggravation.

Larenz's mouth curled into a fully fledged smile, lighting his eyes, turning them to a gleaming sapphire. 'Goodnight, Lady Maddock.'

Ellery stiffened. She didn't use her title—worthless as it was—and it sounded faintly mocking on Larenz's lips. Her father had been a baron and the title had died out with him. Her own was no more than a courtesy, an affectation.

Still, she had no desire to continue the conversation so she merely jerked her head in acceptance and, with another sleepy smile, Larenz turned around and left.

Suddenly, in spite of her best intentions to have him walk away without another word, Ellery heard herself calling out, 'What time do you eat breakfast?'

Larenz paused, glancing at her over his shoulder. 'I usually like to eat early, although, since it is the weekend…would nine o'clock be all right?' His lips twitched. 'I'd like to give you a bit of a lie-in.'

Ellery glared at him. The man could make anything sound suggestive and even sensual, and she certainly didn't need his consideration. 'Thank you, but that's really not necessary. I'm an early riser.'

'Then perhaps we'll watch the dawn together,' Larenz murmured and, with a last wicked smile that let her know he knew just how much he was teasing—and even affecting—her, he left, the door swinging shut behind him with a breathy sigh.

Ellery counted to ten, and then on to twenty, and then she swore aloud. She waited until she heard Larenz's footsteps on the stairs—the third one always creaked—and then she reached for the telephone. It was late, but Lil was almost always ready for a chat.

She picked up on the second ring. 'Ellery? Tell me you've finally come to your senses.'

Ellery gave a little laugh as she brought the telephone into the larder, where there was less chance of being overheard in case Larenz or Amelie ventured downstairs again.

'Just about, after tonight,' she said and Lil laughed, the pulsing beat of club music audible from her end.

'Thank heavens. I don't know why you shut yourself away up there—'

Ellery closed her eyes, a sudden shaft of pain, unexpected and sharp, slicing through her. 'You know why, Lil.'

Lil sighed. They'd had this conversation too many times already. No matter how many times Ellery tried to explain it, her friend couldn't understand why she'd thrown away a busy, full life in London for taking care of a mouldering manor. Ellery didn't blame Lil for not understanding; she barely understood it herself. Returning to Maddock Manor when her mother had been preparing to sell it had been a gut decision. Emotional and irrational. She accepted that, yet it didn't change how she felt, or how much she needed to stay. For now, at least.

'So what happened tonight?' Lil asked.

'Oh, I have these awful guests,' Ellery said lightly. Suddenly she didn't feel like regaling Lil with stories of Amelie and Larenz. 'Completely OTT and high maintenance.'

'Throw the tossers out, then,' Lil said robustly. 'Take a train—'

'Lil, I can't. I have to stay here until—' Ellery stopped, not wanting to finish the thought.

'Until the money runs out?' Lil filled in for her. 'When will that be? Another two weeks?'

Ellery managed a wobbly laugh. 'More like three.' She sighed, sliding to the floor, her forehead resting on her knees. 'I know I'm mad.'

'At least you admit it,' Lil replied cheerfully. 'Look, I know you can't come now, but you are due for a visit. That manor is bringing you down, Ellery, and you need someone to bring you *up*.' Her voice softened. 'Come back to the city, have fun, have a real relationship for starters—'

'Don't,' Ellery warned with a sigh, even though she knew her friend was right.

'Why not? It's not like you're going to meet a man in the bowels of Suffolk, and you don't want to die a virgin, do you?'

Ellery winced. Lil was her best friend, but sometimes she was just a bit too blunt. And she'd never really understood how—or why—Ellery had kept herself from the messy complications of sex and love for so long. 'I'm not looking for some kind of fling,' she said, even as an image—a tempting image—of Larenz flitted through her mind, his tie loosened and his hair tousled…

'Well, how about a girls' weekend, then?' Lil suggested.

'Now *that* sounds lovely—'

'But?' Lil interjected knowingly. 'What's your excuse this time, Ellery?'

'No excuses,' Ellery replied a bit more firmly than she felt. 'I know I need to get away, Lil. I nearly lost my temper with these idiot guests and it's just because I haven't been anywhere or done anything but try to keep things together here—'

'Then next weekend,' Lil cut her off kindly, for Ellery knew she sounded too emotional. Felt too emotional. She didn't like showing so much of herself, being so vulnerable, not even with Lil, and her friend knew it. 'You don't have any guests booked then?'

'Not hardly.' She injected a cheerful note into her voice. 'This lot's only my second. Thanks for chatting, Lil, but I can tell you're out on the town—'

A peal of raucous laughter sounded from Lil's end. 'It doesn't matter—'

'And I'm exhausted,' Ellery finished. 'I'll talk to you later.' After she'd disconnected the call, Ellery sat there, the receiver pressed to her chest, the manor house quiet and dark all around her. She could hear the wind blowing outside, a lost, lonely sound.

The phone call had made her feel a bit better, and she was *definitely* going to go to London next weekend, but in the meantime this weekend—with its two guests—still yawned endlessly in front of her. Sighing, Ellery rose and replaced the telephone before heading to bed.

Upstairs, Larenz took his two glasses, the ice cubes clinking against each other, and walked past Amelie's door. She'd taken the best bed for herself—of course—and Larenz knew the only way to enjoy such comfort was to share it. When they'd gone upstairs together, Amelie still chattering on about how perfect this wreck of a house would be for the launch of Marina, Larenz had known with a certain weariness that the moment was coming.

And so it had, with Amelie pausing in the doorway of the best bedroom, giving him a kittenish little smile that might have amused him once, but now just annoyed him.

'It's awfully cold in here, you know,' she said in a husky murmur.

'You could ask Lady Maddock for a hot-water bottle,' he replied dryly, stepping back from Amelie's open doorway just so she got the message.

She did, smiling easily. That was one good thing about Amelie; she caught on quickly. 'I'm sure she's using it for herself,' she replied. 'It's probably the only thing that ever shares her bed,' she added with that touch of malice Larenz had never really liked.

'Well, at least you have lots of covers,' he replied lightly. From her open doorway, he caught a glimpse of an ornate four-poster piled high with throw pillows and a satin duvet. It looked a good deal more comfortable than the spartan room he'd had to settle for.

Still, he wasn't even tempted. Especially not when his mind—and other parts of his body—still recalled the way Ellery Dunant's violet eyes had flashed at him, the way she'd jerked in response to his lightest touch. She wanted him. She didn't want to want him, but she did.

He turned back to Amelie, the friendliness in his voice

now replaced with flat finality. 'Goodnight, Amelie.' He turned away and walked to his own bedroom without looking back.

Back in his own room now, Larenz grimaced at the faded wallpaper and worn coverlet. Clearly, Lady Maddock had not got around to redecorating the other bedrooms.

He put aside his glass with the precious ice—it had been no more than a pretext to see Ellery Dunant again—and pulled the covers down from the bed. A gust of wind rattled the windowpanes and Larenz felt the icy draught. He grimaced again. What on earth was Ellery Dunant doing in a place like this? Clearly her family had fallen on hard times, but Larenz couldn't fathom why she didn't sell up and move somewhere more congenial. She was young, pretty and obviously talented to some degree. Why was she wasting away in the far reaches of Suffolk taking care of a house that looked about to collapse around her ears?

Shrugging the thought aside, Larenz began to undress. He normally slept in just his boxers but it was so damned cold in this place he decided to leave his shirt and socks on, making him look, he suspected, rather ridiculous.

He doubted Ellery Dunant's room was properly heated. He pictured her in a white cotton nightdress, the kind that buttoned right up to her neck, a pair of fuzzy slippers on her feet, clutching a hot-water bottle. The image made his lips twitch in amusement until he found his mind leaping ahead to the moment when he unbuttoned that starchy nightgown and discovered the delectable woman underneath.

She'd been affected by him; there could be no denying that. Larenz recalled the way her skin had felt, as soft as silk and faintly cool. Her fingernails, he'd noticed, had been bitten to the quick. She was undoubtedly worried about finances; why else would she be renting out this decrepit place?

He knew just how to take her mind off such matters.

He stretched out in bed, wincing at the icy sheets. Again,

he found himself imagining Ellery there with him, warming the sheets, warming him.

And he could warm her… He would take great pleasure in thawing the ice princess, Larenz thought, folding his hands behind his head. Sleep seemed a long way off. From outside he heard a telltale creak of the floorboards and hoped it wasn't Amelie making a last-ditch effort. Surely she had more pride than that; their working relationship was too important to throw away on an ill-conceived fling.

His mind roved back to Ellery. He wondered whether she was pining away for some prince while she waited in her lonely manor. Was she hoping for some would-be knight to rescue her? Well, he was no knight or prince, not in the least. He was a bastard through and through and there was surely no way Lady Maddock would consider him as husband material for a second, which suited him fine.

But as a lover…? Larenz smiled and settled more deeply into the bed.

Then he heard the floorboard creak again, past his room, and the sound of a door closing somewhere at the other end of the hall. It must have been Ellery, on her way to bed.

Larenz stretched out, trying to make himself more comfortable despite the rather lumpy mattress and the coldness of the room. Had Ellery walked past his room on purpose? Was she curious? Longing?

He hoped so, because he had just decided that she most definitely needed to be seduced.

CHAPTER TWO

ELLERY woke early, determined to fill the day with chores and errands. If she kept herself busy and productive, she'd have less time to think. Imagine.

It had been imagining that had kept her up last night, restless with a nameless longing that had suddenly risen up inside her, a tide of need. She'd replayed the moments with Larenz, the feel of his fingers on her skin, over and over again, hating herself for doing so. Hating him.

She needed to focus, she told herself as she tied an apron around her waist and reached for a dozen eggs from inside the fridge. Focus on getting work done now and then having a weekend away, as she'd promised Lil. She tried to imagine herself in London at some random club or bar, having *fun*, but the image remained both blurry and vaguely depressing.

'It *would* be fun,' Ellery insisted in a mutter as she cracked six eggs into a heavy china mixing bowl and began to whip them into a foamy froth. 'We'd talk and laugh and dance—' And Lil would try to convince her—again—to come back to London.

When Ellery had told her friend she was returning home in an attempt to make Maddock Manor a success, Lil had looked at her as if she'd gone completely mad.

'Why on earth would you want to go back *there*?'

Ellery hadn't been able to answer that question. She'd only

visited her home once or twice a year since her father had died; her mother usually preferred to meet her in London. She had never even had much affection for the house, really; four years at boarding school and another three at university had made her a stranger to the place, and she still remembered the shock slicing through her at its decrepit state when she'd returned after her mother had announced she planned to sell it. When had the paintings been sold? When had the grounds gone to ruin? Had she never noticed, or had she simply not cared? Or, most frighteningly, had their family's slide into financial ruin happened a long time ago, her father hiding the truth from her, as he had with so many things?

Yet, despite the Manor's decrepit state, Ellery had been determined to keep it for as long as she could. Somehow the prospect of losing it—losing her childhood memories there—had forced some latent instinct to kick in and so she'd rushed into this unholy mess. Even now she couldn't regret it, couldn't shake the fear that if she lost the Manor, she lost her father. It was a stupid fear, absurd, because she'd lost her father long, long ago…if she'd ever really had him.

Grimacing, Ellery reached for a tomato from the windowsill and began to slice it with a bit too much vigour. She didn't like to dwell on memories; if she thought too much about the past she started wondering if anything was true… or trustworthy.

'Careful with that. You're liable to lose a finger.' Once again, Ellery jumped and whirled around, the chopping knife still brandished in one hand. Larenz stood in the doorway, looking even better than he had last night. Even in her pique, Ellery could not quite keep herself from gazing at him. He was dressed in a pair of faded jeans and a worn grey T-shirt. Simple clothes, Saturday slumming clothes, Ellery supposed, yet Larenz de Luca looked far too good in them, the soft cotton and faded denim lovingly hugging his powerful frame, emphasizing his trim hips and muscular thighs.

'I'm fine, thank you,' she said crisply. 'And, if you don't mind, I'd rather you knocked before coming into the kitchen.'

'Sorry,' Larenz murmured, sounding utterly unrepentant.

Ellery made herself smile and raised her chin a notch. 'May I help you with something, Mr de Luca? Breakfast should be ready in a few minutes.' She glanced pointedly at the old clock hanging above the stove. It was a quarter to nine.

'Why don't you call me Larenz?' he suggested with a smile.

Ellery's smile back was rather brittle. 'I'm afraid it's not the Manor's policy to address guests by their first names.' That was a complete fabrication and, from Larenz's little smile, she could tell he knew it. He was amused by it.

'The Manor?' he queried softly. 'Or Lady Maddock's?'

'I don't actually use the title,' Ellery said stiffly. She hated her title, hated its uselessness, its deceit. As if she was the only one who deserved it. 'You may simply call me Miss Dunant.' Listening to her crisp voice, she knew she sounded starchy and even absurd. She wished, for a fierce unguarded moment, that she could be someone else. Sound like someone else, light, amused, mocking even. She wished she could feel that way, as if things didn't matter. As if they didn't hurt. Instead, she just bristled and it made Larenz de Luca laugh at her.

'Miss Dunant,' Larenz repeated thoughtfully. 'I'm afraid I usually prefer to be a bit more informal. But if you insist...' He took a step closer, still giving her that lovely lazy smile, and Ellery's heart began to beat like a frightened rabbit's. She sucked in a quick, sharp breath.

'Will Miss Weyton be joining you for breakfast?'

'No, she won't.' Larenz's smile widened. 'As a matter of fact, Miss Weyton is leaving this morning.'

'What...?' Ellery couldn't keep the appalled shock from her voice. She realized she was disappointed, not simply to lose the money, but to lose the company. Larenz de Luca, the most intriguing and infuriating man she'd come across in a long time. She was actually disappointed that he might be leaving.

'Yes, she has to return to work,' Larenz continued, sounding anything but regretful. 'However, I'll be staying for the rest of the weekend.'

Ellery's breath came out in a slow hiss. 'You'll be staying?' she repeated, and heard how ridiculously breathy her voice sounded. Inwardly, she cringed. 'Alone?'

Larenz had been moving slowly towards her so now he was less than a foot away. Ellery could smell the clean citrusy tang of his aftershave, and she found her fascinated gaze resting on the steady pulse in his throat. The skin there looked so smooth and golden.

'Well, I won't be alone,' Larenz murmured. He reached out to tuck an errant tendril of hair behind her ear and Ellery jerked back in shock; her skin seemed to buzz and burn where his fingers had skimmed it. Her senses were too scattered to make a reply and, seeing this, Larenz clarified, 'I'll be with you.'

She took a step backwards, away from both danger and temptation. She didn't want to be tempted, not by a man she couldn't even like. Not by a man who looked poised to use her and discard her—and any other woman—just as her father had her mother.

Or perhaps Larenz de Luca wouldn't even get that far. Perhaps he was simply amusing himself with her, enjoying her obvious and inexperienced reactions. Perhaps he never intended to act on any of this. She didn't know which was more humiliating. 'I'm afraid I'll be busy with my duties most of the weekend,' she told him crisply, 'but I'm sure you'll enjoy the relaxing solitude of Maddock Manor…especially such a busy man as yourself.'

Larenz watched her stumbling retreat with a faint, mocking little smile. 'Am I so busy?' he murmured and Ellery shrugged, spreading her hands wide, forgetting she was still holding a rather wicked-looking knife.

'I'm sure—'

'Watch that,' Larenz murmured, his voice still lazy despite the fact that the knife's blade had swept scant inches from his abdomen.

'Oh—' Ellery returned the knife to the worktop with an inelegant clatter. Her breath came out in an agitated shudder. She hated that this man affected her so much, and she hated it even more that he knew it. 'It's probably better,' she managed, turning back to her bowl of eggs so she didn't have to face him, 'if you leave me to finish making breakfast.'

'As you wish,' Larenz replied. 'But I'm going to hold you to showing me the grounds later today.' He left before Ellery could make a response, but she already knew she had no intention of showing Larenz de Luca anything while he was here. She intended to stay completely out of his way.

The weekend seemed as if it were getting longer by the minute.

Larenz wandered through the empty reception rooms as he waited for Ellery to make his breakfast. The heavy velvet curtains were still drawn against the light, although pale autumn sunshine filtered through the cracks and highlighted the dust motes dancing in the air.

Larenz gazed around the drawing room, with its high ceiling and intricate cornices, a beautiful marble fireplace and long sash windows. It was a stately, elegant room, and if he tried he could almost see it as it had once been, grand and imposing, despite the faded carpets and moth-eaten upholstery, the peeling gilt and wide crack in the marble surround of the fireplace.

He thought he could hear Amelie upstairs rather forcefully throwing her things back into her suitcase. She had been less than pleased to be summarily dismissed from the manor.

Larenz had caught her coming out of her bedroom—she looked as if she'd had a better night's sleep than he had—and said with a little smile, 'I've been thinking about your idea of using the manor as the location for Marina's fashion shoot. It's a good one.'

Amelie's lipsticked mouth curved into a satisfied smile. 'I knew you would.'

'And,' Larenz added in an implacable tone, 'I need you to head back to the office this morning to start the paperwork. I'll deal with Ellery.'

'Ellery, is it?' Amelie noted, her eyes narrowing. She forced a smile. 'Well, I for one will be glad to see the last of this hovel for a little while at least.' Larenz felt only relief as he headed downstairs.

Now, wandering restlessly through the drawing room, Larenz thought of how Ellery had whirled around when he'd come into the kitchen that morning, surprised and jumpy and aware, and he smiled, all thoughts of Amelie wiped clean away. This weekend was going to be very interesting and, he had no doubt, very pleasurable, as well.

Ellery placed the scrambled eggs, fried mushrooms, bacon, stewed tomato and a heap of baked beans on a plate, grabbed the rack of toast and a bottle of ketchup with her free hand, and made her way into the dining room.

Somewhere in the distance a door slammed and Ellery winced at the sound of a car starting, along with the telltale spray of gravel. More ruts in the road.

'That would be Amelie leaving,' Larenz said pleasantly. He stepped from the shadows of the dining room where he'd been standing. Hiding, more like, Ellery thought. At least this time she didn't jump.

'In a hurry, is she?' she asked dryly. She ignored the sudden pounding of her heart and the fact that her mind—and body—were very aware that she and Larenz de Luca were now alone. She placed the food on the table and turned around to fetch the coffee. 'I'll be right back.'

'You are getting a plate for yourself, I hope?' Larenz enquired. A frisson of feeling—could it possibly be hope—shivered through Ellery. She stiffened, her back to him. 'I prefer not to eat alone,' Larenz clarified, a hint of laughter in his voice.

'I eat in the kitchen,' she said without turning around.

'Then allow me to join you.'

She heard Larenz reach for his plate, the clank of cutlery as he scooped up his dishes, quite prepared to follow her into the kitchen. Slowly Ellery turned around. 'What exactly do you want from me, Mr de Luca?'

'Is friendliness not part of the weekend special?' he asked lightly. He didn't answer her question.

'I like to be friendly *and* professional,' she replied curtly.

'As a matter of fact, this is professional,' Larenz returned. 'I have a business proposition to put to you.'

Ellery didn't bother hiding her disbelief. The idea of this wealthy man having anything to do with her or Maddock Manor was utterly absurd. 'You can't be serious—'

Larenz gave her a playful, mocking smile. 'Is that your reaction to most business propositions?'

She gritted her teeth. She'd been doing that quite a bit since Larenz de Luca and his lover had arrived—although now she was gone, no doubt dismissed by Larenz. He'd discarded one woman—and why? To move on to another?

To move on to her?

Ellery pushed the alarming—and tempting—possibility

away. Surely there had to be another reason for his continued presence. He was far too wealthy to enjoy staying in a place like Maddock Manor; he was clearly used to five-star hotels with matching service. Amelie had told her as much yesterday, and everything Ellery had noticed about Larenz de Luca confirmed this opinion, from the navy-blue Lexus he'd driven up in last night to the way he stood there, arrogantly relaxed in his supposed Saturday slumming clothes. He was, Ellery noticed, wearing buttery-soft loafers of Italian leather that had to have cost several hundred pounds at least. The man reeked of power and privilege.

Maddock Manor was way, way beneath him. *She* was way, way beneath him. And yet he stayed?

It made her nervous, anxious and even a little bit afraid.

'You're clearly a very wealthy, important person,' she finally said with frank honesty. 'I can't imagine any business proposition of yours that would involve me or Maddock—'

'Then you're wrong,' Larenz said softly. 'And my breakfast is getting cold.' He lifted the plate once more. 'Shall we?'

Ellery capitulated. She realized she had little choice, for Larenz was clearly the kind of man who was used to getting his own way. And she was tired of fighting; she was exhausted already. After breakfast she'd fob him off with the list of errands she had to do. She couldn't quite see him tagging along while she dug for the last potatoes or raked over the gravel that Amelie had sprayed everywhere.

'Fine,' she said curtly and then, because it was obvious he had no intention of being an ordinary guest, she threw over her shoulder, 'we can eat in the kitchen.'

Ellery fixed herself a plate of eggs and mushrooms while Larenz took a seat at the big scrubbed pine table. He popped a mushroom into his mouth and surveyed the huge room with its original fireplace big enough to roast an ox and the bank of windows letting in the pale morning sunshine.

'I'd say this was quite cosy,' he murmured, 'except this table could seat a round dozen. And I imagine it once did, in this house's heyday.' He smiled, raising his eyebrows. 'When was that?'

Ellery stiffened. 'The house's heyday?' she repeated and then, to her surprise and dismay, she sighed, the sound all too wistful and revealing. 'Probably some time in the seventeenth century. I think the Dunants were originally Puritans in good standing with Cromwell.'

'And did they lose it all in the Restoration?'

Ellery shrugged. 'I don't think so. They changed sides a dozen times or more.' She reached for two heavy china mugs and poured coffee. 'The Dunants aren't particularly known for being faithful.' Too late she heard the spite and bitterness in her voice and closed her eyes, hoping Larenz hadn't heard it, too. Yet, even without turning around, she knew he had; he was far too perceptive for his own good—or hers.

'Here.' She placed a mug of coffee in front of him on the table and then walked around to her own seat, all the way on the other end of the table. It looked a little ridiculous for them to be sitting so far apart but Ellery didn't care. She wasn't about to give Larenz any excuse to touch her.

Even if you want him to...

Ellery just barely kept from closing her eyes again. It was a good thing Larenz de Luca wasn't capable of mind reading—except when she looked at him and saw that faint knowing smile on his face she felt as if he was.

'Thank you,' he murmured and took a sip of coffee. Ellery began to eat her eggs with grim determination. She didn't want to talk to Larenz, didn't want him to flirt or tease or tempt her. Yet, even as these thoughts flitted through her mind and her eggs turned rubbery and tasteless in her mouth, Ellery knew she was already tempted. Badly. She thought of how Larenz's flutter of fingers on her wrist, skin sliding on skin, had jolted her, an electric current wired directly to her soul.

Except, Ellery thought as she speared a mushroom, souls had nothing to do with it; the temptation she felt for Larenz de Luca was purely, utterly physical. It had to be, for he was exactly the kind of man she despised. The kind of man her father had been.

She glanced up from her breakfast to look at Larenz, to drink him in, for he really was the most amazingly beautiful man. Her gaze lingered on the straight line of his nose, the slashes of his dark brows, those full moulded lips—she imagined those lips touching her, even somewhere seemingly innocuous, like where his fingers had been, on her wrist—and she nearly shuddered aloud.

'Is something wrong?' Larenz asked. He lifted his mug to take a sip of coffee and his eyes danced over its rim.

'What do you mean?' Ellery asked sharply. She returned her fork to her plate with a clatter. She'd been caught staring, of course, and she pulled her lip between her teeth, nipping hard, at the realization.

Larenz lowered his mug. His eyes still danced. 'It's just you looked a bit—pained.'

'Pained?' Ellery repeated. She rose abruptly from the table and grabbed her plate, moving to scrape the remains of her mostly uneaten breakfast into the bin. 'I'm afraid I have rather a lot on my mind,' she explained tartly. Too much on her mind to be thinking about Larenz the way she had. Too many worries to add temptation to the mix, especially when she knew he could only be amusing himself with her. The thought stung.

'Breakfast was delicious, thank you,' Larenz said. He'd moved to the sink, where Ellery watched in surprise as he rinsed his plate and mug and placed them in the dishwasher.

'Thank you,' she half mumbled, touched by his little thoughtfulness. 'You don't have to clean up—'

'Amazingly, I am capable of putting a few dishes away,' Larenz said with a wry smile that reached right into Ellery and twisted her heart. Or maybe something else. She turned away again, busying herself with the mindless tasks of wiping the table down and turning off the coffeemaker. From the corner of her eye, she saw Larenz lean one shoulder against the door, his hands in the pockets of his jeans. 'So it looks to be a beautiful day out. How about you show me the grounds and we can discuss this business proposition?'

Ellery jerked around, the dripping dishcloth still in her hand. She'd completely forgotten about his business proposition—what kind of proposal could he possibly have?

'I'm really rather busy—' she began and Larenz just smiled.

'I promise you, it'll be worth your while.' He reached out almost lazily and took the dishcloth from her hand, tossing it easily into the sink where it landed with a wet thud. 'An hour of your time, no more. Surely you can spare that?'

Ellery hesitated. Larenz stood there, relaxed and waiting, a faint smile curving those amazing lips, and suddenly she had no more excuses. She didn't even *want* to have any more excuses. She wanted, for once, an hour to enjoy herself. To enjoy temptation instead of resist it. To see what might happen, even if it was dangerous. An hour couldn't hurt, surely? That was all she'd give Larenz—or herself.

She let her breath out slowly. 'All right. But we ought to wear wellies.' She glanced pointedly at his leather loafers. 'It rained last night and it's quite muddy out.'

'I'm afraid,' Larenz murmured, 'I didn't bring any— wellies—with me.'

Ellery pursed her lips. She could just imagine the kind of clothes in the case Larenz had brought inside last night, and it didn't run to rubber boots. 'It's a good job that we have plenty for guests,' she returned, and Larenz quirked one eyebrow in question.

'We?'

'I mean I,' Ellery clarified, flushing. 'The boots are from when I was growing up—when we had house guests.' Her throat suddenly felt tight. She tried not to think of those days, when she was little and Maddock Manor had been full of people and laughter, the rooms gleaming and smelling of fresh flowers and beeswax polish and everything had been happy.

Had seemed happy, she mentally corrected, and went to the utility room to fetch a pair of boots she thought might be in Larenz's size.

Larenz followed Ellery out of the kitchen door to the walled garden adjacent to the Manor. He took in the remnants of a summer garden, now bedraggled and mostly dead, the grass no more than muddy patches. He wondered if the parsnips for last night's soup had come from here. He imagined Ellery harvesting the garden by herself, a lonely, laborious task, and something unexpected pulled at his heart.

He felt a single stab of pity, which was most unlike him. He'd worked too hard for too long pulling himself up from the gutter to feel sorry for an aristocrat who'd fallen on hard times, no doubt in part due to her family's extravagant living.

Yet, as he watched Ellery stride ahead of him, the boots enveloping her slender legs, her back stiff and straight, he realized he did feel a surprising twist of compassion for her.

She would be horrified if she knew. Ellery Dunant, Larenz thought with amusement, possessed a rather touching amount of pride. She seemed to love this heap of hers about as much as she disliked him, and was, he knew, most reluctant to spend time with him. She resented the attraction she felt for him, that much was obvious, but Larenz did not think she could resist its tug for long.

He certainly had no desire to. He wanted to release that platinum fall of hair from its sorry scraped little bun; he wanted to trail his fingers along her creamy skin and see if it was as soft as it looked—everywhere. He wanted to transform the disdain that pinched her face to a desire that would soften it. And he would. He always got what he wanted.

'Did you plant a garden this summer?' Larenz asked, nudging a row of withered runner beans. Ellery turned around, her hands deep in the pockets of her waxed jacket.

'Yes—a small one.' She glanced around the garden, remembering the vision she'd once had, the rows of hollyhocks, the cornucopia of vegetables, the neat little herb garden. She'd managed only a few potatoes and parsnips, things that were easy to grow, for she'd learned rather quickly that she did not have much of a green thumb. 'It's difficult to manage on my own,' she explained stiffly. 'But one day—' She stopped, letting the thought fall to the ground, unnourished. One day what? Every day she stayed at Maddock Manor, Ellery was conscious of how futile her plans really were. She would never get ahead on her own, never have enough money to make the necessary repairs, much less the renovations, never be able to see Maddock Manor restored to the glory it had once known. She tried to avoid these damning realizations, and for the most part she did, simply living day by day. It was Larenz de Luca, with his knowing smile and pointed questions, who reminded her of the futility of her life here.

She turned away from the garden to lead Larenz out to the half-timbered barns that flanked the rear of the property. 'So just what is this business proposition?' she called over her shoulder.

'Let me see the barns,' Larenz returned equably, and Ellery suppressed a groan. She'd only agreed to show Larenz the grounds because she'd already discovered how persistent he could be, and in a moment of folly—weakness—she'd wanted to spend time with him. She'd wanted to feel that dangerous, desirable jolt again. Even—especially—if it went nowhere; there was nowhere for it to go.

Yet, now that they were actually outside, Larenz inspecting the overgrown gardens and crumbling brick walls, Ellery felt no enjoyment or excitement, only the ragged edge of desperation as a man who looked as if he'd never known a day of want or need strolled through the remnants of her own failure.

'A lovely building,' Larenz murmured as Ellery let him into the dim, dusty interior of the barn that had once stabled a dozen workhorses. She blinked in the gloom, the sunlight filtering through the cracks.

'Once,' she agreed, and Larenz just smiled.

'Yours is hardly the first stately home to fall into disrepair.'

Ellery nodded rather glumly. It was a story being told all over England: estates crippled by rising costs and inheritance taxes, turned over to the National Trust or private enterprises, hotels or amusement parks or even, in the case of a manor nearby, a zoo.

Larenz stepped deeper into the dimness of the barn and ran his hand over a bulky shape shrouded in canvas tarpaulin that took over most of the interior. 'Have you ever thought of turning the place into a park or museum?'

'No.' She'd resisted letting Maddock Manor become anything but the home it once had been—her home, her mother's home, a place that had defined them—because she was afraid if she lost the Manor she'd have nothing left. Nothing that pointed to who she was—what she was. Her father's daughter. 'Letting rooms out for holidays is the first step, I suppose, but I couldn't bear it if someone put a roller coaster up in the garden or something like that.'

Larenz turned to her, his eyes glinting with amusement even in the musty dimness of the barn. 'Surely you wouldn't have to do something so drastic.'

Ellery shrugged. 'I don't have the money to renovate it myself, not on a large scale, so the only choice would be to turn it over to developers.'

'Have you had any offers?'

That was the galling bit, Ellery thought with a sigh. She hadn't. Manor houses, it seemed, were all too available, and Maddock Manor was in enough disrepair to make developers turn away. At least they hadn't been pestering her. 'No, not really. We're a bit off the beaten track.'

Larenz nodded slowly. 'I'm amazed Amelie found this place, actually.'

Ellery bristled; she couldn't help it. 'I do have a web-site—'

'Mmm.' Larenz pulled at the canvas tarpaulin. 'If I'm not mistaken, there's a car under here, and probably a nice one.'

Ellery's heart seemed to stop for a second before it started beating with hard, heavy thuds. 'A Rolls-Royce,' she confirmed as Larenz pulled the tarpaulin away to reveal the car. They gazed silently at the vintage vehicle, its silver body gleaming even in the dim light. Ellery wished she'd taken Larenz to another barn. She'd forgotten the car was kept in this one. Actually, she'd forgotten about the car completely, yet now she found the memories rushing back and she reached one hand out to touch the gleaming metal before she dropped it back to her side.

'A Silver Dawn,' Larenz murmured. He ran his hand over the engine hood. 'From the nineteen-forties. It's in remarkably good condition.'

'It was my father's,' Ellery said quietly.

Larenz glanced at her. 'Has he passed away?'

She nodded. 'Five years ago.'

'I'm sorry. You must have been quite young.'

'Nineteen.' She gave a little shrug; she didn't want to talk about it, especially not with Larenz, a virtual stranger. She didn't like talking about her father to her closest friend. She certainly wasn't about to unburden herself to a man like Larenz.

'You could sell the Rolls,' Larenz commented as he covered the car back up; Ellery felt a sudden pang of loss. She'd ridden in that car as a child, stuck her head out of the window and laughed with joy as her father had motored down the narrow country lanes, waving at everyone who passed.

She'd also stood on the front steps and watched the Rolls disappear down the drive when her father had gone on his alleged business trips. She'd never known when he would be coming back.

'Maybe I don't want to sell it,' she said, her voice coming out in something of a snap.

Larenz glanced at her, unperturbed. 'It must be worth at least forty thousand pounds.'

Forty thousand pounds. Ellery had no idea the car could be worth that much. She felt foolish for not knowing and yet, even so she knew she would never sell it. Another emotional and irrational decision, but one she couldn't keep from making. She turned away, walking stiffly out of the barn. 'Some things aren't for sale,' she said quietly after Larenz had followed her out and she had closed the big wooden door, sliding the bar across.

'Forty thousand pounds would make a big difference to a place like this,' Larenz remarked mildly. 'You could mow the lawn a bit more regularly, for starters.'

Ellery whirled on him, suddenly furious. 'Why do you care?' she demanded. 'You've been here less than twenty-four hours. You already think my home is a wreck. And,' she added, real bitterness now spiking her words, 'I don't recall ever asking you for advice.' She turned on her heel—her boots splashing through a rather large puddle and, she noted with satisfaction, spraying mud onto Larenz's jeans—and stormed back to the house without once looking back at her guest.

CHAPTER THREE

BACK at the house, Ellery rinsed off her boots and lined them up on the stone step outside. Anger still pulsed through her, making her hands tremble as she opened the back door. She was angry with herself for being angry with Larenz; he wasn't worth the emotional energy she'd already wasted.

Not to mention her physical energy. It was late morning and she hadn't dealt with the breakfast dishes, or made the beds, or done any of the half-dozen demands that required her attention on any given day.

Stupid, arrogant Larenz de Luca had completely thrown off her day, she thought furiously. He'd thrown more than her day off; he'd unbalanced her whole self, making her see Maddock Manor in a way she tried not to. She kept herself so busy working and trying and *striving*—all for something she knew she could never gain or keep. And Larenz, with his expensive car and clothes, his smug little smile and knowing eyes, made her realize it afresh every second she spent in his presence.

What was even more aggravating was her body's treacherous reaction to a man she couldn't even like. She knew just what kind of man Larenz was, had known it from the moment he'd driven up the lane in his sleek Lexus and tossed the keys on the side table in the foyer as if he owned the place. She'd seen it in the careless way he treated his lover, Amelie, and

the way she responded, with a distastefully desperate fawn-
ing. And, most damningly of all, she saw it in the way he
treated her, with the sweeping, speculative glances and the
lazy voice of amusement. He was toying with her and enjoying it. The fact that Ellery's body reacted at all—betrayed
her—was both infuriating and shaming.

'I'm sorry.'

Ellery whirled around, her thoughts lending the movement
a certain fury. Larenz stood in the doorway of the kitchen;
he'd removed his boots and there was something almost en-
dearing about seeing him in his socks. One of them sported
a hole in the toe.

'You're sorry?' she repeated, as if the words didn't make
sense. They didn't really, coming from Larenz. It was the
last thing she'd expected him to say.

'Yes,' he replied quietly. 'You're right. I shouldn't be
giving you advice. It's none of my business.'

Ellery stared at him; his eyes had darkened to navy and
he looked both serious and contrite. The sudden about-face
disconcerted her, made her wonder about her own assumptions. Now she was left speechless and uncertain, not sure if
his words were sincere.

'Thank you,' she finally managed stiffly. 'I'm sorry, as
well. It's not my usual practice to insult my guests.'

A smile quirked Larenz's mouth and his eyes glinted again,
as sparkling and blue as sunlight on the sea. The transfor-
mation made Ellery's insides fizz, and she felt faint with a
sudden intense longing that she could not, for the life of her,
suppress. It rose up inside her in a consuming wave, taking
all her self-righteous anger with it. 'I'm not really a usual
guest, am I?' he teased softly.

'A bit more demanding,' Ellery agreed, and wondered if
she was actually flirting.

'Then I must make up for my deficiencies,' he replied.
'How about I make us lunch?'

His suggestion caused another frisson of wary pleasure to shiver through her. Ellery arched her eyebrows. 'You can actually cook?'

'A few things.'

She hesitated. They were stepping into new territory now, first with the little flirtatious exchange and now with the idea of Larenz actually making lunch—cooking—for her. Dangerous ground.

Exciting ground. Ellery hadn't felt so alive in ages, not since she'd first buried herself here in the far reaches of Suffolk, and probably far before that, too. She sucked in a slow breath. 'All right,' she finally said, and heard the mingled reluctance and anticipation in her voice. Larenz heard it, too, or she assumed as much from the wicked little smile he gave her.

'Fantastic. Where are your cooking pots?'

Smiling a little bit, a bubble of laughter threatening to rise up inside her and escape, Ellery showed him where everything was. Within a few minutes he was playing at executive chef, dicing a few tomatoes with surprising agility as a big pot of water bubbled on the stove. Ellery knew she should go upstairs and make the beds, but instead she found herself perched on the edge of the table, watching Larenz move around the kitchen with ease and grace. He was wonderful to watch.

'How did a man like you learn how to cook?'

His shoulders seemed to stiffen for a single second before he threw her a questioning glance. 'A man like me?' he repeated lightly. 'Just what is that supposed to mean?'

Ellery shrugged. 'You're wealthy, powerful, entitled.' She ticked the words off on her fingers, not meaning them as insults although, from the still stiff set of Larenz's shoulders, she had the uncomfortable feeling that he took them as such.

'Entitled?' he repeated wryly. 'I'm afraid not. You're the one with the title.'

Was she imagining the bitter undercurrent in his voice? Surely she was. 'I don't mean an actual title,' she said. 'Useless as they are—'

'Are they?'

'Mine is.' She swept an arm to encompass the whole Manor, her whole life. 'It's just a courtesy anyway, because my father was a baron. Besides, what's good about being Lady Maddock, besides having to pay death in taxes?'

'Nothing is certain except death and taxes,' Larenz murmured as he minced two fat cloves of garlic.

'Exactly.' Ellery paused, both unable and unwilling to voice how this new side to Larenz had surprised and even unsettled her. 'Men like you don't usually learn basic life skills,' she finally said.

'Men like me,' he echoed thoughtfully. 'And that's because someone is always doing it for us, I suppose?' He paused in his slicing and dicing. 'Fortunately, my mother had a more prosaic view. She made sure I learned all of life's necessary skills.' He slid her a sideways smile that did strange things to her middle; it was as if something were opening and closing inside her, like a fist.

'I see,' Ellery murmured. She felt herself blushing, her whole body heating from just a single look. Suddenly the kitchen felt very warm.

'We can eat as soon as the pasta is done,' Larenz told her. 'No more than a simple tomato sauce, I'm afraid. My skills are indeed basic when it comes to the kitchen.' Yet his playful emphasis suggested that his skills were both more advanced and adept outside of the kitchen.

Such as in the bedroom.

Or was that where her own desperate thoughts were taking her? She was mesmerised by the way his hands moved so quickly and skilfully as he prepared their lunch; she watched the sunlight play on his dark curls as he bent his head to his task and felt nearly dizzy with need.

She needed to stop this, Ellery told herself. She had no intention of getting involved—in any way—with Larenz de Luca. She might feel a brief and admittedly intense attraction for him—intense simply because she'd denied her body for so long—yet she had absolutely no interest in acting upon it. She couldn't.

The thought of being intimate—vulnerable—with someone like Larenz actually made her shudder. She would not be beholden to a man like Larenz de Luca, a man who would surely turn his back on her without a second thought. A man who, by all evidence, treated women as playthings, as amusements. And surely he was merely amusing himself with her in an effort to while away a long lonely weekend. Was that why he had stayed? For his own bored amusement? Surely the supposed business proposition was no more than a pretext.

Larenz peered into the pot. 'I believe it's done.'

Ellery forced her thoughts—and their natural direction—away. 'Isn't it supposed to stick to the wall?' she asked, half-teasing, and he grimaced.

'Foolish folk tales. An Italian knows when the spaghetti is done simply by looking.'

'Where did you grow up in Italy?' Ellery asked. It was an impulsive question, breaching the wall she'd erected between servant and guest. Tearing down the self-defences she'd made despite her resolve not to be involved. Interested.

Yet somehow she kept asking the questions, somehow she stayed. Her mind and body were clearly at war.

Larenz drained the pasta and ladled it into two bowls before replying. 'I'm originally from Umbria,' he finally said. 'Near Spoleto, but really in the middle of nowhere.'

'Your family is still there?' Ellery asked.

Another pause. She felt as if the questions were becoming intrusive, although she'd meant them to be innocuous. 'Not any longer,' Larenz finally answered, and brought the bowls to the table. 'Now let's eat.'

He'd placed the bowls on one end of the table, leaving Ellery little choice but to sit next to him instead of her earlier, safer place at the far end. It would surely be offensive—and obvious—to move her bowl to the other end of the table.

Still, Ellery hesitated and Larenz glanced at her, clearly amused. 'I don't bite, you know. Unless asked, of course.'

Ellery rolled her eyes. 'Oh, please.' She sat down and, from the fleeting little grin he gave her, she knew he'd been outrageous on purpose; it had, strangely, put her at ease.

They ate for a few moments in a silence that was surprisingly companionable. Larenz's knee occasionally pressed against hers, and Ellery wondered if it was accidental. He seemed unaware of the times when they touched, although surely he could see how those brief brushes affected her? Several layers of fabric separated their skin and yet, every time his knee pressed against hers, her whole body tensed as though preparing to resist an assault.

And it was an assault, an onslaught of the senses, for each time he touched her she felt her body—and her resolve—weakening further. She felt pleasure and need flood her body, overwhelm her senses, so that she couldn't think about anything but the purely physical joy of being touched.

She wanted this. To be touched, desired, loved, even if it was only for a moment's amusement.

No. The realization was far too shaming. She could not allow herself to think this way. Feel this way. Yet her body disagreed; every nerve blazed to life, every sinew singing with reawakened awareness. Her body wanted more.

And so her body betrayed her. Without being even fully cognizant of what she was doing, she moved her foot so it brushed against Larenz's leg. She felt taut muscle under her toes. He didn't even pause, and Ellery felt a ridiculous flaring of disappointment. What on earth was she doing? Was she actually playing footsie under the kitchen table?

And the most galling part was Larenz didn't even notice.

Maybe he really hadn't meant to touch her, the brushing of their knees no more than an accident. Perhaps his attraction, just like her own need, was all in her head. In her body, now stirring to life with suppressed longings and taking over her common sense. Larenz looked as if he felt nothing at all. And while that should relieve her—keep her safe—Ellery discovered, to her annoyance, that it simply made her feel frustrated.

He raised his head to smile at her, and Ellery knew she'd been caught staring. She turned resolutely back to her pasta. 'So tell me about this business proposition of yours, if there really is one at all.'

'You doubt me?' Larenz asked, sounding amused. Ellery shrugged. 'As a matter of fact, I own a chain of department stores—De Luca's.' He raised an eyebrow. 'You've heard of them?'

Ellery nodded. Of course she'd heard of them; there was a De Luca's in nearly every major European city. She'd hardly call it a department store, though. It was too upmarket for that. She certainly couldn't afford anything there. She supposed she should have made the connection earlier, when she'd learned what Larenz's last name was. Yet, even though she'd known him to be rich, she hadn't quite realized just how powerful and wealthy he truly was.

He really was slumming here, staying at the Manor, flirting with her. Amusing himself, and that only a little.

'Amelie scouted your Manor for a fashion shoot,' Larenz continued. 'The shoot will launch a new line of haute couture I've commissioned, and I'd like it to be done here.'

Ellery stared at him in disbelief, her lunch—and even

her longings—momentarily forgotten. 'You want to stage a fashion photography shoot here?'

Larenz smiled, steepling his fingers under his chin. 'Is that so strange?'

'As a matter of fact, yes. There are dozens—hundreds—of manor houses in this country, houses that are in better shape than Maddock.' It hurt to say it, even though it was glaringly obvious. 'Why would you choose a third-rate place?'

He was still smiling that faint mocking little smile that drove her just about crazy. Ellery bit the inside of her cheek. 'You don't think much of your home.'

'I'm honest,' Ellery returned flatly. 'Something I don't think you're being.'

'Maddock Manor has a certain…ambience…we'd like for the photo shoot.'

Ellery stared at him for a full minute, trying to grasp what he was saying. She was missing something, she was sure of it, because there was no way one of Europe's most elite stores would want to market their new high-end fashion label at a falling-down wreck of a house in deepest Suffolk. Was there? She narrowed her eyes. 'This is pity, isn't it?'

'Pity?' Larenz repeated questioningly, as though the word was unfamiliar to him. Before Ellery could make any kind of reply, he reached over and touched his thumb to the corner of her mouth, pressing lightly against her skin.

Ellery's lips parted instinctively and she heard her breath escape in a tiny, soft sigh that betrayed her utterly. Larenz's smile deepened and he murmured, 'You had a bit of sauce there.'

Ellery felt a flush burn its way up her body, right to the roots of her hair. She'd always blushed easily and she hated it especially now, for surely Larenz saw how he'd affected her—how he'd meant to affect her, touching her so provocatively.

Or perhaps it hadn't been provocative; perhaps he'd merely

been wiping away a dab of sauce, and she'd read more into it because she was so desperate with longing.

She rose from the table, reaching for the dishes almost blindly and bringing them to the sink, her back to Larenz.

'Ellery?' he asked, his voice mild yet questioning.

Ellery dumped the dishes into the sink and watched almost impassively as a bowl broke cleanly in half. She hated how confused she felt, sensuality and self-protection warring within her while Larenz seemed completely unaware of the pitched battle going on.

She heard him rise from the table; she sensed him standing close behind her, felt his heat and his strength. She even inhaled the now familiar tang of his aftershave. 'Why are you doing this?' she asked in a low voice. She realized she no longer cared if she embarrassed herself. She needed to know why. Was he even aware of how much he affected her? Surely he had to be. Surely he was enjoying this little game.

'Doing what?' Larenz asked. His voice was carefully bland.

Ellery turned around. 'Teasing me,' she said, her voice still low. 'With this ridiculous business proposition, with—' She swallowed, unwilling even now to admit how much his careless little touches and flirtations affected her. 'Are you amusing yourself for the weekend because your lover left early? Since nobody else is available, you've decided I'll do?' The accusations poured out, scraping her throat raw. 'I don't need your pity, Mr—'

He pressed a finger to her lips, silencing her. 'You think I pity you?'

'I know you do.' She drew in a ragged breath; his finger was still on her mouth, and she tasted the salt of his skin. 'I see it every time you look around this place. You think it's a hovel, a mouldering wreck like your…your *mistress* called it last night!' Ellery was breathing hard and fast now;

she was angry, angrier than the situation merited, and she knew why. Larenz reminded her of her father. Larenz treated Amelie—and her—like her father had treated her mother. Someone to take or leave, as he desired, with no regard for the sorrow or heartbreak he caused. Fresh rage poured through her.

'Amelie is not my mistress,' Larenz said calmly.

Ellery snorted in disbelief, despite the ridiculous lurch of hope she felt at his words. He had to be lying. 'You really expect me to believe that?'

He gave a negligent little shrug. 'I suspect you will believe what you will. I confess I had no idea you were making such assumptions about me. But, in point of fact, Amelie is the head of public relations for my company. That's why she was here at all, trying to find a place suitable for the fashion shoot—'

'You cannot expect me to believe that anyone finds this place suitable.'

'Obviously you don't.' He dropped his voice to a lulling whisper. 'Why are you here, Ellery? Why do you stay? I wonder if you even like this Manor of yours very much.'

Ellery recoiled. The questions were too revealing, too close to the truth. She was not about to answer them, or give Larenz any more information that his sense of perception had already gained him.

She tried to turn away but his finger was still against her lips, and now he touched her chin, forcing her to look at him.

'Ellery, I do not pity you. I must admit, I would find it hard going to take care of this place on my own as you do, but that hardly translates to pity.'

'When it sounds, looks and feels like pity, it generally is,' Ellery retorted. She tried to jerk her chin away from Larenz's grasp but he held on, smiling as he dipped his head so their faces—and lips—were no more than a breath apart.

'I assure you,' Larenz murmured, '*this* isn't pity.' And, before Ellery could process or protest that statement, his lips met hers and he was kissing her in a way she'd never been kissed before.

He was kissing her in a way that made her forget every resolution or regret she'd ever had.

Ellery remained unmoving under his caress for the briefest of seconds; she was too dazed to do or think anything, her mind and body both frozen with surprise. Then her senses took over, flooding with sweet, warm pleasure, and her body spurred into action, responding of its own accord, without the permission of her still-resistant mind.

Her arms came up and twined around Larenz's shoulders, her fingers splaying across the taut muscles of his back, her head falling back and her body arching, as sinuous and sensual as a cat. She heard herself make a sound she never had before, part of her incredulously aware of how wanton she was being. She moaned, the sound trembling on her lips, reverberating through her body.

Larenz deepened the kiss.

His hands had drifted down her back and now cradled her hips, drawing her closer to him, the contact intimate and revealing. His hand moved upwards to stroke her breast through the thin fabric of her T-shirt, his lips still on hers, tasting and exploring, and the sudden nerve-tingling jolt the caress caused made Ellery stumble back, coming hard against the sink.

The moment, hazy with desire, had now turned crystal-clear with cold reality. Ellery felt sick and when she swallowed she tasted the acidic bite of bile.

'Don't—' she whispered. Her heart thudded as if she'd run a mile and her whole body still tingled with the aftershocks of his kiss.

Larenz smiled. Besides his hair being a bit rumpled,

he looked remarkably composed. 'Don't what?' he asked pleasantly. 'Don't stop?'

'Don't tease me,' Ellery burst out. 'Don't toy with me.'

For a moment Larenz looked genuinely nonplussed. 'Why am I toying with you, Ellery?' She liked how he said her name, the trace of an accent in the caress of the syllables. 'I want you. You want me. Really, it's very simple.' His expression hardened for a single second as he added, 'It doesn't have to be difficult.'

She shook her head. She felt her throat clog and her eyes fill damningly with tears. She couldn't speak without giving herself away, so she bit her lip—hard—instead. It wasn't simple at all. Not to her, at least. Yet she could hardly explain that to Larenz, especially when she barely understood it herself. All she knew was that giving herself to a man like him now—like this—would not be the simple physical pleasure he seemed to think it would.

It would, Ellery knew, be the selling of her soul.

She shook her head again, managing to get one word out of her constricted throat. 'No,' she said and, pushing past him, she fled from the room.

Larenz stood in the quiet of the kitchen, trying to process the last few minutes. What had started so promisingly had ended, he realized ruefully, rather disastrously. Ellery Dunant had looked, damn it, near to tears. Had such a simple little kiss really affected her so deeply, so terribly?

It didn't bode well for his planned seduction.

Moodily, Larenz wandered to the bank of windows that overlooked the walled garden. Sunlight made the puddles shimmer, and the dew-spangled grass looked as if it were gilded with silver. There was a strange, almost ethereal beauty to the Manor grounds, and Larenz could see why Amelie had thought it would be such a spectacular backdrop for the new couture gowns De Luca's would be showcasing next spring.

Ellery was a bit like her beloved Manor, he thought with a philosophical bemusement. She shrouded herself in plain clothes and unflattering hairstyles but she still couldn't hide the beauty underneath, the beauty he saw in her bruise-coloured eyes and elegant bone structure. And not only beauty but desire; he'd seen it in the way her eyes darkened to storm clouds, the way her body had trembled and yielded to his when he'd kissed her.

He hadn't even meant to kiss her right then. Leaning against a kitchen sink was hardly the most comfortable place for seduction. Yet in that moment when he'd felt the velvety softness of her lips against his finger—skin on skin—he hadn't been able to think of anything else. Want anything else. Kissing her hadn't been an indulgence; it had been a necessity.

Larenz expelled his breath in a frustrated sigh. Yet what had that kiss been to Ellery? Judging by her response, he would have thought it an awakening. Yet, remembering the shattered look in her eyes as she'd fled from the room—and from him—Larenz wondered if it had, instead, been, bizarrely, a betrayal.

He pushed the thoughts aside. He didn't want to wax philosophical about an insignificant little kiss; he certainly wasn't going to *care*. All he wanted was a weekend of pleasure and if Ellery Dunant couldn't handle that then he'd leave her damn well alone.

She was, Larenz decided firmly, nothing special. And, since he didn't mix business with pleasure anyway, he should just forget all about her. Go and pack. Move on. He was good at that.

Yet still he remained staring out at the unkempt garden and in his mind's eye all he saw was the hurt flaring in Ellery's violet eyes.

CHAPTER FOUR

ELLERY didn't see Larenz for the rest of the day. After she'd run from the kitchen like a frightened girl—shame and anger warring within her—she'd gone upstairs to deal with the dirty sheets. She needed to work, to do and not to think. She needed to regain some balance and some common sense.

Yet she found neither when she stepped into the Manor's master bedroom, with its tangled sheets and the cold ashes of a fire in the grate. Ellery sagged against the bedpost, her mind replaying the images she'd envisioned last night—Larenz and Amelie in that bed, before the fire…

Firmly she pushed such thoughts away—along with the accompanying absurd jealousy—and stripped the sheets from the bed. An expensively cloying perfume she recognized as Amelie's drifted up from the sheets. Ellery grimaced.

She bundled them into a pile to take downstairs to the rather ancient washing machine, another appliance on the brink of collapse, stopping only when she saw the door to the room next to Amelie's was ajar. She kept the doors to all the bedrooms firmly closed in a somewhat futile effort to maintain some warmth in the main sections of the house.

Now she stepped inside, gazing around in surprise at the neatly made bed; a pair of shoes—men's dress shoes—were lined up at its foot. The bag Larenz had carried in last night was on the divan by the window and she could see his woollen trench coat hanging in the wardrobe.

Had Larenz slept here? Had he and Amelie had a fight? Or had he actually been telling the *truth*?

Ellery took a step closer to the bed and reached down to smooth the faded counterpane. Then, on impish impulse, she bent and sniffed the pillow. It smelled of a citrusy aftershave. It smelled of Larenz.

Ellery straightened. She felt strangely unsettled, relief and uncertainty mixing uncomfortably within her. She also knew she did not want to be caught snooping in Larenz's room. Quickly she backed out of the bedroom and hurried to pile the sheets in the washer.

Yet all afternoon vague unsettled thoughts drifted through her mind like wispy clouds, insubstantial and yet still greying her day. Had she misjudged Larenz? What kind of man was he, really? She wondered just how much of her assumptions had been based on her own experience and how much on what she saw and heard from the man himself.

'So he had a fight with Amelie,' she muttered as she went to the kitchen to see about dinner. 'He slept in another room, and she flounced off in a huff. It doesn't change anything.' It shouldn't change *her*.

Kissing a man like that—*wanting* a man like that—still felt like a betrayal of who she was and every hard lesson she'd learned from another betrayal—her father's.

The sun had started its descent and the gardens were already cloaked in dusky shadows. Larenz had left earlier that afternoon, speeding off in his Lexus, and he still hadn't returned. Ellery had no idea if she should make a proper dinner or settle for her usual tinned soup or beans on toast. Yet if Larenz did return, he would undoubtedly expect a meal. The thought of waiting on Larenz alone in the huge, shadowy dining room made nerves leap low in her belly.

She pushed the feelings aside and made herself a cheese

sandwich, eating it alone at the kitchen table as darkness claimed the grounds. Although she lived alone for most of the year, tonight she was especially conscious of the empty house all around her, still and silent, room after cavernous room yawning into infinity.

Ellery snorted in disgust at her own fanciful thoughts. She was getting maudlin again. She could go down into the village, visit a fellow teacher from the secondary school where she taught part-time. Get out of the Manor, and out of her own head. Yet she knew she wouldn't. She was too restless, too wary. And, she acknowledged ruefully, she was waiting for Larenz to return.

She stood up abruptly and put her dishes in the sink. A gust of wind rattled the windowpanes and the boiler started clanking again.

She thought of Larenz's knowing questions that afternoon: *Why are you here, Ellery? Why do you stay? I wonder if you even like this Manor of yours very much.*

The questions pointed to a grim truth: sometimes she hated this house. She hated the memories made here that caused her to doubt who she was; she hated that she stayed because this house felt as if it was all that was left of who she was. She hated how her life was sucked into taking care of its empty rooms and endless repairs, and yet the thought of giving it up—selling her only home—was akin to selling her soul.

Just like kissing Larenz had been.

Ellery groaned. 'Stop it,' she said aloud. Living alone, she was used to talking to herself. Yet the words had little effect. She couldn't stop thinking about that kiss, or how it had reached deep down inside her and shaken up all her longings and fears until she didn't know which was which. She couldn't stop remembering how it felt to be held in Larenz's arms, to have his lips on hers, to feel touched and treasured and dare she even think it—loved.

Ellery didn't consider herself enough of a dupe to imagine

even for a second that love had anything to do with what Larenz wanted. It didn't have anything to do with what *she* wanted.

Love was dangerous. Frightening. Forbidden. Especially with a man like Larenz.

No, all she wanted—all she could want—was a moment, a night of pleasure like Larenz had promised.

So why had she hightailed it like a scared rabbit or, more appropriately, a shy virgin after her first kiss? Why couldn't she enjoy what Larenz offered? Why couldn't she take what he offered without feeling afraid or, worse, used? Betrayed?

Why did it have to mean anything?

Tired of the questions that ran around in her head in useless circles, Ellery left the kitchen. There was still plenty for her to do: paperwork and paying bills, not to mention the general housekeeping she'd neglected for much of that day. The downstairs reception rooms needed a good dust and polish, and she'd been slowly—very slowly—plastering some of the cracks in the walls of the foyer. Yet her endless DIY list held little appeal as she wandered from room to room, wondering just how—and when—the house she'd once adored as a child had become an impoverished prison.

Of course she knew the answer, even if she didn't like to think about it. It had started when her father had chosen to live two lives rather than one.

Larenz pulled up in front of Maddock Manor and groaned aloud. Under the sickly glow of a waxy moon the place looked even more decrepit than usual. He'd spent the afternoon driving around the country, motoring down narrow twisting lanes and through quaint sleepy villages—what had he been looking for? Another place for Amelie's photo shoot? Or had he just simply been trying to forget?

Forget the look in Ellery's eyes when he'd kissed her.

Forget the feeling of her in his arms—fragile, precious, unforgettable.

Of course he couldn't forget.

Even a whisky at the local pub—the man behind the bar had been particularly closed-mouthed when Larenz had casually asked about Lord Maddock and his damned Manor—had only blunted the raw edge of desire that had been knifing through him all afternoon.

Muttering a curse, Larenz slammed the door of his Lexus and stalked towards the Manor. He stopped halfway to the front portico for a light had flickered in the corner of his vision, somewhere in the gardens behind the house.

Larenz's mind leaped ahead to intruders, thieves, murderers, rapists. He thought of how isolated Ellery Dunant was here, mouldering in her Manor all by herself, and when he saw the light flickering again—it looked like a torch in someone's hand—he swung around and began to stalk towards the barns.

'Damn it to hell,' he said aloud, for he knew his earlier determination was shot to pieces. He did care.

Ellery pulled the tarpaulin off the Rolls and stared at it under the sickly yellow glare of her torch. She let her breath out slowly; funny how even after years stored in a barn the car still retained its gorgeous gleam. Funny too how she'd almost forgotten it was here, how she'd made herself forget.

Until Larenz had forced her to remember.

Slowly she let her hand run along the antique car's mudguard. The metal felt like hard silk under her fingers. Without even realizing she was doing so, she let out a small choked sound that was far too close to a sob.

Damn her father for making her love him so much. Damn him for hiding so much from her. Damn him for dying, and damn him for making her the kind of woman she was now, alone and afraid to love.

Damn. Damn. Damn.

Ellery lifted her hands to swipe at the revealing moisture at the corner of her eyes. She drew in a desperate breath and let it out again; she needed to regain some composure, some control. Ever since Larenz had breezed into her life—just a little over twenty-four hours ago—she felt as if both had been slipping away from her. Why did he affect her so much? Why did she let him?

She let out another long, slow breath and then resolutely covered the Rolls back up. Perhaps she would sell it. Forty thousand pounds would, as Larenz had said, go a long way.

As she turned towards the barn door, feeling her way with careful slowness, the pale beam of the torch barely cutting a swathe through the unrelenting darkness, she wondered where he was. Was he coming back? Had he breezed out of her life as quickly and easily as he'd breezed into it, simply because she wasn't the easy affair he'd counted on?

Why was she disappointed?

Then every thought flew from her head as a body tackled her, slamming her hard against the barn door, and the torch fell from her hand.

Ellery didn't realize she'd screamed—and was still screaming—until a hand covered her mouth. Even in the midst of her terror and shock she was conscious of a familiar citrusy scent.

'Larenz?' she said, the words muffled against the hand still covering her mouth.

She heard what could only be a curse muttered in Italian. The hand dropped from her mouth, and she saw Larenz bend to pick up the torch. He shone it in her face, and she squinted in the sudden light.

'What are you doing—'

'What are *you* doing,' Larenz demanded, his voice sounding almost raw, 'out in the barn at one o'clock in the morning? I thought you were a thief—or worse.'

'And you didn't think to ask questions first?' Ellery retorted. She rubbed her shoulder, which had hit the door hard. She would most certainly have a bruise.

'Where I come from, you ask questions second,' Larenz said roughly. He shone the torch up and down, inspecting her body. Ellery was uncomfortably aware that she was wearing her dressing gown and wellies. Not the most enticing combination. 'Are you all right?'

'A bit bruised,' she admitted. 'Didn't you consider I might be inspecting my own property?'

'In the middle of the night? No.' Larenz paused, the torch still trained on her body. 'I'm sorry. The last thing I wanted was to hurt you.'

Ellery stilled, surprised and even moved by the contrition in Larenz's voice. 'It's all right,' she said after a moment. 'I was about to go inside, anyway.'

She started to move away from the door but Larenz stilled her, one hand on her shoulder. 'Ellery, why were you out here? Were you looking at the car?'

Ellery heard a note in his voice she didn't like, couldn't like. It was the gentle note of compassion, and it spoke of a song she couldn't bear to hear. Tears stung her eyes and she blinked them furiously away.

'Perhaps I am thinking of selling it,' she said roughly and pushed past him.

She couldn't make her way in the dark without stumbling and possibly even hurting herself more so Ellery was obliged to wait for Larenz to catch up. Silently, he handed her the torch and she took it with stiff dignity. They walked back through the muddy gardens without speaking.

Once in the kitchen, Ellery shed her boots and went automatically to the big copper kettle on the range. She desperately needed a cup of tea, or perhaps something even stronger.

'You should ice your shoulder.'

She stiffened. 'It's really not necessary.'

'I slammed you rather hard against the door,' Larenz replied evenly. 'If you don't ice it, it will bruise.'

'I can handle a bruise.'

'Why are you so touchy?' Larenz murmured. That sleepy, hooded look Ellery was beginning to know well—and to both dread and desire—had come into his eyes, turning them a deep glinting navy. 'Besides, I know for a fact there's a big bag of peas in your chest freezer. I saw it last night when you so thoughtfully fetched me some ice.' He smiled and Ellery's heart turned over. Or squeezed. Or something, making it suddenly rather hard to breathe.

Larenz moved to the freezer, opening it and rifling through the contents before emerging with a bag of peas. 'There. Plonk that on your shoulder for a bit.'

It would be easier, Ellery knew, to simply give in. If she iced her shoulder for a few minutes, perhaps then Larenz would leave her alone. Although half of her—more than half—didn't want him to leave her alone. A good, and growing, part of her wanted him to stay…and more. So much more. She couldn't deny the insistent need spiralling deep within her, pushing away any thoughts of regret or betrayal.

She swallowed and looked away. 'Fine,' she said and grabbed the bag of peas, pressing it against her shoulder. It was hard to do without wrenching her other shoulder, not to mention looking entirely awkward and, seeing this, Larenz took the bag from her. 'Why don't I do it?' he murmured.

'No—'

'Are you worried I'll kiss you again?' His words were no more than a breath against her ear as he leaned down to press the bag of peas against her shoulder; his head was bent so his jaw was no more than a whisper away from Ellery's own lips.

And, just like that, the mood in the room changed, awareness replacing annoyance, the atmosphere more charged than ever before.

'I wouldn't say worried,' Ellery managed. She moved her head back, away from the temptation of Larenz's skin. Her heart slammed against her chest and her mouth had turned bone-dry. She was conscious of Larenz's breath feathering her cheek. No, she wasn't worried. She was wanting.

Wanting him.

She felt desire pool languidly in her limbs, felt her body and mind soften and open into possibility. At that moment she didn't know why Larenz affected her so much, why her body responded in such a basic and overwhelming way to his. She didn't care. All she knew was that she did want him to kiss her again, and more, and she was so very tired of fighting it. Her body acted of its own accord, leaning into him, her senses straining once more for his touch. He was so close; she could brush her lips against the warm, rough skin of his jaw and it would practically be an accident…

The kettle began to whistle shrilly, and Ellery jerked back as if it had actually scalded her. The bag of peas fell to the floor, splitting open so the peas rolled everywhere.

Larenz glanced down in bemusement. 'Oh, dear.'

Ellery turned off the stove, her back to him, her blood and heart pumping far too fast. That had been close. So very, very close…

'Why were you in the barn, Ellery?'

'Would you like a cup of tea?' She turned around, the tin of tea held to her chest like a shield.

Larenz smiled and shrugged. 'I don't usually have tea at this time of night, but why not? Especially if there is a drop of brandy to go with it. You could use some, I'm sure.'

'There's a bottle somewhere,' Ellery mumbled, turning back to the kettle. Larenz moved closer.

'Why were you in the barn?'

'I told you, I was checking up on things,' Ellery replied stiffly. She reached for two mugs and her hand trembled. 'Why do you care?'

Larenz didn't answer for a long moment—long enough for Ellery to pour the tea and hand him his mug. She stared at him, surprised at the way his eyes had darkened with shadows, the angles of his face suddenly seeming harsh.

'I don't know why I care,' he finally said thoughtfully. 'I've been asking myself that all evening.'

Ellery felt that curious squeezing sensation in her chest once more and for a few seconds it was difficult to take a breath. She rummaged in a cupboard for the requested brandy. 'I think it's here somewhere…' She was so very conscious of Larenz behind her, of the tension tautening between them and uncoiling in her own belly. She was conscious of her own rising need; the intervening moments had not stemmed it. She still felt. She still wanted.

She tried to keep her voice light as she asked, 'Where were you all afternoon? Did you go touring?'

'You could say that. I drove.'

'Drove where?' The conversation was utterly inane and made even more so by the fact that she didn't care what his answers were. Speaking was simply a way of keeping herself from doing something far more desperate—and desirable.

She finally found the brandy in the bottom of the pantry, the bottle dusty but the amber liquid still glinting in the light. 'Here you are.'

Larenz took it, his fingers wrapping around the neck of the bottle and over Ellery's own hand. His gaze locked with hers, dark and unrelenting, and every thought flew from Ellery's head. She was trapped by that gaze and she had the strange sensation that Larenz was as trapped by it—by this—as she was. Ellery didn't move. She couldn't. She knew if he kissed her now she wouldn't resist. She wouldn't want to.

And why should she? She'd been locked up in this Manor,

keeping it like some kind of shrine to a family, a life that had never really existed, for six long months. She wanted to stop, if only for a night. Stop thinking, fearing, hiding.

And start living. Larenz was here, his eyes were on hers, his lips parted, his expression hungry and intense, and suddenly Ellery knew exactly what she wanted.

This.

She let go of the bottle, not thinking of it or anything but her own need and the answering look in Larenz's eyes, and somehow it slipped, shattering at their feet. Yet neither of them even reacted to the broken glass and spreading liquid, the pungent smell of alcohol rising up towards them. Something far more dangerous was happening.

Ellery didn't know who kissed who first. She didn't care. All that mattered was that she'd found her way into Larenz's arms and he was kissing her, his lips hot and hungry on hers as her arms wound around his neck, her fingers threading through his hair as she pulled him closer, and closer still—how she needed this...

'The glass—'

'I'll clean it up later,' she mumbled, turning her head to find his lips once more, eager and greedy. She felt Larenz smile against her mouth.

'I prefer not to need to have stitches,' he murmured, and in one easy graceful movement he'd swept her into an embrace, carrying her out of the kitchen and up the Manor's sweeping staircase. He held her easily, as if she were weightless, and Ellery felt like a doll in his arms, small and treasured.

'Where's your bedroom?' he asked, and then shook his head. 'On second thoughts, forget it. If your bedroom was anything like mine last night, I don't want to go there.'

'Worse,' Ellery admitted.

'What's the warmest place in the house?'

Ellery's heart squeezed again. Yes, she wanted this—she really did—but, now that the heated moment in the kitchen had cooled just a little, she was left wondering and afraid once more. Just what was she getting herself into? 'The master bedroom, I suppose,' she answered after a moment, 'or the drawing room when the fire is on—' Her voice wobbled just a little bit. Ellery closed her eyes in embarrassment.

'You're getting cold feet, aren't you?' Larenz placed her back on the floor so her body slid sensuously against his, his hands still on her shoulders, until her feet touched the ground. She swayed towards him and he reached up to tilt her chin with one finger so she was forced to meet his gaze. 'Ellery?'

'Not cold,' she corrected with a shaky laugh as her gaze slid away from his. 'A bit cool, perhaps.'

She felt rather than saw his smile, and they stood there in the dark and quiet, the house full of empty shadows all around them, the only sound their own breathing.

It took Ellery a moment to realize that Larenz was not speaking on purpose; he was not trying to convince her with words or, far more persuasive, with kisses. He was giving her time. He was letting her decide.

Slowly she leaned in and rested her forehead against his chest; he slipped his hand down and laced his fingers with hers. They remained that way, silent and swaying, for several moments. A thousand thoughts tumbled through Ellery's head. She realized she had no idea what she was doing…or why. She was afraid and excited and, strangely, a little sad. Yet she also knew if she could stretch this moment out into eternity, she would. She'd be happy just standing here in the dark, touching Larenz, feeling his breath and his heat, his hand gently—so gently—squeezing hers.

He wasn't the man she'd thought he was. The realization slipped into her mind slyly, like a secret, yet a good one. She'd assumed Larenz de Luca was an entitled, womanizing bastard—and yes, he'd seemed like it at first—but, even so, Ellery knew she'd leaped to conclusions because she was afraid. Afraid that any man who touched her—touched her heart—might turn out like her father, leaving her as brutally betrayed as her mother had been. Leaving her alone.

She'd never been willing to take the risk.

Yet Larenz had shown her too many small, surprising kindnesses for her to rest on her assumptions. To hide behind them. And right now she didn't want to. Right now she wanted to forget...and to feel.

She tilted her head upwards, her eyes still closed, and found Larenz's lips with her own. Her kiss was no more than a brush, but it served as an answer to the question Larenz's silence had posed.

Yes.

His arms came around her and he pulled her against him; Ellery went unresisting, without trepidation or fear.

'Come with me.'

CHAPTER FIVE

ELLERY followed him back downstairs, his fingers laced with hers as he led her through her own house, walking with the confidence of a man who knew exactly where he was going. And Ellery followed without needing to know where, or why. Now that she'd made her decision, she felt strangely, surprisingly at peace; she was content to rest in the moment, in being with Larenz, without jumping ahead to the what-ifs or why-nots.

He led her to the drawing room with its huge marble fireplace, now lost in shadow, the only light a gleam of lambent silver from the moon high above, visible through the gap in the heavy curtains at the windows.

'I assume this fireplace works?' Larenz said. He'd slipped his hand from hers and now crouched in front of the hearth.

'Yes, although I usually just use the electric—'

'This?' Larenz unplugged the three-bar electric fire she'd placed in the great old hearth with obvious contempt. Ellery found herself smiling. The electric fire had been sensible, or so she'd thought; she kept the firewood for guests. Yet now she found she was pleased as Larenz reached for the birch logs piled up next to the fireplace and began, quite expertly, to lay and then light a fire.

Within a few minutes a comfortable, friendly blaze was

crackling away, the flames casting long orange shadows around the room and over Larenz's face, making him look a little devilish. A little dangerous.

'Things getting cool again?' Larenz teased softly, and Ellery couldn't help but laugh, in spite of her lingering nerves, for he'd read her perfectly.

He knows me so well. The thought was ridiculous, absurd, for of course Larenz de Luca didn't know her at all. She'd only met him yesterday. Yet Ellery couldn't keep herself from thinking it—and perhaps even believing it.

'Come here,' Larenz said.

He was kneeling in front of the fireplace, his face half in light, half in shadow, and his voice sounded both teasing and a little raw.

Ellery went to him.

She stood in front of him, a little uncertain, a little breathless. Larenz tugged at her hand, and she dropped to her knees in front of him. The logs crackled and shifted, scattering some sparks across the carpet. Larenz brushed it with his fingers.

'We can't ruin another rug of yours,' he murmured, and Ellery tried to smile. She felt so nervous.

'At least this one's not an Aubusson.'

'You know all the antiques in this house of yours?' Larenz asked. His hand slipped along the nape of her neck, his fingers rubbing her tense muscles.

'Yes…my mother catalogued everything in this house.' Ellery's breath hitched. She was finding it difficult to concentrate with Larenz's deft fingers on her. 'She left a list… I went over it when I first came back.'

'How long ago was that?'

'Six months. My mother was going to sell this place and I couldn't—' She stopped suddenly, her throat tight. Larenz finished the thought for her.

'Couldn't imagine life without Maddock Manor in it somewhere?'

'Something like that.'

'Where is your mother now?'

'In Cornwall.' Ellery managed a smile. 'She lives in a lovely little thatched cottage and is happier than she's ever been.' Happier than she'd ever been with her father, Ellery added silently. She was glad her mother had found her place, her peace. She just needed to find hers.

She didn't want to talk any more, not about her house or her history, and Larenz must have sensed that for he smiled and reached to take the clip from her hair.

'I've been wanting to see your hair down ever since I first met you.'

'All of twenty-four hours ago?' Ellery joked, but it came out a bit flat.

'It's been a very long twenty-four hours,' Larenz replied and he released her hair.

Ellery almost always wore her hair pulled up any which way; it was more practical and there was never anyone to impress. Now she felt surprised by her own sensual response to the fall of her hair as it shimmered about her face and shoulders in a pale cloud. She shivered when Larenz threaded his fingers through it, his thumb brushing her cheek and the fullness of her lip.

'Beautiful…just as I imagined. Or perhaps better. You look like The Lady of Shalott.'

'You know that poem?' Ellery asked in surprise, for Tennyson's ballad was one of her favourite poems.

'You know it was based on an Italian story? *Donna di Scalotta*. I like the English version better, though.' He quoted softly, '"There she weaves by night and day, A magic web…"' He brushed his lips against her jaw. 'You've certainly woven some kind of magic around me.'

Ellery thrilled to his words, even as another more logical part of her was insisting that surely she was not like that doomed lady, isolated and imprisoned in her island castle, pining for the handsome Lancelot. Surely, unlike the sorrowful Lady of Shalott, she had a surer hand in her own destiny—and a happier fate.

Then all thoughts fled Ellery's dazed mind for Larenz was kissing her again, his lips moving slowly over hers, exploring every contour as he pulled her closer, and closer still, and she surrendered herself completely to the caress.

She wanted to forget. She wanted to feel. To feel and not to think.

Larenz's hands slid along her nightgown, deftly undoing the row of buttons down the back. 'I dreamed of you wearing something like this,' he murmured into her neck. 'Yards and yards of white flannel… I can hardly wait to unwrap you.'

Ellery gave a shaky laugh. 'It keeps me warm.'

'Good thing I lit a fire,' Larenz replied and gently pushed the nightgown off her shoulders. The garment slid from her body, landing in a heap of cloth, which Larenz kicked aside. All Ellery wore was a pair of thick woollen socks. She was uncomfortably conscious of her own nakedness, even though in the dim light, her body bent, her hair hanging down, Larenz could hardly see her. Yet she couldn't help but notice that he still wore all his clothes.

'This feels a little uneven,' she said, trying for a teasing note, and Larenz cocked his head, his eyes gleaming in the half-light.

'So it does. How should we remedy the situation?'

And Ellery knew exactly how. Smiling a little bit, emboldened by her own desire—and Larenz's—she reached for his T-shirt. 'I think I can help.' She pulled the T-shirt from his torso while Larenz obediently raised his arms, watching her with a sleepy half-smile. His chest gleamed bronze in the firelight and Ellery sucked in her breath. He was a beautiful man. And tonight he was hers.

Cautiously, she reached out and touched the taut muscle

of his chest, letting her hand drift down to the waistband of his jeans. And there she stopped.

She glanced back at his face and saw him watching her with a knowing—and almost gentle—little smile. Her fingers played with the button of his jeans. She let out a little ragged laugh.

'Shall I help?'

'I'm a bit…new…to this.' It was as close as she was willing to admit to just how new she was.

Larenz's hand covered her own and, emboldened once more, Ellery undid the button.

Just a few seconds later he'd been divested of all his clothes—and Ellery of her socks—and they were both naked, stretched out in front of the fire, the flames casting dancing amber shadows over their bodies.

Larenz ran a hand along her calf, to her thigh and then her hip, before cupping the fullness of her breast. 'You're beautiful,' he said with such sincerity that Ellery felt tears come to her eyes.

She didn't believe him. Couldn't. She was nothing special—blonde hair and odd-coloured eyes and an average body. She didn't want Larenz's platitudes or sentiments aimed at seduction; she couldn't stand lies.

She turned, covering his mouth with her own to keep him from speaking, her arms twining around his body as she pressed closer to him and felt her own feminine softness come up against his hard chest and thighs. Larenz responded, deepening Ellery's desperate kiss, his hands roaming over her nakedness and, as Ellery closed her eyes, she let pleasure take over, stealing through her veins like a drug, blotting out all remembrance and regret.

It was all too easy to give herself up to the moment, to let her body's need take precedence over her mind's fear, and as Larenz caressed her, kissing and touching and loving every inch of her body, Ellery writhed and moaned and cried out his name, her fingernails snagging on the worn carpet, her mind blissfully blank.

A moment came when Larenz hesitated, his body poised over hers. 'Are you protected?'

'Nnn…no,' Ellery stammered, thinking of her heart. Her heart was all too dangerously exposed, and yet of course Larenz meant her body. He rolled off her, rifling through his clothes, and Ellery felt a pang of something that was halfway between hurt and disappointment.

'You were prepared.'

'Let's say hopeful,' he murmured, slipping on the condom he'd taken from the pocket of his jeans. Ellery pushed all her thoughts away and gave herself up to pleasure once more.

She experienced a brief flicker of pain as Larenz pushed past her innocence, and she heard his own sucked-in breath of surprise. She closed her eyes and pushed back, opening herself up to him, and after a tiny second's pause Larenz embedded himself deeply inside her, groaning against her lips in both need and satisfaction. Ellery felt the flickers of pleasure blunt the pain in both her body and heart, and then the flickers turned to waves that crashed over in a tide of satiation and the pain was—for the moment—utterly obliterated.

Afterwards, they lay in a tangle of limbs, their skin golden in the light of the few dying embers left in the grate. Larenz traced circles on her skin with his fingertips as Ellery laid her head against his shoulder.

'You should have told me you were a virgin,' he said. Although he spoke in a lazy, sensual tone, Ellery sensed a different undercurrent. Disappointment, perhaps. She tried not to tense. Had she not been a good enough lover?

'I didn't think it was important,' she said with a little shrug. Her virginity, strangely perhaps, had not even crossed her mind when she'd considered whether to give herself to Larenz. It had been her heart and soul's safety and innocence she'd been more concerned about, rather than her body's.

Larenz's fingers stilled on her skin. 'A woman's first time is always important. If I'd known—'

Ellery propped herself up on one elbow, daring to look down at Larenz's brooding face. 'You would have taken more care? Or perhaps you wouldn't have bothered in the first place?'

He let out a sigh that wasn't an answer at all. 'I just wish I'd known.' Gently, he pushed Ellery's head back down on his shoulder and, as she resettled herself, his fingers stroked her temples. Ellery closed her eyes. She suddenly felt almost sleepy.

'I didn't think it really mattered,' she said after a moment. 'I decided I wanted you, and that was it.'

'Oh, was it?' Larenz teased, sounding amused. 'And here I was thinking I was the one who decided I wanted you.'

'Well,' Ellery said, barely suppressing a yawn, 'I suppose it was mutual.'

'Yes, indeed, *dormigliona*.'

She laughed a bit and snuggled deeper into the silken warmth of his shoulder, content to lie there for ever in Larenz's half-embrace.

Yet they remained like that for a moment, no more, and then in one deft movement he rose, scooping her up and taking her with him. Ellery was too sleepy and sated to do anything but curl into him and let him take her where he would.

Larenz strode through the darkened empty rooms of the Manor, naked and magnificent, and upstairs to the master bedroom, which Ellery had laid with fresh sheets only that afternoon. He peeled back the satin duvet and laid her on the bed. In the darkness she could not read his expression or even see his face, but Ellery smiled up at him, waiting, expecting him to slide into the bed next to her and take her in his arms once more.

He didn't.

He hesitated, or seemed to, although in the darkness Ellery couldn't be sure. Then he bent and brushed a kiss on her forehead. As his lips grazed her skin, he whispered, 'Sweet dreams, my Lady of Shalott.' And then, before Ellery could even draw a breath, he was gone. She heard the click of the door closing and then the sound of Larenz's footsteps down the hall.

Alone in the darkness Ellery was conscious of the cold slippery sheets against her naked limbs and, far worse, the coldness creeping inside her, stealing straight to her heart. Why had Larenz left so suddenly?

Yet, even as she asked herself that question, Ellery knew the grim answer. Tonight had been simply that: a night. And now it was over.

She never should have expected a single thing—or a single moment—more.

Minutes before, she had been content to drift into a satisfied sleep but now, lying there, she felt cold and unhappy and most definitely awake. She rose from the bed, grabbing one of the complimentary dressing gowns she'd hung in the wardrobe herself, a rather cheap attempt to make Maddock Manor more upmarket than it was or ever could be.

Enveloped in thick, rough terrycloth, she stole downstairs, not wanting to alert Larenz to her presence. Yet he wasn't downstairs; he seemed to have disappeared completely. Ellery half-wondered if he'd actually left the Manor itself, and that brief kiss had been her only goodbye.

She forced the thoughts away, keeping her mind determinedly blank. Yet, as she entered the drawing room and saw their scattered clothes and the ashes of the fire Larenz had laid, she heard the raw tearing gasp of her own pain. Wrapping her arms around herself, she took several steadying breaths and then turned to go to the kitchen.

She needed that cup of tea.

Yet the abandoned mess in the kitchen told its own

sorrowful story; the scattered peas and shattered glass glared at Ellery as she stood there, silent condemnations of her own folly. She drew another breath; it sounded like a shudder, halfway to a sob.

She set her chin and threw her shoulders back as she went for the broom and dustpan. None of this, she told herself, should come as a surprise. This was what she'd expected, even wanted, when she'd allowed herself to kiss Larenz. A night of pleasure, a chance to forget—for a moment.

Now she was just dealing with the remembering. And the regret.

Ellery bent to her task of cleaning up the mess in the kitchen, allowing the menial nature of the chores to numb her mind and keep the thoughts at bay.

She'd risen to empty the dustpan in the rubbish bin when she caught sight of her face in the darkened windowpane. Her face was ghostly pale, her hair streaming over her shoulders in a pale river. Just like the doomed Lady of Shalott. Then, unable to stop herself, Ellery let the tears trickle slowly down her cheeks.

Alone in his bedroom, Larenz let out a moody sigh, the sound entirely at odds with the sleepy satiation stealing through his body.

Yet, even as his body tingled and remembered and longed for more, his mind was coldly listing all the reasons to walk away from Ellery Dunant right now.

Tonight had been a mistake. A big one. He chose his bed partners carefully, made sure they knew exactly what to expect from him: nothing. Nothing beyond a night of pleasure, maybe a week. Yet when Ellery had snuggled into his arms, when he'd felt the way she'd fitted so perfectly, he'd realized she would expect a good deal more than that. He'd felt it in her soft, pliant body, in the satisfied little sigh she'd given.

In the fact that she had been a virgin. Larenz hadn't expected *that*; she had to be in her mid-twenties at the least. Yet she'd chosen to give herself—her innocence—to him? On the floor of her own wrecked home?

Larenz turned away from the window, unable to deal with or even accept the scalding sense of shame that poured through him. He didn't bed virgins. He didn't take them on the worn floors of their ancestral homes.

He didn't break their hearts.

Yet, alone in his bedroom, conscious of the creak on the stair, Larenz realized he might have done just that. Or he would, given time. He had no intention of sticking around for Ellery Dunant to fall in love with him, to think of him as Sir Lancelot to her tragic Lady of Shalott. There was no happy ending to that story, and there wouldn't be one here, either. Larenz knew very well that happy endings like the one Ellery was undoubtedly envisioning didn't exist. He knew it from the hard reality of his own life, his own disappointments… and he had no intention of experiencing that kind of rejection again. He would never give himself the opportunity.

Yet, even as he made these resolutions, his face set in grim lines, Larenz couldn't quite keep his mind from picturing Ellery's violet eyes, from his body remembering how soft and silken she'd felt in his arms. And he couldn't keep both his mind and body from wanting more.

Ellery Dunant was a luxury—and a liability—he couldn't afford. Resolutely, Larenz closed his mind from thinking about her. From remembering how she felt in his arms. Even so, sleep remained a long way off.

CHAPTER SIX

THE next morning Ellery awoke to bright sunlight and a hard, glittering frost covering the ground. She rose from the bed, groggy and dazed. She must have slept, although she did not feel like she had. She certainly did not feel rested.

She fumbled for her clothes, trying to shake the fog that enshrouded her since Larenz had left her last night. She told herself she had no reason to feel this way; she had surely expected no more. She shouldn't feel *hurt*.

Dressed, her hair pulled into a tight bun—no Lady of Shalott for her this morning—Ellery headed downstairs. She had no idea whether Larenz would expect or even want breakfast, but she had every intention of keeping this morning as normal as possible. Even if the very idea made something inside her shrivel.

She paused on the threshold of the kitchen; all vestiges of the evening before had been cleaned away by her own hand just a few short hours ago. The kitchen suffocated her with its normality, for it looked as if nothing had changed. As if *she* hadn't changed. Yet Ellery knew she had; she felt it in the slight soreness between her thighs and the far more persistent ache in her heart. She hadn't expected that.

With grim determination she set about cracking eggs and slicing toast. She wondered if Larenz would even come downstairs. Had he gone? The house echoed emptily around her.

She wouldn't think about him, she told herself. She wouldn't think about him at all. She'd fill her mind with the trivial details of her day, with the to-do lists and DIY worries that had occupied her until he'd come into her life—there, she was thinking about him again. Ellery groaned aloud.

She left the eggs bubbling on the stove and went to fetch the two pints of milk the local dairy delivered every other day. As she opened the kitchen door, the sunlight hit her in the face, a brilliant yet cruel reminder that nothing had really changed over the course of one night, even if she had; if anything, the weather had just got better.

'Good morning.'

Ellery whirled around, the pints of milk clutched to her chest nearly sliding from her suddenly nerveless fingers. She tightened her grip and swallowed dryly. Larenz stood in the kitchen, dressed in a navy-blue suit, a coat hanging over one arm. He was, Ellery knew, coming to say goodbye.

Larenz gazed at Ellery, the milk clutched to her chest, the sun creating a golden nimbus around her cloud of pale hair. She looked like something out of a Constable painting, with the sunlight pouring in from the half-opened kitchen door, the wild gardens and crumbling brick wall visible behind her.

Her eyes were wide and shocked, the same colour as the shadowed circles underneath them. Of course, she couldn't have got very much sleep last night. Neither had he.

Still, despite his resolve to leave this morning, leave this woman and all her unnecessary and unwanted complications, he found himself now standing there, speechless, a growing tightness in his chest. Ellery looked so lovely, so fragile and yet with an inner strength he knew she possessed, radiating out from her despite the hurt and pain hiding in her eyes.

He'd hurt her. This was what happened when you opened

yourself up to anything more than brief physical pleasure. You got hurt. He'd taken something from her, something precious, and he would hurt her now, by leaving. Even if he didn't want to hurt her…even if he didn't want to leave.

Even if the thought of leaving hurt *him*.

'Good morning,' Ellery replied. She aimed for a brisk tone and just about managed it. She kicked the door closed behind her and put the milk in the fridge. She tried to think of something to say, but even the usual banal inanities seemed loaded with meaning: *sleep well*? didn't have quite the right ring. 'It's a beautiful day out,' she finally said, now sounding perhaps a little too brisk. She turned to the eggs; they'd overcooked and gone rubbery. 'Would you like the full fry-up this morning?'

Larenz hesitated and Ellery braced herself. Of course he didn't want a full breakfast, she told herself furiously. Not like yesterday morning, when he'd asked her to share his breakfast, when she'd still been an interesting and unknown challenge. Now he just wanted to leave.

'If you're making it,' he finally said, his tone neutral, but Ellery heard pity.

'If you'd rather just have coffee,' she told him with a bright, rather glittering smile, 'that's fine. The eggs look a bit overcooked, anyway.'

Smiling faintly, Larenz glanced in the pan. The eggs had congealed to its bottom. 'How about a compromise? Coffee and toast.' He paused. 'If you'll join me.'

She threw him a startled glance; he smiled, his face so very bland. How good he was at wiping away all expression, she thought resentfully. She had no idea what he was thinking, and she had an awful feeling that she was all too transparent. 'Very well.' She poured two mugs of coffee and fetched the toast. Larenz hung his coat over a chair and they sat across from each other, the awkwardness palpable, unbearable.

Ellery took a sip of coffee and burned her tongue. 'You're

off?' she enquired in that same awful brisk voice. 'I don't even know where you live. Are you returning to Italy or…' She let the sentence trail away for it occurred to her that perhaps he didn't want her to know where he lived. She hardly wanted to come across as some sort of stalker.

'I divide my time between Milan and London,' Larenz replied quietly. He hadn't touched his toast or coffee; he simply stared at her across the length of the table, his expression solemn now and perhaps even a little sorrowful.

Ellery took a bite of toast. It tasted like dust in her mouth. 'Sounds lovely,' she finally managed after she choked it down. 'Quite the jet-setting lifestyle.'

'Quite.' Larenz lifted his coffee mug, then placed it back on the table without taking a sip. 'You could come with me.'

Ellery stared at him, sure she must not have heard him correctly. 'Pardon?' she said politely, and waited to hear what he really must have said.

'You could come with me,' Larenz said again, and he sounded surprised, as though he hadn't expected to say it. Staring at him, Ellery was quite sure he hadn't.

She shook her head slowly, confusion and hope warring within her. 'Come with you? Where?'

'To London, and then to Milan,' Larenz stated matter-of-factly. He seemed to have recovered from his surprise. 'I have some business to do, but it could be…nice…to have company. It might do you some good, too. You don't have any guests booked for the next week or so, do you?'

'No, not yet,' Ellery said after a moment. The words *week or so* seemed to echo through her mind. Was that as long as this…affair…would last? 'I teach at the local school,' she added. 'But it's actually half-term this week.'

'Then why don't you come with me?' Larenz smiled and took a sip of coffee. 'You could use a break, I'm sure, and we could hammer out the details of the fashion shoot—'

'The fashion shoot?' Ellery repeated in disbelief. 'You still want to have it here?'

'Of course. My head of PR is quite set on this place.'

She shook her head slowly. The idea of a fashion shoot at Maddock Manor made no sense to her, but it hardly seemed relevant now. 'So you want to bring me to London and Milan to discuss business,' she said a bit flatly. 'Surely a week's trip isn't necessary for that.' She heard the slight edge to her voice as she added, 'You could just take me out for dinner.'

'I could,' Larenz agreed, smiling faintly, 'but this trip isn't about what's necessary.' He put down his mug and met her gaze directly, with an open honesty she hadn't been expecting, a vulnerability that reached right down inside her and grabbed her heart.

No. Don't reach me. Don't touch me like that, with your eyes. Don't make me hope, don't make me fall—

'I want you to come with me because I want to be with you,' Larenz said steadily. 'What happened between us last night—it was good.' He raised his eyebrows. 'Wasn't it?'

Ellery looked down. 'Yes, it was,' she whispered. It seemed such a simplification of the night they'd shared, not to mention the pain and sorrow she'd felt afterwards, but she could hardly voice that sentiment.

Larenz rose from the table, coming around to her side. He reached down and took her hand, tugging her upwards. Ellery didn't resist. She stood up, savouring his closeness, the scent of his aftershave, the heat and strength of him. He'd already become familiar. He laced his fingers with hers. 'Come with me, Ellery.'

'For a week?' she said, and Larenz paused.

'Yes.' He spoke steadily, flatly. 'That's all I have to offer.'

So those were his terms. A week, take it or leave it. A week, and then he would leave her for ever and she would return here, to the half-life she'd made for herself. Ellery knew she should say no. Agreeing would be opening herself up to all sorts of pain, hurt, sorrow. A week of being used, because surely that was all it was? A week was not a relationship.

She opened her mouth and yet still she didn't speak. The definite *no* didn't come. For, despite every logical reason to refuse, she still *wanted* to go. She wanted to escape this house and her life, and she wanted to be with Larenz.

'Ellery?' Larenz prompted gently, and she remembered how he'd let her decide last night. He'd waited then, and he was waiting now.

What if it didn't have to be like that? she wondered suddenly. What if she made these terms hers, instead of just Larenz's? She wasn't interested in love. She didn't even want a relationship; she'd kept herself from such things on purpose, out of self-protection.

What if *she* decided on a week's fling? What if she was in control?

The thought was powerful. Persuasive. Her mother had been at her father's whim, waiting hopelessly for his return, for his careless favour. Yet Ellery didn't have to be like that. She could take this week, enjoy it to the full, and when it was over she could be the one to walk away, her heart intact.

This, she thought suddenly, could be just what she needed. In so many ways.

She squeezed Larenz's fingers. 'Yes,' she said. 'I'll go with you.'

Larenz waited in the kitchen as Ellery went to pack. He felt restless, edgy and even a little hopeful. A strange mix. He had no idea why he'd asked Ellery to come with him to London. He'd had no intention of doing so; he'd been coming to say goodbye.

And then he'd found himself saying something else instead, and wanting it. Wanting her.

The thought was just a little bit alarming.

Of course, it didn't have to be. He'd made it very clear to Ellery what his terms were, what this week would mean—and especially what it wouldn't mean. And even if he'd broken all of his rules—bedding a virgin and mixing business with pleasure—he wouldn't break that one.

After a week, it was over. After a week, he would leave.

They left right after breakfast. It felt strange to pack a single case—she had few dressy clothes left over from her London days—and then to lock up the Manor, leaving it emptier than ever.

Larenz waited by his car; Ellery sensed his impatience, even though he didn't say anything or even glance at his watch. He was ready to go. To move on. And in another week, he'd be ready again. Well, so would she.

'Do you need to notify anyone?' he asked as Ellery slid into the front passenger seat of his car. 'I suppose things will just tick over for a few days?'

Ellery nodded. 'I was just planning on doing some maintenance around the house this week.' She smiled wryly. 'But I suppose it can wait.'

'Good,' Larenz said firmly and started the engine.

'It feels strange,' she admitted with a little laugh, as Larenz drove down the Manor's sweeping lane, 'to leave, even for just a little while.' She wanted to be clear that she understood the rules. That they were hers, too.

Larenz slotted her a quick sideways smile. 'It will do you good.'

Ellery stiffened. That was the second time he'd said that. 'Don't see this as some kind of mercy mission,' she warned him. 'I'm going with you because I want to. It's my choice.' She met his gaze directly. 'A week is all I want, as well, Larenz.'

Surprise flashed across his features, followed by what

could only be satisfaction. His mouth tightened. 'Good,' he said again, and just as firmly.

Ellery settled back in the seat, glad she'd made herself clear. *A week is all I want*, she repeated to herself, and she believed it.

They didn't speak again until they'd left both the Manor and village behind and the road stretched out in front of them, glittering under a bright autumn sun.

Larenz steered the conversation to more innocuous matters, talking lightly about films and books and even the weather; Ellery enjoyed chatting about such simple things.

'So you teach,' he commented as they turned onto the motorway. 'I can see you giving one of your stern looks to a classroom full of unruly boys.'

Ellery chuckled. 'Actually, it's an all-girls school. I taught full-time in London, but I gave that up when I came out here. Fortunately, I found a part-time job. One of the teachers was going on maternity leave.'

'And when she comes back? What will you do then?'

Ellery shrugged. 'I don't know. I don't have a long-term plan, to be honest.' She made herself smile. 'I know I can't hold on to Maddock Manor for ever.'

Larenz glanced sideways at her, speculative and a little compassionate. 'Then I suppose the question is—why hold on to it at all?'

'That is indeed a good question. I haven't yet found a good answer.' She stared out of the window at the trees lining their side of the motorway, their stark branches stripped of leaves and stretching towards the sky. 'Have you ever not been able to give something up, even though you know you probably should?' Larenz didn't answer, and so Ellery finished, 'That's how I feel about the Manor. I'm just not ready to let it go yet. All of my friends think I'm mad, of course.'

'Well,' Larenz said quietly, 'I think you're brave. Not

everyone is able to actually *do* something the way you have. Most people would just let it go and be sad.'

'Perhaps that's better.'

Larenz glanced at her again. 'Do you really believe that? Wouldn't you rather act and really live life than let it go by?'

Ellery swallowed, surprised by the intensity in his voice. Yes, she wanted to live life. She wanted to act. Wasn't that why she was here? She was taking control.

They lapsed into silence, and an hour later Larenz pulled the car up to the front of The Berkeley, an impressive-looking hotel in Belgravia.

He tossed his keys to the valet while a porter helped Ellery out of the Lexus. Larenz ushered her into the hotel's sumptuous lobby; she thought she saw a celebrity she recognized disappear into one of the exquisite dining rooms.

Ellery was breathless, overwhelmed by the luxury she had never experienced and yet should have expected. After all, Larenz de Luca was a wealthy, powerful man. And she was never more conscious of it than when he strode through the hotel lobby, the staff nodding and bowing to him. He was quite obviously a regular customer. The very idea that she was here with him seemed ludicrous, so much so that Ellery had to stifle a laugh of sheer amazement and wonder as she followed him through the sumptuous lobby.

'You come here often?' she asked as he gestured for her to enter the lift before him.

'I reserve a suite for my personal use,' Larenz replied with a shrug.

'Reserve?' Ellery echoed. 'You mean always?' The thought of paying thousands of pounds a night for a hotel suite to be on reserve seemed not only incredible but rather wasteful, especially in light of her own desperate financial situation. She could not imagine ever being so wealthy or privileged.

Larenz shrugged again. 'Not always,' he allowed. 'If I know I'm going to be out of the country for some time.' He gave her a knowing little smile. 'I'm not a spendthrift, Ellery. I didn't get to where I am by throwing money away.'

The statement, delivered in such a matter-of-fact manner, intrigued her. 'Get to?' she repeated. 'Where did you come from, then?'

The lift pinged and the doors whooshed open. Larenz gestured for her to enter the suite first. 'I told you before, near Spoleto,' he said lightly, but Ellery felt quite certain that he knew she'd really been asking something else.

Yet all thoughts of their conversation evaporated in light of the splendour of the suite Larenz reserved for his occasional use. Rooms stretched out in every direction, and Ellery silently marvelled at the polished marble and mahogany, the sumptuous carpets, the graceful Grecian columns that flanked the doors leading out to a private terrace.

She peeped in what was clearly the master bedroom and swallowed. 'It's gorgeous.' She'd become so used to the tattered state of Maddock Manor that the luxury and opulence left her nearly speechless. 'I can't believe I'm here,' she admitted with a little laugh.

Larenz came up behind her as she stared silently at the king-sized bed piled high with silk throw pillows and rested his hands lightly on her shoulders. Ellery shivered under his touch.

'I want you to enjoy it,' he murmured. 'Enjoy this. Let me spoil you, Ellery. I want to.'

His words caused a fingertip trail of unease to ripple down her spine. *Spoil* had such unpleasant connotations, she thought distantly, like rotting food. To be ruined, perhaps, for anything else.

Yet as she gazed around at the suite with its beauty and its finery, its handmade chocolates and a bottle of Krug champagne chilling in a silver bucket in the sitting room, she told herself that a week of being spoiled could do no harm...or at least not much. Surely she deserved a week out of time, out of reality. A week of this...and she wanted it. Just one week.

Whether it was right or wrong, good or bad, she wanted a week with Larenz. She wanted to be wined, dined, romanced and seduced. She wanted to be immersed in the wonderful whirlwind, to let it pick her up and take her where it would.

Eventually—in a week—she'd land with a thump, and when she did she'd go back to life, to reality, happy and satisfied. She *would*.

She turned around so she was facing Larenz and, with a little cat-like smile she'd never felt on her face before, she wound her arms around his neck. 'All right,' she agreed in a husky murmur as Larenz pulled her closer, 'if you insist.' And, by Larenz's answering smile, she knew he was pleased by her response.

They ate a late lunch of lobster bisque and caviar on crackers in their room, washed down with several glasses of champagne. By mid-afternoon Ellery was feeling wonderfully relaxed and even a little sleepy.

'I have to check in with a few things,' Larenz told her as a maid slipped in to clear their discarded dishes. 'But why don't you have a rest and a bath? We have reservations at the restaurant downstairs tonight.'

'All right,' Ellery agreed. Mentally, she went through the few clothes she'd packed and doubted whether the cocktail dress she'd worn to her college's May Ball four years ago would be elegant—or expensive—enough. Still, a rest sounded good; she was exhausted.

She stood in the centre of the suite's master bedroom with its huge king-sized bed piled high with pillows, its doors to the private terrace outside, and listened to Larenz moving through the living room.

Ellery slipped off her shoes and peeled back the satin duvet. As she slipped into the bed with its slippery sheets, she felt another shaft of amazement that she was here at all slice through her. A few seconds later she heard him speak in a low voice and knew he must be on the telephone. Who was he calling? What business did he need to check? Lying there, Ellery was forced to acknowledge just how little she knew her lover, her only lover.

Her lover for a week.

Her terms, she reminded herself fiercely. Those were her terms. It wasn't as if she was looking for *love*, and especially not from a man like Larenz de Luca: rich, entitled, uncaring. All he felt for her—could feel—was a brief physical pleasure; she *knew* that. She was not yet so desperate or deluded to think that anything would happen as a result of this week out of time, or that she even wanted anything to happen. She knew what loving someone—a man—did to you. She'd seen her mother wither and shrivel from her father's lack of love. Ellery didn't want that kind of life; she didn't want any man to have that kind of power over her. It was why she'd been a virgin until last night, why she'd avoided serious relationships at university and beyond, why even now she guarded herself from anything—or anyone—that could touch her heart. It was why she would end up alone.

But it was also why Larenz's offer of a single week suited her perfectly.

CHAPTER SEVEN

WHEN Ellery awoke the sky was banked with violet clouds and the room thick with shadows. She heard a rustle of satin at the edge of the bed and she knew Larenz was there. She sensed him, smelled him and, when he rested a hand on her leg, she felt the comforting heat of him even through the thickness of the duvet.

'Hello, *dormigliona.*'

She snuggled deeper into the duvet; Larenz let his hand rove a little higher on her thigh. 'What does that mean?'

'*Dormigliona?* I suppose in English it would be sleepy-head. You've been asleep for over three hours.'

'Have I? Goodness.' Ellery sat up, self-conscious now that she was fully awake. 'I hardly ever nap. There's too much to do.'

'All the more reason for you to nap here,' Larenz replied easily. 'All you have to do is enjoy yourself.'

Ellery smiled and stretched under the covers. 'Sounds simple.'

'It is.' In the twilit dimness of the room she couldn't make out the expression on Larenz's face, but she was achingly aware of the charged atmosphere growing between them, the need spiralling deep inside herself. She leaned forward, expectant, waiting. Larenz removed his hand from her leg.

'I ran you a bath,' he told her as he rose from the bed. 'You didn't even stir when I came in here to do it, but I thought you'd like a nice soak before dinner.'

Ellery leaned back against the pillows, disappointment eroding her brief happiness. She'd wanted Larenz to kiss her, and more than that. She wanted to be in his arms again, to have him make her both forget and remember at the same time, in such a sweet, sweet mix of both longing and satisfaction...

'Come on,' he said lightly, 'it's getting cold.'

And then he left the room.

After a moment Ellery swung her legs over the side of the bed and pushed open the door to the en suite bathroom. A huge jacuzzi bath in sumptuous silvery-grey marble had been filled with fragrant foaming bubbles, a fluffy towel laid neatly on the side. Just the sight of that bath made Ellery feel every aching muscle; lukewarm showers and hot-water bottles back at Maddock Manor simply didn't compare.

'This hotel must have an amazing boiler,' she said aloud as she stripped off her clothes and a few seconds later sank gratefully into the silky, steaming water. She lay her head back against the marble and closed her eyes; she didn't know how long she lay there, relaxed enough to be in a half doze, when she heard the door open and her eyes flew open.

'Hello.' Larenz stood there, the sleeves of his crisp white shirt rolled up to his elbows.

Ellery sank deeper into the water, grateful for the foaming bubbles that hid her from view. Even though it was rather ridiculous to feel shy now, she still did. She wasn't used to this. She didn't even know how lovers were supposed to act. She barely knew how to flirt.

'I thought I could help you wash your hair,' Larenz said. He sat on the edge of the tub, and Ellery was conscious of both his nearness and her own nakedness.

'I don't—' she began, but Larenz smiled and shook his head.

'Trust me, it would be my pleasure.' He reached out to wipe a stray bubble from her cheek. 'Ellery, are you shy with me now? After what we've done—and been—to each other?'

Ellery shook her head as a matter of instinct. Yet the question Larenz had asked was a loaded one, and she wondered if he'd done it deliberately. Just what *had* they been to each other?

'All right,' she finally managed, scooting forward so he could access her hair, which she'd piled rather untidily on top of her head with a plastic clip. Realizing she sounded a bit grudging, she added, 'Thank you.'

Smiling, Larenz reached out and took the clip from her hair. It cascaded down her back in unruly waves, the ends trailing in the water. Ellery saw that Larenz had an arrested, almost mesmerized look in his eyes as he reached down and cupped his hands. She felt the pull of his gaze like a magnetic force between them, growing stronger in the steamy heat of the room. 'Lean back a bit.'

She did, conscious of how vulnerable she felt as Larenz cradled her head in the crook of his arm. She closed her eyes as he poured the warm water over her head until her hair was completely wet. He reached for the shampoo by the side of the tub and then began to lather her hair, his strong fingers massaging her skull and temples, eliciting a low moan of relaxed pleasure from her lips. His hands slid down to her shoulders, massaging those muscles as well, his thumbs skimming the top of her breasts.

'Time to rinse,' he murmured, and Ellery arched back so the water wouldn't get in her eyes, her head still cradled in Larenz's hands. She was achingly conscious of how intimate an experience this was, how it filled every sense with longing. 'Ellery…' On his lips her name was no more than a raw plea and Ellery's eyes flew open, stunned and gratified to know that he felt it, too, to see the flame of need turning Larenz's eyes to blazing sapphire.

Her lips parted but she couldn't think of a thing to say except, 'Kiss me.'

Larenz obeyed, leaning down to claim her lips with his own and Ellery's hands came up of their own accord, fisting the collar of his shirt, careless of how soaked he became.

The kiss went on endlessly, and yet it still wasn't enough. When Ellery felt Larenz lift his mouth from her own, she must have made some protest for he murmured, a sleepy laugh in his voice, 'I don't want to drown you.'

Easily, he scooped her up and carried her out of the bathroom, just as he'd carried her downstairs at the Manor. Ellery, wet and naked, curled into him; she'd never felt so safe, so cherished as she did in Larenz's arms.

Except, perhaps, for when he lay her down on the bed and gazed at her not with hunger, but with wonder. Something shifted inside her then; she felt her soul opening in a way it never had before, even when her body had yielded to his. Yet she didn't dare question just what it was she felt; the physical need was too great. And it had to be enough.

She reached up and twined her arms around his shoulders, bringing him to her, needing him near her, skin upon skin.

'Too many clothes,' she mumbled and, laughing, Larenz pushed away briefly to remove his clothes; his shirt was damp in patches from where he'd held her.

Then, as he returned to her and she felt the beauty and bliss of his skin on hers, their bodies aligned perfectly, no more objections—or even thoughts—came to mind.

Afterwards, they lay in the room, now nearly dark, their limbs in a satisfying tangle, when Larenz glanced at the clock and murmured, 'If we don't get moving, we're going to miss our dinner reservation.'

Larenz swung his legs over the side of the bed and was

now striding through the room, magnificently naked. Ellery watched as he threw open the doors of the wardrobe and reached for a crisp white shirt. She saw her own clothes had been hung up there as well, no doubt by the same maid who had cleared their dishes.

As Larenz began to dress, Ellery was strangely moved by the intimacy of the scene; they'd just risen from bed and were now dressing. It felt like something a couple would do, even a married couple, and the realization that they really were just two strangers made Ellery feel disconcerted, even disappointed, as if what they'd just shared was sordid rather than sweet. She pushed such thoughts away and rose from the bed.

'I'll just go dry my hair,' she said and, without turning around, Larenz nodded.

By the time she'd returned to the bedroom, Larenz had gone into the living room, although Ellery could still smell a faint citrusy whiff of his cologne. She dressed quickly, grimacing slightly at the rather plain black dress she'd brought. It was a classic, if rather inexpensive, LBD, which was why she'd bought it, but she'd realized afterwards that the cut was too severe and black made her look rather washed out. Sighing, Ellery pulled her hair into a chignon of sorts, not as tight a bun as she normally would have but still a severe hairstyle. She grimaced again. She looked like a disapproving housekeeper. At least her shoes were pretty: a pair of sparkly black open-toed stilettos she'd bought only a few weeks ago. She'd travelled to Ipswich to run errands and had seen them in a shop window. It had been an impulse buy and surely a ridiculous one, for she didn't usually wear heels and had no call to don a pair while living at Maddock Manor. Besides, they'd pinched her toes even in the changing room. Still, gazing in the mirror, she focused on her feet and decided any pain was worth it. They were fun, frivolous and entirely unlike her, but she loved them. And they gave her the courage to walk out of the room and into this strange—and amazing—new world.

Taking a deep breath, she headed out into the living room. Larenz turned around as soon as she entered, although Ellery had hardly made a sound. He looked magnificent in a beautifully tailored suit of grey silk and his gaze swept over her, taking in the plain unflattering dress, the severe hairstyle and ending at her feet. He smiled.

'Nice shoes.'

Ellery grinned. She couldn't help it. It was the best thing he could have said—the kindest and the most honest—and she gave a little laugh as Larenz's glinting gaze met hers and he smiled back.

'Shall we?' He held out his arm and Ellery took it.

'Yes.'

The restaurant was as opulent and luxurious as Ellery had suspected, yet on Larenz's arm the insecurities over her own attire faded to nothing. She was smugly conscious of the covetous looks a few women shot her, as well as a few curious and assessing glances by the men.

She felt like a movie star.

'The usual, Signor de Luca?' a waiter murmured, and Larenz gave a brief nod. Within minutes—seconds, even— the waiter had returned with a bottle of Krug and two delicate crystal flutes.

'I've never had so much champagne,' Ellery confessed after the waiter had left and Larenz raised his glass in a silent toast. She followed suit.

'I must admit, I am partial to it, especially when travelling. At home, of course, I drink only the best.'

'Which is?' Ellery asked, taking a sip of her champagne. The bubbles fizzed crisply on her tongue.

'Italian wine, of course. One of my interests is in supporting local vineyards. Drink up.'

Ellery took another sip; she had a feeling that on a rather

empty stomach the alcohol would go right to her head. Still, it relaxed her and surely that could not be a bad thing. All around her she heard the clink of crystal and the murmur of conversation. She glanced down at the menu, taking in the decadent offerings: caviar, truffles, filet mignon.

'So many choices,' she murmured, and Larenz glanced at her.

'Surely you've been to restaurants such as this before,' he said almost sharply. Ellery glanced up, surprised by his tone.

'Not really,' she said. She paused, wondering how much to reveal. How much she wanted to reveal. 'There wasn't much money growing up,' she finally said. 'The house is really the only thing of value we ever owned.'

'And the Rolls,' Larenz reminded her gently. He was looking at her with a shrewd compassion that seemed far too perceptive, too understanding, when Ellery reminded herself he didn't know anything about her. Not really. 'Tell me about him.'

The menu slid from her fingers. 'Who?'

'Your father.'

She shook her head too quickly. 'There's nothing really to tell.'

Larenz arched one eyebrow in blatant, if kindly, scepticism. 'There is always something to tell.'

The waiter had returned with a basket of flaky rolls and Ellery avoided Larenz's knowing gaze by devoting herself to selecting one. Yet, when the waiter had gone, the silence remained, and Ellery just shredded her roll onto her plate while Larenz waited.

'He was one of those people,' she finally said, her throat suddenly tight, 'who was larger than life. Charismatic, you know? Everyone loved him. He was everyone's friend, from the gardener to the greatest lord.' She looked up, smiled. 'My mother said she fell for his charm.' She stopped there because she didn't really want to talk about how her mother had realized that that was all she'd fallen for, how her father had deceived and destroyed them both, how hard it was to forgive, how even now she couldn't let anyone close. She found she just wanted to remember the good things.

'How did he die?' Larenz asked quietly.

'Cancer. It was very quick, just three months from diagnosis to—' She stopped again, shrugging.

'I'm sorry. It is hard to lose a parent.'

'You've lost one?' Ellery asked, for he spoke as though from experience.

Larenz paused, and Ellery knew he didn't want to tell her about himself, his family. God knew, she had her own secrets. Would it really surprise her that Larenz had some, as well? Yet she couldn't suppress a little wave of sorrowful longing that he didn't want to tell them to her, which was silly since she had not told him the whole truth either.

'My father,' he said at last. 'But I was not close to him. In fact, we were…estranged.'

'Estranged? Why?'

Larenz shrugged and took a sip of champagne. 'Why do these things happen? I could not say. It is only after—when it is too late—that you wonder if perhaps you should have been a bit more forgiving.'

They both lapsed into silence; Ellery found herself taking Larenz's words to heart. Should she have been more forgiving of her father? She'd only learned of his deceit upon his death, yet the truth had brought up so many painful memories, recollections of the times he'd disappeared, the birthdays he'd missed, the promises broken, the endless rounds of hope and disappointment, and all the while he'd been—

No. She wouldn't think of it. She didn't want the past to spoil the present, this one golden week. Ellery glanced down at her bread plate; her poor roll was no more than a pile of shredded crumbs. She pushed it to the side. 'Well,' she said, 'no use being gloomy. What do you suggest I order?'

'I'm partial to the wild sea bass,' Larenz replied, picking up his own menu and glancing at it, 'but the Angus fillet is very nice, as well.'

'I'll stick with steak,' Ellery decided. 'I'm afraid I'm not the most adventurous eater.'

'There are different ways to be adventurous,' Larenz murmured as he set his own menu aside. 'Coming with me for a week was certainly in the spirit of adventure.'

Ellery's cheeks warmed. 'Foolish, perhaps,' she said, and Larenz's eyes narrowed.

'Ellery, why do you say that? Do you regret your decision?'

She lifted her chin. 'No, of course not.' She smiled, keeping her tone light. 'But the house is going to go to rack and ruin in the week I'm away. I'd been planning to replaster the front hall this week, you know. I'd even gone out and bought the proper tools.'

'Very impressive,' Larenz murmured. His eyes danced. 'However, I have no doubt this week will be far more entertaining.'

Ellery pursed her lips thoughtfully. 'Well, I don't know. I was really looking forward to it, you know.'

Larenz laughed aloud, which made Ellery grin. He reached over and squeezed her hand. 'I love it when you smile. A real smile. You look far too sad sometimes.'

'I feel far too sad sometimes,' Ellery admitted quietly. The waiter came to take their orders before either of them could say anything more and she was glad. She'd said too much already.

'What made your mother decide to sell Maddock Manor?' Larenz asked eventually, his tone one of casual curiosity.

Ellery arched her eyebrows. 'You've seen the place, haven't you?'

He gave a small smile. 'Still, it's your ancestral home. Hard for her to let go of, I would think.'

'I suppose my mother had had enough,' Ellery said after a moment. 'She didn't have too many happy memories there.'

'You didn't have a happy childhood?'

Ellery shrugged. She didn't want to explain the endless cycle of disappointments, how her father's sudden, prolonged absences had affected her. 'Happy enough. But their marriage—' she took a breath '—went downhill after a while.' She took another breath, let it buoy her courage and met Larenz's gaze directly. 'That's why this suits me perfectly, Larenz. After seeing my parents' marriage fall apart, I'm not interested in relationships.'

Larenz didn't say anything for a moment, just watched her thoughtfully. 'Good,' he finally said and took a sip of champagne. He still gazed at her from over the rim of his glass. 'Because neither am I.'

'Good.' Ellery reached for her own glass. She felt wound up inside, everything held together so tightly, so tensely, and she couldn't explain why. Or why she felt just the tiniest bit disappointed. Hadn't they just cleared the air? Weren't they in agreement?

'You're an only child,' Larenz said after a moment. 'Aren't you? I haven't heard you mention any brothers or sisters. So I assume the line will die out with you?'

Ellery felt the tension twang inside her, ready to snap. Why was he asking *that*? 'Yes,' she said quietly, too quietly, 'I'm my parents' only child.' The silence ticked on for several seconds before Ellery forced herself to look at Larenz. He was studying her with a rather brooding expression, his brows drawn darkly together.

'Enough about me,' she said as lightly as she could, 'and my concerns. What about you? You said you were from Spoleto. Were you happy there?'

Larenz shrugged. 'I left Spoleto when I was five or six years old. I'm actually a city boy. My mother raised me in Naples, near her family.'

'And your father?'

Larenz paused, his expression turning obdurate. 'He wasn't in the picture,' he said flatly.

Ellery nodded, accepting, even though she wanted to ask about the sorrow his scowl seemed to be hiding, and why he didn't like the kind of probing questions he'd asked her any better than she did. She wanted to know more about Larenz, to understand him, yet she was also realistic enough to know that wasn't what this week was about. They were enjoying each other; that was all.

As the silence stretched between them, it suddenly seemed very little.

Ellery caught sight of the waiter heading towards them with two silver chafing dishes. She smiled at Larenz, throwing off the pall of gloomy remembrance that had briefly enshrouded them both. 'It looks like our starters have arrived,' she said lightly, 'and I for one am starving.'

They kept the conversation light for the rest of the meal, chatting about inconsequential matters, and yet even so Ellery felt as if neither of them had escaped the hold of the memories their earlier talk had stirred up. Certainly Larenz seemed a bit more preoccupied than usual, his expression sometimes distant and even dark.

By the time the dessert had been cleared and they both had refused coffees, Ellery was glad for the evening to be over. They headed back up to the suite in silence, each of them lost in their own thoughts.

Back in the suite, Ellery waited uncertainly in the living room; she had no idea what to do, having never been in such a situation before, and she couldn't read Larenz's mood at all. He'd shrugged out of his suit jacket and loosened his tie, but his back was to her and he hardly seemed aware of her presence.

She wished she could sashay up to him and take off his tie, smile sexily and head for the bedroom. She knew she couldn't. She simply stood there, as tongue-tied and uncertain as a teenager on her first date, wishing she knew the protocol. The expectations.

'Thank you for the lovely dinner,' she finally said.

'Of course. You know it's my pleasure.'

'All the same…' She trailed off, for Larenz had not turned around. He was staring out of the French windows at the view of Knightsbridge, although there wasn't much to see. The windows of the building opposite were dark.

Ellery stood there for several moments, hesitating, uncertain, before she finally—belatedly—caught on to the rather obvious signal Larenz was sending her. He wanted to be alone. Her presence, she acknowledged with a trace of bitterness, was no longer wanted or required.

Well, that was fine. *Fine.* She was still tired from her sleepless night and, in any case, they hardly had to live in each other's pockets all week. She was hoping to see Lil some time while they were here. It was fine if Larenz wanted to be alone. She could use a little space, too.

'I think I'll turn in,' she finally said, her voice stiff with dignity. 'Even with that nap, I'm rather tired.'

She turned around, heading for the bedroom and it was only when she'd reached the door, her hand on the door, that she heard Larenz's quiet, even sorrowful, answer.

'Goodnight, Ellery.'

Larenz remained where he was, facing the windows, for several moments. He heard the bedroom door close and then, more distantly, the sounds of Ellery getting ready for bed. He imagined her taking off that awful dress, kicking those decadent heels from her feet, the outfit as much a contradiction as

Ellery herself was. Beautiful and uncertain. Frightened and fierce. Brave and shy. He let out a ragged sigh. Even now he wanted to be in there with her, slipping the shoes from her delicate feet and tracing the bones of her ankles, sliding his hands higher…and yet he kept himself from following his base need.

A far more dangerous need had led him to do things he never did with a woman tonight: to ask questions, to want to know. He kept his lovers at an emotional distance for a reason. Larenz did not deceive himself about that. He didn't want them close because, inevitably, someone would get hurt, and he certainly didn't intend for it to be him.

Even now, he recalled his mother's defeated look whenever he'd asked about his father. He'd seen the pain in her eyes, had felt it in himself. And he remembered the blank, brutal look his father had given him, the one time he'd ever seen him face to face.

I'm sorry. I don't know you. Goodbye.

Muttering a curse in Italian, Larenz pushed open the doors to the terrace and stepped out into the cool, damp night. Why had he washed Ellery's hair? Why had he asked about her father? Why had he started an intimacy he professed never to want?

And yet, tonight, he *had* wanted it. He'd wanted to be with her, to know her secrets, to allay her fears. It was so unlike him, so unlike anything he'd ever wanted with a woman, and that couldn't be good. It alarmed him. Scared him, even, if he was to be honest.

He didn't like it.

He should never have asked Ellery along for the week, he reflected moodily. It had been a sudden impulse, the suggestion taking him by surprise as much as it had Ellery. He'd broken his rules in doing so, and he'd broken another one tonight. *Don't let them come close. Don't ask questions. Don't need.*

He'd seen it in her eyes this morning; she'd been expecting him to leave with a thank you and a goodbye. *He'd* been expecting to leave. His car keys had been in his hand. Why had he stayed? Why had he asked?

The answer, of course, was all too obvious. He'd wanted more—wanted Ellery—and a single night wouldn't satisfy. Well, that was fine; women had certainly lasted longer than a night. He'd been with several lovers for a month or even more. Yet, Larenz knew, that cold fear rippling unpleasantly through him once more, they'd lasted because they had been so undemanding, wanting nothing but physical pleasure and a few trinkets, tokens of his affection, which he carelessly gave away.

They didn't ask him questions, they never made him think. Want. Need.

Remember.

Ellery did. He didn't know how those clear violet eyes reached right inside him and clutched at his soul, made him want to tell her things he'd never told another person. When she'd asked about his father, he'd wanted to tell her about the fourteen-year-old boy he'd been, humbled, humiliated, *heartbroken* when his father had turned him away with a flat, forbidding stare. He'd never told anyone—not even his mother—about that. He'd never remotely wanted to.

He doubted Ellery was even aware of her effect on him. And while part of him longed to surrender himself to that want and need, to revel in it even, another larger part knew that would be the most dangerous thing to do.

He wouldn't do it.

He couldn't.

Larenz gripped the wrought-iron railings that surrounded the terrace and let a damp wind blow over him. Behind him, he saw the light in the bedroom wink out, and he imagined Ellery lying in that huge bed, uncertain and alone.

He'd go in there, he told himself, and make sweet love

to her again. He would do it to reassure her, and to reassure himself that physical pleasure was all they had. A week of pleasure, nothing more. Nothing less.

Wasn't that why he'd brought her along, after all? Yes, to get enough of her, but also to give her something. He'd felt bad—guilty—for taking her innocence so carelessly, a thoughtless seduction. A week of sex and spoiling, he'd thought, would assuage both his own sense of guilt and any sorrow she might feel over their union.

Besides, Larenz acknowledged with a bitter twist of his mouth, after a week she might get tired of mucking with the lower classes. *She* would tire of *him*.

Suppressing the sudden stab of fear that thought caused him, Larenz turned back inside. He headed towards the bedroom with cool determination, only to pause with his hand on the knob. From inside the darkened room he heard an alarming sound, something between a sniffle and a sob.

Larenz cursed again in Italian and whirled away from the door. He paced the living room, restless, anxious and half-wishing he'd never met Ellery Dunant.

CHAPTER EIGHT

ELLERY woke suddenly, her eyes snapping open. All around her the bedroom was dark and silent. She had no idea what had awakened her but she was now achingly, painfully conscious of the smooth, empty space next to her in the bed. A glance at the clock told her it was two o'clock in the morning and Larenz still hadn't come to bed. At least he hadn't come to *her* bed; he might have availed himself of one of the many other beds in the hotel suite.

She lay there for a few minutes, the implications of this unwelcome possibility sinking into her. Why wouldn't Larenz come to her? This was her first night away with him. Could he have tired of her already? And, if so, why not just tell her to leave? That it was over?

Yet he hadn't. So, if he hadn't tired of her, what other reason could there be for keeping himself from her? Ellery found herself thinking back to their dinner conversation and how the questions about his past had sent him into a brooding silence. She didn't know what memories held Larenz captive; she only knew how painful her own were. Was it the regrets and remembrances of the past that were keeping Larenz from her now? Was he lost in unhappy memories, just as she'd been?

Knowing she could be horribly, humiliatingly wrong, Ellery decided to find out. She slipped from the bed, dressed only in the same fleece nightgown she'd worn at the Manor. She had no other pyjamas, much as she would have liked to don a silk teddy—if she even had the courage to wear such a thing.

She left her bedroom and tiptoed down the hall to the living room. A single light burned by the terrace and she saw Larenz sitting in an armchair, his back to her, his head bent.

Her heart turned over. He looked so serious, so intent, so... sad. Or was she simply being fanciful, jumping to conclusions based on her own earlier thoughts?

She crept closer, afraid to disturb him, yet yearning to talk to him, to touch him. She was behind his shoulder when she saw what had been making him look so serious.

'You're doing *Sudoku*?'

Larenz stiffened, startled, then swivelled slowly to face her. Despite his still-serious expression, Ellery felt a bubble of laughter rise up her throat; she managed to swallow it back down but she still felt a silly smile spread over her face.

'I'm sorry if I disturbed you.'

'No, no, I...I couldn't sleep.' She swallowed, for now that Larenz was facing her, she found he still wore an intense look that had nothing to do with his seemingly innocuous activity. She wasn't sure she wanted to know what it had to do with.

She let her gaze slide away from his and pointed to the top right grid of the puzzle. 'That should be a six.'

'What?' Surprised, Larenz turned back to his book.

Ellery leaned over his shoulder, one finger pointing to the page. 'That should be a six. See? You've made it a two, but it can't be a two because there's one already—there—' She tapped the number with one finger before withdrawing rather self-consciously. She'd wanted to keep things light, afraid of Larenz's intensity, but now she wondered if he would be annoyed or even offended. Some people were serious about their Sudoku.

Larenz stared at the puzzle for a long moment before he let out a chuckle. 'So you're right. You must be quite good at Sudoku to suss that out so quickly.'

'Well, I spend a lot of evenings alone.'

'By choice, though,' Larenz said quietly.

Ellery came around to the front of his chair, hesitating for only a second before she sat on the sofa opposite, her legs tucked up underneath her nightgown.

'Yes, by choice. I never thought living at Maddock Manor would be a social whirl.'

'Will your mother sell it one day?'

Ellery let out a slow breath. Sometimes she was amazed her mother hadn't insisted on selling it already. Even in its dilapidated state, the house was worth well over a million pounds. The very fact that her mother was willing to hold on to it made Ellery think she missed the happy times they'd once had, or believed they'd had, before her father had exposed it all as a sham. A lie.

'Probably,' she finally said. She glanced away, letting her gaze rest on the darkened silhouettes of the building opposite. Above them a pale slender moon glowed dimly through the clouds. 'I never thought I'd live there for ever.'

'Then what will you do when the place eventually goes?'

Ellery turned back to look at him rather sharply, wondering why he cared. Would it assuage his uncomfortable conscience, when he said goodbye, to know she had something ahead of her other than mouldering away at Maddock Manor? Was he pitying her? Was that why he'd brought her here at all?

The thought that she might be some sort of charity case was both humiliating and repellent. 'I suppose I'll go back to teaching full-time,' she said, injecting a cheerful, brisk note into her voice. 'I enjoyed it.'

'Did you? What did you teach?' Larenz was looking at her with that sleepy, heavy-lidded gaze that Ellery had come to know well. It meant she wasn't fooling him for a moment.

'English literature.' She gave him a pointed look. 'Including Tennyson's *The Lady of Shalott*. One of my favourite poems, although I don't think I like being compared to her.'

'Oh?' Larenz cocked his head to one side; if anything, his tone and look had become sleepier. 'Why not?'

'Well, she didn't have much of a life, did she? Imprisoned in her tower, only able to view life through an enchanted mirror, falling in love with Lancelot from afar, and he never even noticed her—'

'He did at the end,' Larenz objected softly. He quoted from the last verse of the poem: '"But Lancelot mused a little space; He said 'She has a lovely face—'"'

'Not much, though, is it?' Ellery interjected, and heard the sudden bitterness in her own voice. 'Considering all she gave up for him.'

A silence descended that was both oppressive and awkward. Ellery had meant to show Larenz how fine she was by joking about that wretched poem, but she felt now she'd done the complete opposite. Annoyed, she glanced away.

'It's late,' Larenz said finally. 'You should go to bed.'

Ellery turned back to him, her eyebrows raised in challenge. 'Are you coming?'

Larenz hesitated. His gaze slid away from hers and Ellery's heart sank. 'Soon.'

She walked from the room in stiff silent dignity.

When she awoke the next morning, Ellery saw that the other side of the bed was still smooth and untouched. Either Larenz had not slept at all or he had not slept with her.

Determinedly ignoring the little painful pang this thought caused, Ellery rose from bed, showered and dressed. When she came out into the living room, she saw Larenz was already there, dressed in a business suit, a cup of coffee at his elbow as he scanned the day's headlines on his laptop.

'Good morning,' he said, barely looking up from his computer. 'There's coffee and rolls if you'd like. I'm afraid if you want the full fry-up you'll have to go downstairs.'

'Coffee is fine,' Ellery replied. She poured herself a cup from the cafetière and took a roll, still warm, from the basket before sitting down opposite Larenz.

They sat in silence for a few minutes, Larenz busy with his laptop and Ellery doing her best to sip her coffee with an air of insouciant unconcern. It looked to be a lovely day; bright autumn sunshine poured through the terrace doors and bathed the room in crystalline light.

'I'm afraid I have to go into the office today,' Larenz said. He glanced up from his computer briefly, his gaze resting on Ellery for only a few seconds before he turned resolutely back to the screen. 'A few things have come up that I have to deal with.'

'Nothing too serious, I hope,' Ellery replied. Her voice, she heard with relief, stayed light.

'No. Just the usual minor crises. But I hope you can amuse yourself for the morning?' He glanced up from the screen once more. 'I have accounts with most of the major stores here, as well as all the important designers. And of course, you can buy anything you want at De Luca's.'

'Of course,' Ellery murmured. She pictured marching into that sophisticated shop and asking for a boiler.

'So you should be all right? I'll be back after lunch, I hope.'

Annoyance streaked through her. 'I'll be fine, Larenz. I hardly need to be minded like a child. And as it so happens, I already have plans.'

'Oh?' Larenz hadn't moved or changed expression but he suddenly seemed wary and alert. Dangerous.

'Yes,' Ellery answered, courage firing through her. 'I used to live here, you know. I'm going to have lunch with one of my university friends.' She hadn't actually rung Lil yet, but she knew her friend would make time for her.

'Oh, really?' Larenz gave her an almost chilly smile. 'I hadn't realized you'd made such plans. What if I hadn't been busy?'

Ellery shrugged. It felt good to be in control for once. She'd agreed to this week because she thought she'd *be* in control, but she'd been spinning out of it ever since they'd arrived in London. It felt good to snatch a little back. 'I assumed you'd have business to take care of and, anyway, we can hardly be in each other's pockets all week, can we? From what I saw between you and Amelie, you don't particularly enjoy a clinging female.'

Larenz frowned, his eyes narrowing to navy slits. 'I already told you, there was nothing between me and Amelie.'

Ellery shrugged, refusing to argue. She wished she hadn't mentioned Amelie; the wretched woman hardly mattered any more. 'Even so.' She finished her coffee and rose from the table. 'You can't be cross I have plans, surely, when you've already said you'll be busy? Why don't we meet for afternoon tea downstairs? I read that The Berkeley puts on a good do.'

'*Tea?*' Larenz nearly spluttered. He sounded outraged.

'Or pre-dinner drinks,' Ellery suggested with a smile. 'You're right, I can't quite see you balancing a teacup and a scone.'

She turned towards the bedroom and, from behind her, she heard Larenz say tightly, 'Fine. We'll meet for drinks. But at least spend the afternoon shopping. I want you to wear something suitable this time.'

Ellery didn't answer. She'd tried for a light, unconcerned

tone to show Larenz she didn't care. She knew she wasn't meant to care, didn't even *want* to care, but he would never know how much it cost her. As she turned the knob of the bedroom door, her hand trembled.

Two hours later, Ellery stood in front of a soulless office building of glass and concrete in the heart of the city, waiting for her friend Lil to emerge. She was grateful Lil had been available for lunch; in fact, she'd been thrilled to hear from Ellery and insisted on treating her. Her friend's familiar bubbly warmth was a balm to Ellery's damaged dignity. The parting jab Larenz had given her regarding her clothes had added insult to grievous injury. Miserably, she wondered why he'd invited her along at all if he was going to avoid or ignore her both day and night.

'Ellery!' Small, curvy and red-headed, Lil Peters hurried across the skyscraper's forecourt and enveloped Ellery in a tight perfumed hug. 'I'm so happy to see you!'

'Me too,' Ellery replied after Lil had released her and she'd got her breath back. 'It's been too long.'

'And whose fault is that?' Lil asked, wagging a finger in front of Ellery's face before she linked arms and half-dragged her down the pavement. 'I booked us a table nearby. I don't want to wait in some wretched queue—we've got loads to say to each other, I'm sure. And I need a drink.'

Ellery smiled as she let her friend barrel her along. 'I do, as well,' she said. 'Let's order a bottle.'

Ten minutes later, they were comfortably seated in a French bistro, a bottle of Chardonnay opened between them and two glasses already poured.

'So what brings you to London?' Lil asked as she took a healthy sip of her drink. 'I thought our girls' weekend wasn't until next week.' She arched her eyebrows. 'Please tell me it's because you've finally sold Go-Mad Manor and are coming back to London to live a proper life.'

Ellery grinned. 'Not yet, I'm afraid.'

'Ellery, what are you waiting for? I understand family loyalty, of course I do, but that place is falling down around your ears.'

'Actually, I think it's reached my shoulders.' Ellery smiled and Lil just shook her head. They'd had this conversation too many times already. 'I can't sell it yet, Lil. I don't know why.' She pressed her lips together. 'I know I have to sell it eventually, but I'm not ready yet.'

Lil shook her head. 'Your father really did a number on you, Ell. It's been five years since he died, you know.'

'I know.' Her throat was tight, the two words forced out. She looked away.

'I know learning about…well, I know it was a shock,' Lil said gently. 'But surely you can let it go? You need to.'

'I've let it go,' Ellery said flatly. She tried for a smile, a lighter tone. 'It's just the house I'm holding on to.'

Lil smiled back, although Ellery knew her friend was neither satisfied nor convinced. 'So what are you doing here, then? And please don't tell me it's to buy something dreadfully boring, like curtains for your drawing room.'

'No, nothing so tedious, although I could use new curtains.' Ellery glanced down at her glass, a few bubbles bursting against its sides. 'Actually, I'm here with someone. A… man.'

'A *man*?' Lil squawked and several patrons shot her amused and curious glances.

Ellery flushed, rolling her eyes. 'Lil—'

'It's just I'm so pleased.' Lil leaned over the table, her eyes alight. 'Tell me about him. Is he the local squire in Suffolk? Or a *farmer*? I always thought they were dead sexy when they did that programme about bachelor farmers—'

'Neither.' Ellery held up a hand to stop her friend's gushing monologue. 'Actually, he is—was—a guest.'

'A guest? How romantic. Who is he? I want all the details.'

Lil's eyes widened comically. 'He's not the one you mentioned this weekend, is he? The high-maintenance one?'

'Actually, yes. But he's not as high-maintenance as I thought.' She paused. She didn't really want to mention Larenz by name; he was, she knew, somewhat famous. 'Just a man. A gorgeous man, actually.'

'Gorgeous? Really? Oh, Ellery, I'm so happy for you.' She reached over to squeeze her hand.

'It's not going anywhere,' Ellery said quickly. 'I mean it. It's just for fun. A…fling.' The word sounded awkward, coming from her. Lil, of all people, knew how few flings she'd had: zero. And how cautious she'd been with men.

'A fling,' Lil repeated thoughtfully, then gave a little shrug of acceptance. 'Sounds fabulous. And he brought you to London for a dirty weekend?'

Ellery flushed once more. 'A dirty week, actually,' she managed and took a sip of wine. 'After this, we're going to Milan.'

'*Milan!*' Once again, a few patrons glanced Lil's way but she didn't even notice. 'Just who is this man, Ellery?'

Looking at her friend's excited, animated face, Ellery knew she couldn't keep the truth from her, and she didn't even want to. Lil was her closest friend; she'd come to her father's funeral, she'd been there when her world had fallen apart.

And it might be about to fall apart again.

The thought slid into her mind slyly and Ellery forced it away. *No.* She was not going to get hurt, because she was in control. She was having a fling, a silly fling, and that was all. 'His name is Larenz de Luca.'

Lil's mouth dropped open so theatrically that Ellery found herself chuckling. The waiter had brought them two huge bowls of steaming pasta and she reached for her fork. 'Close your mouth. And don't shout his name from the rooftops, please. We're trying to be…discreet.'

'*Larenz de Luca,*' Lil hissed, the name still managing to carry to several tables. 'Ellery, he's just about the most eligible bachelor in Europe!'

'Is he?' Ellery felt a ripple of unease. She hadn't realized Larenz had quite that much notoriety. And yet he'd chosen *her*. 'How come I hadn't heard of him, then?'

'You don't read the gossip mags like I do,' Lil replied as she dug into her own pasta. 'And, all right, perhaps he's not the *most* eligible bachelor—there has got to be a minor prince or two that fits that title, but honestly—Larenz de Luca! He's always in the tabloids, you know, usually with some bimbo on his arm—*oh!*' She bit her lip, her blue eyes wide and contrite. 'I did *not* mean you. You know that.'

'Of course not.' Ellery's smile wavered only the tiniest bit. Lil wasn't telling her anything she hadn't known already. She'd suspected Larenz was a playboy, a womanizer; she'd gone into this with her eyes wide open. She *had*. 'I suppose he's deviating from his usual this time round, eh?'

'I suppose.' Although Lil smiled back, her eyes were still clouded with anxiety. 'I don't want you to get hurt, Ellery.'

'I'm not going to,' Ellery replied firmly. 'I told you, Lil, this is a fling. I don't want a relationship.' She smiled, reaching for her wine glass. 'Don't you know me well enough to know that?'

'Ye-es,' Lil admitted slowly, 'but I also know when you *do* fall, you'll fall hard.'

Ellery's expression hardened. 'I'm not going to fall.' Fall in love. She had no intention of doing that. No intention of stumbling into it either. Love was off-limits, for both her and Larenz.

'Why on earth was he staying at that Manor of yours?' Lil asked. 'I mean, I would have expected him to want a bit more luxury. No offence, of course—'

Now Ellery laughed with genuine amusement, the sound

a relief. 'None taken, I'm sure. I'd be the first one to admit Maddock Manor is not the pinnacle of luxury. We can't even say we have hot water any more.'

'Oh, dear.'

Ellery shrugged. 'He was there with his PR person, scouting out a photo shoot.'

'A photo shoot? At your house?' Lil looked intrigued, and Ellery laughed again.

'I know, it sounds ridiculous, doesn't it? But apparently it has some ambience.'

'And have you agreed? To the shoot?'

Ellery paused. She had neither agreed nor disagreed; the subject hadn't come up again, and she wasn't sure she wanted it to. If she agreed, she'd surely see Larenz after this week was over. That wasn't part of their agreement; it wasn't one of their terms. And yet…was it something she wanted? He wanted? 'I don't know,' she said slowly. 'Perhaps. The money would certainly help.'

'Ellery…' Lil reached over, her hand on Ellery's arm. Ellery looked up, saw the concern and compassion in her friend's eyes. 'Are you sure you know what you're doing? Larenz de Luca is…well, he's not exactly a safe bet. You know?'

'Yes,' Ellery replied lightly, 'I know.'

Lil frowned. 'Are you sure this is just a fling?'

Ellery arched her eyebrows. 'Lil, this is Larenz de Luca we're talking about.'

'No,' Lil said, 'I'm talking about you. I'm damned sure Larenz de Luca only wants a fling. But what about you, Ellery? Are you sure that's what you want?'

'Yes,' Ellery said quickly. Too quickly. And not firmly enough. For, as she gazed into her friend's face, she was suddenly struck with the alarming—and frankly terrifying—possibility that it wasn't what she wanted at all. That she wasn't in control.

That she'd been lying to herself all along.

'If you're sure,' Lil said doubtfully, and Ellery nodded.

'I'm sure.' Yet already her mind played over the conversation from last night, the way she'd been seeking Larenz out, trying to understand him, *know* him. That was not agreeing to the terms. It was not the way to keep from getting hurt. The only way to protect her heart, Ellery knew, was not to have it involved at all. And surely with a man like Larenz—a known womanizer—it shouldn't be too hard.

Except for the times when he didn't seem like the man the world knew, the playboy of the gossip magazines. When he asked her questions, when he made her lunch, when he washed her hair…

Ellery closed her eyes. She couldn't think about *that* man. She couldn't take that risk. She certainly couldn't change the terms.

She opened her eyes and gave her friend a rather hard smile. 'Don't worry, Lil. I know what I'm doing. This really is just a fling.'

At six o'clock that evening Ellery made her way into the hotel bar, her new stilettos clicking across the parquet floor. She'd bought a dress to match the shoes, a slinky number in spangled grey silk that clung to every dip and curve and shimmered when she moved. The stilettos gave her another three and a half inches at least. She'd left her hair long and loose and she'd stopped by the make-up counter at Selfridges— she'd avoided De Luca's—for a free makeover. When she'd only bought a lipstick the saleswoman had looked rather put out, but Ellery wasn't using the de Luca account. She'd pay her own way, at least for this.

She saw Larenz waiting at the bar, his back to her, his hand clenched around a tumbler of whisky. He looked tense, she thought, and stressed. Had it been a bad day at work? She didn't care. She wouldn't ask.

She knew the rules. Larenz didn't want her to ask about his day; he wanted her in bed. And she wanted him in bed. That was all they had, all they could ever have. All they wanted.

Ellery had been reminding herself of it all afternoon. Last night she'd let herself care; she'd even let herself be hurt. And that was not going to happen again.

Tonight she was going to be just what Larenz wanted—his lover. Only his lover. Not his love.

'Hello, there.' Her voice came out in a husky murmur that she'd never used before. She dropped her beaded clutch on the bar and slid onto the stool next to Larenz.

He turned, his eyes widening and then narrowing as he took in her appearance, from her tousled hair to her red pouty lips, to the dress that hugged her body, finally ending on her feet, one stiletto now dangling from one newly pedicured toe.

His mouth tightened. 'Nice shoes.'

Ellery beckoned to the bartender with one finger—she'd had her nails done too—and let her lips curve in a provocative smile. 'Why, thank you.'

'I didn't really take you for having a thing about shoes,' Larenz said. He took a long swig of his drink. The bartender came over and Ellery ordered the first cocktail she could think of—a screwdriver. Larenz's eyebrows rose but he made no comment.

'Well,' she said, jiggling her foot so her stiletto dangled a bit more, 'there are a lot of things you don't know about me.'

'So it would appear.' He glanced at her again, looking even more displeased with her appearance. Ellery felt a stab of frustration; what did he *want*? She was showing him she understood just what kind of relationship—for lack of a better word—he expected, and it still didn't satisfy him. She wondered if she ever could.

'So what did you get up to today?' Larenz finally asked, and she gave a little shrug.

'Lunch, shopping.'

'You made good use of my accounts, I see.' He didn't sound particularly annoyed but, even so, Ellery didn't feel like pointing out that she'd spent her own money. Suddenly it didn't matter. Larenz was making her feel as ridiculous as a little girl playing at dressing-up. Her cocktail arrived and Ellery took a sip. She just kept herself from making a face; she didn't normally drink hard alcohol and it tasted bitter.

Larenz shook his head slowly. 'Why are you doing this, Ellery?'

'Doing what?'

He gestured to her outfit. 'Dressing like this. Acting like this. Like a…a femme fatale!'

'Really, Larenz,' Ellery murmured, 'you give me too much credit.' She let out a husky little laugh that had several men's heads turning.

'Stop it,' Larenz bit out. 'Stop pretending. I don't know what you're trying to prove to me, but it isn't working. It isn't,' he finished coldly, 'enticing. At all.' Then, without another word, he got up from his stool and left the bar.

Ellery sat there alone, her made-up face flushing with humiliation. She felt curious and even pitying stares and, taking a deep shuddering breath, she straightened her shoulders, lifted her drink and said to nobody in particular, 'Cheers.'

Then she took a long swallow before erupting into a fit of coughing as the vodka burned down her throat.

Up in the suite, Larenz paced the room as desperate and angry as a caged panther. He didn't even know why he was so angry, why seeing Ellery like that sent him into such a rage.

The dress and make-up—hell, even the shoes—had all been high quality, well made. She'd looked sophisticated, sexy.

Coy. Like all the other women he'd taken to his bed. And, Larenz realized with a savage lurch of despair, he didn't want to put Ellery in that category.

Ellery was different. *He* was different when he was with her. And when she'd sashayed into the bar and spoken to him in that husky, honeyed voice he'd felt as if she'd cheapened what was between them, made it no more than a…a *fling*.

Yet it was a fling. He'd made it clear; they had a week together and that was all. He didn't *do* relationships, he wasn't looking for love.

If Ellery had been sending him a message, he should have been relieved to receive it.

Not furious.

Not *hurt*.

Fury rushed through him—fury at himself for allowing himself to care. To feel. He was breaking more rules, the most important rule of all.

Never let your heart become involved.

Ellery let herself into the suite quietly, glad at least that Larenz had given her a key that morning. She had no idea what to expect. The living room was dark, as was the bedroom. Had Larenz gone? she wondered. Checked out? Had she driven him away for good?

Perhaps it was better that way, Ellery thought wearily. She kicked off her heels, careless of them now. She didn't have a thing for shoes. She didn't have a thing for dresses or makeup or any of this. She realized she'd been pretending, playing a part because she'd thought—mistakenly, stupidly—that it was what Larenz wanted. That it was what *she* wanted.

She'd dressed like this, acted like this to convince herself more than Larenz that she understood the terms. The rules.

Yet now, disheartened and weary, she didn't care any more. It was all too confusing, too complicated. Even if he made her body sing, her heart was miserable.

She wanted to go home. Except she wasn't even sure where that was any more.

She flicked on the light in the bedroom, glancing out of the doors to the terrace as she did so. She stiffened, for a lone figure stood by the railing, hands clenched, head bowed.

Larenz.

Without considering what she was doing or why, Ellery opened the doors and stepped out into the cool night.

CHAPTER NINE

LARENZ must have heard the door open but he didn't turn. He didn't even move.

Ellery surveyed him for a moment, surprised by the calm that had stolen over her, replacing her earlier resignation. She didn't care any more so it no longer mattered what she said. This was the secret, she thought. This was what she'd wanted all along. Not to care. If you didn't care, you couldn't get hurt. She drew a breath. 'If you wanted to make a scene, that was one way to do it.'

'I'm sorry.'

She shrugged, even though Larenz hadn't turned and couldn't s
ee her. 'I didn't realize buying a dress would annoy you quite so much.'

'And shoes.'

She thought she heard a thin thread of amusement in his voice and she chose to match his tone. 'Oh, was it the shoes? I wondered if the heels were too high.' She came to join him by the railing, gazing out at the Georgian buildings of Belgravia with a sense of cool detachment.

'I'm sorry, Ellery.' His head still lowered, Larenz turned to look at her. 'I acted like an ass.'

Ellery let out a sigh. She supposed she'd wanted an apology but, now that she had it, it didn't seem to matter or mean very much. 'I'm sorry too, I suppose,' she said after a moment. 'I don't get what it is you're trying to tell me, Larenz. I'm not…good at this.'

'What do you mean?'

'Only that I've never had this kind of no-strings affair before.' Of course he knew that; he knew she'd been a virgin. Still, Ellery tried to explain. 'I agreed to this week because, like you, I'm not interested in a relationship. I'm happy alone.' The words sounded hollow but Ellery continued anyway. 'I just don't understand how flings—'

'Don't use that word.'

'Flings?' She shrugged. 'Fine. Whatever this is…between us…I don't understand how it works. What I'm supposed to do.'

'I just want you to be yourself,' Larenz said in a low voice.

'And yet when I was myself, you stayed in the living room all night,' Ellery replied a bit sharply. 'I think I know enough to realize that when you take your lover to London, you don't sleep on the sofa.'

Larenz let out a long weary sigh and rubbed a hand over his face. 'No,' he said quietly, 'you don't.'

'So what's going on, Larenz?' Ellery asked quietly. 'Why did you get so angry? I thought I was playing by the rules.'

'Forget the rules.' Larenz cut her off, his voice nearing a savage roar. 'Forget the damn rules. Why do there have to be rules?' He turned to her and, in the sickly yellow lights from the buildings around them, Ellery thought she saw a trace of desperation in his eyes. He pulled her to him, the movement abrupt and almost rough. 'There are no rules between you and me,' he said against her mouth, and then he kissed her.

Ellery was too startled by the kiss to respond at first, and her mouth stayed slack under his as his words echoed through her. *There are no rules between you and me.*

Before she could consider that snarled statement or what

it meant, her body had kicked into gear and she responded to the kiss in instinct and need, her arms coming around Larenz's shoulders, pulling him closer to her.

Larenz kissed her like a drowning man, and her touch was his only anchor. In all the times he'd kissed her, she'd never felt so needed. So necessary. And so she kissed him, imbuing it with all the hope she felt, hope that now buoyed up within her even though, moments ago, she'd been as near despair as Larenz seemed to be.

He swept her into his arms in one easy movement and Ellery couldn't help but laugh. 'You know, you do the Rhett Butler thing very well,' she murmured. 'I haven't been carried so much in my life.'

'Sometimes grand gestures are needed,' Larenz replied and took her into the bedroom.

After that, there was little need for words.

Ellery must have dozed after they'd made love, for when she awoke, slowly, blinking in the darkness, she saw it was near ten o'clock at night. Too late for the dining room but, as her stomach gave a rumble, she realized she was starving.

Next to her, Larenz stirred—he must have slept, too—and lifted his head to glance at the clock. When he saw the time he groaned and fell back on the pillows.

'I take it we missed our dinner reservation?' Ellery teased, and he smiled and reached for the telephone on the bedside table.

'Room service it is, then.'

They ate in bed, feeding each other bits of this or that, for Larenz had seemed to order at least a dozen dishes.

'We'll get crumbs all over the sheets,' Ellery protested, laughing, and Larenz just gave her a wicked smile.

'I can think of worse things. Besides, I don't intend for us to do much sleeping.'

Yet eventually—nearing dawn—they did sleep, Ellery's

head on his shoulder, his arm wrapped protectively around her. As she tumbled slowly into sleep, Ellery found herself wondering how everything had changed—for it surely had—and how, when only hours before, things had felt so confused and unhappy and *wrong*, they could now feel so wonderfully right.

Her eyes fluttered closed and she refused to think about it any more. For surely that could only lead to doubt, and then to fear.

No, she would trust whatever had happened, whatever had changed, and she would enjoy this precious new bond with Larenz…for however long it lasted.

The next morning Ellery awoke in Larenz's arms as he dropped a kiss on her head and said, 'Wake up, *dormigliona*. We need to catch an eleven o'clock flight to Milan.'

'What?' Ellery struggled towards consciousness; several nights in a row of only a few hours' sleep—if that—had left her feeling groggy and disorientated.

Larenz, she saw a bit resentfully, pushing her tangled hair behind her ears, looked fresh and energised.

'I have a business meeting late this afternoon,' he told her as he headed towards the en suite bathroom. 'And then a party this evening for the launch of Marina. I want you to wear one of its signature gowns.'

'You do?' Ellery drew her knees up to her chest, her mind spinning and her heart thudding at the sudden turn of events.

'Yes, so get dressed!' He popped his head out of the bathroom door. 'The shower is big enough for two, you know.'

Two hours later, they were sitting comfortably in first class as the jet rose into a dank grey sky, breaking though the clouds to dazzling blue. It was an apt metaphor for her own life, Ellery reflected as she gazed out of the window, for she felt as if the clouds and cobwebs enshrouding her own mind and heart had been swept clean away. For now. She slid a glance at Larenz, who was reading the paper. He looked, Ellery thought, rather adorably serious, yet he must have felt her eyes upon him for, after a few seconds, he glanced up, smiled and reached for her hand.

They remained holding hands as Ellery settled into her seat and watched the last of the clouds disappear below them, no more than forgotten wispy shreds.

Once in Milan, Larenz ushered Ellery into a waiting limo; within minutes they were speeding away from Milan's Linate Airport towards the city centre.

'I have a suite at the Principe di Savoia,' Larenz told her. 'I'll need to go straight to the office but I've booked a set of spa treatments for you this afternoon.' He touched her hand briefly. 'I want you to feel completely pampered.'

'I already do,' Ellery murmured. Larenz smiled and squeezed her hand.

The limo pulled up in front of the impressive white facade of the Hotel Principe di Savoia, one of Milan's oldest and most luxurious hotels. And Larenz, Ellery soon found out, had the most luxurious suite.

He hadn't even got out of the limo when it pulled up to the hotel, so Ellery was escorted to the Presidential Suite on her own. She stood in the centre of the living room, turning in slow circles as she took in the panelled ceiling, the priceless art work and the windows that overlooked the suite's private swimming pool with its muralled walls and marble pillars, the dolphin mosaics giving it the look of a decadent Roman bath.

In the bedroom, her feet sank into the cushy comfort of a plush carpet that had clearly been modelled on the Aubusson design; this one, however, wasn't threadbare like Maddock Manor's.

Amazed, laughing, Ellery fell onto the king-sized bed,

revelling in the wondrous luxury, only to sit bolt upright when a knock sounded at the door of the suite.

She opened it to find a sleek-looking young woman smiling at her. 'Signorina Dunant? I am here to begin your spa treatments.'

Ellery had never had any kind of spa treatment; the entire notion was alien to her and conjured vague images of something halfway between pleasure and pain. She soon found out she'd been quite wrong.

Stretched out by the Pompeiian-style pool, she had an hour-long massage that nearly put her to sleep, followed by a set of facials and waxings and mineral therapies that left her feeling as shiny and sleek as one of the dolphins depicted in the mosaic. Every inch of her glowed or even sparkled.

She felt utterly rejuvenated, both inside and out.

A staff member had brought her lunch; another one had provided the finest selection of magazines. The young woman, Maria, who had first greeted her, tucked her into bed several hours later, informing her that she would return to dress her in two hours.

Ellery fell promptly asleep.

She woke to another knock at the door and, before she could even call out, Maria slipped into the room, a gown swathed in plastic draped over one arm.

'*Buona sera, signorina,*' she called out cheerfully. Then, in English, 'I come to dress you.'

Ellery slipped out of bed and watched as Maria first took out the most delicate, exquisite undergarments she had ever seen. 'These first.'

Ellery obeyed, exchanging the robe she'd slept in for the fragile lace. They felt like gossamer on her body, like silken cobwebs. She tried to glance in the mirror but Maria, smiling, shook her head and wagged a finger at her.

'Not yet. Wait until the whole ensemble, it is finished.

Now the dress.' She undid the plastic to reveal the most beautiful and breathtaking dress Ellery had ever seen.

Made of shimmering lavender silk, it fell in a waterfall of colour from a simple strapless design, ending in a discreet yet dazzling row of lighter violet ruffles. It was a fairy-tale dress, a Cinderella dress, a dress in which to feel like a pampered princess. And Ellery couldn't wait to wear it.

Maria helped her into it, advising her to sit carefully so as not to crush the gorgeous material. She styled her hair into a loose chignon, allowing a few artful tendrils to frame Ellery's face. And then came the make-up: Ellery had never worn so much, yet, when she finally looked in the mirror, she didn't look overly painted, just a better and more beautiful version of herself.

She looked, Ellery thought as she took in her own appearance, amazing. The dress hugged her bust and waist before swirling around her; Ellery turned in a quick, dizzying circle and laughed as the dress flew out around her.

'Signor de Luca sent these,' Maria said, holding up a magnificent pair of diamond teardrop earrings. They were real, Ellery knew, and had to be worth around half a million pounds. She fastened them in her ears with shaking fingers. 'And these,' Maria added. 'He selected them in particular, apparently.'

Ellery opened the box to stare, smiling, down at the pair of diamond-studded stiletto sandals. Although they would hardly be seen under the gown, they still complemented the outfit perfectly and were the most amazing shoes she'd ever seen. She put them on and Maria handed her the final touch: a gauzy wrap in pale violet. Ellery slid it over her shoulders.

'Signor de Luca will meet you in the hotel lobby.'

Ellery gave a shaky little laugh. She could hardly believe that any of this was real, that she—like this—was real. A few days ago she'd been scrubbing the kitchen floor, and now she was Cinderella about to go to the ball. And, at some point, whether tonight or tomorrow or five days from now, like Cinderella, she would most certainly lose all these gorgeous trappings. This had to end. Yet she didn't want to think that way. She didn't want to ruin the most magical night of her life with worries or fears. She just wanted to enjoy. To revel. She smiled at Maria. 'Thank you for all of this.'

As she came out of the lift into the hotel's opulent lobby, she saw Larenz right away. How could anyone fail to notice him, she wondered, for he was by far the most breathtaking man in the room. His curly hair had been tamed and combed back from his face and his powerful frame was perfection in an exquisitely fitting tuxedo. He turned when she left the lift, as if he'd sensed her presence, and then all of time and life itself seemed suspended as her eyes met his and held his gaze for an endless, enchanting moment.

Larenz took in her hair, her gown, her feet in one single sweep of his eyes that left Ellery breathless when she saw the blatant admiration and appreciation glinting in their navy depths.

He strode towards her, curling one arm around her waist to bring her into contact with the hard wall of his chest. Ellery lifted her face for a kiss but he brushed a kiss across her forehead instead. '*Magnifica*. I don't want to spoil your make-up.'

'Don't worry—'

'That gown matches your eyes perfectly. We should call that colour "Ellery".'

'You can't—'

Larenz arched an eyebrow. 'No? Perhaps a little more mystery is required. Do you know, when I first saw you I remarked on your eyes? I thought they were the colour of a bruise, but that is far too sad. They are happy now,' he whispered in her ear, 'the colour of the most beautiful sunset I have ever seen.'

Ellery let out a little bubble of laughter. 'Is this the famous Italian charm?'

'You've only noticed now?' Larenz pretended to sound hurt. 'Come, our car is waiting.' He bent his head to murmur in her ear, 'And, as always, nice shoes.'

The party was held in another of Milan's best hotels but, so dazzled by everything, Ellery could barely take in the glinting chandeliers, black-suited waiters circulating with champagne, the clink of crystal and melodious tinkle of a piano offset by the low steady murmur of a hundred different conversations. Yet they all stilled to silence when she entered the ballroom on Larenz's arm.

Ellery felt herself freeze as five hundred pairs of eyes seemed to train right on her. 'They are wondering who this Cinderella is,' Larenz murmured. 'And, of course, the men are jealous of me.'

'And the women?' she tried to joke.

'Wish they were so beautiful,' Larenz replied smoothly, 'of course.'

Yet the unreality of the evening didn't fade as Ellery circulated through the ballroom, glued to Larenz's side, watching as he chatted and laughed easily—mainly in Italian—with hundreds of different people.

After two hours Ellery had a headache from the constant noise, and a raging thirst from having consumed nothing but two glasses of champagne since they'd arrived. Her beautiful dress felt a little tight under her arms and her shoes pinched her toes. Besides that, all she'd had to eat since noon was a salad and she was starving.

Standing next to Larenz as he joked in Italian with a balding businessman, she had an intense, insane desire to be tucked up in bed with a bowl of popcorn and a good book.

'Dinner is about to be served,' Larenz told her. 'You have been so patient, enduring all these business conversations.'

Ellery tried to smile. 'It's nothing.'

'Still, I'm sure you're hungry.'

'Yes… I'll just nip to the loo first. I'd like to freshen up before we sit down.'

She made her way through the maze of people, grateful for the blast of cooler air when she finally emerged from the crowded, overheated ballroom. A waiter directed her to the ladies' room, which was blissfully empty. She had just gone into a stall when she heard two women enter, speaking for once in English.

'Have you seen de Luca's latest?' one woman asked, her voice sounding bored and laconic.

'That wilting flower? She won't last long.'

Ellery froze, then leaned forward to glimpse the two women now reapplying their lipstick in front of the huge gilt mirror.

'They never last long with Larenz,' the first woman observed. 'Yet he seems to be giving this one the star treatment. That gown is from his new line of fashion, and did you see those earrings? She looks like such a little mouse. Larenz must have given them to her.'

The second woman let out a trill of sharp laughter. 'Payment for services rendered. She must not be such a mouse in bed.' She smacked her lips and capped the tube of lipstick. 'He always gives them the star treatment before the axe falls.'

'Well, this one should be gone by tomorrow, then. I thought he was seeing someone else—a Greek girl, Al-something.'

'That heiress? No, he sent her packing ages ago.' The woman shrugged and capped her lipstick. 'Oh, well. I'm sure we've just about seen the last of this mistress. I wonder who he'll be on to next.'

Ellery didn't hear the rest of the conversation; the buzzing in her ears was too loud. She waited until they had gone and the room was empty again before she left the stall. In the mirror, her face looked pale and shocked.

The gossip hadn't surprised her; she'd known, of course she'd known, that Larenz had had plenty of women. She'd even known they didn't last long. And whether or not *she* would last long—well, she knew just how long she was meant to last.

No, none of the casual yet vicious gossip had surprised her; it was the word the woman had used so carelessly.

Mistress.

She was Larenz's mistress—a woman to be used and discarded. Just like her father had used and discarded both his wife and his own mistress—the woman who had shattered both her and her mother's worlds.

These clothes, these jewels, these *shoes*—all of it was... what had the woman said? Payment for services rendered. She was a bought woman, a scarlet woman, a *slut*—

This wasn't just a fling; she had no control. These rules, these terms, were not hers. This wasn't, Ellery realized numbly, remotely what she'd wanted. She'd been such a fool, thinking it was. Convincing herself it was. And, worse, she'd been fooling herself in believing that Larenz might now feel more for her than a passing fancy—

He always gives them the star treatment before the axe falls.

Standing there, gasping, reeling from pain, Ellery felt it had already fallen.

CHAPTER TEN

SOMEHOW, Ellery made it back to the ballroom; by that time everyone was filing out towards the dining room. She couldn't see Larenz and for once she was glad. She had no idea what she would say to him.

She was horribly conscious of the curious gazes and speculative stares, and now they no longer held admiration or even jealousy but malice or pity. Everyone here—the cream of European society—knew that she was Larenz's mistress. Expected her to be on the way out of the door. Accepted that she had received this gown, these jewels, everything—for sex.

The only reason she was here was because she'd had sex with Larenz de Luca.

Of course. It was obvious; she couldn't understand how she'd not made the connection before. She'd deceived herself so unbearably, Ellery thought. A hard knot of misery lodged in her middle, spreading outwards and taking over her whole body. She'd told Larenz, told Lil, told *herself* that she'd wanted a fling. She'd believed it. At least, her mind had.

Her heart wanted something else entirely. Her heart wanted a relationship. Her heart, she realized despondently, wanted love.

And, with the word *mistress* echoing horribly in her mind,

she fully understood just how much of a fool she'd been, how empty what she had with Larenz—she couldn't even call it a relationship—was.

Blindly, she left the crowds heading into the dining room, hurrying through the lobby so fast she nearly slammed into someone and one of her stiletto sandals slipped from her foot. Ellery barely noticed until a young porter grabbed it and caught up with her.

'Signorina! Signorina! Vostro pattino!'

Ellery took it blindly, mumbling, 'Grazie... grazie...'

'Just like Cinderella, eh?' The porter said in English, and Ellery flashed him an utterly mirthless smile.

'Yes, just like Cinderella,' she replied woodenly. She'd already turned into a pumpkin and it wasn't even midnight.

She took a taxi back to the Savoia. At the concierge desk, she asked for another room and the man behind the desk frowned at her.

'It is not necessary, signorina—'

'Yes, it is,' Ellery said firmly. 'How much is your...most basic...room?'

The man frowned again and quoted a price that Ellery could never afford. Swallowing, she said, 'Scusi...you're right, it's not necessary.'

She needed to get her things from the Presidential Suite anyway, and she should at least write Larenz a note and explain.

Yet how could she explain? How could she articulate that she'd agreed to his damned terms, to this whole wretched fling, because she'd thought she'd be in control? She'd thought she wouldn't be like her mother then, waiting and pining and miserable. She'd thought she could handle it.

Yet, hearing those women in the ladies' room, Ellery had realized she wasn't like her mother at all. She was worse. She was like her father's mistress. That was what this fling was: accepting presents, staying in gorgeous hotels, being wined and dined and *spoiled*, just as Larenz said, and all because she was his lover. His mistress. Payment for services rendered. An agreement whose terms he had chosen.

She felt like an idiot for not making the connection before, for not realizing what it all meant. *Of course* she was Larenz's mistress. Of course a fling with a rich and powerful man would end up being like that.

Yet she'd been so determined not to act like her mother, she'd ended up acting like something far worse instead: the woman she despised, the woman who had stolen her father's heart, not only from her mother but from her, too. The woman who had taken everything from her, even her memories, leaving her only Maddock Manor.

That was why she stayed.

And it was why she had to leave now. She couldn't be that kind of woman. She couldn't even pretend to be that woman for a moment.

Ellery dragged herself up to the suite, fumbling with the key card, and finally managed to unlock the door, kicking off her hated sandals as she entered the living room.

'What the hell were you doing?'

Ellery froze in shock. Larenz stood in the centre of the living room and he looked furious.

'How did you get here?' she managed numbly.

'I saw you running from the party and took a taxi back here.'

'And got here before I did,' Ellery noted, still dazed. The wrap slid from her shoulders and puddled on the floor.

Larenz shrugged one shoulder. 'You don't know Milan. The driver most likely took a longer route to earn a few more euros.'

'I see,' she managed, moving into the room like a sleep-walker.

'Well, I don't,' Larenz retorted and, even in her shocked state, she heard the current of pulsing rage in his voice. 'Why did you leave the party without even telling me? Do you real-ize how many people saw you? Including a few journalists—it will be in all the papers tomorrow, how de Luca's mistress ran out on him!'

Ellery froze. She turned slowly to face Larenz. Even in the face of his obvious anger, she felt suddenly, eerily calm. 'That's the first time you've used that word with me.'

Larenz looked nonplussed. 'What are you talking about?'

'Mistress. You called me your mistress.'

A certain wariness replaced his anger. 'It's just a word, Ellery.'

She took a deep breath; this was something she under-stood. 'No, it's not, Larenz. It's an attitude.'

He let out an exasperated breath. 'Fine. Whatever. Why did you leave the party?'

Ellery just shook her head. She couldn't believe how much had changed, or how flimsy the bond between them had really been. She'd thought everything had changed last night, when Larenz had told her there were no rules. Yet there were still rules—just rules for her and not for him. 'I left because I received a much-needed wake-up call,' she finally said.

'A wake-up call? What are you talking about, Ellery?'

'I heard two women in the ladies' room,' Ellery said, her throat tightening, 'talking about *me*—'

Larenz cursed under his breath. In two strides he'd reached her and his hands clasped her bare shoulders. His skin was warm. 'Ellery, you must know it is just gossip. Malicious—'

'Oh, yes, I know that,' Ellery choked out. 'Of course I do. I may have been a naive virgin, but I'm not completely stupid.'

'Then what—'

'I'm your mistress, Larenz, aren't I? That's what this week is.' Somehow she found the strength to twist away from his grasp. She walked to the doors of the terrace and gazed out at the darkened sky. 'I came with you to London, to here, thinking it was just a fling, some fun. Thinking I could handle it. And I admit it's my own fault for being so stupid. For not seeing the forest for the trees.'

'You are not,' Larenz gritted out, 'making the least bit of sense.'

'No, I know I'm not,' Ellery agreed. Her voice sounded so reasonable, yet she knew underneath that thin veneer of calm was a boiling river of hurt and shame. 'And I freely admit that my reaction to that word—mistress—is purely emotional,' she continued in that same reasonable voice. 'Irrational, even. It doesn't change how I feel, I'm afraid.'

Larenz shrugged impatiently. 'I don't understand any of this.'

'And I finally understand everything,' Ellery returned. 'These lovely earrings—' She took off the precious earrings and dropped them onto the coffee table. 'And these—' She kicked off the sandals. 'All of it, payment for sex. Because, if I weren't sleeping with you, I wouldn't be here.'

'This is ridiculous. What are you saying, Ellery? I can't give you things? *Gifts?*'

'But they're not gifts. Our relationship—if I could even call it that—isn't equal. Because you're calling the shots, Larenz. When you tire of me, whenever that is, you'll send me packing. Discard me…like…' She bit back the words she'd been going to use: *my mother*. 'Like an old shoe.'

Larenz stilled. 'When I invited you to come with me, you knew the terms of the arrangement—'

'Oh, yes, I knew the rules. And they *do* apply, don't they? You're the only one who is allowed to break or change or even forget them for a moment.' She drew in a ragged breath. 'Yes, I knew them. But I didn't realize how they would make me feel.'

'You agreed,' Larenz said, his voice quietly icy. 'You

made it quite clear, in fact, that they suited you, too. You weren't looking for a relationship, Ellery. Or love. Or did you deceive me?'

'I deceived myself,' Ellery said flatly. 'Because I thought that's what I wanted. Or could want, at least.'

'I see.'

'No, you don't.'

All of a sudden all the self-righteous anger drained out of her, leaving her only weary and depressed. 'I knew,' she said quietly. 'And so it might not seem fair that I'm changing my mind. But I can't do this, Larenz. I can't be your—or any man's—mistress.'

'I tell you, Ellery, it is just a word!' Larenz exploded. 'Why let it upset you?'

'Because it's more than just a word to me.' Ellery smiled at him sadly. 'Perhaps I should tell you why I stay at Maddock Manor.'

Larenz regarded her warily. 'Fine.'

She drew a breath, knowing she needed to explain and yet not wanting to expose herself, not to Larenz when he was like this, so cold and angry and hard. And she'd actually been afraid—for a little while—that she might fall in love with him.

Letting out a little sigh, Ellery sank onto the sofa. Her dress—her gorgeous dress—poufed all around her. 'I told you I loved my father,' she began. She stared out of the window, not wanting to look at Larenz or attempt to read his emotions. 'He was charismatic, charming, larger than life.' She spoke dully, reeling the list off as if reading from a script. That was all it had been: the script of her father's false life.

'He was never good with money,' she told Larenz. 'He inherited everything from his father, although the property and title aren't entailed. Looking back, I suppose the Manor fell slowly into disrepair over the years, slowly enough that I never really noticed. When I was little, it was my home and

I loved it. When I got older, I was too busy with my own life to notice or perhaps even to care.'

Larenz gave a little shrug. Although he was listening, he still seemed impatient. 'It is always so with the young.'

'I suppose. Anyway, that's not the point of what I'm telling you. I just want you to understand…everything.' She looked at him then but saw his expression hadn't changed. She made herself continue. 'My father used to go away on trips. Business trips, he called them, although he didn't have a job as such. He had investments—concerns, he said.' She gave a sudden bitter laugh that had Larenz raising his eyebrows although he said nothing. 'Yes, concerns. Two of them, in particular.' She broke off, drew a breath and then looked at Larenz directly. 'He'd be gone for days, sometimes weeks at a time. My mother always told me he was doing it for us, to make sure we could stay in our lovely manor house. I think she genuinely believed that—that he was working on these investments of his. At least she made herself believe it, although, looking back, I know she suspected…something. She was certainly unhappy. But neither of us found out the whole truth until he died, when I was nineteen.'

Larenz narrowed his eyes. 'What happened then?'

'My father's secret was revealed,' Ellery said flatly. 'Both of them. He had a *mistress*, you see. A mistress and…' her voice hitched '…a son.' Larenz's mouth tightened but he said nothing. 'A son.' She shook her head, reliving the shock and horror she'd felt on that day, still numb from grief, when her father's *other* family had come to Maddock Manor and she'd realized how they had been as grief-stricken and *loved* as she and her mother. 'He visited them,' she explained dully. 'When he was gone. He had a whole other life—a whole other family. They lived in Colchester, in quite a nice house, which he provided—part of the reason why the Manor was falling into such disrepair. Funding two separate existences is quite expensive.'

She let out her breath slowly. 'We didn't believe them at first. Wouldn't someone have known? Wouldn't someone have said something? After all, tooling around Colchester in a vintage Rolls isn't exactly cloak-and-dagger.' She tried for a laugh and failed. Her fear was that people *had* known and had kept the secret out of pity. 'Anyway, the woman showed my mother photographs taken throughout the years. Birthdays, even Christmases when my father said he just had to be away. A whole life.'

Ellery had stared at those photographs with a numb sense of disbelief; she'd gazed at the pictures of her father playing football with the son he'd always wanted—and had had. Her mother's face had closed in on itself as she'd looked at several snaps of her husband kissing another woman and, worse than that, far worse than that, were the photos of the kind of family life they'd lost years ago, that her father had been enjoying all along. With someone else. It had been the worst kind of betrayal, for both of them.

'What is her name?'

Ellery glanced at him, startled. 'You mean my mother…?'

'No,' Larenz replied flatly, 'your father's mistress. What is her name? Did you know? Do you remember?'

She stared at him, nonplussed. 'Diane,' she said after a moment.

'And the son?'

Ellery didn't speak for a moment. 'David,' she finally said quietly. 'He's just a year younger than me. Why do you want to know?'

Larenz shrugged. 'No reason.' He paused, the silence tense and impatient. 'I don't see what this has to do with you or me.'

You or me. Not *you and me.* Perhaps there wasn't a *you and me* any more, that essential *us*. There never had been.

Ellery swallowed. 'Because I want you to understand…I

agreed to this week, Larenz, because I thought it would be different. *I* would be different. I've spent most of my adult life trying not to be like my mother, pining away for a man who wouldn't love her. It's why I avoided relationships, why I was a virgin.' She gave a tiny humourless laugh. 'And so I came on this fling because I thought it would be a way to take control. To choose for myself. To *not* be like her. And,' she added fairly, 'I wanted to. I wanted to be with you.' Larenz said nothing and Ellery finished painfully, 'But I ended up being something worse than my mother. I ended up being like my father's mistress. A mistress,' she repeated, her words filled with self-loathing. 'I can't be that.'

'But I'm not married,' Larenz said flatly. 'It's not the same.'

'No,' Ellery agreed, 'not exactly. I realize that. But it's not…we're not…equals, are we? And this whole thing—' she flung her arm out to encompass the discarded earrings, the sumptuous king-sized bed, everything '—isn't what I wanted. It isn't me.'

'What you're really saying,' Larenz said in a voice whose quietness still spoke of an underlying fury, 'is that you do want a relationship.' He spoke the word with scathing disdain. 'Love, even.'

Ellery blinked. She didn't want to admit it. She didn't want to be so vulnerable, and especially not with Larenz when he looked like this, so cold, so contemptuous. He certainly didn't want love, not from her, not from anyone. 'I don't know what I want,' she finally said in a small tight voice. 'Just not this.'

Not this, and yet she still wanted Larenz. Her body ached with the memory of his touch, and her heart ached, too. Even now, when he stared at her so coldly, unmoved by her sordid little story, she wanted to love him. To be loved. The thought was terrifying. She'd been fighting it all along, denying it to herself, yet the truth was so appallingly obvious that Ellery wondered how she'd managed to dupe herself—not to mention Larenz—for so long. Silly, stupid her.

She was a very inconvenient mistress.

'Anyway, I'm sorry for being difficult,' she finally managed, half amazed by her own apology. The feelings surely ran too deep for a simple sorry, yet she didn't know what else to say, how to bridge this chasm that had opened between them, wide and yawning. 'I know this wasn't what we agreed on.' She wondered why she'd told him at all. He *was* right; her father's past—her past—had nothing to do with Larenz and her. It was just *her* problem, her baggage, and the reason why she was standing here alone, the heart she'd sworn wouldn't get involved now breaking, just as her mother's had.

Larenz watched Ellery's slight shoulders slump, her head bowed, the pain he knew she'd been holding inside for far too long now spilling out, even though she tried to keep it back. From him.

His heart twisted, it tore, for he knew what kind of heartache she'd experienced in her father's betrayal. He understood all too well how it made you alone and afraid. Afraid to trust, to love. Staying alone was safer.

Wasn't he the same?

And yet he was, Larenz thought, all too different. What she'd told him tonight confirmed that.

Even so, he wanted to take her in his arms, to smooth the hair from her forehead and kiss the tears shimmering in her eyes—she blinked them back, bravely—and tell her the past didn't matter at all.

But of course he couldn't, because it did. The past mattered very much, and it was what kept them both here, suspended in silence, neither of them able to cross the chasm that now yawned between them.

And he was furious—*furious* that she'd reneged on their terms and broken their rules.

And furious with himself for doing the same.

'I'll go and change,' Ellery whispered, her voice breaking, and Larenz stifled a curse. He didn't want it to end like this, broken and despairing. He didn't want Ellery to leave.

He wasn't, Larenz knew, ready to let her go. Even if at some point it was inevitable. Even if letting her go now would be the smartest—and safest—thing he could do. For both of them.

'Wait.' He spoke gruffly, his throat tight. He didn't know what words to say, what would help. What would be enough and yet not too much for, God knew, he didn't know even now what he was capable of feeling. Giving. 'Let me help you,' he finally said.

She turned, surprised, wary and perhaps a little hopeful. Larenz forced his face into a smile. He didn't know what he wanted. He didn't know what he wanted to *feel*.

'Let's not end it like this, Ellery.'

Her mouth turned down at the corners, drooping, and so did her eyes. 'I'm not sure I really see the point of going on.'

'There are…' Larenz paused, his throat drying, tightening, and he forced the words out '…there are things I have to tell you, too.' He could hardly believe he was saying the words. Ellery may have trusted him with her secrets, but he had no intention of revealing his.

Did he?

Why did this woman make him want to share his tightly held self, reveal the parts of himself he kept hidden from the world?

He felt as if he were teetering on the edge of that chasm between them and he couldn't bridge it. He could only jump.

'You do?' Ellery asked softly, and Larenz jerked his head in the semblance of a nod. He felt far too close to breaking, to falling. And he had no idea if he would tumble into the abyss below, or if trust—and love—would help him to fly. It was a frightening feeling, this uncertainty, this defencelesness. He didn't like it.

'Later,' he said almost roughly. 'There will be time for it later.' And Larenz didn't know whether that was a threat or a promise…or simply a hope.

She nodded slowly, accepting and, reaching for her hand, Larenz led her into the bedroom. He didn't trust himself to speak; he had no more words.

When Ellery awoke the next morning her body ached as if she'd been climbing a mountain. She felt as if she had and the summit was nowhere in sight. As she lay there, the morning sunlight bathing her face, she wondered just how long she'd been climbing; it surely wasn't a matter of a single day.

So much of the last few years had been caught up in that ceaseless striving, trying to make sense of her life when her father's revelations had scattered all the truths she'd built her very self on.

This is my family. This is who I am. I am loved.

She rolled over to look at Larenz; he was still sleeping. She wasn't sure what had happened last night, if somehow she and Larenz had found a way forward. They hadn't spoken much after she'd told him about her family. Words were too dangerous, the bond between them too fragile. Ellery had gone to bed alone, only to wake up in the middle of the night to find Larenz sleeping next to her, as he was now.

She gazed at his face, the lines and angles softened in sleep, his lashes touching his cheeks. She wondered what thoughts hid in his head, what hopes in his heart. She wondered if she would ever have the courage to ask, or if he would have the courage to tell her.

She wondered what was going to happen next. Now.

Then, quite suddenly, his eyes opened and Ellery was caught staring.

'Good morning,' Larenz said, his voice husky with sleep. 'You're looking at me as if I'm a puzzle and you're trying to work me out.'

She knew she could never do that, or at least not yet. She didn't have all the pieces. 'Nothing so dramatic,' Ellery said, keeping her voice light. 'I just like watching you sleep.'

Larenz caught her hand and pressed it to his lips, his eyes on hers. Ellery's heart turned over at the gesture, and what it could possibly mean. She didn't dare ask. She simply accepted it for what it was rather than what it might be. 'I want to show you some of my life,' he said.

His life. His *self*. Hope fluttered inside her. 'I want to see it,' she said, her hand still caught in his. 'Where are you taking me?'

'De Luca's and then, perhaps, Umbria. Where I'm from.'

And Ellery knew this was his way of giving her something, perhaps of bridging the chasm that had opened between them—the chasm between a fling and a relationship.

They drove in a chauffered limo to De Luca's flagship store in the centre of Milan. Housed in an art nouveau building, it was five storeys of sumptuous elegance. The crowds parted like the Red Sea for Larenz and staff flocked to his side, eager to do his bidding. Ellery simply marvelled at it all: the soaring marble pillars, the fabulous jewellery and linens and clothes, the feeling that she'd been catapulted into a film or a dream.

He showed her everything; he knew everything. Every worker's name, every piece of merchandise. He owned the store, not just in the literal sense but in a spiritual way, as well. It was utterly his.

'How do you know so much?' Ellery asked as they rode

the old-fashioned lift upstairs, complete with brass grille and uniformed attendant.

Larenz gave a little shrug. 'It's my job to know everything.' He paused. 'I started as an errand boy for the head of a department store. Marchand's, it was called. I watched everything there and I saw all the waste and corruption and greed. And I knew—even then—that I wanted to start something better, bigger. Something that celebrated the beautiful without making you feel ugly.' He gave a little self-conscious laugh, a sound like nothing else Ellery had ever heard from him, and she knew this was another gift. He was showing her himself.

Over the course of the afternoon he took her to every department at De Luca's, and not once did he offer to buy her anything. Ellery knew it was intentional, knew he was keeping her from feeling like a dreaded mistress. Funny, how this lack of gifts could feel like a gift in and of itself; how much she appreciated the true gift Larenz was giving her: his time, his self.

And it was, she knew, making her fall in love with him. Love. The forbidden word, the word she could only whisper to herself because it made her so afraid. Love was scary. Risky. Love was a big, dangerous unknown.

And she couldn't think about it for too long.

At the end of the day they returned to the hotel, weary, foot-sore, happy. Larenz ordered food in and they ate in the soft glow of candlelight in the sitting room. They didn't speak much, as if they both knew that words could break this precious, fragile bond that had emerged between them, tenuous and tender.

When Larenz simply reached for her hand and led her to the bedroom, Ellery went. She didn't ask questions, not of Larenz, not of herself. She simply did. She simply was.

They made love silently, slowly, and it felt like the purest form of communication. The joining of bodies, of minds, of *hearts.* As Larenz entered her, his eyes fixed on hers, Ellery felt tears start to come. She blinked them back, unnerved, undone because, even now, she hadn't expected *this*.

She hadn't expected Larenz to reach her, to find her, and yet he had. As she lay in his arms afterwards she didn't let herself wonder, question, regret. She simply lay there, listening to the sound of their breathing; even their lungs found an innate mutual rhythm. And she let herself be at peace.

The next morning they drove out of Milan in Larenz's silver Porsche, the sky high and blue above them. After an hour or so of driving, Larenz turned off the motorway and took a narrow road through the rolling hills of Umbria, now russet and ochre with autumn, bathed in sunlight.

'Just where are we going, exactly?' Ellery asked. They hadn't spoken much in the car. Words were still dangerous, fraught with possibility. Silence, Ellery reflected, was truly golden.

'A palazzo near Spoleto,' Larenz replied. 'My home, of sorts.'

After another hour of driving, he finally turned up a long tree-shaded drive; at its end Ellery could see a magnificent palazzo, two dozen windows glittering in the sunlight.

So this was where Larenz grew up, she thought as he parked the car and turned off the ignition. A child of power and privilege. His shoes crunched on the gravel as he came around to open her door.

'Does anyone live here now?' Ellery asked as she followed Larenz to the palazzo's main entrance. There was a strangely empty feel to the place; the windows looked blank and, although everything was excellently maintained, it felt sterile and barren. Lifeless.

'No.' Larenz took a key from his pocket and opened the door. Ellery heard the rapid beeping of a security alarm before he shut it off. 'Come in,' he said with a wry, rather twisted smile, 'to my Maddock Manor.'

Ellery stepped into a soaring hall, the floor tiled in gleaming black-and-white chequered marble. Above her a huge crystal chandelier glinted in the sunlight streaming from the diamond-paned window above the front door. She gave a little laugh. 'This is nothing like Maddock Manor.'

'I suppose I was speaking figuratively,' Larenz replied. He tossed the key on a marble-topped table by the door and turned around in a slow circle. 'Do you know, I've never been in here before.'

'What?' Ellery turned to face him, her mouth slackening in shock. 'What do you mean? Isn't this your home?' Yet, even as she said the words, she acknowledged that Larenz didn't have a home. He lived in hotels—temporary, impersonal, luxurious. Now she wondered if there was a reason for that…and if he was going to tell her now.

'This is my father's home,' Larenz corrected. 'He died three years ago, which was when I bought it.' His mouth twisted in something like a smile, although the expression still chilled Ellery. It held so much darkness, so much pain. 'Our fathers, you see, were very similar.'

'Larenz…how…' Ellery trailed off uncertainly, for there was something forbidding about his expression, something bitter in his voice. She didn't know what to say, what questions to ask. He was giving her another gift, another part of himself, and she was afraid to receive it.

'Come on,' he said in that same bitter, brittle voice. 'We might as well see what my money has bought.' He strode off towards one of the reception rooms and, after a moment, uncertainly, Ellery followed.

Larenz walked up and down the drawing room, inspecting the priceless antiques and artwork with a critical eye. Ellery stood in the doorway and gazed around the room; everything was burnished, polished and in perfect condition. The air

smelled faintly of lemon polish and it looked as if a maid
had just left the room.

Yet Larenz had never lived here? *No one* lived here?

It was, Ellery decided, strange. Unsettling.

'Larenz? What's going on? Why have you never lived
here?'

He stood in front of what looked like an original Gaugin
and studied it for a moment. 'Not bad, I suppose.'

'Larenz—'

'I never lived here because I was never allowed,' he said,
cutting her off, his voice sounding curiously unemotional.
'This was my father's home…and he did not recognize me
as his son.'

Ellery's breath came out in a rush. 'What do you—'

'You see, we're from opposite sides of the blanket, Ellery,'
Larenz said with a strange little smile. 'Yet the same sordid
story.' Ellery just shook her head, not understanding, yet
knowing somehow that what Larenz was telling her was terribly, horribly important. 'My mother,' he clarified, 'was my
father's *mistress*.' His delicate emphasis on the word made
Ellery flinch.

It's just a word.

Was this the reason he believed that? Was this the reason
he never let anyone close? She felt blood rush to her face as
she thought of all the bitter, damning things she'd said about
her own father's mistress, and that mistress's *son*.

A man like Larenz. Luckier than Larenz, for at least her
father's son had been acknowledged. Loved. Larenz, Ellery
knew then with icy clarity, had not.

'And what happened?' she whispered.

Larenz shrugged. 'My mother worked in the kitchen here.
Classic story, you know?' He gave a little laugh, almost as
if it bored him. Yet Ellery heard—and felt—the hurt underneath and knew his father's rejection had wounded him the
same way hers had. He'd felt the same fierce betrayal, felt it

now, and the thought filled her with a deep, sudden sorrow. 'She got pregnant, she was let go, my father gave her a little money.' His mouth twisted. 'He didn't set her up in a nice little house in Colchester, that was for certain.' His voice caught, tore. 'He didn't spend birthdays or Christmases with his other little family. No holiday snaps, I'm afraid.'

Ellery blinked back tears. They gathered at the corners of her eyes, threatening to spill. She'd been so callous, lost in her own sad little story without a single thought for Larenz's. If only she'd known. If only she'd asked. 'Did she love him?' Ellery asked quietly. She wanted to ask—*did you*? Had Larenz—in his own different way—been as disappointed by his father as she had been by hers? Or perhaps even more? He'd received nothing from his father. At least she had memories, tarnished as they were.

Larenz shrugged. 'Who knows? She doesn't talk about it very much. She was ashamed—an unmarried pregnant woman in rural Italy a generation ago was a very hard thing to be.' He walked over to the window, leaning one shoulder against its frame as he stared out at the gardens, manicured to the point of sterility. 'That was why she moved to Naples—her sister was there and she wanted to get away from the gossip.'

'And what about you? Did you ever meet your father?'

Larenz tensed; at least Ellery thought he tensed, although he didn't seem to move. She felt it in the air, suddenly taut with suppressed emotion. 'Once.' The single word did not invite more questions, yet Ellery longed to ask. To know.

'And this house?' Ellery asked for a moment. 'How did you come to own it?'

'Now that's an interesting question.' Larenz turned away from the window. 'Why don't we go ahead and see the rest of it?'

Wordlessly, Ellery followed Larenz out of the drawing room. He headed up the curving marble stairs and then down a hallway lined with wood-panelled doors. Their steps were silent on the sumptuous carpet. He barely glanced in the bedrooms, each one decorated, as far as Ellery could tell from her hurried glances, with the utmost elegance and luxury.

If this was his Maddock Manor, she thought rather ruefully, it looked a lot better than hers.

Back downstairs, he paused in a library, the walls lined in leather-spined books. He trailed one finger along the titles, a look of dispassionate calm on his face. It made her ache, for she knew how that blank expression could hide so much feeling. She'd felt it on her own face, and the turbulent, boiling emotions underneath, as well. 'Larenz—' she began, but he just shook his head. He didn't want to talk. He was shutting her out with his silence, and she couldn't bear it. She wouldn't let him.

'So?' she finally asked, her voice sharp. 'Does it live up to your expectations?'

Larenz dropped his hand from the shelves. 'No,' he said after a moment. 'I don't know what I expected to feel the first time I walked across that threshold, but...' He shook his head slowly. 'I don't really feel anything.' He gave a sad little laugh. 'Stupid, eh? Pathetic. I bought this house when my father died as a way to show I was worthy of it. At least I suppose that's why, if I'm going to indulge in a little psychoanalysis.' He let out a long weary sigh. 'Just like your father, mine was terrible with money. By the time he died, I was able to pick this place up for a song. And his family, of course, was furious.' Ellery heard the way he scornfully emphasised *family* and felt the sting of tears once more.

She realized that in all of her maudlin musings on her father's double life, she'd never considered how his other family felt; how hard it must have been to feel like the impostors, hidden away, unable to claim him as their own. She'd felt betrayed, yet they must have, as well.

And so must Larenz, whose own father had never even

acknowledged him. Had his father's rejection made him the man he was, Ellery wondered bleakly, unwilling and perhaps even unable to love, or even to have a relationship longer than a few weeks? And, if that was the case, how could she reach him? How could they ever find a way forward—if there was even one to begin with?

They were so different, yet so unbearably alike, crippled by their families' failures, holding on to the one tangible thing that proved they'd had families at all: *houses*. And, while Larenz's palazzo was in immaculate condition, it was as much a millstone to him as Maddock Manor was to her.

'Larenz—' She took a step forward, hope lurching inside her, making her almost stumble. She would not give way to despair; she'd done that for too long, and so had Larenz. At least they were alike. They were the same at least in this, and knowing that made her realize this impossible chasm could, in fact, be bridged. What had seemed to keep them apart could, possibly, *hopefully*, draw them together.

If they were willing to take the risk. If she was.

'What is it?' Lost in his own thoughts, he turned to her as if he'd forgotten she was even there. He looked blank, bored, and she knew he was closing himself off again.

And then Ellery understood what she needed to do—and what Larenz needed to do. She closed the space between them and reached up to touch his shoulders, letting her hands slide along the silk of his suit, drawing him to her. He tensed, resisting, and she let her own body relax into his, daring him to accept her own surrender. She wouldn't let this separate them. She wouldn't let either of them back off, shut down. Stay safe. 'Take me to your real home,' Ellery said. 'In Naples. Is your mother still there?'

'Yes—'

'Take me there,' Ellery implored quietly, her body still nestled into his. 'Show me your home, not this…this mausoleum. Show me *you*.'

Larenz shook his head, the movement one of instinctive denial and self-protection. 'I've never taken anyone there.'

'Take me.' Ellery held her breath, knowing how much she was asking. Her heart bumped against her chest, against Larenz's, and the silence stretched on. 'Please,' she whispered and, tilting her face up so she could see his, she saw expression after expression chase each other across Larenz's features. Denial, fear, uncertainty, hope. She knew them all herself. Felt them deeply, these painful feelings that could in fact—maybe, *please*—bind them together. After an endless moment Larenz finally answered.

He put his arms around her, drawing her even closer into the shelter of his own body, and buried his face in the warm curve of her neck, his lips grazing her skin. This was, she knew, his own surrender. 'All right,' he whispered, and Ellery closed her eyes in relief and gratitude as the sun's rays slanted through the long elegant windows of the palazzo and bathed them in warmth and light.

CHAPTER ELEVEN

DARKNESS was falling by the time they reached Naples. It had been a long day driving, for Naples was at least four hundred miles from Milan, and yet, for all the time they'd spent in the car, Larenz and Ellery had hardly spoken. The memories were too thick, too suffocating, and yet, even in the midst of them Ellery felt a small strong ray of hope. She'd felt it in Larenz's arms and she clung to it now, even through the silence, the growing tension. The memories were strong but she wouldn't let them win. She would not be defeated.

Larenz glanced at Ellery, her profile pale against the darkened window. She looked tired and a little sad, and he could hardly blame her. The last few days had been a hell of a roller coaster; he felt their toll in every part of his body, especially his heart.

He'd never wanted this. To care—and, perhaps, God help him, even more than that. He couldn't voice it. He wasn't sure he could even feel it, and he wasn't about to tell Ellery any of it, and yet the thought of her leaving…

Larenz's fingers tightened on the steering wheel. Taking Ellery to Naples—to his past—was surely a way to guarantee that she *would* leave. He might exhibit the trappings of wealth and privilege now, but he certainly didn't come from it. Even his mother, ever proud, refused his offer of a house in the better part of town. She still lived in the cramped flat he'd grown up in, much to Larenz's dismay and even disgust.

And perhaps Ellery's, as well… Most women, he'd found, weren't interested in anything but the man he'd become. Not the man he'd been. Not even the man he was. Yet, from nearly the moment he'd met Ellery, he'd been revealing the man he truly was, as if he *wanted* to be known.

It was maddening. Frightening. Why—and how—did she make him reveal his secrets, make him long for that dangerous vulnerability? What would she really think of the boy whose father had told him he didn't know him, who had turned him away from his door—the same door Larenz had opened that morning? Possessing the palazzo was an empty victory; the man he'd been trying to impress was already dead. Yet Larenz hadn't realized that—fully understood the futility of his grand gesture—until he'd shown the place to Ellery. Until he'd seen the grand empty rooms through her eyes.

Sighing, Larenz steered the Porsche through the narrow streets of one of the city's solidly working-class neighbourhoods. This was his childhood, his home, and he felt its shabbiness keenly. Ellery gazed at the apartment buildings with their peeling paint and shutters askew, her face impassive.

It wasn't much different than her Manor, Larenz supposed, although there weren't any Aubussons here, threadbare or otherwise. He nudged the Porsche into a street parking spot, a few inches on either side of the bumpers. 'Here we are.' His voice sounded tight and strained even to his own ears.

'Will your car…' Ellery asked hesitantly.

Larenz pressed the lock on his key, smiling grimly. 'No one would dare touch my car here,' he said. 'They know me. And they know my mother.' He saw her flicker of surprise and wondered how she would react to his mother's cramped flat, her oppressively working-class background, her refusal to accept the world Larenz now inhabited. Would Ellery feel as stifled by that life—that love—as he did?

He'd rung his mother from the road to say he was coming home; she'd crowed with delight and promised plenty of pasta. Now, leading Ellery down a narrow alley to one of the buildings in the back, he wondered if he was making the biggest—and most heart-wrenching—mistake of his life.

This wasn't what she'd expected. Perhaps she should have expected it, Ellery acknowledged, although, considering Larenz's own wealth, she hardly thought his mother would still live in a crumbling apartment building in what was certainly not one of the finer neighbourhoods of Naples. Judging by the tight set of his jaw, Ellery wondered if Larenz wished his mother lived in more comfortable circumstances. Had she refused his money? For a proud man like Larenz, who must have worked his way up to his current stunning level of success, that must have been hard to accept.

She was beginning to understand why he hadn't taken anyone here, why he'd been reluctant to take her. She was beginning to understand so much of this man she'd once judged as simply entitled and shallow. He was, she knew now, anything but.

'Buon sera! Buon sera!' The door in front of them had been thrown open, and a woman in her fifties, her curly greying hair pulled back from her smiling face, stood there. She grabbed Larenz by the shoulders and kissed him soundly on both cheeks. Ellery didn't understand the sudden stream of Italian the woman fired at her son but, from the wagging finger and teasing frown, she suspected Larenz's mother was telling him he didn't visit or eat enough. From their embrace, she knew their relationship had to be warm, yet she could still feel the undercurrent of something—tension? resentment?—tautening the air.

'Mamma, this is Ellery Dunant, Lady—'

'Nice to meet you,' Ellery interjected hurriedly. Why on earth would Larenz use her stupid title now? Was he *trying* to emphasize their differences? She wanted to focus on the similarities. 'Please, call me Ellery.'

'And I am Marina de Luca. It is a pleasure,' Larenz's mother said in halting English. Ellery gave Larenz an involuntary startled glance when she heard his mother's name. Marina. He'd named his line of haute couture after his mother. The realization made her heart twist.

Marina shooed them both inside. 'Come in, I've kept dinner.'

'Of course,' Larenz murmured to Ellery and she smiled. It was good to see Larenz out of his element, and yet also in it. Good and unsettling, too, because he most certainly wasn't the man she'd once thought he was, the man he wanted the world to believe he was.

In the past few days he'd been—willingly, even—showing her someone else. The man he really was. And that man, Ellery knew, was someone she could love.

She swallowed, pushing the thought away. It was too much—too frightening—to deal with now, even though the thought kept creeping up on her mind, twining its way around her heart.

She gazed around the small tidy living room with its framed embroidery, the sofa and chair covered in crocheted slipcovers. The room was cosy in a worn way; it was a million miles from Larenz's luxuriously sterile hotel suites. It was his home.

Marina took a huge dish of rigatoni out of the oven in the tiny kitchen and brought it to the small table in the dining nook. 'Here. Eat. You must be hungry.'

'This looks delicious,' Ellery murmured as she sat down. 'I'm sorry I don't know any Italian, but your English is very good.'

Marina beamed. 'Larenz, he teach me,' she said.

'Really?' She shot a quick speculative glance towards Larenz, but he simply shrugged. He seemed uncomfortable here, almost embarrassed. Ellery knew he didn't like showing her this part of himself, his true self, and she wanted to show him it was okay. She accepted it; she accepted him.

'Eat,' Marina said again and, knowing that food could be love, Ellery did. It was indeed delicious.

Afterwards Marina plied them with tiny cups of espresso and meltingly scrumptious slices of *panetta*.

'Larenz, he never brings anyone to see me,' she said as she watched Ellery eat her cake. 'I sometimes think he is ashamed.'

'Mamma, you know that's not true,' Larenz said quietly. His own cake was untouched.

She shrugged pragmatically. 'I know how far you've come in this world. I can understand how this is a step down for you.'

'It's not,' Larenz said in a low voice. Ellery's heart ached at the intensity she heard.

Marina turned to Ellery. 'Larenz, he wanted me to live in a big place on the outskirts of town. A palazzo! Can you imagine? What would the neighbours say? Who would visit me then?'

Even though Ellery understood the older woman's predicament, she felt a shaft of sympathetic sorrow for Larenz. He'd tried to provide for his mother, and she wouldn't take his money, his love.

Marina glanced at her son, bemused and affectionate. 'Besides Larenz. And he only comes a few times a year, if that.'

'I'm sure Larenz is very busy,' Ellery said quietly, smiling at him, but he only looked away and Marina let out a laugh.

'Oh, yes,' she agreed, 'very busy. But no one should be too busy, eh?'

'I need to make a few calls,' Larenz said and excused himself from the dining area.

A silence stretched between the two women. Ellery couldn't tell if it was friendly or not. Marina gazed at her in an assessing way as Ellery toyed with her fork. Her mind buzzed with all the new things she'd learned today, all the parts of Larenz that he'd shown her. Now she had to process them. Accept them. 'This was all so delicious,' Ellery finally said. 'Thank you.'

'He's never brought a woman to see me,' Marina said quietly. 'You know? A woman...friend.'

Ellery glanced up, blushing. 'Oh. Yes.'

'But you. He brings you.' She shook her head slowly. 'English girl. I don't know...'

'It's not...' Ellery began, having no idea what to say or how to explain. She didn't know what her relationship to Larenz was; the uncertainty was overwhelming, on both sides. She wanted more—at least, part of her did—but even now she was afraid. Everything had happened so quickly, so intensely, and she didn't know whether to trust it. Trust Larenz, trust herself.

Marina leaned forward, her eyes narrowed. 'You don't break his heart, eh? I know he has money, but inside? He is just a poor city boy. That's all he ever was, and he can never forget it.' She sat back, sighing. 'I know how many mistakes I've made,' she said quietly.

'I don't want to break anyone's heart,' Ellery said, her throat turning tight. She didn't add, *and I don't want mine broken either*. They didn't speak again until Larenz came back in the room.

'I reserved us a room at a hotel in town,' he said. He reached down to kiss his mother's cheek. 'It's late, Mamma, and we drove all day from Milan. But tomorrow we'll come back. Perhaps we can take a walk in the city gardens?'

'Why would I want to walk?' Marina said a bit grumpily. 'You know how it makes my feet ache.'

'What about those new trainers I bought you? They're supposed to help.'

Marina shrugged, and Larenz gave a tiny sigh. 'They weren't that expensive,' he said quietly, and she just shrugged again.

Outside, they didn't speak as Larenz unlocked the car and opened Ellery's door before sliding into the driver's seat.

'Thank you for taking me,' Ellery finally said, and he shrugged.

'Now you know.'

Know what? Ellery wondered as Larenz pulled away from the kerb and headed towards the historic district of the city. Know where he came from? Know what he'd experienced and endured? Know that even though he had money, and power, and prestige, he still was that poor city boy underneath, and she loved that about him?

Loved.

Ellery swallowed. *Now you know.* Yet, despite all this, despite how full her heart and mind both were, she still felt as if she didn't know anything. Every thought, every assumption and belief she had was shaken, overthrown, leaving her with nothing more than a handful of doubts. And hope, too, tiny and precious.

They drove in silence to the Hotel Excelsior, yet another luxury hotel, this one on the Bay of Naples. As Ellery took in the stunning architecture, the opulent lobby and, of course, the magnificent penthouse suite, she realized she felt only tired. This wasn't her; this wasn't even Larenz. It was just a way—a luxurious way—to keep from really living.

She had so many unnamed hopes, yet she could not give voice to them, even to herself. She was too afraid. Too much had happened too quickly. She couldn't trust if it was real, if it even existed at all. She sank onto the bed and closed her eyes.

Yet why did the thought of leaving him make her want to cry?

'Don't cry, *cara*,' he said softly. Ellery felt the feather-light touch of his finger on her cheek and opened her eyes.

Larenz knelt in front of her, his face full of such a sorrowful compassion that another tear slipped down her cheek. She hadn't even realized the first one had fallen. She let out a little choked sound, halfway between a laugh and a sob. 'I don't know why I'm crying.'

'It's strange, is it not?' Larenz said. He brushed the second tear from her cheek. 'So much has happened in so little time. It is hard to know what to think.'

Ellery swallowed. *Or what to feel.* Yet, as they sat there in the half-darkness of the room, the only sound their unsettled breathing, she was reminded of that night at Maddock Manor when he'd held her so close, when he'd let her decide.

When they'd made love. And, perhaps, when she'd fallen in love.

For surely she loved him? Surely this was love, this restless churning, this fierce hope, this deep need? She rested her forehead against his and let the realization—the hope and the need—trickle slowly, certainly, through her.

She loved him. Perhaps since she'd first seen him walking so arrogantly into her home and resented him for it; certainly later, when she'd seen the little thoughtfulnesses that betrayed the man he truly was. A man with humble beginnings, who still cared for his mother. A man who washed her hair and wiped away her tears. A man as afraid of love and the hurt it could cause as she was.

Or perhaps more.

Yet still she loved him. The thought was wonderful. Terrifying. For she had no idea if he loved her back, and she was afraid—so afraid—to find out. Afraid to test the weight of the bridge Larenz had built across this chasm between them.

Ellery drew a shuddering breath. She drew back just a little. In the shadowy room she couldn't quite see Larenz's expression. She wanted to say something of what she felt but the words clogged in her throat. Fear kept them in.

Larenz lifted a hand to touch her cheek again. A shaft of moonlight bathed his face in silver, illuminating his expression of hungry hope, almost like desperation. 'Ellery—'

His mobile phone buzzed like an angry insect in his breast pocket and, with a muttered curse, Larenz reached to turn it off.

And then Ellery spoke, not from the love rising inside her but from the fear that was determined to keep it down. 'No, you should answer it. It might be your mother—'

Larenz gave her a strange look, his lips thinning, and then he glanced at the little glowing screen of his phone. 'It's just a business call,' he said flatly.

Ellery rose from the bed. She barely knew what she was saying, only that she was so afraid to make this jump, to let herself feel. Love.

Be hurt.

'Then you should certainly get it,' she said, her voice sounding absurdly false and light. 'It's bound to be important.'

'You want me to answer it?' Larenz said, and he sounded incredulous.

Ellery forced the single word through numb lips. 'Yes.'

'Damn it, Ellery—' His voice turned raw, ragged, and Ellery nearly broke inside. Yet the numbness and fear still held and she shook her head.

'Answer it, Larenz.' She knew she was telling him much more than to answer a call, and it made her heart break. She was pushing him away and she didn't know how to stop.

With another muttered curse, he punched a button on his phone and spoke tersely into it.

Ellery left the room.

Larenz snapped the phone shut and tossed it on the bedside table. A stupid business call, and it had ruined what had been one of the most important moments of his life. Almost.

He felt rage course through him and, worse, far worse than that, hurt.

He was hurt. He was a blind, stupid fool, for he'd let someone get close enough to hurt him and he *never* did that, not since the day he'd walked up that endless drive to his father's palazzo and raised the heavy brass knocker. Not since his father had, reluctantly, seen him, his eyes shrewd, his face cold.

I'm Marina de Luca's son, Larenz had said. He'd been fourteen, tall and bony and awkward, not yet a man. *I've been wanting to meet you.*

I don't know you.

He'd tripped over his words in his haste to explain, to reassure. *I don't want anything from you. I know...how it is. I just wanted to see you...* The longing in his voice! Larenz closed his eyes now as he remembered. There had not been a shred of pity or compassion in his father's face. Yet there had been knowledge. Larenz had seen that. His father had recognized him, or at least had known who he was.

I don't know you. Goodbye.

He'd closed the door in Larenz's face. A moment later, one of the staff had escorted him from the property, making it quite clear that Larenz was never to return again, unless he wanted trouble.

From that moment on, Larenz had hardened his heart. He'd done it methodically, deliberately, knowing full well what he was doing and why. He'd never let anyone get close, never cared when he was mocked or teased, as he had been for that one hellish year at Eton. His mother had told him he'd won a scholarship; it was only later he'd learned that his father, in a moment of guilt, had funded his sorry education.

Larenz had walked out the moment he'd learned. He wouldn't take a penny from anyone, and certainly not from the man who'd sired him.

From then on he'd kept acquaintances, employees, mistresses. Not friends, not lovers. No one came close. No one touched him, no one made him need or even want.

Except Ellery.

Somehow Ellery had slipped past his defences without even knowing she was doing so. She'd touched him with her bruised eyes and fierce pride and sweet abandon in his arms. He'd begun to believe it could all *mean* something.

And in that treacherous moment he'd been about to say— what? That he *loved* her? Larenz didn't know what words had been about to come out of his mouth, from deep in his heart, but they would have meant something to him. Too much.

And she'd told him to answer a damn call.

Larenz glanced at his discarded mobile. He felt his head clear, his heart harden once more. It felt good. Right. Safe. This was who he was—who he'd made himself be. Who he had to be. He let out a long slow breath. He'd just come very, very close to making a terrible mistake.

Thank God he hadn't made it.

In the living room, Ellery sat on the sofa and stared sightlessly out of the window. Her mind was spinning, seeking answers to questions her heart was demanding. Why had she made Larenz take that call? Why hadn't she let him speak?

Had she been afraid he was going to tell her that he didn't love her…or that he did?

Which was more terrifying?

Love was so scary, Ellery thought with a distant numbness. Opening yourself up to all kinds of pain. And with a man like Larenz…

He's not that kind of man. That's just your excuse, because you're so damn frightened.

She let out a shuddering sigh that was far too close to a sob. Larenz came into the room and she felt his silence, heavy and oppressive with unspoken words. She couldn't bear it. She had to say something, anything. 'I've had quite the whirlwind tour of Italy,' she made herself say, her voice cringingly bright. 'I haven't been here since my sixth-form year, on a school trip—'

'Ellery.' She stopped, alarmed by his tone. It was flat and final and unlike anything she'd ever heard from him before. 'It's over.'

Ellery opened her mouth soundlessly and then closed it again. Her mind spun in empty circles. She couldn't think of a single thing to say, so she just repeated his own word. 'Over?'

'Yes.' Larenz didn't look at her as he crossed to the suite's minibar and poured himself a whisky. 'I have to get back to work. I'll put you on a flight back to London in the morning.'

Ellery blinked. She supposed she should have expected something like this and yet, considering what had just happened…what she'd been afraid was going to happen…

What she'd *wanted* to happen.

She swallowed, her mouth turning terribly dry. 'Just like that?'

He shrugged, his back to her. 'You knew the rules, remember?' The words sounded like a sneer.

'And you told me there were no rules between you and me,' Ellery flung back, her voice breaking, the sound of vulnerability, of need. This was what she hadn't wanted, this hurt and pain, but now that it was here, coursing through her, she found a new kind of courage, the kind borne of desperation.

She drew a breath. 'Larenz, I know I acted…strangely…a few moments ago, when I told you to answer the phone, but I was scared… This is all so new to me… I've never felt…' She was babbling, unaware of what she was saying, the words coming from the well of need and fear—a far greater fear—that a life without Larenz in it was far worse than the pain of rejection.

'It's over.' Larenz's voice was low, savage. 'Don't embarrass yourself, please.'

Embarrass herself? Was that what she was doing? Ellery blinked hard, as though she'd been slapped; her head reeled as if she'd been hit. Hurt. Suddenly she wondered if, in her own desperation and desire, she'd completely misread the situation. Maybe that conversation really *had* been about a phone call.

Maybe Larenz was used to these intense, crazy week-long affairs, maybe this was how he always acted with his *mistresses*.

She'd fallen for his damn *lines*.

And then another line came to her: *She hath no loyal knight and true, the Lady of Shalott.*

There was too much damn truth in that wretched poem, Ellery thought bitterly. Too much truth, and she was tired of it. She wouldn't be Larenz's failure; she didn't buy the unhappy ending or the sentimental tragedy. She felt cold, and clear, and quietly angry. She rose, standing before him; his back was still turned. 'Fine,' she said, and her voice sounded as flat and final as his. 'Since it's over, you can sleep on the sofa.'

She'd made it to the bedroom door before Larenz spoke again. 'By the way, that was my assistant calling to tell me Amelie wants to start the photo shoot next week. The normal fee is ten thousand pounds. I'll send you a cheque.'

Ellery stiffened. Her hand shook as she reached for the doorknob. 'Fine,' she said, and went into the bedroom.

CHAPTER TWELVE

ELLERY must have slept, for she awoke in the morning, gritty-eyed, her body aching, her heart like lead inside her. Sunlight poured through the windows and in the distance the Bay of Naples sparkled like a diamond-scattered mirror.

The world was moving on.

She swung her legs over the side of the bed and sat there for a moment, her head bowed, her hair hanging down. She let herself feel the agony of rejection, the intense pain of loss, and then she pushed it all down, deep down inside.

She was moving on, too.

Dressed in a pair of jeans and a woollen jumper—Maddock clothes—she came into the living room with her bag packed, her manner brisk.

Larenz was already showered and dressed, a mobile clamped to his ear. His sweeping gaze took in her clothes, her bag, her purposeful expression, and then he turned away.

Ellery poured herself a cup of coffee from the cafetière left on a tray and took two bitter sips. Larenz shut his phone. 'I called you a taxi.'

Ellery put her cup down. She felt worse than a mistress; she felt like a whore. 'Thanks, but it's not necessary. I can find my own transport.'

An emotion flickered across Larenz's face, darkening his

eyes, but Ellery couldn't tell what it was. She made herself not care.

'I booked you a flight to London, first class. You change in Milan.'

'Again,' Ellery replied, her voice crisp, 'it's not necessary.'

Now she recognized the expression on Larenz's face: impatience. 'Ellery, you don't need to make a point. You can't afford a plane ticket—'

'Actually, I can—' Ellery cut him off coolly '—considering I'm ten thousand pounds richer.'

'And shouldn't that money go towards the house?' Larenz demanded, and Ellery faced him with blazing eyes.

'I hardly think,' she told him coldly, 'that you're in any position to offer me advice.'

Larenz exhaled impatiently, and Ellery reached for her bag. The fact that her heart was breaking and he just looked tired and impatient made her feel both furious and pathetic. He was done. Well, so was she.

'Goodbye, Larenz,' she said coolly, without looking at him, and then she walked out of the door.

Larenz stood in the centre of the suite, the sound of a door closing echoing through his empty heart. Except it wasn't empty any more; it was far too full.

He'd cut off Ellery to keep himself from getting hurt and it hadn't worked. He ached all over, inside and out. He was crippled with pain.

And that, he told himself savagely, was surely a sign that he'd made the right decision. Even if it was agonising.

Ellery booked the cheapest flight to London, which required three changes and took twenty-four hours. By the time she stumbled out of Heathrow, she was exhausted and yet she had another journey to make.

She took a train to Bodmin and then hired a taxi for the journey to her mother's cottage near Padstow. Anne Dunant rented a modest place on the outskirts of the town where she worked as a librarian. In the six months since her mother had left Maddock Manor, Ellery had only been there once. Now she took in the neatly tended garden, the welcome mat in front of the door, the vase of flowers in the window and was glad her mother had made a life for herself, away from the Manor. Away from the memories.

Her mother opened the door before she could knock and enveloped Ellery in a quick, fierce hug before she uttered a word. 'I'm so glad you came.'

'Me too,' Ellery said. It had been a sudden and surprising decision during the long hours of her endless flight from Naples, but one she'd realized she needed to take before she got on with her life.

'Come in, I've made tea.'

'Thanks. I'm exhausted.'

'I'm sure you are. What on earth were you doing in Italy?' Her mother, still elegant at fifty, and in jeans and a jumper, moved into the cottage's tiny kitchen. It was all such a far cry from the space and elegance of Maddock Manor—at least in its glory days—but Ellery knew that wasn't a bad thing.

It wasn't a bad thing at all.

'I was on holiday of sorts,' she said after a moment. 'With a man.'

Anne paused, the kettle in her hand. 'Promising?' she asked and Ellery smiled wearily.

'No.'

'I'm sorry.' She made the tea and brought it over to the sitting room that led directly off the kitchen. 'I worry about you, you know, stuck up in Suffolk all alone.' Her mother gave her a rather shaky smile. 'I know you wanted to keep that place, Ellery, and I understand, but—'

'It's all right.' Ellery smiled back and took a sip of tea.

'I wanted to thank you for letting me stay there, actually. I realize if you'd sold it you could have been a lot more comfortable—'

Anne waved a hand in dismissal. 'Ellery, I'm fine. And how could I sell the only home you knew? It's your inheritance. It's not mine to give away.'

Ellery nodded, her mug cradled between her hands. 'Still. Thank you. I realize…' Her throat suddenly ached and she took another sip of tea. 'I realize I needed to live there for a while. I needed to…think about things. And,' she added, swallowing past the tightness, 'I needed to get away. Get some perspective.'

'And did you?' Anne asked quietly.

'Yes.' Ellery nodded and put her mug down. 'Yes, I did. It wasn't easy or comfortable, but I did. In fact, I have some ideas I wanted to talk to you about.'

Anne smiled and reached for Ellery's hand. 'I can't wait to hear them.'

Growing up, Ellery had loved her father more than her mother; he had taken up all the space in her heart with his booming laugh and bear hugs, his absences making her, predictably, love him all the more. Her mother had been remote, removed, lost, no doubt, in her own secret heartache. Yet, in the five years since his death, they'd slowly and steadily drawn closer, brought together by her father's betrayal, by their own disappointments and now, Ellery hoped, by their determination and desire to build new and better lives.

The past was done. She was moving on.

As the taxi turned up the Manor's sweeping drive, Ellery's jaw dropped in soundless shock. The lawns were covered with camera crews and their endless equipment, and a trailer had been parked on the gravel in front of the house.

'Something going on, luv?' the driver asked as he pulled up. Ellery took a few pound coins from her purse.

'I suppose so,' she said and got out of the car.

She'd spent the weekend at her mother's cottage, a relaxed respite from her current cares, and yet clearly life had gone on, plans had been made and put into action without her approval or even her permission.

As the taxi disappeared down the drive, Ellery saw Amelie come around the corner of the house, swathed in faux fur, a mobile clamped to her ear. When she caught sight of her, she snapped the phone shut, her mouth curving into a horribly false smile.

'*Sweetie!* We've been wondering when you'd get back.'

'I was in Cornwall, visiting my mother,' Ellery said tightly. 'What on earth is going on?'

'The photo shoot, of course.' Amelie tucked her arm into Ellery's; she'd never been so close to the woman before, and her perfume overpowered even the crisp scent of leaves and frost in the air. 'We need to have the photos out by Christmas.'

'What if I hadn't come back?' Ellery couldn't help but ask. Amelie's arrogance was unbelievable.

'Oh, I knew you would,' Amelie replied cosily as she steered Ellery towards her own front door. 'After all, where would you go?'

There was no malice in the question, and Ellery felt too tired to bother mustering a sense of affront.

'So could you open the house?' Amelie asked, depositing Ellery on the portico. 'We've been doing the outside shots but we need to get inside.'

'Amelie, I just got back. This is a bit inconvenient—'

'Trust me, sweetie, ten thousand pounds is worth a little inconvenience.'

Ellery shook her head in disbelief. Even now, Amelie was acting as if she owned the place, as if a bit of money made that much difference. Yet she couldn't seem to get angry; she was too weary and careworn.

So she smiled instead as she unlocked the door. 'I suppose you're right. That money will make a huge difference.'

'Won't it just,' Amelie agreed and breezed past her into the hall. Ellery said nothing. She wasn't about to tell Amelie Weyton about her plans.

She spent the next two days holed up in her bedroom, spending the time on her laptop and mobile, arranging her affairs. Occasionally she'd go downstairs for something to eat and see the models' make-up being done in the kitchen; if she wandered to the window, she saw shots being posed from a distance. The models looked artfully lethargic, their beautiful faces blankly bored.

It wasn't until the last day of the shoot that she realized just why Larenz had decided on Maddock Manor. She'd stayed out of the rooms they were using for actual photography yet, curious for once, she peeped into the drawing room to see a model splayed in front of the fireplace—*their* fireplace—and her jaw dropped. Her heart ached.

The room had been transformed, and terribly. Fake cobwebs hung from the chandelier and bookcases, and everything had been coated with some kind of imitation dust or grime. The curtains at the windows, while shabby, had been in decent condition; they were now replaced with utter tatters.

It looked, Ellery realized, like the mouldering wreck Amelie had claimed it was. It looked like a ghost house, a ruin, a *hovel*. She felt a tight burning in her chest.

'Isn't it amazing?'

Ellery spun around to see Amelie smiling happily at her. 'They did *such* a good job with the cobwebs. We hired a film-set designer. Look how the gown stands out,' she murmured, turning Ellery back around again. Ellery gazed at the blank-faced girl in a gorgeous fuchsia gown splayed against the now grimy marble. Yes, the colour did stand out against all the gloom and dust; Ellery was level-headed enough to see that there was indeed something artistic about the shot. Beauty and the Beast.

But this was her house. Her *home*. The place she'd been trying to keep afloat for the past six months, and this photo shoot felt like a mockery of everything she'd made of it, everything she'd been.

And Larenz had known all along.

She took in a deep breath and let it out again. She was moving on, past the house, past the hurt. She thought of the money and where it was going and she turned to Amelie with a cool smile. 'Yes,' she agreed, 'very artistic. Today's the last day?'

Amelie had the audacity to pat her cheek. 'We'll be out of here before teatime, sweetie. That's a promise.'

And they were. Ellery watched as they packed up their cameras and vans, the models climbing almost sulkily into a waiting limo. They'd removed all the trappings of decay, and Amelie had even arranged for a professional cleaning service to come and restore the rooms they'd used to their former glory. If there had been any mocking irony in her voice, Ellery hadn't heard it.

Amelie was, apparently, among other things, a professional.

Ellery turned from the window and went to the kitchen to make herself a much-needed cup of tea. The house felt very empty now, and she was glad she would be leaving again soon.

'Hello, Ellery.'

Ellery whirled from the sink where she'd been filling the kettle. Larenz stood in the kitchen doorway; a gust of cold air blew in from the open door and rattled the windowpanes.

'What are you doing here?' Ellery managed. She couldn't think of anything else to say, for she was too busy drinking him in greedily, her eyes lingering on his crisp curling hair, his glinting eyes, the hint of stubble on his jaw. He wore a woollen trenchcoat and held a pair of leather gloves in one hand. His cheeks were reddened with cold.

'May I come in?'

Ellery realized she'd left the tap running and turned it off. 'Yes. I suppose… Why are you here, Larenz?'

'I came to give you the cheque.'

'Oh.' It was ridiculous to feel disappointed. For a moment—seeing him again—her spirits had buoyed, sailing far too high as her heart forgot every hurtful thing he'd done and said.

Now she remembered.

She grabbed the kettle and plonked it on the stove. 'You could have posted it, you know.'

'I didn't want it to go astray. It's a lot of money.'

'Not to you.'

'Just because I have a lot of money,' Larenz said, 'doesn't mean I don't value it.'

'Oh, well, at least that's something you value.' Ellery closed her eyes, her back still to Larenz. She sounded far too spiteful and hurt, and she didn't want to be. She *wasn't*. She was moving on, forgetting Larenz, forgetting the foolish hopes she'd once had, so briefly—

'Ellery—'

'Thanks, anyway.' She turned around quickly and held out her hand.

Larenz didn't move. His gaze held hers, intense and even urgent, yet he didn't say anything and neither did she.

'I'm sorry,' he finally said quietly, 'for the way things happened.'

It was so little. So damned little. He made it sound as if it had been an accident, a twist of fate or nature, rather than his coldblooded decision to end things in such a callous way, to treat her as no more than the mistress she'd always been.

Ellery smiled coolly. 'The cheque, please, Larenz.'

'Ellery—'

'Why did you come here?' she demanded, her voice only a little raw. 'What did you hope to gain? There's nothing between us, Larenz. There never was. You made that quite clear when you dismissed me from your presence—'

'It wasn't—'

'Oh, but it was. And coming back here and seeing this photo shoot you authorised? Turning my home into some kind of mouldering mockery—Amelie explained it all—'

Larenz flinched. 'It's just a photo shoot, Ellery, and I knew the money—'

'Damn the money! And damn all your *justs*. It's not just a photo shoot, or just a word, or just a fling. Not to me.' Her voice shook and she strove to level it. 'I suppose that's how you keep your distance, how you justify it all to yourself. Everything—everyone—is *just*. No one comes close enough to be more than that.'

'Don't,' Larenz said quietly, but the word still sounded dangerous, a threat.

'I won't,' Ellery replied simply. 'I'm done. I thought, for a little while, that I loved you. Or at least that I *could* love you, which was quite a big deal for me. That's what made me so afraid that night, when I told you to answer the phone. I thought you were going to tell me you loved me—silly me—and I was afraid. Afraid of being hurt.' Larenz's lips tightened but he said nothing. She took a breath, spreading her hands wide. There was nothing left to hide now. 'I know it's all a bit tired and trite, but I've always had a difficult time trusting men. I didn't want them to leave the way my father always did, so I never let them get close. And when I learned about his double life, well, that sealed the deal. My heart was off-limits.'

'Sometimes,' Larenz said in a low voice, 'it's better that way.'

Ellery nodded. 'Yes, you would say that, wouldn't you? We're of the same mind, apparently.' She let out a mirthless laugh. 'That's one thing we agree on, I suppose.' She held out her hand. 'I'll take the cheque now.'

Slowly, Larenz withdrew an envelope from his breast pocket. 'What will you do with it?' he asked. 'Mow the lawns a bit more or fix the heating?' There was a glimmer of the old amusement, the old Larenz in his voice and it hurt to hear it.

'I've already arranged those,' Ellery replied flatly. 'I sold the Rolls.'

Larenz raised his eyebrows. 'You did?'

'Yes.' She crossed the kitchen and took the envelope without touching his hand. She was afraid that even that little bit of contact would weaken her resolve. She'd start to cry, or beg, or worse. She slipped the envelope into the pocket of her jumper. 'This money is actually going to charity.'

Larenz's mouth dropped open; it was, Ellery, thought, a rather satisfying sight. 'What?'

'I'm selling Maddock Manor,' she told him. 'It's time.'

'But it's your home—'

'Just like that empty palazzo is yours?' Ellery shook her head. 'I don't think so.' She paused, her gaze resting on him, taking him in and memorizing every curve and line of his face and body because she knew she would never see him again. 'They say home is where the heart is,' she said quietly, 'and it's not here.'

The words seemed to fall into the stillness, to reverberate in the silence of the room. Larenz took their double meaning for he nodded once, in acceptance.

'Goodbye, Ellery,' he said and he turned around and walked out of the kitchen.

Standing in the emptiness of the room, it occurred to Ellery that they'd both had a turn at leaving each other.

And that they were both still, and always, alone.

CHAPTER THIRTEEN

IT WAS snowing when Ellery left the school. It didn't look as if it would stick, but the thick white flakes glittered under the London street lights as she walked down the road, busy with people leaving work, their heads lowered against the falling snow.

She'd been lucky to find a job so quickly; a literature teacher had been taking maternity leave, and the school had been glad to have a qualified teacher willing to work for just a few months. Ellery didn't mind the temporary nature of the position; she needed time to decide just what her next step would be.

Even after a month in the city, she wasn't used to the noise of the traffic, the crowds on the streets. She enjoyed going out with friends again and her regular lunches with Lil, yet she missed the one thing she thought she'd wouldn't't: the peaceful solitude of her life at Maddock Manor.

She paused in front of a newsagent's; the shopkeeper was busy hauling papers and magazines back into the tiny shop, out of the wet. One glossy cover caught her eye, the splash of colour against gloomy grey all too familiar.

She reached for it, a heavy fashion magazine she'd never bothered with before.

De Luca's Delicious Designs, the cover read. On it, a model lounged against the fireplace, resplendent in fuchsia.

'You going to pay for that, miss?' the shopkeeper asked, a hint of surly impatience in his voice.

Ellery hesitated, and then she smiled and put it back. 'No,' she said, 'no, I'm not. Thanks, anyway.'

And she moved on.

The snow was coming down more heavily now, the grass clumped with white. Perhaps it would be a white Christmas after all; it was just a few days away. Ellery was spending the day with friends and then going down to Cornwall for Boxing Day. Afterwards, she would head back to Suffolk, to see how the renovation was going. She was looking forward to that—to seeing Maddock Manor put to good use.

In front of the block of slightly shabby mansion flats where she'd found a short-term let, she fumbled for her key. The light in front of the doorway had gone out a few weeks ago and no one had bothered to replace it, so the entryway was cloaked in darkness.

And from that darkness a voice drifted out, an achingly familiar voice that had Ellery stilling even as her heart rate kicked up a notch and her hands, still fumbling for her key, began to tremble.

'Nice shoes.'

Her fingers closed around the key as she glanced down at her wellies. She'd exchanged her school flats for the sensible boots when she'd headed out into the snow.

She lifted her head, trying to peer into the darkness. Could it really be—? 'They're just boots,' she said.

'I think I first fell in love with you when you were wearing wellies,' Larenz said, and stepped out of the darkness.

He looked so wonderfully the same, the same curly hair and glinting eyes, and yet something was different. There was a sorrow to him now, Ellery thought, a sadness in the shadow of his eyes, in the slight slump of his shoulders.

Then his words registered and her heart bumped harder.

I fell in love with you. 'You didn't,' she said, her voice no more than a whisper.

'I didn't fall in love with you?' Larenz filled in. His hands were shoved deep in the pockets of his coat and snowflakes dusted his hair. 'Well, I certainly tried to convince myself that I didn't. The last thing I ever wanted was to fall in love with anyone.'

Ellery's throat was tight, the possibility of hope making her dizzy with fear. Even now, she was afraid. 'Why are you here, Larenz?'

'I would have thought it was obvious. I came to say I'm sorry.'

Disappointment welled up inside her, a big dark cloud of sorrow. She nodded tightly. 'Fine. You've said it.'

'Oh, but I have a lot more to say than that,' Larenz told her softly. 'And I said I *came* to say I'm sorry. I haven't really said it yet.'

Ellery blinked hard and the threat of tears mercifully receded for a moment. 'Don't tease me,' she whispered, when what she really meant was, *Don't break my heart. Again.*

'Trust me, Ellery,' Larenz said, his voice low. 'I'm not teasing.'

She didn't trust herself to speak, so she just nodded. She unlocked the front door and led Larenz up the dim narrow stairwell to the second floor.

'It's not much,' she said as she opened the door and switched on the lights. 'It's a partially furnished sublet. But at least the heating works.'

'Indeed,' Larenz murmured. He looked incongruous in the flat's tiny lounge, with its hard ugly sofa and scarred coffee table. Ellery shed her coat and boots, dropping her handbag on the table. The actions covered the lack of words.

'Do you want something to drink?' she finally said. 'A tea or coffee?'

'I don't think what I have to say will take that long,' Larenz said after a moment, and Ellery's heart plummeted.

'Oh, all right then,' she said uncertainly and stood there, awkward in her stocking feet.

'Ellery, I love you.' Larenz met her gaze directly, his own open and honest and so achingly vulnerable. 'I love you so much that the last few months have been a living hell for me. I tried to fight it. God knows, I've been fighting it since I first laid eyes on you.' Ellery opened her mouth, but no words came out. Her mind spun. 'You had me sussed completely,' Larenz said with a small smile. 'I was afraid. I've been afraid for a long time.' He passed a hand over his face as he let out a rather shaky laugh. 'I've never admitted that to anyone— even myself—before.'

'Thank you for telling me,' Ellery whispered.

'I know the moment I decided I wasn't going to let anyone close,' Larenz told her. 'I was fourteen and my mother finally told me who my father was. I went to see him—at the palazzo I took you to. I walked up that long drive and knocked on the door.' He shook his head, remembering. 'It was a foolish thing to do, of course. I wasn't expecting him to embrace me. I wasn't that naive. But I thought…' He paused, swallowing. 'I thought he'd acknowledge me at least. Something. But he didn't. Not a word except "I don't know you". He said that twice. And, as I was leaving, he had his thugs come out and tell me they'd rough me up if I ever showed my face around there again.' Larenz sighed. 'You said your story was tired and trite, and I suppose mine is, too. We were both at the mercy of our unhappy families and let it cloud our judgement. It made us protect our hearts.'

He took a step towards her. 'But I don't want it to ruin my life. I don't want to live that way any more, Ellery. I think I convinced myself I was happy, keeping everyone at a distance, letting them be no more than a *just*, like you said.

But it's a half life at best and, even so, I think I could have gone on living it…if I hadn't met you.'

Ellery swallowed, her throat aching with suppressed emotion. The fear was crumbling away, leaving something sure and shining and true. Yet, even now, she wondered if she could trust it. 'What are you saying, Larenz?'

'I'm saying,' he said, his voice raw, 'that I'm sorry for treating you the way I did, for pushing you away because I was so afraid to pull you close. For acting like you were just my mistress when I already knew you were the love of my life.'

'Oh, Larenz—' Ellery stopped, her words choking. 'Forgiven,' she managed, her voice no more than a breath, and Larenz crossed the small space between them to pull her into his arms.

Ellery came into the embrace easily, her hands running up his arms to his shoulders and then to his face, relishing and revelling in the remembered feel of him.

'I have more to say,' Larenz told her. 'I love you, and I want to spend the rest of my life with you. It doesn't matter where. Milan or London or that Manor of yours—'

'I told you, I sold it,' Ellery said.

'I know, but we can buy it back. I know how much that house means to you.'

She shook her head. 'No, it didn't mean that much in the end. I was holding on to it because it felt like a validation of my life, my self, but it wasn't. It was just a house, and a rather unhappy one at that. I sold it to a charity.' She smiled, the knowledge still making her happy, even now. 'It's going to be a home for single mothers who need a safe place to stay. It felt like the right thing to do…considering.'

'It sounds like the right thing,' Larenz said and kissed her.

'I also wrote a letter,' Ellery continued quietly. 'To

Diane…and David. I don't know what kind of relationship we can have, but I felt like I needed to reach out to them.'

'That must have been a difficult thing to do.'

Ellery gave a shaky laugh. 'Yes, it was. I haven't heard back yet, though.'

'All these changes,' Larenz murmured. 'I suppose I should tell you I sold my palazzo, as well.'

'You did?'

'Yes, to a family with five children. They were running around the garden even as we signed the deal. It will be a happy place now. Happy and full.'

'That's good,' Ellery whispered. She buried her face in his neck for a moment, breathing in the wonderful scent of him, before she said, 'I suppose we'll need a new place to live, then.'

'Does that mean you're accepting my proposal?'

'Well…' Ellery felt a smile bloom across her face. 'I wasn't aware you'd actually asked.'

'Forgive me,' Larenz murmured and dropped to one knee. Ellery laughed aloud as he pulled a small velvet box from his pocket and flipped it open to reveal a gorgeous antique diamond ring. 'Ellery Dunant, Lady of Maddock, Lady of Shalott, lady of my heart, will you marry me?'

'Yes,' she whispered and then, louder, 'yes, yes, yes.'

She pulled Larenz to his feet and, as he claimed her mouth in a kiss once more, she knew *this* was the happy ending they'd both been searching for. Neither of them were alone or afraid; there was simply love.

Love, and bright shining joy.

**Don't miss Sarah Morgan's
next Puffin Island story**

*Some Kind
of Wonderful*

Brittany Forrest has stayed away from Puffin Island
since her relationship with Zach Flynn went bad.
They were married for ten days and only just
managed not to kill each other by the
end of the honeymoon.

But, when a broken arm means she must return,
Brittany moves back to her Puffin Island home.
Only to discover that Zac is there as well.

Will a summer together help two lovers reunite or
will their stormy relationship crash on to the
rocks of Puffin Island?

Some Kind of Wonderful
COMING JULY 2015
Pre-order your copy today